MAYA FISHER

Reborn In Shadows

From The Ashes

Content Warning

This content contains heavy themes that some readers may find distressing or triggering. It includes:

Bigotry

Transphobia

Misgendering and deadnaming

Graphic violence

Depictions of a transgender individual pre-transition

These topics are portrayed as part of the narrative and may evoke strong emotional reactions. The story is written by a transgender woman living in a southern Appalachian town who has experienced such bigotry firsthand, lending authenticity to its depiction of these struggles. Reader discretion is advised.

If you are sensitive to these subjects, please prioritize your well-being when engaging with this material.

First edition

ISBN (paperback): 979-8-9923460-1-5
ISBN (hardcover): 979-8-9923460-2-2

Advisor: Roy Jesse
Cover art by Sienna Arts
Advisor: Brandon Ratliff
Editing by Felicia Garcia
Narration by Deana Neibert

This book was professionally typeset on Reedsy.
Find out more at reedsy.com

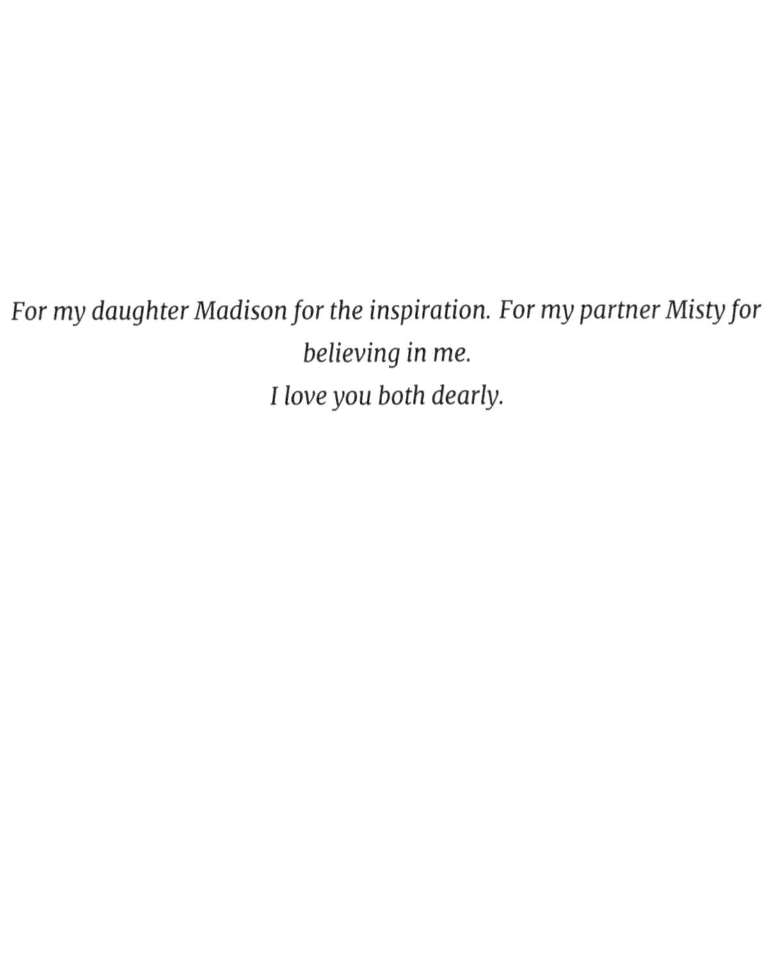

For my daughter Madison for the inspiration. For my partner Misty for believing in me.
I love you both dearly.

I've always been becoming who I am now...

-Maya Dawn Fisher

Contents

Foreword

I have known Maya Dawn Fisher for over twenty years, including her former iteration of herself, when she presented as male under her birth name, which we will not reveal to the public. I have also been friends with her, and her former identity, for over twenty years. We became friends when she was working in a convenience store that I frequented, a line of work I engaged in before going to law school. Her intellect formed the bond of our enduring friendship.

When Maya asked me to read and edit her novel, I was honored. After having done so, I feel even more honored.

Maya has written an incredibly good book. Her writing is impeccable, and her storytelling ability is even better. This novel is innovative, as it explores the enigma of living a transgender existence. Beyond that, the novel is just exciting, fast-paced, and action-packed. I promise you that, once you start reading this fine work, you will not be able to stop reading.

Finally, congratulations to Maya Dawn Fisher on a job that was exceedingly well done. I am very proud of you!

Roy M. Jesse

Roy Jesse is an attorney who has practiced law for over 32 years in Norton, Virginia. He is a graduate of King College, now King University, and the University of Virginia School of Law.

Preface

Why Did I Write Reborn In Shadows?

That's a loaded question. I never imagined myself as a writer. Yet here I am, writing.

I've always been a storyteller—someone who weaves narratives in the moment, captivating friends and family with spoken-word tales. But writing? That felt out of reach. I convinced myself that crafting a novel was for *real* writers, not for someone like me. I doubted whether I had the discipline, the skill, or even the right to put my stories to the page.

Well, I was wrong.

I *can* write. And, to my amazement, people *do* want to read what I've created. It's surreal.

So why *this* story? Why *Reborn In Shadows* as my debut novel?

It started with my daughter, Madison. Over the years, I've loved making up ridiculous stories about how I lost my leg. The truth is, I lost it to medical complications, but my tall tales were always more fun. One day, she asked me, "Have you ever told a story where you lost your leg to the mob?" I hadn't. But within minutes, that question spiraled into an idea—one that felt too big, too rich, too *alive* to remain just another spoken-word tale. It needed to be something more.

It needed a true protagonist.

Enter **Miriam Ryder.**

Miriam is more than just a character. She's a reflection of me, yet also the person I *wish* I could be. She shares my traits—she's transgender, a below-the-knee amputee, and smokes like a fiend—but she's braver. She's sharper. She's the version of myself that doesn't hesitate, doesn't falter, doesn't let fear dictate her choices. Writing her wasn't just about telling a story; it was about *proving* to myself that I had the strength to see this journey through.

Because *Reborn In Shadows* isn't just a book. It's proof.

Proof that I *am* more than just an oral storyteller. That I *can* write something compelling, immersive, and worth reading. That I *do* have something to say.

Proof to my partner, Misty, and my daughter, Madison, that I can accomplish something monumental—something they can be proud of.

Proof to the doubters—the ones who never thought I could pull this off—that they were wrong to underestimate me.

And proof to *myself* that no matter how many times I've been knocked down, I can rise again.

Writing *Reborn In Shadows* has been a cathartic, liberating experience. Through Miriam, I've explored my own struggles, my triumphs, and the strength I aspire to. Her journey is deeply personal yet universal— about survival, resilience, and reclaiming power in a world that often tries to strip it away.

This book isn't just about losing a leg or going into hiding. It's about *rebirth.* It's about transformation. It's about defying expectations— both external and internal—and stepping into the fire rather than running from it.

Miriam Ryder is a survivor. And by writing this book, I've realized that *so am I.*

So thank you. Thank you for letting me share a piece of myself through Miriam and *Reborn In Shadows.* Writing this book has been the most surreal, challenging, and rewarding journey of my life so far.

And I can't wait for you to meet Miri and walk this fiery path with her.

Acknowledgments

No story is ever written alone, and *Reborn In Shadows* is no exception. This novel is the culmination of years of dreaming, writing, and leaning on the extraordinary people who have enriched my life with their love, encouragement, and expertise.

First, to Roy Jesse, my steadfast friend of over twenty years. We met when I was clerking at a gas station, and from the moment we struck up our first conversation, we formed a bond that has only grown stronger with time. Your legal expertise ensured the courtroom scenes in this book are engaging, but your dedication went even further. You took the time to print out my manuscript, read every page, and left thoughtful notes and feedback that enhanced this story in multiple ways. My tremendous respect and admiration for you have only increased over time. Your friendship has been an unchanging light in my life, and I am so grateful for you. Your singing my praises to your family at our lunch in December warmed my heart.

A special thank you to Brandon Ratliff, my lifelong friend and an exceptional attorney, whose legal expertise not only helped me craft a more dramatic and compelling ending but also ensured that it remained legally accurate. Your insights and support have been invaluable throughout this journey, and I am beyond grateful for your guidance in bringing this story to life with authenticity and precision.

To Chasity Patrick, my best friend of twenty-two years. Our story began in 2002 when we first met during my very first training class at Sykes, where you were my trainee. Who could have imagined that the foundation of such a beautiful and enduring friendship was being laid at that moment? Over the years, we've shared countless laughs, meaningful conversations, bra shopping together, and even a boudoir photo session—because why not? You even allowed me to be a bridesmaid, providing a trans girl validation she never knew she needed. Through it all, you have been one of the most loyal and true friends a girl could ask for. Your unwavering belief in me gave me the courage to take the leap and write this book. Without your encouragement, *Reborn In Shadows* might never have made it from my heart to the page. Thank you for pushing me to dream bigger, aim higher, and go for it.

I want to extend my deepest gratitude to my editor, Felicia Garcia, whose incredible insight and keen eye have been instrumental in shaping this story. Felicia, your dedication and thoughtful feedback provided an invaluable perspective that enriched every aspect of the narrative. Your ability to enhance the depth and clarity of my words has truly made this story better than I could have imagined. Thank you for your unwavering support and for helping me bring this vision to life with even greater impact.

To Gregg Dietz, my figurative brother and podcasting partner since 2017. Gregg, thank you for the countless hours we've spent gaming together, from epic D&D campaigns to video game adventures, from laughing our way through Jackbox streams on Twitch to recording a modest yet heartfelt podcast for seven years. You have been my rock, grounding me with your strength and encouragement through every twist and turn. More than that, you have been an unwavering ally throughout my transition, supporting me without hesitation and standing by my side every step of the way. Your humor, creativity, and steadfast friendship mean the world to me, and I'm endlessly grateful for the bond we share.

I want to express my deepest gratitude to my incredible friend,

Natosha Rose, for being such a steadfast source of support and understanding throughout my journey. You've been more than a friend—you're truly part of our family, someone I can always count on for encouragement and love. Your strength, kindness, and authenticity have inspired me in countless ways, and you are the heart and soul behind the character of Dianna Simmons in *Reborn In Shadows*. Thank you for being the amazing person you are and for leaving such a profound mark on both my life and my work.

To my daughter, Madison Fisher, and my partner, Misty Moore—words could never fully express the depth of my gratitude for both of you. Madison, you have inherited my creativity, humor, and passion, and you are a constant source of inspiration. Your question about my leg is what sparked the idea for this book, and your faith in me has been a driving force throughout this journey. Misty, thank you for always accepting me as I am and for loving me unconditionally. Your understanding of my need to transition and your unwavering support through every step of that process has meant more than I can say. Together, the two of you fill my life with joy, hope, and countless reasons to smile. You remind me daily of what it means to truly live and give me the courage to keep going.

This novel is as much a product of my journey as it is a tribute to all of you. Thank you for walking beside me and making this dream a reality. Thank you to each of the GoFundMe supporters, this was made possible by you as well.

With love and gratitude,

Maya Fisher

GoFundMe Backers:

Amanda Fleming

April Austin

Athena Holbrook

Az and Kara

Brandon Ratliff

Brittany Miller

Camellia Kelley

Candace Kelley

Heather Porter

Janella K. Baduini

John Leftwich

Katie Stiltner

Kendra Hootman

Margaret Smith

Mark Carrozza

Nickie McCoy

Noal Edwards

Olivia Dollarhyde

Orson Christian

Rachel Stallard

Randa Sturgill

Roy Jesse

Ruth Greer

Torry Lyles

Will Cooper

And thank you to the numerous anonymous donors!

Prologue

A loud slam echoed through the apartment. *What the fuck was that?* Gabe rolled over and lit a cigarette. The clock on his phone revealed that it was 8:04 a.m. *It's too fucking early!* He sat up slowly in his bed and looked around, gathering his bearings. Suddenly, he heard a noise coming from the living room.

I knew I wasn't imagining that! Gabe slowly stood up and made his way from his bedroom to the living room, stumbling over piles of dirty laundry. To his surprise, he had company.

Leo Rossi stood by the front door looking at Gabe's mail, which was full of bills with 'FINAL NOTICE' stamped in large red lettering. Leo was Gabe's bookie, with whom he had placed bets for over two years. Leo was also a bookie to whom Gabe was heavily indebted. Gabe suddenly broke out in a cold sweat. "Leo... what... what brings you here?"

Leo's face fell, his expression heavy with disappointment. He tossed Gabe's mail aside, snapped his green notebook shut, and said, "Gabe, I wish I could say I was here bringing good news or good tidings and shit, but it's not that kind of visit.

"No, this is a visit in an official business capacity. As I reminded you two months ago, you owe Mister De Luca a lot of money, Gabe. You know how much. You've had time to attempt to make payment arrangements; you've not even tried. You could have entered the employment of Mister De Luca to work your debt off, but you didn't even ask. No, Gabe, we've given you two months to grow a pair and try to do the right thing. But you've not done shit." Leo cracked his knuckles and gestured towards the swivel chair separating Gabe from Leo.

Gabe started toward the chair as he stammered, "I... I... I can do all those things; I can go to Mister De Luca today; I can make this right. I can—"

Another voice emanated from the swivel chair as it slowly rotated to reveal a menacing figure holding a gun and pointing it directly at Gabe. "You don't understand, Gabriel. This isn't a list of offered solutions. This is us telling you that your time has run out."

This voice belonged to a strikingly handsome individual but just as equally intimidating. While not a towering person, standing at 5'10", his chiseled features displayed a cunning guile, and his body language suggested he was serious.

"You! You're... you're... Marco... Marco De Luca... Mis... Mist... Mister De Luca, please," Gabe struggled nervously to find his words. Sweat was running down his face and back. "Plea... please, assure your father that I'll make good on this debt, I swear it. I'll do anything; I just need more time to—"

"Shut the fuck up, Gabriel. As Leo said, you squandered your chances. This is me giving you an ultimatum. You have 24 hours to pay your debt to my father in full, or we'll be back. And we will collect—one way... or another... And Gabriel, pray you come up with the money. You don't want to experience what we do to people who don't pay their debts to the De Luca family." Marco waved the gun from side to side, tilting his head to the right. He continued in a calculated voice, "We paid a visit to a former client in McKees Rocks last week. Let's just say he won't celebrate the 4th in a few days."

Leo chimed in, "24 hours, Gabe. The clock's ticking. See ya

tomorrow." Leo and Marco De Luca exited Gabe's apartment, casting menacing looks on their way out. Leo added a final parting remark. "Clean this place up, it fucking stinks."

Gabe had been holding his breath in fear. His chest heaved as he exhaled and gasped for air, and he struggled to gather his thoughts.

What the fuck am I going to do? 24 hours isn't long enough... I'm as good as dead.

Chapter 1: The House At The Edge Of Tomorrow

Miriam took a long, final drag from her cigarette before putting it out. She slowly turned onto the small dirt road and crossed the solidly constructed wooden bridge that spanned the creek. *This is it,* she thought to herself. *My new life begins now.*

As the dirt and gravel crunched beneath the tires, her chest tightened. *A fresh start, they'd called it. But how do you start fresh when the memories still cling to you like a second skin?* Her fingers absentmindedly brushed against the tender scar on her thigh beneath her jeans—a ghost of a night that had stolen so much from her.

She pulled into the driveway of the two-story house, trying to focus on its charm: the wraparound porch, the sturdy brick foundation, the towering trees. But her mind began to wander as she turned off the car and stared at the house.

For a moment, she wasn't there. She was back in that dingy apartment; the smell of smoke and blood filled her nostrils, and Alex's voice echoed in her ears.

Miriam could still hear him, clear as day. "Let me talk to Leo! He can sort all this out!" Alex had said, his voice calm but desperate, his hands raised in surrender. And then—

The sound of the gunshot tore through her memory. Miriam flinched, gripping the steering wheel tighter as if bracing herself. Alex's body crumpled to the floor, lifeless, before her brain even registered what had happened.

She'd been frozen in her chair, her heart pounding as the lead attacker turned his attention to her. "No witnesses," he'd snarled before the crowbars swung. The searing pain in her leg, the crack of her bones, and the metallic taste of blood were still vivid. She'd tried to crawl, to move, but her body wouldn't listen.

Her breathing quickened. Miriam squeezed her eyes shut and inhaled deeply, forcing herself to anchor back to the present. *It's over. That's not who you are anymore. You're here now. You survived.*

The soft rustle of the wind brought her back. Miriam opened her eyes and stepped out of the car, letting the cool air fill her lungs. She looked at the house again, this time with more clarity. This place was hers. She wasn't the same person lying broken on that floor anymore. She'd chosen to be Miriam Ryder, and that meant something.

She took a deep breath. *Fresh air. Wow, that is some seriously fresh fucking air.* She reached into her purse, withdrew a fresh cigarette and lighter, and then lit it.

The movers should be here soon. She thought to herself as she inhaled and made her way up the steps to the porch. A wooden porch swing at the far end called to her, compelling her to sit as she took her phone out of her purse. It was 11:37 a.m. She was actually early. *That's rare,* she thought. *I'm constantly running late.*

She scrolled through her phone, not really knowing what to look at. She didn't have any social media accounts or use any messaging services. Miriam just looked at various news websites and was instantly disturbed by the current events happening around the country.

"Damn these politicians," she muttered, exhaling her smoke abruptly before placing her phone back into her purse. *Another bathroom bill,* she raged internally. *When are these assholes going to get it through their heads that we just want to fucking pee?*

She put her cigarette out, got up, and walked to the front door. *Time to take a walk-through.* She entered the lock code into the keypad the home's previous owner had left with Rachel: *1-1-2-8.* Miriam heard an audible click, and she breathed a sigh of relief as she opened the door and stepped into her new home for the very first time.

The first room the front door opened into was obviously going to be her living room, as it had signs of clearly being used as such before. Directly to her right was a large open archway leading to another room. *Dining room? Hobby room? I'll figure it out.*

Both the living room and the dining room featured large open archways leading to the spacious kitchen. The wall behind the island on the right was painted black, serving as an accent wall in opposition to the kitchen's white walls. She let out an audible squeal. *I love this fucking kitchen!* She had a dishwasher! There was a large wooden hanging door with glass window panes to the right in front of her. She slid it open to the right on its track to a cavernous pantry.

I love this place so much already, she declared to herself. There were three shelves lining the opposite wall, a small metal table to the left with a microwave, and a large wooden buffet cabinet to the right that seemed to be built into the pantry.

She turned, walked out of the pantry, and looked to her left. French doors with glass panels opened into a large deck in the backyard. A metal-framed gazebo with a canvas top and zipping screened sides was affixed to the deck. *Some wicker chairs and a side table, and here's my reading area. It's perfect.*

She closed the doors and walked back into the kitchen, going down the hallway leading past the living room. A periwinkle blue bathroom was on the right, and she paused to glance at her reflection in the mirror above the sink.

Miriam was tall for a woman, standing at 5'11". She was a curvy, very busty, thick woman, and could be described as plus-sized. Her long, wavy, auburn-brown hair complemented her warm hazel eyes well, framing her face with a natural elegance. She had a commanding presence, carrying herself with a confidence that softened into warmth when she smiled. Her style often leaned toward comfortable yet flattering outfits, accentuating her curves while reflecting her vibrant personality. She smiled at herself and returned to explore the rest of the house.

The utility room was just beyond the bathroom on the right, housing a sleek matching washing machine and dryer with metallic black finishes. At the end of the hallway was another door leading to the side of the house, emptying underneath the sun deck and onto the wraparound porch.

She returned to the living room, where she had her first pause. The stairs leading upstairs needed a handrail. *That's definitely going to have to be rectified quickly.* She looked up, braced herself with her left arm, and carefully proceeded up the stairs.

Aside from being a chain smoker, Miriam was also an amputee. She only had three inches of shinbone below her knee, and she only recently began walking with her new prosthetic leg. She was less than one year removed from the incident that caused her to lose fifteen inches of leg.

People don't realize how much more energy amputees expend on mundane tasks. Her physical therapist told her that a below-the-knee amputee like herself spent forty percent more energy than the average non-disabled person. Climbing stairs was worse. *Fourteen stairs? Fuck me!*

By the time she reached the top, Miriam was out of breath. *The doctors and nurses told me it would take at least a year minimum to regain my former strength. If it ever comes back.* She doubted that she would ever recover that level of strength. Her medications would see to that.

Not only was Miriam a chain-smoking amputee, she was also

transgender. Having recently started hormone replacement therapy, she noticed she had already lost some strength in her body. *Estrogen is truly amazing, but damn if it hasn't weakened me*, she thought as she braced herself at the top of the stairs.

The second floor started with a door to the left leading outside to the sun deck and one long hallway. First on the left was a smaller room, not much larger than the pantry. *Craft room, maybe? Or was this once used as a sewing room? I like this eggshell color on the textured walls.* The next room on the left was the master bathroom, and it was painted a goldenrod yellow. Across the hall from the bathroom was the first of three large bedrooms.

Each bedroom was painted a very light gray and featured a lace-patterned wall texture. *What am I going to do with so much space?* She limped down the hall to check out each bedroom, each quite spacious and having large, walk-in closets. She then became aware that her prosthetic was starting to hurt her. She struggled after a few hours of wearing it and still hadn't gotten her gait down. As a result, she walked with a prominent limp.

She carefully made her way back downstairs and out the front door. *I love that this house has hardwood floors throughout. It will make it easier to sweep.* She glanced at her phone—11:56 a.m. The movers were due at noon. She sat down on the porch swing, awkwardly removed her prosthetic, and began massaging her stump with her right hand while rifling through her purse for another cigarette and her lighter.

"It's not even noon, and I'm already fucking exhausted." The silence rang loudly in her ears. She noticed how peaceful it was. The only sounds were the rustling of the leaves as the wind blew through the trees, the creaking of the porch swing chains, and her boot scraping back and forth on the wooden porch.

Peace... Absolute peace. I can definitely be happy here. It's a welcome change. If Alex could see me now. I wonder what he would think of this place.

As she took another puff on her cigarette, she could see the moving truck turning into the driveway. The day was just getting started.

Chapter 2: Welcome To Jasper Hill

M iriam stood at the side door by the utility room and watched as the tail lights of the moving truck grew smaller and then disappeared. She only had a little for the movers to bring in and set up. *I seriously need to get some furniture soon. I'll have to see what Rachel can help with.*

Miriam opened the door, walked to the other end of the wraparound porch, and sat down in the swing. She pulled her phone and pack of cigarettes out of her denim jacket pocket. It was 2:13 p.m. Lighting her first cigarette in what felt like years instead of two hours, she checked her phone for messages.

There was a missed text. She immediately knew it was from Rachel because Rachel was one of only three people who had this number, and she didn't expect to hear anything from two of them for quite some time. Miriam thumbed her text messages open and read the text silently to herself: *Explore Jasper Hill.*

Well, there's still plenty of daylight; I may as well do that now. Miriam grabbed her purse, made sure she had her keys, double-checked the lock on the front door, and walked to the car.

Her car was a silver 2016 model Honda CR-V, and it had recently been outfitted with hand controls so she could still drive. *The things that I used to take for granted,* she thought, as she cranked the car. She slid the panel under the glass moon roof open to allow a bit more natural light into the car. She turned the car around and proceeded down the driveway's hill.

She tuned the radio to Sirius Liquid Metal, turned it up, rolled her windows down, and put her sunglasses on. She then pulled out of the driveway onto the secondary road which was the first part of her journey into town. *Wow, I officially live in a 'holler' now.* It was one mile to the main road, then five miles to the main county highway. Then another seven miles to Jasper Hill. *Yeah, I definitely live in the fucking sticks.*

On her drive, she thought a lot about what Rachel had told her about Jasper Hill. It was tiny—landlocked and only incorporated four square miles. The last census claimed the population was 1,549, but that was four years ago. The population has since decreased to closer to 1,300.

The biggest shock for Miriam was the town's lack of diversity. 98.5% of the population was white, and 32.4% were over 65. *I've moved to Boomerville.*

The town itself was nestled in the Appalachian mountains of southwest Virginia. Its location was less than twenty minutes from the Kentucky border, forty-five minutes from West Virginia, and roughly one hour away from the Tennessee border. *No one will ever find me here. It's just the way I need it.*

Her first sight of Jasper Hill was a floral shop on her right, and then she passed an out-of-business dry cleaner. Miriam drove around a small curve and was officially in Jasper Hill, where a used car dealership greeted her.

Miriam checked her speedometer to ensure she was driving at the posted speed limit of 25 miles per hour. As she progressed down the street, she turned the music down to avoid attracting unwanted attention.

There wasn't much to the town. It definitely gave off a throwback vibe to decades before. There was a large grocery store at the town's roundabout, along with a large hotel across from it and a small gas station next to a Mexican restaurant. She entered the roundabout. There were three exit options: back the way she came, to the right, leading to the 'business district', and to the left, past the grocery store leading to the next county over.

Wow, this place is incredibly tiny. Miriam counted the possible chain locations in town where you could eat. There was a taco place and a pizza place, and across from those was a place to get subs inside a gas station; just past the lumber supply company on the left was a burger place, and at the town border was another small pizza place and a burger joint that was also inside a gas station.

It looks like I'm going to be cooking a lot in the foreseeable future. Miriam turned around to go the other way and explore the other side of town. She counted ten churches in the span of the two-mile drive through town. There were more places to worship than there were to eat.

Miriam spotted the Jasper Hill Courthouse, a convention center diagonally across from it that looked like it used to be an old single-screen movie theater, and the Jasper Hill Cafe. She decided to pull into a parking space in front of the cafe and went inside. She opened the door, and the tempting smell of greasy burgers wafted through the air to greet her.

The smell of greasy burgers transported Miriam back to late nights with Alex, ordering takeout and arguing over which movie to watch. Her stomach tightened. She pushed the memory aside, but it lingered like a phantom, reminding her of everything she had lost and how much she still had to hide.

Holy shit, she exclaimed in her head, *this place is straight out of that old show 'Happy Days.' Alex would love this place.* The interior of the Jasper Hill Cafe was a tribute to another era. The tile floor sported a red and white checkerboard design. On the far wall, in between the red restroom doors, was a classic jukebox blaring country music. The turquoise walls were decorated with dozens of black and white photos that appeared to be pictures of Jasper Hill in the 1950s. Beneath the photos were red booth-style tables, each with a retro tabletop speaker that was synced to the jukebox.

On the left side of the cafe was a long turquoise lunch counter with twelve red barstools. At the right end of the counter was a cash register, and behind the counter was an open window that allowed patrons to see into the kitchen. Miriam looked around, and there were six other people in the cafe: a waitress, the cook in the back, an older woman who appeared to be in her 60s, another pair of older women, and the county sheriff.

The pair of older women at a corner table glanced her way, their voices dropping to whispers. Miriam felt the weight of their eyes, and the unspoken question was clear: Who was she, and why was she here? She turned back to choose a seat, but her heart raced. Fitting in here was going to be more challenging than she thought.

Miriam chose a barstool at the far-left end of the lunch counter by the front window. This allowed her to watch her car, the front door, the sidewalk, and keep to herself. On the wall in front of her was an elongated mirror with an integrated clock in the center. It was now 2:53 p.m. It took her less than forty minutes to drive to town, drive through town to check it out, and enter the cafe for a late lunch.

I'm absolutely starving, she realized. She had not eaten since the 6:00 a.m. sausage and cheese croissant earlier that day. The waitress came over to her and handed her a spiral-bound laminated menu. "I'll be with ya in just a sec, hun." The waitress turned back to the register, and the lone older woman was ready to pay her bill.

Miriam opened the thick menu and thumbed through the pages. She really just wanted a cheeseburger, fries, and a soda. She placed the menu on the counter and waited for the waitress to collect the old woman's money. Miriam grinned to herself and mused, *"It never fails.*

Old people always have cash, never a card." To Miriam's surprise, the woman began writing a paper check.

Just how many years behind is this town, anyway? She did her best not to stare in awe at the older woman and her archaic payment method. When she glanced further to her right, she met the sheriff's gaze. He was staring intently at her over a cup of coffee with a stern look. He placed his coffee cup on the table, stood up, and approached Miriam, his eyes locked on hers.

Chapter 3: A Taste Of Hostility

Miriam tensed up as the sheriff approached her. His stern gaze was met with an equally determined pace. His massive frame moved with purpose. His forehead was glistening with sweat, running from his thinning gray hair and onto his cheeks. Miriam stared as a bead of sweat amassed on the tip of the sheriff's nose before it dropped to land somewhere on his massive belly. She thought she could smell a hint of alcohol on his breath as he spoke.

"Can I help you... Miss? *Are* you a miss?" His contempt was so thinly veiled that he seemed like he would potentially snap at any moment. "Just exactly *what* are you, and what are you doing here?" He placed his right palm face down on the counter and leaned in close to Miriam while not-so-subtly brushing his badge with his left thumb.

Miriam flashed her most polite smile before replying. She silently counted to five in her head. "Well, officer, if you must know, I wanted a cheeseburger. This place seems like it sells cheeseburgers. So my intention is to order a cheeseburger. And maybe a side of fries. And a Pepsi. Is there a problem with me ordering a cheeseburger? Officer...?"

"It's sheriff. Sheriff Tom Harris. And you didn't answer my question. *What* are you? You one of... them? 'Cause we don't need your kind around here. Y'unnerstand?" The more he spoke, the lower his voice got. The last two words, *you understand*, were uttered through clenched teeth.

Miriam was genuinely shocked. *The fucking audacity!* Her mind was reeling. She balled up her fists and dug her fingernails into her palms. *Yes,* she told herself, *you're transgender, Miriam, and it's the very early stages of your transition. Sometimes, people will notice.*

She took a deep breath before calmly responding, "Yes, Sheriff, I am a transgender woman. I'm a hungry one at that. I am new in town. In fact, I just moved here this morning, and I don't have any food in my house yet, so I came to town to find a place to eat, then get some groceries and go home." With her eyes focused on his face, she was showing Sheriff Harris that she would not be intimidated.

"Well, maybe you should just get your order to go." He stepped back, turned to the waitress, who had been watching the exchange with worry, and said, "What do I owe you for the coffee, Di?"

The waitress, Di, replied, "It's on the house, Tom, the same as it is every day. Can I get you anything else?" Her weight shifted nervously from one foot to the other, and her left hand fidgeted at her side out of sight.

"No, just the coffee today." He shot one final stern glance at Miriam before walking out in a huff. He paused on the sidewalk and looked at Miriam's car, cast one more look at her through the front window, then walked off.

What an asshole. Now, the anger was setting in. Miriam had been misgendered in the past, and the few times it had happened, the offender apologized, corrected themselves, and carried on. She was okay with that, and she could tell those people were making a genuine effort. But this was something entirely new to her, and she did not like it.

Di approached Miriam with a notepad and pen to take her order, but Miriam cut her off. "I'm really sorry, but I'm not hungry anymore. I'll come back another day. Would that be okay?"

"Hun, you're more than welcome to come back any day of the week. Don't let Sheriff Harris get to you; he's all bark with no bite. So please, I heard you tell him you wanted a cheeseburger and fries. What do you want on it?" Di clearly wasn't going to allow her to leave after such an unpleasant encounter.

Miriam smiled and gently lowered herself back onto the barstool. "Yes, I would love a cheeseburger, the biggest one you have. Can you put caramelized onions on it? And mustard? With a side of fries and a Pepsi, please."

"I can do all that but the Pepsi. We have Coke. Will that work?" Di smiled warmly at Miriam as she nodded yes to the Coke. "That's going to take about ten minutes, hun. I'll be back in a flash."

"I'm going to step outside to smoke; I'll be back." Di nodded in acknowledgment as Miriam went outside and onto the sidewalk. She reached into her denim jacket pocket, retrieved a cigarette and lighter, and proceeded to light up. She inhaled. *Damn, there's nothing better to alleviate stress than a good cigarette.*

She pushed the confrontation with the sheriff out of her mind, breathing deeply and allowing calmness to wash over her. As she smoked, she watched cars pass by on the street. It was much different than what she was accustomed to. This was so far removed from the hustle and bustle fast-paced environment she had lived in for ten years prior. She finished her cigarette, extinguished it into an ashtray by the cafe door, and went back inside.

Di emerged from the kitchen with Miriam's food just as Miriam seated herself on the barstool once again. Miriam was delighted by how absolutely delicious the burger smelled, the sweetness of the onions cutting through the air. "Thank you. I know by the look and smell I will enjoy this very much." Di gave her a wink and disappeared to the kitchen.

Miriam grabbed the enormous cheeseburger and lifted it to her mouth, breathed it in for a moment, and then took a bite. *Amazing! This burger is incredibly good!* She delightfully chewed, swallowed, and then repeated with another bite. This cheeseburger was immaculate. It was nearly like a religious experience for her. *I didn't realize how fucking hungry I was.*

She finished her meal, astounded at how tasty it was, and as she glanced over towards the entrance to the kitchen, Di emerged. Miriam gave a small smile as Di made her way towards her. She appeared to be in her mid-40s, was about 5'6" tall, thick and curvy, and had shoulder-length wavy honey-blonde hair and brown eyes. Her eyes and the warm smile she displayed let Miriam know that she had nothing to worry about from Di. This woman was genuinely kind.

"Would you like a slice of pie? We have apple, peach, cherry, blueberry, and key lime."

Miriam grinned and replied, "Key lime, please, that sounds wonderful." Di went back to the kitchen and returned a minute later with a slice of key lime pie.

"I'm Diana Simmons. But everyone calls me Di for short. I'm the owner of the Jasper Hill Cafe. What's your name, hun?" She had such a kind tone to her voice, Miriam thought, as if to imply she was genuinely interested in learning about her new customer.

"I'm Miriam. Miriam Ryder. My friends call me Miri." She continued. "What's up with the sheriff? He seemed to have a stick up his ass." She was relieved when Di let out a chuckle.

"Tom Harris is a hard ass, and he's not a fan of anyone from the LGBTQ+ community. I'm sure he noticed your pin and patch on your jacket, and it really got under his skin."

Miriam was so used to her transgender flag pin on the right breast of her jacket and the Pride patch on her right sleeve that she had almost forgotten they were there. "Oh. Great. Just what I need, an intolerant, ignorant cop on my ass."

"Try not to let it get to you, and I know that it's easier said than done. Tom is a stubborn man, and he's resistant to change and social progress. By abusing his power and privilege, he hounds any of the local college kids he suspects or knows are LGBTQ+ whenever he sees them. My daughter used to be a frequent target of his. It's all I can do to serve the man when he comes in. Just know you aren't alone, and you have an ally in me."

"Thank you, Di. It's comforting to know there is at least one person who isn't a bigot. I always heard there was a higher concentration of bigotry and intolerance in the South, but that was the first time I had experienced it. It's... unsettling, to say the least."

Miriam's smile faded, and sadness crept into her eyes. *Privilege,* she thought. *I have taken that for granted.* It was at this point she understood that she had exchanged her privilege from her former identity. She realized she was still in a better position than a lot of other transgender people, especially people of color, but this encounter had left her shaken nonetheless.

Di could tell Miriam didn't want to discuss the encounter with the sheriff further, so she changed the subject: "So you're new in town, eh? Why did you move to Jasper Hill? Are you enrolling in Mountain View College? Go, Trailblazers!"

Miriam had anticipated this question, and she and Rachel had devised a solid story, she hoped anyway. "There are several reasons, actually. First and foremost, I'm an artist. I thought, what better way to tap into my creativity than to draw inspiration from the natural beauty of Southwest Virginia? And not only that, the countryside seems like a great place for me to heal my mind and body further."

Di glanced downward at Miriam's prosthetic leg. "That looks pretty new, do you mind if I ask how it happened?" Miriam's face lit up; she loved telling new people all about how she lost her leg. She remained calm in her outer demeanor, but inside she was jumping with joy and cackling with laughter. What people didn't know is that it's a new story every time. Only a handful of people know what really happened, and she intended to keep it that way.

"I was catfish noodling in North Carolina last summer. Some friends and I were at Fontana Village in the Smokies, and we wanted to try it after seeing it being done on YouTube. I'm a bit adventurous, so I'll try nearly anything once, twice if I like it." She continued. "So I'm in the shallow waters of a cove on the lake, wearing nothing but my bikini because we had also been swimming, and I'm bent over, feeling around in the water with my hands for signs of a catfish nest.

"My foot landed on something slippery. It turned out to be a moss-covered log, and there was a hole in the top. My foot slipped through the hole and was trapped and lodged in the hollowed-out log, which, unsurprisingly, was a catfish nest. And he was big. And he was home. He bit and clamped down on my ankle, and the barbels in his mouth cut through my leg in multiple places. My friends helped pull me free, and we went back to our cabin. We treated the wounds and went to eat. I didn't think anything else about it.

"Soon after, about a week or two, I got very sick. I thought I had the flu, and my leg started swelling massively. The following day I couldn't put any weight on it, so I called 911, and an ambulance came to get me. After arriving at the hospital, I was informed I had sepsis, and they took X-rays and an MRI. There was a severe infection in my tibia. The doctors said they would have to amputate above the infection and ravaged bone, or else I would die. So they performed emergency surgery.

"In addition to being septic, I had contracted a staph infection and necrotizing fasciitis, also known as flesh-eating bacteria disease. The doctors told me that I was mere hours away from death. They saved my life."

Di stood there, mouth agape, while listening to Miriam's story.

Miriam sold it well. She took pride in her ability to bullshit others, and she was convincing. After a few seconds, Di found her words again. "Honey, that sounds like a horrible ordeal, and I am so glad you survived. The Lord above has a purpose for you; mark my words."

Miriam struggled not to roll her eyes, as she was an atheist but nodded along with the sentiment. "Thank you, Di, I hope you're right."

She looked at the clock on the wall to check the time. Somehow an hour had passed, and then a young couple walked into the cafe and seated themselves in a booth. Di was getting ready to take the couple menus when Miriam asked for her bill. DI responded. "This one is on me, you've been through a lot today, and I want you to know that there are more people here that will welcome you than those that will reject you. Just give us a chance."

Miriam thanked Di, smiled genuinely, and left the cafe for what she felt would be the first of many times.

Chapter 4: A Glimpse Of Normalcy

Miriam departed from the Jasper Hill Cafe and thought about where to go next. She recalled that Rachel had told her there was a small university on the western outskirts of town. She decided she would go check it out.

The college was about two miles away from the center of Jasper Hill yet remained within the town limits, and the difference in the vibes Miriam felt was vast. Whereas Jasper Hill felt like a relic of a time long gone, Mountain View College felt like it was made for modern-day society.

Mountain View College, or MVC as the students and alumni affectionately refer to it, was a public liberal arts college. The campus was home to roughly 1,800 students, with another estimated 700 commuting students from Jasper Hill and other nearby towns. As a result of most students being from northern and eastern Virginia, the campus exhibited a wide range of cultural influences and perspectives. Diversity thrived and flourished at MVC.

There were two entrances to MVC's campus, and Miriam chose the second entrance. What caught her attention first was the campus baseball diamond on the right when she turned into the entrance. It was April 1, and a game was underway. *I bet it's opening day!* Being a fan of baseball, she turned into a small parking lot across the road from the field and walked over to the field entrance.

Tickets were five dollars. Miriam paid, took her ticket stub, put it in her jacket pocket, and chose a seat in the front row. The away team was at bat, and MVC was fielding. It was the top of the third inning, and MVC was trailing two runs to one. The away team wore navy blue uniforms with gold trim and a pirate logo. As she watched the game unfold, she wondered what school they represented.

MVC was wearing white home uniforms with red pinstripes and red hats. The pitcher was struggling on the mound. The away team was making solid contact with a majority of his pitches, putting the ball into play often and giving the infielders and outfielders a very busy day in the field.

He's already gassed, Miriam thought to herself as the pitcher hurled a desperate fastball to the catcher, only to be met with an extremely loud crack as the batter drove the ball over the right field wall. Home run. With one runner on first, that made the score 4-1. And it was still the top of the third inning. *Alex used to love going to the ballpark with me.* Her thoughts shifted back to last summer.

The stadium buzzed with energy, the scent of popcorn and hot dogs wafting through the warm summer air. Miriam, still living as her pre-transition self, leaned against the metal railing of the upper deck, her eyes fixed on the field. Alex stood beside her, his broad smile as constant as the cheering crowd around them.

"I'm telling you, this pitcher is toast," Alex said, nudging Miriam with his elbow. "He's throwing meatballs out there. Watch—next inning, someone's taking him yard."

Miriam smirked, rolling her eyes. "You think you know everything about baseball, don't you?"

"Not everything," Alex replied with mock humility. "But enough to impress you."

She laughed, the sound surprising her in its ease. It had been a long time since she'd felt this carefree. Alex had a way of making the world's weight vanish, even if only for a few hours. She glanced at him, his profile outlined by the stadium lights, and felt a pang of something bittersweet. She wasn't sure how much of her true self she could show him—how much of her he'd understand.

As if sensing her gaze, Alex turned to her, his grin softening. "You're awfully quiet. Don't tell me you're siding with the pitcher."

"I just like to watch," she replied, shrugging. "Doesn't have to be all about stats and predictions."

"Fair enough," he said, tipping his cap in mock deference. "But just wait. I know a bomb when I see one coming."

A loud crack interrupted their banter, and the ball soared high into the night sky. The crowd erupted as it cleared the centerfield wall. Alex whooped, pumping his fist. "Called it! Did I not call it?"

Miriam laughed again, shaking her head. "You're unbearable when you're right, you know that?"

"Maybe, but you keep me around anyway." He winked, then pulled a box of Cracker Jack from his pocket. "Want some? Or are you too dignified for ballpark snacks?"

She took a handful, tossing a piece into her mouth. "I'm only here for the seventh-inning stretch."

"Ah, the highlight of any baseball game," Alex teased. "Where else can you sing off-key with thousands of strangers and get away with it?"

The inning ended, and the players jogged off the field. As they waited for the next at-bat, Alex turned to her, more serious now. "You okay? You've seemed... I don't know, distracted."

Miriam hesitated, the question tugging at a truth she wasn't ready to share. "I'm fine," she said, forcing a smile. "Just soaking it all in."

Alex studied her for a moment before nodding. "Alright. But you know you can tell me stuff, right? Whatever's on your mind."

She swallowed hard, looking back at the field. The game was simpler— runs, hits, outs. Life didn't work that way. "Yeah," she said quietly. "I know."

The crowd roared as the next batter stepped up to the plate, but Miriam barely heard it. She clung to the moment, the shared warmth of the evening, and the fleeting comfort of Alex's presence, even as the distance between them—the truths unspoken—felt insurmountable. A fan sitting behind her screaming at the umpire jerked Miriam back to reality.

Miriam scanned the stands, spotting a small smoking area tucked near the press box. She made her way over, leaning against the railing as she lit her cigarette. The faint buzz of college chatter hummed around her—a trio of students, all carefree laughter and casual shrugs, traded stories about exams and weekend plans. She envied their lightness, their unburdened existence.

"First time here?" one of them asked, catching Miriam's gaze.

"Yeah, just moved to town," she replied, exhaling a thin stream of smoke.

"Well, welcome. Don't let the score fool you—MVC always comes back in the later innings."

Their casual warmth caught her off guard. She offered a small smile, grateful for the unexpected connection, however fleeting. As she finished her cigarette, a sharp crack echoed across the field, drawing groans from the stands—another home run. Miriam chuckled wryly. Maybe MVC wasn't so great at comebacks after all.

Rachel will be happy to see me integrating into small-town life, she mused. *Well, maybe not so much about my run-in with Sheriff Harris.* She lit another cigarette and heard a thunderous crack, followed by a collective groan from the stands. She looked to the field to see the pitcher had given up another home run. *His day is done, they're down 7-1 now.*

Miriam decided to leave early. She still had to get a few groceries, and she wanted to get home soon because her leg was starting to throb.

To compensate for the pain, Miriam shifted more of her weight onto her left leg, but in doing so, she overcompensated and caused lower back pain to manifest. *Great. I'm pushing myself too hard today, and I will be paying for it tomorrow.*

Miriam decided the grocery store could wait. She stopped at a gas station for cigarettes and grabbed some snacks: beef jerky, chips, a candy bar, Skittles, caramel creams, and a pre-made turkey sandwich. She grabbed a bottle of Pepsi and a bag of ice, got her cigarettes, paid for everything, and then headed home.

Once home, she sat on the porch swing to enjoy the fading daylight hours while googling the local comic book shop. Her phone dinged. It was a text from Rachel with the meeting location for tomorrow. *10:00 a.m., car wash, bay number 4.* Miriam committed the location to memory and deleted the text.

She noted it was 7:14 p.m., and she was beyond tired. Going inside, she placed her food in the refrigerator and went upstairs. It had been a very long day, and she was going to bed early.

She eased out of her clothes, the fabric brushing against her skin as she swapped them for the soft embrace of her pajamas. Sitting on the edge of her bed, Miriam removed her prosthetic leg with practiced care. As she did so, a wave of relief washed over her. The ache in her stump lessened immediately, as though the weight of the day—both physical and emotional—had been lifted. She rubbed the tender skin gently, her fingertips tracing over the scars like an intimate ritual, grounding herself in the here and now.

Sliding under the covers, she exhaled deeply, letting her body sink into the mattress. The events of the day replayed in her mind unbidden. Sheriff Harris's sneer, Di's warmth, the crack of the bat at the baseball game—it all felt like puzzle pieces she hadn't yet figured out how to fit together. She considered picking up her phone to distract herself but decided against it. Her thoughts were enough for tonight.

With a small sigh, she set her phone alarm for 6:00 a.m., placed it on the nightstand to charge, and closed her eyes. As she drifted into sleep, her mind lingered on the tenuous hope that tomorrow might offer a smoother path.

Chapter 5: Quarters And Connections

Miriam pulled into the car wash and did a quick scan of the area. There were six wash bays, and she noticed each was numbered above their respective entrances. She was supposed to be in bay four at 10:00 a.m. It was 10:06 a.m. *Incredible, I'm constantly running late.*

Miriam pulled into the bay and shut her car off. She deposited her cigarette into the smokeless ashtray she kept in the console, looked in her mirrors for signs of anyone, and saw no one, so she exited the car. Taking a look at her car, she realized it could benefit from being washed. *That's certainly convenient,* she thought. *I have a reasonably dirty vehicle as is. I'll go ahead and get some change to wash it.*

Miriam walked to the change machine that provided quarters in exchange for bills. Depositing three ones, she scooped up the quarters and placed them into her jacket pocket. Miriam had nearly reached the wash station when she heard Rachel's voice.

"You're late, Miri. Again." There was no reason to deny the exasperated tone Miriam heard in Rachel's voice. She turned around and flashed an apologetic grin.

"I'm really sorry, Rachel. I had a long day yesterday, and I was exhausted, so I didn't unpack last night. I realized it was a bad idea to have skipped it when I had to spend ten minutes digging through my bags looking for additional sock layers for my prosthetic."

Rachel nodded and looked at Miriam's prosthetic leg. She knew that Miriam had only recently begun walking with it, so she said nothing else. "So, what do you think of our quaint little town?" Rachel asked her.

Rachel Lee was a police officer for the Jasper Hill Police Department. She was just a couple of years older than Miriam, thirty-one or thirty-two years old at best. Rachel was at least half a foot shorter than Miriam, and had a slender frame. Rachel had short black hair and brown eyes and was of Korean-American descent.

"I'm not entirely sure yet. I do think the sheriff's a dick, though." Miriam gritted her teeth when she recounted the interaction with Sheriff Harris to Rachel. "The college looks promising, and the cafe is kitschy, but the owner is very nice. I heard about a comic shop that I'm going to check out after I leave here. So, it has some charm but more bigotry than I had anticipated."

Rachel nodded sadly. "It has its share of xenophobia, too. A lot of the 'good ole boy' local cops can't stand anyone who isn't White working as a fellow officer, let alone a woman being on the force. They automatically assumed I was there to work in dispatch when I reported for duty on my first day." She gave Miriam a wry look. "You'll find out on your own soon enough how differently women get treated in a man's world."

Miriam pulled out a cigarette and started to light it. Rachel scoffed, "I just saw you putting one out five minutes ago. Slow down, maybe? I am responsible for your physical well-being, remember?"

Miriam stopped and put the unlit cigarette and lighter back in her jacket pocket. "I know, it's a disgusting habit, and I smoke more when I'm stressed. And the past year has had me really fucking stressed." She looked up, her gaze meeting Rachel's eyes. "But thank you. I appreciate your concern for me."

"It's genuine. Even if it is my job, it's a big deal. It's important to me. And not because it's my job. It's because it's your life. I'm going to protect you. You're going to be able to testify. And those bastards that did this to you will pay their penance." She paused, and when Miriam didn't respond, she continued. "What can I do to help with your living situation? I went to the house yesterday morning. It's pretty secluded, but that's as much a detriment as it is a benefit. You need surveillance cameras. I'm getting those for you in a couple of days. You'll be able to install them yourself, and you can monitor them 24/7 from any internet-enabled device, such as a PC, laptop, or your phone."

"Do you really think I'll need cameras all the way out here? I'm so far out, if something were to happen, and the De Lucas did find me, the response time from the police would make it far too late for me. I'd be dead." Miriam was stony-faced in her response.

"Please don't automatically think of the worst-case scenario. But on the off chance they do find you, with the cameras, we'd have video evidence of assault or, well... murder." Rachel was solemn in her reply. She changed her tone quickly. "What can I requisition from the Marshal Service for you to improve your quality of life?"

Miriam definitely needed some furniture. She needed to replace her PS5, her TV, and more. She smiled at Rachel and said, "Let's make a list."

Miriam finished washing her car. Rachel's words kept echoing in her mind, *assault or, well... murder.* She had been on the receiving end of De Luca violence once before. She vowed she never would be again. She decided to go check out the comic book shop. She lit a cigarette and drove off to the address on her phone.

Trailblazer Comics was located in a shopping center about two miles from Jasper Hill. Nestled between a Mexican restaurant and a GameStop, it featured a brightly colored logo depicting the MCV mascot, Monty the Explorer. She parked her car, finished her cigarette, and went inside. Instantly she felt right at home.

This place has everything! She was taken aback by everything the store had to offer. Wall-to-wall toys, games, model kits, miniatures, paints, tabletop RPGs, novels, manga, tables for gaming, and, of course, comics. A sizeable L-shaped glass display cabinet separated the far left wall from the customer area. It was here that the very valuable books were kept on display, many of them fetching hundreds of dollars in price. The display case itself was filled with vintage toys, Magic cards, dice sets, and more. Behind the counter was a slender male, a couple of inches shorter than Miriam, with dark brown hair, a full beard, and glasses.

Miriam decided to introduce herself. She knew she'd be spending lots of time here. She had been a self-proclaimed nerd all her life. Miriam couldn't wait to look around. She walked up to the counter after the clerk finished a transaction with a customer. "I just wanted to say this store is amazing. I love everything about it!"

The clerk smiled and replied, "Thank you! It's a lot of work and can sometimes drive me crazy, but after spending 15 years here, seeing customer's faces light up and hearing how much joy these various properties give them, it's been worth it."

"I'm Miriam, Miriam Ryder. I just moved here yesterday. I was just wanting to get some comics, but first, I had to tell you how fantastic your store is!" She felt like she was possibly a little too excited and composed herself.

"I'm Elijah Marley, but everyone calls me Eli. I'm the owner of Trailblazer Comics." He continued. "It's April 2, did you move here for MVC? It's a little early to arrive for the summer term."

Miriam said, "No, I'm not a student or a prospective student. I'm an artist, actually. I thought the region was gorgeous and could be inspirational. That, and it would be a good place to heal." She gestured to her prosthetic leg.

Eli's curiosity was too much for him to overcome. "Forgive me if this is too forward, but I have to know. How did you lose your leg?"

Miriam nonchalantly replied in an even tone, "I have a really bad allergy. Turns out, when I hit a guardrail at 60 miles per hour, I break out with a bad case of amputation."

Eli erupted in laughter but quickly gathered himself before apologizing. "That was insensitive of me, I'm sorry."

"No, it's fine, it's funny in hindsight, and I tell it that way so people can laugh. If I can laugh at it, so can others. It's my way of bringing humor to the world. Keep in mind, that not every amputee has a sense of humor and an easygoing personality. Some may be offended by the question." Miriam grinned and walked over to the shelves containing comics. After a few minutes, she grabbed several titles and approached the counter. "Eli, do you have any good indie titles you recommend?"

"As a matter of fact, I do. This book was written and illustrated by a local resident who grew up here. He used to play in bands and was a singer, and it's a coming-of-age tale about growing up here. It's also a bit of a love letter to the area." He grabbed a thick graphic novel and added it to her selections. "Will this be all for you today, Miriam?"

"Yeah, for now, but I'll be back soon. I am always looking for something to read, and I could use a new hobby or two." She paid Eli and grabbed her books.

Eli gestured to a whiteboard near the cash register. "Here's a monthly schedule of all our upcoming events in April. Aside from the scheduled Friday night trading card games, every Wednesday night is tabletop RPG night, and every Sunday is wargaming afternoon. And this Saturday, April 6th, we're having a miniature painting class. You mentioned you were an artist. You should come."

"You know, I love painting. Why not? It sounds like a good time. See you Saturday, Eli!" Miriam waved and left the store. The smell of the Mexican food next door convinced her she needed to get some lunch. It was 11:48 a.m. Miriam carried her items to her car, locked them inside, and went to order some chimichangas.

33

Chapter 6: Reflections And Rituals

Over the next three days, Miriam took care of multiple tasks around the house. Rachel made good on the various requests, and Miriam finally had furniture and entertainment. She had a nice sectional in the living room, a new 65" Smart TV, a PlayStation 5, an entertainment stand, coffee table, and in the former dining room, she had a new PC and PC desk with a nice office chair with locking wheels so Miriam could get out of the chair without worrying about it sliding away and causing her to fall.

Rachel also got a security camera system for her. It was easier to install than she anticipated, and thankfully Miriam had remembered to request a tall ladder which without would have made installing cameras on the second-floor exterior next to impossible. It was tremendously taxing on her body, however, and she spent the entirety of Friday afternoon in bed recuperating. While she lay in bed, she looked into a couple of local contractors online and requested estimates from each one about installing handrails for the stairs. She had nearly fallen off the stairs twice, and the last thing she wanted was to break her good leg or her neck.

She managed to fit some reading in and thought about Trailblazer Comics, recalling Eli's invitation to paint miniatures on Saturday. Curious about miniature painting, she pulled up multiple YouTube videos and watched several different content creators paint tiny plastic figurines while explaining proper techniques. Miriam became enamored and was extremely excited to try this potential new hobby for the first time.

When Saturday morning rolled around, she was pleased to find that she felt better physically, and she proceeded to get ready. She made her way to the bathroom and removed her clothes, followed by her prosthetic leg, precariously balancing on her left leg while awkwardly maneuvering her body to the shower chair in the bathtub. She reached for the handheld shower wand and adjusted the water temperature and pressure, and cleaned up, shampooing her long auburn hair and scrubbing herself clean. After rinsing the conditioner from her hair and soap from her body, she shut off the water and reached for a towel.

This was always tricky. She couldn't balance long or well enough to dry off standing up, so she was forced to dry off partially in the shower chair, then gently lower herself to the bathroom floor, and continue drying her lower half while on her knees. Only when she was completely dry could she put her prosthetic leg on, due to it using a suction system to vacuum seal to the skin of her remaining right leg.

Miriam put her bra and panties on, cranked up some music, and walked into her closet to pick an outfit. She settled on a pair of jeans and a plum-colored v-neck top that plunged just enough to show off some of her more than ample cleavage. She chose a pair of brown leather knee-high boots to wear as well.

Miriam had arrived at the difficult part of getting dressed. First, she had to remove her prosthetic and then slide the proper pants leg over her prosthetic leg. Then she had to unzip the boot and wrestle with the rigid, unyielding foot to get it to slide into the boot. Once she had done these things, she could then put her prosthetic leg back on, and finish putting on her pants. She then put on her other boot to ensure she had an even height to walk on. Finally, she put her top on. After getting dressed, she could now fix her hair and put on her makeup and jewelry.

This entire process took Miriam, on average, two hours to complete, and once she was finished, she checked her reflection in the mirror. *Damn, I look cute AF this morning. Let's go paint some miniatures.*

Miriam was extremely meticulous about her appearance when she left her house and went into public. It was essential to her that when people see her, they see a woman. Being transgender was highly complicated and came with a complex mindset and routine. It was different from one transgender person to the next. In Miriam's case, she spent 29 of her 30 years feeling like one person on the inside but being forced to present as another person socially on the outside. Now, when anyone saw her, there was zero doubt in the minds of others. Miriam was able to pass.

Passing meant that when people looked at Miriam or spoke to Miriam, they both saw and heard a cisgender woman. This was important to her for many reasons: Miriam's feelings of validation and self-confidence helped her mental health and well-being, but most importantly, it allowed her to feel safer and reduced the chances of discrimination and harassment. Miriam only chose to reveal she was transgender to people she was close to, who currently were only doctors and a handful of law enforcement officers. *I know passing isn't the goal for every trans individual, but it's important to me. It doesn't make others any less valid. We should all be allowed to be who we know we are without repercussions.*

Her rituals were more than routine; they were armor. Each stroke of makeup, each perfectly chosen outfit, was a declaration of who she was—a woman, whole and complete. Passing wasn't just about blending in. For Miriam, it was about reclaiming the life she'd always envisioned.

How did my life get so fucked up? Why did I spiral out of control and make the choices I did that led to my amputation? Miriam stared at herself in the mirror. She cleared away the doubt and the brief moment of 'why me?' she was experiencing and said confidently aloud, "Today, I choose to love and accept myself exactly as I am. I am strong, capable, and resilient. My worth isn't defined by my mistakes or flaws. I've overcome challenges before and will do so again. My uniqueness is my strength. I deserve kindness, compassion, and love from myself and others. I embrace my journey, imperfections and all. I am enough. I am worthy. I am loved."

"You'd be proud of me, Alex," she whispered to her reflection. His memory wasn't a weight anymore—it was a light, guiding her through the moments of doubt and fear. He'd always believed in her, even when she couldn't believe in herself.

It took many years for Miriam to reach a level of acceptance, but she found there were things she was still discovering about herself. One of these things was how incredibly sore her boobs always were. Her prior endocrinologist said that the high dosage of progesterone would likely cause increased sensitivity and soreness. She just hadn't anticipated the levels of increased sensitivity and soreness. To Miriam, it was a welcome problem to endure. She chuckled softly, wincing as she adjusted her bra. The sensitivity was an annoyance, sure, but it was also a reminder of how far she'd come. Every ache and soreness felt like a small victory—proof that she was finally living in a body that felt like her own.

She took one final look in the mirror, winked at her reflection, and carefully made her way downstairs. She started a small pot of coffee, and when it was finished brewing, she poured herself a cup, added her creamer and sugar, and then went to the porch swing to smoke and enjoy her coffee.

Today feels like it's going to be a great day. The weather is gorgeous out, and I get to try out a new hobby in a hobby haven, I'm so excited! She finished her first cup of coffee, got a refill, and had another cigarette with it. Afterward, she gathered her jacket and belongings and left for Trailblazer Comics.

As she gathered her things, Miriam felt a spark of something she hadn't felt in a while—excitement. Today wasn't just about painting miniatures; it was about exploring a part of herself she hadn't tapped into before. For the first time in a long while, she felt like she belonged somewhere.

Chapter 7: A Brush With Fate

Miriam walked into Trailblazer Comics and was pleased to see a crowd gathered together for the miniature painting class. She greeted Eli, paid for the six-hour session, and took a seat at the first of four tables. Each table had eight seats, and each seat had been supplied with paper towels, a water cup for rinsing brushes and thinning paint, a dry palette to thin and mix paint, and some brushes of varying sizes. In the center of each table was a large tiered carousel, each filled with numerous colors of paint.

Miriam looked around at the various attendees, and it was pleasantly a diverse crowd ranging in ages from young children to adults. A short woman with fiery red hair spoke in a loud yet gentle voice, "Everyone, may I have your attention, please? Okay, I need everyone to choose a seat… there, thank you. You are all going to be provided with a miniature to paint. Everyone will receive the same miniature. Today we're painting space marines from an extremely popular wargame." As she spoke, Eli handed out a space marine figure to each participant.

She continued, "My name is Ava. I'm an art teacher at Jasper Hill High School, and I am active in various groups associated with Mountain View College. I've been painting miniatures for ten years, and I am here to teach proper techniques for holding your brushes, how to thin your paints, how to mix paints, color theory, wet blending, dry brushing, base coating, recess shading, edge highlighting, zenithal priming, and more! We have six hours, and my assistants Mark and Kyle are at two of the tables. If you need help or have any questions, come up to one of them or myself and we will be happy to help you. Any questions? No? Let's get started!"

Ava began by explaining brush control. She then discussed the properties of synthetic brushes versus sable hair brushes, how to rinse and clean them, and more. Miriam and the rest of the class listened intently to the lecture. When Ava finished speaking, she walked around the room, checking everyone's progress. After doing so, she returned to Miriam's table and sat in the chair across from her.

Miriam had been watching Ava as she made her way around the room. She appeared to be Miriam's age, maybe slightly younger. She was short. Very short. 5'2", and she had a very curvy, voluptuous, hourglass figure. In addition to her fiery red hair, she wore open-toed sandals and a flowy purple dress with an emerald green belt. Miriam noticed that Ava had a carabiner hanging from her belt, and it was orange, pink, and white. *She's a lesbian*, Miriam thought to herself. *Those are the lesbian pride colors.*

Ava had a pierced left eyebrow, the left side of her head was shaved, and she had a tattoo of a phoenix on her right ankle. The red and orange hues contrasted starkly against her alabaster skin. But what Miriam couldn't stop looking at were Ava's eyes. They were the most striking and bright green eyes she had ever seen.

As Ava took her seat, Miriam shifted her focus back to her space marine. She had achieved a very smooth base coat with even coverage. She was happy to realize that she was in love with miniature painting. She was then startled by the sound of Ava's voice addressing her.

"Is this your first time in a miniature painting class? You've got a very clean base coat. It looks great."

Miriam grinned enthusiastically, "It's my first time ever painting a miniature, yes, but I am an experienced painter. I'm an artist. I have done lots of painting throughout the years."

Ava's eyes lit up. "Oh, you're Miriam! Eli told me about you! He said that you were new in town and were an artist. I am so happy you came today!" Ava's eagerness to learn more about Miriam was only matched by Miriam's eagerness to learn more about Ava.

Ava continued, "So tell me, Miriam, what in the world prompted you to move to Jasper Hill, here in southwest Virginia, of all places? Most people come here for two reasons, either they come to go to college, or they're born here. And Eli said you weren't a student. Did you move here for family?"

Miriam smiled. It gave her a warm feeling to know that the store owner remembered her name and told the class teacher specifically about her. She wasn't used to this warm feeling, which she felt deeply in the pit of her stomach. *What the hell? Why are my cheeks hot? Are those butterflies? Am I experiencing butterflies in my stomach?*

"No family here, no. I don't have any family to speak of. And I'm not enrolling in MVC. As you're aware, I'm an artist. I needed a fresh start after my amputation. I felt like I needed a change of pace, scenery, lifestyle... all those things. I thought I could draw inspiration from the natural beauty of the area and, most of all, heal. Both my body and my mind." She unzipped her right boot to reveal her prosthetic leg. Ava nodded and continued to listen as Miriam spoke. "I was living in Baltimore for the past decade and change. I was a freelance artist, so I did a lot of side jobs to support my art habit. Working as a fishmonger at the docks and seafood markets. I did a lot of delivery driving for Uber Eats and DoorDash. I worked in catering services, and housekeeping for Airbnbs, too, all to supplement myself so I could do what I truly love. Which is to create. Whether it be sculpting or painting oil canvases, creative outlets are my passion."

"So when I lost my leg, I couldn't work for a while. I then had to find somewhere to live that was affordable, and fast. So I did tons of legwork, in a manner of speaking, to find an idyllic place that could both be a home to me and inspire me and also fit into my budget. I found my house listed, and it was just outside of Jasper Hill. I bought it on the spot because the price was too good to be true."

Ava looked as if she wanted to ask a question, then stopped. Finally, she just asked, "How did you lose your leg, Miriam? Is it okay to ask that? Or is it too sensitive a topic? I'm sorry. I don't want to trigger any trauma. Never mind, forgive me." Ava's face was bright red with embarrassment. She put her head down and tried to avoid Miriam's eyes. She was relieved when Miriam responded.

"Ava, I promise you that you're fine. You haven't offended or upset me, and it's natural to be curious. Please don't be embarrassed." She paused and waited for Ava to look up before she continued. "It's a sad story and stupid on my part. I dropped a glass in my kitchen one night, and it shattered. I didn't have socks or shoes on, and in trying to clean it up, I stepped on a very thin long piece of glass in the bend of my toe. It was nearly two inches long, and it struck the bone. It was excruciating."

Ava winced in empathy at the thought of the glass piercing Miriam's toe. She listened as Miriam spoke. "It didn't bleed much, I doused it with peroxide and washed it with soap and water, put a bandage on it, and that was that. Or so I thought." She paused, collected her thoughts, then moved forward. "After several weeks, I began to feel really sick and nauseous. I began vomiting. I vomited anything and everything. I tried drinking water, Gatorade, and Sprite, but it all left me within minutes. But I was so thirsty. I kept trying to get any liquids to stay down. Nothing would. I had zero appetite. This started on a Friday afternoon. I didn't stop vomiting until late Tuesday night. And the entire time, I was shivering in cold sweats, huddled under a blanket in July. I thought I had the flu."

"After the vomiting stopped on Tuesday, I tried to force myself to eat. I made myself force down one cup of chicken broth. Wednesday morning, I again tried to force myself to eat something. As I made it to the kitchen, I noticed burning pain in my foot and looked down to see it swollen the size of a football. I was extremely worried but too weak to take myself to the emergency room, I figured I would eat, rest, and get my strength up so I could drive myself to the ER. The next morning, I couldn't stand. That Wednesday was the last night I ever walked on my entire natural leg. So I called 911 and begged for an ambulance to come get me. Tests, X-rays, and MRIs showed significant bone damage due to infection."

"I was suffering from a staph infection, I had necrotizing fasciitis, also known as flesh-eating bacteria disease, and I was in septic shock. I was about to die. The doctors amputated 15 inches of my leg to save my life." She looked at Ava, who had tears streaming down her cheeks. Miriam began to apologize, "I'm sorry, I didn't mean to upset you with that. I know it's gross, I was stupid for not going to the doctor when I cut my toe, I should have gone to the ER on the first day... there are so many things I should have done differently. But, I lived, I'm here now, and I want to live my life at a slower pace and heal now."

"That is so sad, yet so inspiring. You're so resilient and strong, to go through that and come out with the mindset you have. It's so admirable. Thank you for sharing your story with me." Ava smiled and then hurriedly looked away. She then said, "I need to go check everyone's progress, I'll be back."

Miriam nodded and replied, "I'm going to go smoke, I'll be back in a few."

She reached a bench outside and sat down. The smell of Mexican food from the restaurant next door permeated the air, and her stomach rumbled loudly. She lit a cigarette and recounted everything she just experienced. *I really like this woman. Holy shit, I felt something in there that I have NEVER felt before. I really like her. And I just lied to her about nearly everything. I hate that I just couldn't be honest with her. God damned witness protection program. I get that I have to maintain my cover for my own safety, but why can't I be honest with the people I meet here? We're nearly 400 miles from where I was. Damn it! Alex would know what to do. If only he were here. He'd probably tell me to ask her out.*

She finished her cigarette and went back inside the comic shop. She glanced around and saw how engaged everyone was in their painting and their conversations, and she made a decision. She looked for Ava and saw she was just returning to her seat. Miriam sat down, and as soon as she did, she asked Ava a question. To her surprise, Ava asked her precisely the same question.

"Do you want to have dinner with me?"

Chapter 8: The Art Of Vulnerability

Miriam was ecstatic. Outside she was noticeably smiling, but inside she was squealing and turning cartwheels. She was going to dinner with Ava. They both agreed to go to the Mexican restaurant next door to Trailblazer Comics immediately following the painting class. Ava was walking around assisting a couple of kids with huge smiles on their faces. As Miriam continued to paint her miniature, her thoughts went into overdrive. *I'm excited, but I am so frustrated. I've already started this friendship with nothing but lies. If I want to build on this, I have to maintain my cover. And if I maintain my cover, I am building a potential relationship on nothing but lies. What happens when I tell her the absolute truth? What if she finds out before I can tell her myself? But if I tell her now, I would be in violation of the witness protection program for revealing my status. I'd be removed from the program.* She was struggling with the ramifications of everything losing protection would bring her.

If I tell Ava before I get clearance from the US Marshal Service, I'm out. If I'm out, not only do they remove me from their protection, but they remove me from my house. They take away my stipend. They are paying for my gender-affirming care and laser hair removal as part of crafting my identity. A lot of strings were pulled to make that happen. I'd lose my hormone replacement therapy. I'd lose everything that makes me Miriam Ryder. Miriam continued painting and looked up to see Ava flash a quick smile at her. She returned the smile, then refocused and continued to paint.

I hate lying to her. I despise it. But I don't have a choice. If I had told her now and lost all that, the De Luca family would indeed have found me and finished what they started in July. And I'd rather live and get to know her better. Gods, this fucking isn't fair.

Before Miriam realized it, she was finished with her mini, and she took a few minutes to admire her work. She looked around to see everyone else finishing up and asked Eli if he needed a hand to put the paint supplies away. Eli welcomed her assistance, and the two gathered the supplies from the tables. Miriam noticed Ava was near the store's exit, talking to several of the class participants.

"You're quite enamored with Ava, I see," Eli smirked at Miriam as she shot a look of surprise back.

"Oh shit, was it that obvious? I figured everyone was so busy painting they would assume I was asking for help or tips or something."

Eli chuckled, "Trust me, it was beyond obvious. You two could be standing on the moon and people would be able to see how infatuated you two are with each other, and they wouldn't need a telescope to do it."

"Do you really think she's infatuated with me?" Miriam's voice had a noticeable twinge of hopeful curiosity when she asked the question. She followed Eli with her load of supplies through a door in the back of the shop to a storeroom. They unloaded the various supplies onto some shelves before Eli responded.

"I've known Ava for ten years; she's been my customer for that long and a good friend for almost as long. She started coming here when she first moved to Jasper Hill. And I know her well. She's been in several of my RPG campaigns. And it's clear as day to me that she's just as interested in you as you are in her. Hell, she asked you to dinner. She told me she was going to when you were outside. Make no mistake,

Miri my friend, Ava likes you."

Miriam finished helping Eli, thanked him for holding the painting class and inviting her, and said goodbye. She walked outside to find Ava waiting on the bench for her. Ava grinned, "Did you enjoy yourself today?"

Miriam smiled back, "I'm still enjoying myself. Ready to go eat?" Ava nodded, and the two walked the short distance to the Mexican restaurant next door, El Monterrey's Fine Mexican Cuisine.

The interior of El Monterrey's buzzed with life, its vibrant decor a kaleidoscope of bold reds, yellows, and greens that reflected the lively energy of the packed space. The aroma of sizzling fajitas and freshly baked tortillas mingled with the hum of laughter and conversation. Colorful banners fluttered gently from the ceiling. Servers wove expertly through the crowded tables, balancing trays laden with steaming plates and frosty margaritas, their cheerful smiles matching the upbeat rhythm of the Latin music playing in the background.

It was 7:00 p.m. on a Saturday night in a small town, so to Miriam, it made sense that it was packed. There was a fifteen-minute wait for a table, so Miriam asked Ava if it was alright if she went outside to smoke. "I'll join you if that's okay. We have a pager to let us know when our table's ready."

The pair walked outside, and Miriam reached into her jacket pocket to remove her cigarettes and lighter. Ava asked, "May I have one, too?"

Miriam handed Ava a cigarette and extended her lighter so that she could light it. Miriam then lit her own, and they returned to sit on the bench. Miriam raised her eyebrow in surprise, "I didn't realize you smoked; you didn't during the class."

"Girl, I'm a teacher. I'm used to going several hours without a cigarette. But now I'm off the clock, so to speak, so it's my time to relax." Ava continued, "You're a really good painter. For your very first miniature, you did an amazing job. How did it make you feel?"

Miriam responded, "I loved it so much! I never knew how therapeutic painting a tiny sculpted two-inch tall figure would be. I think I've found my new favorite hobby."

"Well, you've certainly found an expensive one. I've spent thousands on the hobby myself the past decade." They finished their cigarettes just as the pager lit up to alert them their table was ready. They returned inside, and the hostess took them to their table. While they waited for the waiter or waitress to arrive, they revisited their conversation. This time, Miriam was asking questions.

"How long have you been teaching?"

Ava replied, "Six years. I got my Bachelor of Fine Arts degree from MVC in 2018. I graduated in June, and in August, I started teaching art classes at Jasper Hill High School." She stared into Miriam's hazel-colored eyes. "I really enjoy it. When I moved here in 2014, I never pictured myself staying. I came here to attend Mountain View College, and then the plan was to go back home to Richmond and get a teaching position there. But that didn't happen."

"I fell in love with the area. The college, the town, the people, I didn't want to leave. I decided I wanted to build a life here. But only if I had a teaching position by the time I graduated. Fortunately for me, there was an open position, and I was hired during my interview the day before I graduated." She gazed into Miriam's eyes some more. Miriam's cheeks felt hot. "My parents were sad I wasn't moving back home, but they are happy for me, happy that I have a career, a nice apartment, a dependable car, a bank account, a savings account, and more. They're proud that I ticked off all the boxes in the adult category."

"What do your parents do for a living?" Miriam was taking in every detail, listening intently while staring into Ava's green eyes. "Mom's a pediatrician, and she has her own private practice. Dad's a former attorney turned social justice activist. I think that's where I get it from, my passion for helping those in need and those that are maligned. They influenced me from a young age."

They were interrupted by their waiter to take their order. Miriam ordered chicken chimichangas and a Pepsi, while Ava ordered El Pollo Loco with a sweet tea. The waiter entered their order and returned with their drinks and a basket of chips and salsa. Then Miriam revealed to Ava, "I need to tell you something. I don't want to keep this from you. But... I'm transgender."

Ava smiled, "Truthfully I thought you were, you're wearing a transgender flag pin on your jacket. You're also very tall, and you have a very sultry voice, similar to Kathleen Turner. And guess what? I'm a lesbian. But you already knew that because of my carabiner on my belt." She grinned enthusiastically. "I don't have any issues with you being transgender. Do you have any issues with it?"

"Aside from the bigotry, the harassment and discrimination? No. I love who I am. I'm proud of who I've become. I've grown and evolved emotionally and mentally, and I'm continuing to do so. I do struggle at times, I'm definitely a work in progress, both literally and figuratively." Miriam reflected on Ava's words and carried on. "When I say a work in progress, I mean... I haven't had bottom surgery yet. It's a long process and a longer wait time. And I don't want you to be uncomfortable with me for any reason."

Ava paused, smiled, and answered, "We don't have to figure that out right now. And I'm extremely comfortable with you. I feel like I can tell you anything without any fear of judgment or repercussions, and I want you to know you can do the same with me. I like you, Miriam. I like you a lot. It's day one. I want to take things extremely slowly and allow us both to learn everything about each other. Is that okay?"

"Of course it is, I just worry so much about others' perceptions and expectations of me. I feel like that part of me is a deal breaker for most people. I don't want it to be one with you, is all. Because I really like you too, Ava. And I wish I could just tell you everything here and now, but I know I can't, I have to allow this to unfold naturally, and we take time to learn about each other, rather than just info dump our life stories onto each other and expect something of significance to develop. So let's do exactly what you said; let's take it extremely slowly and enjoy each other's company while we get to know each other."

Ava leaned across the table and gave Miriam a small kiss on her left cheek. "Thank you. That means more to me than you can imagine. I've never met anyone like you, Miriam. Hell, I don't even know your last name yet, and you don't know mine. So, I'm Ava Marie McCormick. I'm 28 years old. And I was born on August 7th, 1995. One interesting fact about me is that not only do I paint and teach, but I'm also a violinist. Your turn."

"I'm Miriam Dawn Ryder, Miri for those who care about me, and I'm 29 years old. I was born on April 18th 1994. And aside from my birthday being in twelve days, one interesting fact about me is that I never tell the same story twice about how I lost my leg."

They laughed, and then Ava said, "Hey, does that mean your inspirational story you told me was made up?" Miriam lied, "No, the version I told you was the truth."

Chapter 9: Finding Comfort

A va and Miriam continued to enjoy their dinner, exchanging information and generally enjoying their time together, when Ava suddenly dropped her fork to her plate and muttered, "Oh no. Not tonight." Miriam looked around and saw a large burly man in his mid-20s strolling toward their table.

The approaching man was broad, about 6'3", 230 pounds, with a muscular build, icy blue eyes, and shortly cropped blonde hair. He didn't seem to have concern for the personal space of other patrons of El Monterrey's because he bumped into a young child and told her to watch where she was going. He grabbed a chair from a neighboring table, turned it around, and straddled it while placing his elbows firmly onto Miriam and Ava's table. He emitted a loud "AHEM" to announce his arrival.

Miriam glanced at Ava, who had begun to gather her things. "Let's go, Miri. I've lost my appetite."

She started to stand up, but the large, burly man grabbed her by the wrist and said in a commanding tone, "Sit down. You've not introduced me to your friend here, Ava. That's rude." Miriam scoffed; the irony was clearly lost on this guy.

"Take your hand off of me, Beauregard. That's the last and only time I will tell you." Ava declared angrily, staring Beauregard in the face. He released her arm and got defensive.

"Whoa, no need to flip the bitch switch, Ava. I just wanted to make acquaintances with your new friend here. Settle down." Rage was rapidly rising in Miriam. In her pre-transition days, she wouldn't have hesitated to get physical with guys like Beauregard, but she wasn't that person anymore, and she couldn't afford any legal troubles.

"Miriam, this is Beauregard Harris, aka Bubba. Or, as I like to call him, Deputy Dipshit."

Miriam flashed a look of recognition. She asked, "Harris? As in Sheriff Tom Harris?"

Bubba gave a wolfish smile. "Oh, you've met my daddy. Met him at the cafe on Monday. That's right, he told me. And I'm here to tell you somethin' right here and now: this town don't need no people like you. We won't stand for it." Miriam shot Bubba a death glare. He went on, "B'Sides, Ava here's all mine anyway."

Miriam unclenched her jaw and spoke in a steely tone. "Ava's not into men, sorry to disappoint you."

Bubba scoffed and retorted, "Says the guy in a dress. Did you honestly think you had a chance with this rug muncher? She don't like people that can piss standing up." He looked at Ava, "Not yet, anyways. She knows she just needs a taste of a real man."

Miriam responded calmly and cooly, "I may be new in town, but just because you're a cop doesn't give you the authority to talk to women the way you just did. It doesn't give you the right to place your hands on a woman when she didn't consent to do so. And just to give you an education beyond the 5th grade that your daddy requires to hire your ignorant ass, trans women are women. Ava, would you like to add anything to that?"

Ava nodded and gave way to restraint, "Beauregard, if you ever touch me, speak to me or Miri the way you just did again, you will have to start wearing dresses because I'll rip your scrotum off. Now get out of our fucking way!" She grabbed her things as Miriam grabbed hers.

They were almost to the front door when Miriam stopped their waiter. "Excuse me, everything was lovely tonight, but we have had an emergency. But Beauregard Harris over there said he will happily pay for our meal." And then the duo left.

Once outside, Ava tried to salvage the evening. "I'm really sorry for those awful things he said about you. Can we get some coffee and try to get this awful moment out of our minds? I don't want what has been a wonderful day to end on such a terrible note."

Miriam replied, "I'm sorry he spoke to you and grabbed you. I hate that he thinks he can do that. I would love to get coffee. But let's go to my house. We can sip coffee on my porch swing while we smoke, talk, and stare at the stars. Deal?"

Ava smiled, "Deal."

As Ava and Miriam made their way back to their cars, the warm buzz of shared laughter from the restaurant faded into the cool stillness of the evening. The streets were unusually quiet, with only the soft hum of distant crickets breaking the silence. They paused by Ava's car, which was parked a few spots ahead of Miriam's.

Ava gave Miriam a soft smile. "Thanks for standing up to that creep tonight. I hate that it even happened, but you handled him like a champ."

Miriam chuckled, though her eyes darted around the lot instinctively. "I think you handled him better. I'm pretty sure Beauregard will be nursing his bruised ego for a week after that scrotum comment."

Ava smirked. "Let's hope he stays out of our way from now on. Drive safe, okay? Coffee on your porch sounds perfect. I'll meet you there."

Miriam nodded, her unease creeping in as she watched Ava climb into her car. She made her way to her own car, parked further back in the dimly lit lot. Sliding into the driver's seat, she started the engine and checked her mirrors. Her stomach tightened when she spotted a car parked at the far end of the lot, its headlights clicking on just as she pulled out.

It's nothing, Miri. Coincidences happen. But as she turned onto the main road, the car pulled out behind her, its headlights steady and uncomfortably close.

Miriam's fingers tightened on the wheel as she glanced at the dashboard clock. Ava would already be halfway to her house, oblivious to the sinking feeling that someone was following her.

Another turn. The car stayed with her.

Miriam's pulse quickened. She grabbed her phone, debating whether to call Ava and warn her, but what could she say without raising questions? Ava didn't know about her past, her new identity, or the shadows she'd tried to leave behind.

Not yet.

Instead, Miriam sent a quick text. *Running a little behind. I'll be there soon.*

The response came almost instantly: *Everything okay?*

Miriam hesitated, her foot pressing harder on the gas as she took a detour. The car behind her did the same. She swallowed hard and typed back with one hand. *Yeah, just had to get cigarettes. See you soon.*

She turned onto a quieter street, away from the route home. The car followed again, its headlights unwavering. Miriam's heart pounded as memories of the night she had been attacked flooded her mind. She knew she had to stay calm, but the sinking feeling in her chest grew heavier with every mile.

Miriam's porch and their promised coffee seemed miles away now.

Another turn. The headlights stayed close. This time, Miriam decided to test them. She veered into a small gas station, pulling into a well-lit spot near the entrance. The car behind her drove past, continuing down the road without hesitation.

Miriam exhaled sharply, her hands shaking as she gripped the wheel. Was it just her imagination? A coincidence? Or was someone really watching her?

Her phone buzzed. It was Ava. *Miri? You okay?*

Miriam stared at the screen, her thumb hovering over the keyboard. She typed back: *Fine, on my way now.*

But as she pulled out of the gas station and turned back toward home, the uneasy weight in her chest remained. She glanced into her rearview mirror one more time, half expecting to see those headlights again.

If someone really *was* following her, she couldn't let Ava find out—not yet.

Ava sipped her coffee and smoked a cigarette while swinging gently back and forth with Miriam. Resting her head on Miriam's shoulder, she said, "Miri, when did you first know when you were a girl?"

Miriam gave a sad smile. "When I was 4 years old. I knew. I didn't know that I was transgender, hell, I don't even know if that term was used then in society. I just knew I didn't feel like a boy, even though my parents insisted I was. I told them I was a little girl, that I wanted to wear dresses and pigtails, play with Barbies, and wear makeup. It fell on deaf ears."

"The day I turned 18 in my senior year, I left in the middle of the night. I haven't seen or spoken to them since." She took an extra long drag from her cigarette before going on. "What's wild is I'm geographically closer to them than I have been in twelve years, and they wouldn't know me if they saw me."

Ava sat upright, "Wait, how close are we talking about?"

Miriam replied, "The last I knew of, my mom was living in Kentucky, just across the border. I'm pretty sure my dad is still in Northeast Tennessee. He and my mom divorced when I was 5. Yet here I am, less than an hour from either one of them."

"Do you ever think about trying to reconnect with them?"

Miriam was silent for a few moments before finally replying, "No, there's too much bad history there. I don't intend to ever speak to either one of them again."

Ava nodded solemnly. She took one final drag from her cigarette and finished her coffee. She snuggled up next to Miriam as Miriam put her left arm around her. "Other than the incident with Bubba, this has been a truly wonderful day."

Miriam chuckled, "Well, he was nice enough to pay for our meal." She then began shaking with laughter, and Ava did the same. They laughed for several minutes until their sides hurt, and when they stopped, they were staring longingly into each other's eyes. Ava tilted her neck upward as Miriam lowered herself, and they shared a tender kiss. After what Miriam felt was an eternity, they stopped.

They sat in the swing for another fifteen minutes, neither saying a word, each just focusing on the presence of the other, cuddling together and savoring the moment. Ava broke the silence first. "I don't want to leave."

Miriam's heart raced, pounding in her chest. "You don't have to leave. You can stay."

Ava smiled and said, "I'd like that. Thank you." They continued to sit in the swing as Miriam offered Ava another cigarette, and Ava accepted. They sat holding each other while finishing their cigarettes and going inside.

Ava spotted the TV remote, turned it on, and selected a channel that played music. She selected one that played slow songs. Miriam nodded in approval and extended her hand to Ava, who, in turn, accepted. The two stood face to face, Ava put her arms around Miriam's neck, and Miriam placed her arms around Ava's waist. Then they slowly danced in the living room, staring into each other's eyes, not saying a word.

After two songs, Miriam began wincing in pain. She had been wearing her prosthetic for over twelve hours at this point. Ava noticed she was favoring her leg and motioned to the couch. Miriam nodded. Miriam couldn't take her prosthetic off without removing her pants. She didn't want to cause Ava any moment of discomfort, so she said, "I don't want to alarm you, but in order to take my prosthetic off, I have to take my jeans off. But I have a pair of pajamas in the bathroom down the hall. Would you be willing to get them for me so I can change? I don't think I can walk anymore; my leg is aching and throbbing terribly."

Ava gently smiled and nodded, left the room, and returned a few seconds later with Miriam's pajamas. She then said, "I'm going to start some coffee while you change, okay?"

She went to the kitchen and began to make coffee and Miriam began the process of getting undressed to remove her prosthetic leg. First, her left boot, then undoing her pants, pulling them down to the knees so she could access the vacuum-sealed sleeve on her thigh. She rolled the sleeve down her thigh to release the grip of the prosthetic and proceeded to remove her stump leg. She could then finish removing her jeans from her left leg. She carefully pulled on her pajama shorts and changed her low-cut v-neck top for her pajama top. "I'm changed, Ava."

Ava returned to the living room carrying two cups of coffee and placed them on the coffee table. She sat down and looked into Miriam's eyes, then down to her stump leg. Miriam began massaging the areas of her stump that were bothering her while Ava looked on. After a few moments, Miriam felt relieved and leaned back into the couch, all the physical stress of wearing her prosthetic for such a lengthy time vanished. Ava leaned in and put her head onto Miriam's right shoulder and reached her right hand across her body to place it on Miriam's stump leg. She gently massaged her leg while cuddling next to Miriam, allowing Miriam to wrap her arms around her and draw her closer. After several minutes, Ava spoke. "How badly does it hurt?"

Miriam replied, "I'm not sure how to describe it. Imagine wearing a pair of extremely snug hiking boots, and you wear them non-stop for about two days while traversing the most difficult terrain the entire time. You become fatigued and feel soreness like you've never experienced, and your feet are burning like they're on fire. It's similar to how that would feel. But taking it off... the relief, the rush of cool air to the skin, the alleviation of constant pressure, it's a genuine feeling of bliss."

"Like taking your bra off at the end of the day?" Ava responded.

Miriam grinned, "Actually, that's not a terrible comparison, but the level of relief of one versus the other is leagues apart." She reached forward and took a sip of her coffee. Ava did the same.

Ava nodded solemnly and asked, "Why is it so uncomfortable?"

Miriam grabbed her prosthetic to show her the inside of the socket that fits around her stump. "When they make the socket, they shape it around a plaster cast of my stump. But I can't just rest the bottom of my leg into the bottom of the socket; it would literally be like walking on the bone. So they mold it so it locks in below my kneecap at the patella on what's left of my tibia. It cradles my stump and holds it in place with pressure. After a few hours, it's agonizing." Ava looked sad, but Miriam interjected. "Some things are absolutely worth the agony. And as much pain as I'm in currently, it's been beyond worth it today. Truthfully this has been the best day I've had in I don't know how long."

Ava smiled warmly, snuggling deeper next to Miriam. She felt at peace and safe, but she also felt very sleepy. Miriam, on top of her exhaustion, also felt tired. The two sat on the couch, curled up in each other's arms, listening to the music, and drifted off to sleep.

Chapter 10: The Price Of Being Different

Miriam awoke the following day to Ava gently nudging her. "Good morning. It appears we fell asleep on the couch."

Miriam stretched and groaned. She was absolutely aching from the events prior to the day. She asked, "Would you like me to make some breakfast? I can make pancakes and sausage links. Would you like that?"

Ava nodded and said, "Yes, I'll go start the coffee." Before she got up to make coffee, she leaned in and gave Miriam a good morning kiss.

Miriam smiled and grabbed her phone. She texted Rachel four words: *Need to meet. Urgent.* Miriam then began removing the boot and jeans from her prosthetic leg so she could assemble herself as she liked to joke and go make breakfast. She started frying up some sausage links and then mixed some pancake batter while the griddle was warming. Then, she watched as Ava danced around the kitchen, humming to herself and grabbing plates, silverware, and glasses. Miriam finished cooking and made three pancakes and four sausage links for each of them. She plated their meal and set the plates on the table as Ava returned with orange juice and coffee.

"Your pancakes are delicious; thank you for making breakfast, Miri."

Miriam said, "You're welcome. What do you have planned for the day?"

Ava sighed, "As much as I want to stay and hang out with you, I have to go home and grade exams then do my lesson plan for this week. That's how I usually spend my Sundays. What about you?"

"I think I'm going to go to Trailblazer and pick up some miniatures and paints. You have me hooked on the hobby. Other than that, I just intend to chill today." They finished their breakfast, and Ava gathered her things to leave. She looked up at Miriam and gave her a kiss as Miriam opened the door for her. Ava then walked to her car, waved goodbye, and departed.

I have to tell Rachel. I have to get clearance to tell Ava I am in witness protection and why. I refuse to lie to her anymore. Alex would tell me this is the right thing to do. She checked her phone to see that Rachel had texted her back. *I'm coming over now.* The text read.

Ten minutes later, Rachel knocked at the door, and Miriam let her in. "Are you okay? What's wrong?" Rachel's concern was evident in her tone of voice.

"Yes, Rachel, I'm fine. In fact, I'm more than fine. I'm better than I've been in forever. Years, really." Miriam was going for it. *Now is the time. Don't fuck this up, Miri.* "Rachel, I've met someone. I've met someone who is incredible, and sweet, and confident, and intelligent, and she's into art, and teaches art at the high school, and—"

Rachel cut her off, "You're talking about Ava McCormick. How did you meet her? What happened?"

"How did you know I was talking about Ava?"

Rachel looked surprised that Miriam had asked. "It's a tiny town, Miri. Everyone knows each other." Miriam then recounted the events of the prior day, leaving out no details. Rachel noticeably winced about the confrontation with Beauregard Harris and listened as Miriam finished up her story.

Miriam ended with, "I'm telling you all of this because I am in witness protection, as you're aware. You're my contact. I want approval to let Ava know about me being in witness protection. I can't keep lying to her, and it's tearing me apart inside, Rachel. Please."

Rachel sighed. "You've been in town for a week, today is day seven, and you're already wanting to risk your cover? Even if I said it was okay to tell her, which isn't my call, by the way, US Marshal Thompson is not going to consider this request, especially after a week."

Miriam grew frustrated. "Rachel, please, I am begging you. Vouch for her. You know who she is. You know her character. Go to bat for me. I genuinely see a future with her. It scares me, but I want this. Please."

Rachel was silent for a full minute. She looked back at Miriam, who was quite despondent, and finally replied. "Alright. I'll put in the request with Marshal Thompson. I will vouch for Ava's character. But if he says no, and be prepared, he's probably going to say no. You have to promise me you won't violate your protection agreement and tell her. We're trying to protect you for a reason." Miriam silently nodded in agreement. She sank into the couch, feeling defeated. She knew as well that Thompson would deny her request. But she thought she had to try regardless.

"Look, Ava is a compassionate and considerate human being. If what you're telling me is entirely true, when you do get approval to reveal the truth, I'm confident she'll be understanding." Rachel gave Miriam one final look, said goodbye, and left her to contemplate their conversation. What Rachel couldn't see was the tears streaming down Miriam's cheeks after she left.

Miriam, now reassembled and presentable for the public, pulled into the parking lot of Trailblazer Comics. She wasn't sure what type of crowd to expect but recalled Eli saying Sundays were wargaming days. Miriam saw about a dozen people gathered around the gaming tables, each with battle mats and terrain and brightly painted plastic armies. She could hear the rolling of multiple dice and whoops of joy and moans of despair.

Eli was watching casually from behind the counter. He looked up and saw Miriam and greeted her hello. Miriam grinned and walked over. "So, how was dinner?" Miriam told Eli about the events of the evening and morning. Eli smiled, "I had a feeling you two would hit it off and be friends, but this surpassed anything I anticipated. So what brings you by today?"

Miriam said, "I wanted to get hobby supplies, everything I need to build and paint miniatures." Eli led her to the miniatures and explained the difference between each type. Some were single cast, some came in parts on sprues that had to be cut out and built, some were made from plastic, some from resin, and more. In the end, she picked up a box of space marines, a box of bugs, a couple of single-piece fantasy minis, and a dragon. She then grabbed glue, sprue cutters, brushes, and paint. In the end she ended up spending over $250. *My therapist has always said I'm impulsive, and Ava wasn't kidding when she said this hobby wasn't cheap.*

Miriam thanked Eli and decided to grab lunch at the Jasper Hill Cafe and see how Di was doing. She parked in an accessible parking spot and walked in. She was met with lots of chatter and loud country music playing on the jukebox. To Miriam's surprise, every booth was occupied, and only two barstools were available. One next to the cash register and one next to the front window. Miriam chose to sit by the window. Di saw Miriam, waved hello, and said she'd be over momentarily to take her order. Miriam looked over the menu and decided on a grilled chicken club sandwich and a side of fries with a Coke. Di came to take her order, placed it with the cook, and went back to check on customers.

After a few minutes, Di returned with Miriam's food and said, "How was your date last night?"

Miriam responded with a shocked look on her face. "How do you know about that?"

Di laughed, "Hun, this is Jasper Hill. It's tiny. Everyone knows your business before you do."

I'm beginning to figure that out. She was about to answer Di when the door chimed and in walked Sheriff Tom Harris and his son, Deputy Beauregard Harris. Miriam's heart sank into her stomach, and a sense of dread started gnawing at her. She braced her mind for the inevitable confrontation.

She ate, attempting to enjoy her meal, which had lost its appeal as soon as the father and son duo arrived. Various customers were finishing their meals and paying, Di bid them a good day, and the process repeated until there were only four other customers in the cafe. Along with Sheriff Harris and his son Bubba, there was a well-dressed old man and a man who appeared to be close to Miriam's age. As soon as the last of the other customers left, Sheriff Harris addressed Miriam from across the room. "So, the transgender thinks it can talk to an officer of the law any old way it wants, is that it?" Bubba laughed as his father continued. "Now you listen here, whatever you are, I don't give a shit what you do in your own home. Wear a dress, prance around with your face painted, sit down to pee, I don't care. That's your home, and as strange as that kind of mental illness is, it's your right to do so."

Miriam's stomach twisted, but she forced herself to sit still, her hands tightening around her coffee mug as if it could anchor her. She glanced at Di, who had frozen behind the counter, her face pale as she clutched a tray. For a moment, Miriam thought Di might intervene, but she hesitated, her eyes darting to the sheriff's badge. The weight of authority kept her silent, and Miriam's heart sank.

"But this here's Jasper Hill. This is our town. We were here long before you. You alphabet mafia aren't welcome here. You're not wanted here. People like you disgust the good people of Jasper Hill. And you damn sure aren't no woman. Y'unnerstand?" The sheriff picked his teeth with a toothpick and then began to chew on one end while the other stuck out of his mouth.

Miriam's pulse thundered in her ears, her mind racing. *He's trying to provoke me. Stay calm. Don't give him a reason to escalate this.* But beneath her resolve, fear clawed at her chest. What if this was more than just hate? What if he knew about her past? About WITSEC? She couldn't afford to slip, not here, not now.

"Excuse me, Sheriff Harris," Miriam began, her voice steady despite the trembling in her hands. "I think you'll find that the 'alphabet mafia' you're so fond of disparaging are actually human beings deserving of respect and dignity. And as for your claim that people like me 'disgust the good people of Jasper Hill,' I'd wager that there are plenty of good people in this town who don't share your bigotry.

"As for your assertion that I'm not a woman, I'd say that's a matter of opinion – and one that's been settled by the medical community, the law, and most importantly, by my own sense of self. You're welcome to your opinion, Sheriff, but I'm not going to let you dictate how I live my life or how I identify myself.

"And by the way, Sheriff, I think it's interesting that you feel the need to police my identity and my presence in this town. It says a lot more about you than it does about me."

Bubba started to rise from his seat, his chair scraping loudly against the floor, but Sheriff Harris motioned for him to remain seated. "Careful now," the sheriff said, his voice low and menacing. "You've got a sharp tongue for someone who just got here."

Sheriff Harris laughed. "Listen here, you've been here a week. Things may work differently where you're from, but they don't fly in Jasper Hill. We don't use pronouns. We don't accommodate mental illness. We don't let groomers like you pee where a little girl can be assaulted. You get me, pedo?"

The words hit Miriam like a slap, her vision blurring as a surge of anger rose in her chest. She clenched her fists under the countertop, willing herself not to react. A single misstep could put everything at risk. She glanced at Di again, who was gripping the edge of the counter so tightly her knuckles had turned white. But she still didn't move. Miriam took a deep breath, forcing herself to maintain her composure. "I am none of those things," she said, her voice measured but cold. "And for someone in your position, Sheriff, I'd think you'd know better than to spread such hateful and unfounded accusations."

Bubba laughed, his voice loud and mocking. "Look at it trying to act all proper. Like you belong here." His father joined in, their laughter echoing through the nearly empty cafe. "That's enough, Bubba," Sheriff Harris said, though the smirk on his face betrayed no real authority in the order. He leaned forward, fixing Miriam with a look that sent a chill down her spine. "You'd best keep your head down, *Miss* Ryder. Don't go thinking you can make this town bend to your will. People who stand out too much around here tend to regret it."

Miriam's heart pounded as she met his gaze, refusing to look away. She couldn't let him see her fear. "I'll keep that in mind," she said evenly, though her hands trembled under the table.

Sheriff Harris said, "Mayor Winston, you care to introduce yourself to this pedo?"

The old man spun in his seat and stood up. He was a thin, frail-looking man of about 70, but his voice was anything but frail. "It's like Tom said. You're not welcome here. We won't have groomers like you poisoning the minds of our youth. You're a freak. And as mayor, I will make changes. You won't be able to use the ladies restroom. You won't be able to do a lot of things; just you wait."

The sheriff stood, tossing two one-dollar bills onto the counter. "Come on, Bubba. We've made our point."

As they left, Bubba turned to Di and sneered. "She's paying for all our meals, Di." The four men left, and Miriam sat crushed upon her barstool, tears streaming down her face.

Chapter 11: A Coalition Is Born

Miriam sat on the barstool of Jasper Hill Cafe, trembling. Her mind was reeling about what just happened. Di immediately rushed to Miriam's side and put her hands on her upper arms to console her, then when Miriam turned to Di, she allowed Di to hug her. Di stood there and let Miriam sob for several minutes. Miriam finally pulled away and composed herself. "Thank you, Di. I'm sorry you had to see that."

Di replied, "Nonsense, Miri, absolute nonsense. There's no damned reason for those four to be such assholes to a girl. I can't get over how close-minded people still are in this town, especially with the university here in town and all the revenue the kids bring to this town. Kids from all walks of life, genders, races, sexuality, and such. It makes my heart hurt to actually see firsthand that bigotry used against another soul." Miriam shuddered, dried her tears with a clean napkin, and looked at her now cold, partially eaten meal.

She started to reach for her sandwich when Di stopped her. "Miri, stop. Let me make you a fresh meal. That's what you came for. And don't you worry about paying for their meals. I'll invoice the mayor's office for them. No good bastards." She disappeared into the kitchen for a few minutes while Miri went outside to smoke.

They called me it. Not even misgendering me but actually dehumanizing me. How cruel. I've never felt such humiliation before. I've never felt so powerless before... well, almost never. There was last July, after all. The events that led me here to begin with. She was on the verge of tears again. *Stop this. No. You're not going to lose it right now. These are small-town bigots, not the De Luca family.* She imagined Alex saying, *You belong just as much as they do. So show them.* She finished her cigarette and went back inside. Di was just bringing her food out to her.

"Di, do you have cameras in here?" She crossed her fingers and hoped the answer was yes.

Di shook her head no. "Sorry, Miri, I never thought about installing them before, but I wish I had. You'd have a lawsuit on your hands for sure." Di cleaned away the dishes from the sheriff's and his cohorts' tables. "I'm no lawyer, but it's worth talking to one anyway, see what they say."

Miriam nodded. She then thought to ask, "Do you get a lot of college kids in here?"

Di chuckled, "I have lots of college kids in here all week long. Why?"

Miriam beamed, "I think I have a plan."

Miriam texted Ava, *Just checking in, call me when you're free.* She added a smiley face emoji. She was curious to know if she was doing that right or not. She never used emojis. Her conversation with Di had given her an excellent idea. Mountain View College was within the town limits. It was home to approximately 1,800 registered voters. Voters who had likely never voted in the Jasper Hill elections. And if she could get them to vote, she was sure she could get Sheriff Tom Harris and Mayor Harold Winston voted out. She texted Rachel, *Any word yet?* She lit a cigarette, cranked her car, and headed home.

Miriam gripped the steering wheel tightly as she drove home, the events at the cafe replaying in her mind like a haunting loop. Her eyes flicked constantly between the road ahead and the rearview mirror, scanning for anyone following her. Every shadow sent a jolt of panic through her chest. Was that truck back there slowing down when she did? Were they turning the same corners on purpose, or was it just her imagination? She swallowed hard, trying to steady her breathing, but the tension refused to ease.

Turning into her holler, Miriam didn't relax until she saw the car behind her continue past. Even then, she stayed in the car for a moment, her heart racing as she surveyed the road and the tall trees around her home. Was someone out there watching? Or was she just letting fear take over? She finally stepped out, her keys clutched tightly in her hand, and hurried inside, locking the door behind her with trembling fingers. The comforting smell of coffee still lingered from earlier, but tonight even her safe space felt fragile.

Once home, she changed into more comfortable clothes, a pair of gym shorts and a tank top, and organized a hobby space to work on miniatures. She had to shake the feelings she experienced, and she could do this through painting. Her phone dinged; it was Rachel responding to her text. *Denied.* She was prepared for this. She would call US Marshal Arthur M. Thompson herself tomorrow morning. Then her phone rang. It was Ava. She answered, "Hey, how's the lesson planning going?"

"It's fine. Are you okay? I wasn't expecting to hear from you until later." Miriam told her about the four men bullying her in the cafe. Then she asked the question to which she needed an answer.

"You said you were involved with various groups at MVC; what groups, and how can we recruit them to help us fight social injustice?"

Ava responded, "I have a couple of friends I can call. Would it be cool to bring them by your house this evening around 7:00 p.m.?" Miriam said yes, and they hung up on each other.

At 7:00 p.m., Miriam heard several cars. She checked her cameras to see Ava had arrived. With her were Eli, Di, and two people she hadn't seen before. She opened the door to greet them.

Ava gave Miriam a hug and a kiss on the cheek as she entered. Then came Eli, who carried three pizzas, followed by Di and the two she hadn't met. Miriam smiled, welcomed them all, and invited them to sit down. She retrieved two 2-liter sodas from the refrigerator, one Pepsi and one Mountain Dew, and some glasses. Ava helped her carry some paper towels and plates. Everyone sat down, and Ava spoke. "Everyone, this is Miriam, aka Miri. She's new in town, and I really like her a lot. And I want to help her. And I wanted you all to meet her and get to know her and how amazing she is, so maybe you would want to help her, too." She reached over and squeezed Miriam's hand. Miriam cleared her throat and began.

"Hi everyone. I've already met Eli and Di and even gave them some of my money today," everyone laughed, "I haven't met everyone yet, so I will introduce myself, and then if you would tell me about yourselves, we can get into what's going on. As Ava said, I'm Miriam Ryder, but my friends and people I love call me Miri. I'm an amputee, and I'm a transgender woman. I just moved here from Baltimore on Monday. It's the first Sunday since then. I am an artist, and I love painting, sculpting, and I just discovered miniature painting. And I'm happy you all brought pizza."

A young, brown-skinned woman with vibrant blue hair spoke next. "Hi, Miri, I'm Julia Craft, but I go by Jules. I'm a senior at MVC, and I'm majoring in graphic design. I'm president of the MVC Design Club, and I also volunteer at the campus LGBTQIA+ Resource Center. I'm 22, I also love to paint minis and I love to play wargames."

Everyone turned to the last person. "Hi, I'm Noah Sawyer. My pronouns are they/them. I'm a sophomore at MVC, majoring in social work. I'm originally from Richmond, and I play guitar and sing in a band."

Eli spoke next: "All of you know me, but Miri, allow me to give you some more insight about me. I'm gay and have always strived to create a safe haven for the LGBTQIA+ community. Many of us live here and on campus, and I am here to support you."

The last speaker was Di: "Diana Simmons, or Di to everyone. I'm the owner of the Jasper Hill Cafe. I'm an ally. I'm a divorced mom of four kids and two grandkids, and I know everyone in town. I know who you can count on as allies and who we're up against."

Di sighed as she grabbed some pizza, pausing for a moment before looking Miriam in the eye. "You know, this isn't the first time I've seen Sheriff Harris and his crew go after someone like that," she said, her voice tight with emotion. "My youngest daughter, Lauren, came out as a lesbian when she was just sixteen. The sheriff made her life hell. Pulling her over for no reason, 'randomly' searching her car, and spreading rumors that she was a bad influence on other kids in town. She was just a teenager, for God's sake, and they treated her like she was a criminal for simply being who she was. It broke her spirit, Miri. She couldn't wait to leave Jasper Hill, and she hasn't been back since." Di's hands trembled as she gripped the tray. "I stayed quiet back then because I was scared—scared for her and for my other kids. But seeing what they did to you today, I can't keep quiet anymore. If you're going to stand up to them, you can count on me to help. No one else should have to go through what Lauren did."

Jules and Noah glanced at the others, and both displayed looks of resolve and determination. Miriam smiled and spoke again. "My first day here, I was insulted and belittled by Sheriff Tom Harris. Yesterday on my and Ava's date, we were assaulted verbally and physically by his son, Deputy Beauregard 'Bubba' Harris. This afternoon, in front of Di, I was dehumanized and shamed by the Harrises, as well as Mayor Harold Winston. They've made veiled threats, encouraged me to leave town, assured me I'm not welcome here, and the mayor vowed to enact discriminatory policies targeting me. I am here to let you all know that I'm going to take them down."

"How? They're corrupt, and they've got everyone scared to death." Jules inquired. Miriam asked Jules, "What's the number of campus residents at MVC?" Jules responded, "Approximately 1,800. Why?" Miriam smiled and continued, "Di, what's the official census population of Jasper Hill?" Di tapped her phone, then spoke slowly and concisely, "1,549. But that was four years ago; the actual population is closer to 1,300 now."

Miriam elicited a tiny whoop and carried on, "It's an election year. The mayor is up for reelection. The sheriff is, too. It should be easier to get the votes needed to topple the mayor in a town election. But the sheriff will be more complex because that's a county election. We can get a surge in votes against him, but he has a lot of influence and will be much more difficult to replace.

"That's why I asked Ava to bring you here. So we can organize; so that we can fight! We aren't going to allow them to revoke our rights and tell us where to pee or refuse to hire us because we're gay or any litany of policies they want to try to enact. Today, Sunday, April 7th, 2024, we say enough is enough. I want to start an organization named the Jasper Hill Equality Coalition. We will strive to bring equality, acceptance, and inclusivity to Jasper Hill. Who's with me?" Everyone in the room raised their hands. Thus, the Jasper Hill Equality Coalition was born.

The group spent the next couple of hours eating pizza and discussing strategies, intermingling, and sharing details about each other to get to know one another better. Miriam learned that Eli was not only the owner of Trailblazer Comics, but after he graduated from MVC, he attended a famous art school taught by a legendary comic book artist in New Jersey. She learned that Jules was actually in the process of writing her own graphic novel exploring themes of identity and social justice based on her own experiences as a young bisexual Black woman. Di was not only the cafe's owner, but she also lived on a farm. Noah's grandparents were active in the 1960s folk music scene, and his love of music is influenced by them. She loved learning more about each of her new friends. Then, Jules asked the question that had been on her mind since she arrived, "Miriam, how did you lose your leg?"

Ava, Di, and Eli had all heard a version of the story before, but only Ava knew she never told the same version twice. Miriam gave a sad smile and began. "I used to live in Pittsburgh pre-transition, and I was a pizza delivery driver. I was working like crazy and saving all of my tips for the many surgeries I wanted. I was depressed and suffering from severe gender dysphoria, so I started gambling in hopes that I would hit a series of payoffs to advance my savings.

"I was using a guy who a co-worker introduced me to as a bookie. At first, I won a few small bets, but the payoffs weren't enough to make a significant contribution to my funds. So I made increasingly riskier bets, and I started losing. And I lost big. I eventually lost enough to owe $100,000. What I didn't realize was that the bookie was part of a crime family, and they wanted their money. One night, they sent some goons to collect. My friend who introduced me to the bookie was at my place with me when they arrived. They were beating me up, and he tried to intervene, and they killed him right in front of me. They beat me with crowbars and broke my leg in six places, broke eight ribs, damaged my larynx, lacerated my face, and broke my left arm. They left me for dead.

"My leg was so mangled the doctors decided that amputation would be the best route for my leg because the risk of infections was too great. I gave them the okay. And the next morning, they amputated. That's the true story of how I lost my leg." Miriam looked around the room; everyone had a stunned look on their faces. Eli broke the silence first, "You joked you had hit a guardrail with me!" Di added, "She told me it was a catfish noodling accident!" Ava revealed, "Miri's told me that she never tells the same story twice as part of her warped sense of humor. This one was super tragic, though." Miriam said nothing. She had done something for the first time. She had just told the true story about how she lost her leg.

74

Chapter 12: Pittsburgh

"Seventeen fucking cents? Fucking cheapskates." Gabriel was angry. Here he was, delivering pizza in the pouring rain, a $41.83 order, and they actually said to keep the change from $42.00. He angrily threw the hot bag into the passenger seat of his green 2005 Honda Civic and headed to his next delivery stop. Tips had been shitty all night. So far, he had only made $18.45, and that was for ten deliveries. It was going to be a long night. He lit a cigarette, put the car into first gear, and peeled out of the slick driveway, spinning his tires in the process. *Shit, that wasn't intentional, but I guarantee they call to complain to my manager. Good fucking job, Gabe.*

Gabe Wilson worked for a small regional pizza franchise local to Pittsburgh. He had been living in Pittsburgh for about ten years now and had been working for this particular employer for almost eight years. The job paid well enough, $15.00 per hour, plus commission and tips. There were many nights Gabe took home an average of $150 and up to $200 on weekends. He loved the job for the money, the perks, and the women. He got half-price pizza whenever he wanted, could listen to music as loudly as he wanted, could smoke in his car on deliveries, and Gabe took home a lot of phone numbers. He had a notebook filled with addresses and names of women who went out with him and tipped well so he could never forget to be extra charming. Pittsburgh was a prominent place. It took a lot of work to remember the best tippers and even harder to keep the names straight of the multiple women he took on dates.

Gabe pulled into the driveway of his next delivery and gave the customer their food. At least the two kids at this house tipped $5 on a $20 order. *That's more like it. Good kids.* He backed out of the driveway and headed back to the store. With commission, that delivery brought his running total up to $24.95, which was well under the average for eleven deliveries at that point. Commission was $1.50 per delivery, which was $16.50 of his $24.95. That meant out of eleven houses, he had been given tips totaling $8.45, one house was a $5 tip, and another was for $2. *It's been a lousy night.*

Gabe arrived back at the restaurant and went in, leaving his car running in case there were more deliveries ready to go. There weren't. But his manager, Dan, was waiting for him. "Get your sign, you're going home." He knew it, when he spun his tires pulling out of that driveway on the wet pavement, the customer had called to complain. He placed the hot bags back on the storage rack and went to retrieve the car topper that lit up and displayed the restaurant's name and phone number. Shutting his car off, he went back inside.

Dan already had his delivery totals summed up. He was definitely in a bad mood. Gabe turned in the store's money and pocketed his earnings, $24.95. *What a pathetic night.* "Clock out and get out of here. Pull any more stunts like this, and you'll be lucky if all James does is suspend you for two weeks."

Gabe attempted to defend himself, "Dan, the driveway was an incline and it's raining. I drive a lightweight front-wheel drive car; it's a 5-speed manual transmission. Of course, the tires spun out. It was an accident, I'm sorry."

Dan gave Gabe a confused look and responded, "What are you talking about? Do you think a customer complained? No, this is about your bookie coming to collect while you're on the clock. He said you'd already placed and lost three bets tonight since 6:00 p.m. You came to work at 4:00 p.m. So you have been accused of illegal gambling on company time. James wanted to fire you then and there, but I managed to get it changed to a two-week suspension, you're welcome by the way." Gabe looked gutted. Dan continued, "Look, Gabe, you're a good delivery driver, you're a decent person, but you have a serious problem, and you have a history of making bad decisions. Take these next two weeks to sort your shit out and get your head on straight, okay?" Gabe nodded and left.

On the drive home, Gabe felt uneasy. He kept checking his mirrors to see if anyone was following him, but it was difficult to be sure in the rain. Shortly thereafter, he arrived at his first-floor apartment. Gabe wasn't at all surprised to find his friend Alex waiting for him. After looking around the parking lot, he exited his car.

Alessandro "Alex" Bianchi was Gabe's best friend. They met three years ago when Alex started working at the restaurant, and Gabe trained him to be a delivery driver. Alex was about five years younger than Gabe, being 24 to Gabe's 29, and he looked up to Gabe and would do anything for him. Alex stood at 5'8", had a thin build, and he had light brown hair. He spoke, "Dan told me you were getting suspended. What happened?"

Gabe was frustrated. "Your cousin Leo happened. He came by the store and made me look bad in front of my boss."

Alex was surprised, "What did Leo do that for?"

Gabe unlocked his apartment door, cast a desperate look over his shoulder at the parking lot, and the pair went inside. "Because I owe him money. I owe him a lot of money," Gabe admitted the ugly truth.

"So, what, like a grand? I can float you that much; I've got savings." Alex pulled out his phone. " What's your PayPal?"

Gabe sighed, "No, not like a grand. I wish it were just a grand. No, it's more. A lot more."

Alex asked, "So ten? Fifteen?"

"One hundred." Gabe barely emitted the number; it was caught in his throat and just above a whisper.

Alex dropped his phone. His mouth was agape in disbelief. "One hundred... thousand? Dollars? How?"

Gabe shook his head, "I wish I knew. I've been out of control for a while now, but I didn't realize it was this bad. I've been placing riskier and riskier bets and wound up losing and digging a deeper hole for myself. Then, two months ago, I bet $20,000 on a horse in the Kentucky Derby. He lost. I don't know what to do."

Alex was concerned. "Let me talk to Leo, I'm sure I can get him to see reason, get him to cut you some slack, maybe. It's worth a shot." Alex added, "Don't worry, I won't tell Ma. I know how much she hates you. She's insistent that you're a terrible influence on me."

Gabe winced at the mention of Alex's mother. He knew precisely how Francesca Bianchi felt about him. "She's never going to forgive me for the pumpkin pie."

Alex laughed, then offered, "Nah, dude. Ma has tried to control my every move lately. It's like she doesn't want me to be around you at all. I didn't tell her I was coming here tonight, so don't fret." He continued, "Still, fucking Leo..."

Gabe was perplexed. He knew Alex was naive and didn't want him to see the truth about his cousin Leo. Leo Rossi was his bookie, and he was best friends with Marco De Luca, the son of Mario De Luca, head of Pittsburgh's most prominent crime family. The De Luca family just happened to be the financial backers of Leo's illegal gambling operation. So, if one gets indebted to Leo, they're actually indebted to the De Luca family.

Gabe fidgeted nervously. "No, Alex, I got myself into this mess, I'll figure something out to get out of it. It's my problem; I don't want to make it yours too." He shrugged it off and said, "Wanna play some baseball?" He powered on his PlayStation 5 and started MLB The Show 2023. Selecting his team and handing Alex a controller, he pushed the gambling mess out of his mind. "Shohei Ohtani's gonna make you cry tonight."

Alex grinned and replied, "Not if Acuña takes you yard!" The two entered a competitive game, trash-talking each other and sharing laughs. But as the innings wore on, Gabe found himself losing focus. His fingers faltered on the buttons, and Alex's taunts started to fade into the background. His mind was elsewhere.

Alex paused the game and gave Gabe a curious look. "Alright, man, what's up? You've been acting weird all night. Is it the suspension? Or Leo?"

Gabe hesitated, his hand tightening around the controller. He took a deep breath. "No, it's... something else. Something I've been meaning to tell you for a while.

"I've been feeling like... like I'm living a lie, Alex," Gabe began, his voice trembling. "Every time I look in the mirror, it's like I don't even recognize the person staring back at me. It's not me."

Alex frowned, trying to piece it together. "What do you mean? Like... existential crisis stuff?"

Gabe shook his head. "It's deeper than that. I've felt this way my whole life.

"Alex, do you know what gender dysphoria is?"

Alex was confused, "I think so? Isn't that like when a person thinks they're a dude when they have the body of a chick, and vice versa?"

Gabe shook his head, "It's more complicated than that, dude; it's the distress a person experiences due to a mismatch between their gender identity, or rather their personal sense of their own gender, and their sex assigned to them at birth."

Alex responded, "How is that any different from what I said?"

Gabe patiently explained, "Well, Alex, your definition simplifies it to just a matter of 'thinking you're a dude or a chick.' But gender dysphoria is more about the emotional pain and discomfort that comes from feeling like your body doesn't match who you truly are. It's not just about 'thinking' you're something; it's about feeling it deeply and having that feeling conflicted with the sex you were assigned at birth."

Alex looked puzzled. "I don't get it. If someone feels like a guy but is actually a girl, why can't they just... I don't know... be a guy?"

Gabe took a deep breath, trying to find the right words. "It's not that simple, dude. For people like me, our gender identity is a fundamental part of who we are. It's not something we can just 'be' or 'not be.' And when our bodies don't match that identity, it can cause a lot of distress and discomfort."

Alex nodded slowly, starting to understand. "I think I get it. It's like... your body and your mind are two different things, and they're not matching up?"

"Exactly. And I suffer from that." Gabe confessed and continued, "I want to act on these feelings. I want my outward appearance to reflect how I feel and who I am at my core. I'm going to transition to be a woman. I wanted to tell you first because you're my best friend."

Alex was silent for two minutes, his mind pondering the information he just learned. He finally spoke.

"Whoa, Gabe... dude... I... I don't know what to say. I'm glad you told me, though. I'm here for you, no matter what. I just... I don't understand all this, but I want to. You're still the same person to me, you know? But I guess that's not the point, huh? The point is that you're not feeling like yourself, and that sucks. So, um, what does this mean, exactly? You're going to... start dressing differently and stuff?"

"Yes, but it's more than throwing on a dress and makeup and buying a purse. There's gender-affirming care. Hormone replacement therapy. Laser hair removal. Voice training." Gabe took a deep breath, trying to break it down in a way that Alex could understand. "So, when

I say I want to transition, I'm talking about a whole process that helps my body align with my gender identity. It's not just about changing how I look on the outside but also about feeling more comfortable in my own skin.

"Hormone replacement therapy, or HRT, is a big part of that. I'll start taking estrogen and anti-androgens to help my body develop more feminine characteristics. That means my voice will get higher, my hair will get softer, and I'll start to develop curves.

"Laser hair removal is another part of it. I'll have to go through several sessions to get rid of most of my body hair. And voice training will help me learn how to speak in a way that feels more natural for me." Gabe continued, "It's a lot to take in, I know. But for me, it's about feeling like I'm finally being true to myself. It's scary, but it's also kind of exciting."

"My dysphoria has made me desperate, and that's why I've been gambling so heavily. This process takes years. And it's not fucking cheap."

Alex nodded. "So, do you have a name picked out you want to be called when you transition? What do you want to be called?"

Gabe did have a name. He had picked it out and was ready to go in preparation for this conversation. He revealed his chosen name to Alex.

"Mi—"

Just then, there was a knock at the door. "Who could that be?" Alex asked as he got up and walked over to answer the door.

Chapter 13: Impetum

Alex opened the front door, this was typical behavior because Gabe viewed Alex as his only family and allowed Alex to treat the place as if it were his own. Alex looked outside, took a few steps back, and shouted, "GABE!"

Six men wearing all-black clothes, complete with black gloves, boots, and ski masks, and carrying crowbars entered the apartment. The last one inside shut the door behind him. The lead masked man spoke. "Mister De Luca said you owe him one hundred grand. He told us to come get it, and if you didn't have it, take it out of you. So, which will it be, kid?"

Gabe stammered, "I... I... I..."

Alex interjected, "Let me talk to Leo; he can sort all this out. There's no need to—"

Alex never saw the bullet coming. One of the masked men walked right up behind him, pulled a .38 caliber pistol out, and shot Alex right through the back of his head. "No witnesses."

Gabe sat horrified, frozen in his chair at the sight of his best friend's life ending in an instant. He managed to speak. "Al... Alex..." His voice was barely a hoarse and raspy whisper. The lead masked man reared back with his crowbar and swung it like a baseball bat to Gabe's right shin. Gabe felt his tibia snap, and he cried out in agony, speaking unintelligibly as a second blow snapped his tibia in another place. *No... A* third blow, *no...* followed by a fourth, *no...* then a fifth, *just stop...* and a sixth. *I'm going to die...* His ankle was completely shattered, he tried to stand, but his leg crumpled under his body weight like tissue paper. *This is it,* Gabe thought. *This is how I die.*

As Gabe pulled himself across the floor, he felt a hard blow to his head. *Gotta get away...* The masked men closed a circle around him and began raining blows from their crowbars on Gabe's body. *Move, Gabe...* They stomped him and kicked him repeatedly. Gabe's entire body felt as if it was on fire, a burning sensation permeated throughout. Even his fingertips were burning. *It's no... it's no use...* He couldn't focus, his vision was blurred, and he was seeing red. And after what felt like forever, it stopped. The men left and closed the door.

The entire attack took eighty-seven seconds. Gabe tried to breathe, but it felt like he was underwater. He heard a woman's frantic voice while he tried to crawl. *Who's that? Oh no, Alex...* After a few seconds of trying to crawl to Alex, he lost consciousness.

Gabe opened his eyes. He struggled to look around to see where he was. Instantly he realized he was in a hospital. He saw the IV inserted into his left hand and watched as the bags slowly dripped whatever solution they contained into the tube that fed into his arm. He then noticed his left arm was immobilized in a cast. He attempted to stretch because he felt stiff, but his body protested as pain shot through him from head to toe. He saw the nurse's call button on his bed and managed to grab it and press it.

A minute later, a nurse entered the hospital room and began checking his vitals. She was an older woman with graying hair, and she wore glasses. After recording Gabe's vitals, she spoke. "You've been through something beyond belief, and you're in tremendous shock and pain. Please try to remain motionless for the time until the doctor gets here. She's on her way now." Gabe oddly didn't hurt too badly to be in the hospital. He thought back to the attack; much of it was a blur, but the biggest thing that stood out in his mind was seeing Alex killed while trying to reason with the attackers.

Gabe was alerted by a knock on his door, followed by a doctor entering with a clipboard. The doctor, who was approximately 5'7" and of Indian descent, had black hair and brown eyes. She exhibited a very calm demeanor and a kind bedside manner. "Hello, Gabriel. I'm Doctor Anaya Kapoor. I'm glad to see that you're awake. How do you feel?"

Gabe struggled to speak, and when he did, he found it painful, "Thirsty, but otherwise okay, I guess?"

Dr. Kapoor replied, "You feel okay because of the amount of painkillers coursing through your body right now. Do you realize where you are?" Gabe nodded, and Dr. Kapoor continued, "You suffered a brutal attack, according to police reports. Eyewitnesses reported seeing six masked men leaving your apartment that night. They left you clinging to life with significant injuries."

Gabe struggled to speak again, "How bad?" was all he could manage to get out.

Dr. Kapoor began softly and clearly, "Gabe, I want to take a moment to discuss the extent of your injuries. When you were brought into the hospital, our team immediately began assessing the damage. Unfortunately, you've suffered significant trauma.

"You have six compound fractures below your right knee, which will require extensive surgery and rehabilitation. In addition to that, you've sustained eight broken ribs, which punctured your left lung. We've been able to stabilize the lung, but you'll need to be closely monitored to ensure there are no further complications.

"You've also suffered a break in your upper left arm, just above the elbow. We've immobilized the arm to promote healing, and you'll need to undergo physical therapy to regain strength and mobility in the affected limb.

"You've also suffered damage to your larynx and throat, which has affected your ability to speak. Our speech therapist will work with you to help regain your vocal strength. Furthermore, you have facial lacerations, which will require stitches and possibly further surgery.

"The CT scans also revealed a concussion, which we're treating with rest and observation. Lastly, the tissue damage to your lower right leg is extensive, and we'll need to perform multiple surgeries to repair the damage and promote healing.

"I know this is a lot to take in, Gabe. But I want to assure you that we're doing everything in our power to ensure you receive the best possible care. We'll work together to get you through this difficult time and help you regain your strength and mobility."

"Just take it off," Gabe said. Dr. Kapoor asked, "What do you mean?" Gabe sat upright painfully, his ribs giving a sharp reminder they were broken. "My leg. Just cut it off. It's not going to heal properly. Wouldn't that be easier?"

"Gabe, I understand why you might think that amputation would be a more straightforward solution, given the extent of your injuries. And I agree that, in the short term, it might be the best option for your leg. The damage is severe, and amputation might be necessary to prevent further complications and promote healing.

"However, I want to be transparent with you: amputation is not an easy solution. It's a major surgical procedure that comes with its own set of risks and challenges. You'll face a long and complex recovery process, including physical therapy and rehabilitation. You'll also need to adapt to a prosthetic limb, which can be a significant adjustment.

"I want to make sure you understand that amputation is not a decision we take lightly. But I also want to assure you that we'll be with you every step of the way, providing the best possible care and support to help you through this difficult time."

Gabe absorbed Dr. Kapoor's words. *So what if I lose my leg, I'm barely alive. Speaking of alive... I have to know.*

"My... my friend...Alex? Is he... is he..." Gabe couldn't bring himself to finish the question.

Dr. Kapoor was very somber with her reply. "I'm so sorry, Gabriel. When the paramedics arrived to find you and your friend, they did everything they could to resuscitate him. There was nothing that they could do. He didn't survive."

Gabe nodded. *They did it. They killed Alex. Why didn't they finish me off? Why did I have to live?* He then said, "I'll sleep on the leg decision." And then he passed out again.

When Gabe awakened next, he was unsure how much time had passed. He paged a nurse. After a couple of minutes, the same nurse from before returned to his room. "Good afternoon, Gabe. It's good to see you awake. How do you feel?"

"Like hammered shit." He could definitely feel the painkillers weren't as effective as when he was awake last. "How long have I been here?"

The nurse gave him a solemn look, "Eleven days. You were unconscious for the first eight days, you woke up briefly and met me and Dr. Kapoor, she disclosed your injuries, and you passed out again, this time for three days." The nurse checked the IV and noticed it was ready to change, then left the room.

Eleven days. He'd lost the past eleven days. Alex was dead and probably buried by now. He'd missed the funeral. He wondered how his mother was reacting to the loss of her son. *I caused this,* Gabe thought; *my gambling caused this. My obsession with trying to win money instead of saving it got my best friend killed. Mrs. Bianchi would kill me for this. I just want to die.*

Why can't I just die?

"WHY CAN'T I JUST DIE?"

Chapter 14: Revelations

Miriam said goodbye to Eli, Di, Jules, and Noah and closed the door. She looked at Ava, who was seated on the couch, with a very concerned look on her face. *To hell with lying anymore, I'm telling her everything. She deserves to know the truth, and Marshal Thompson can't prove I told her prematurely. I'm gonna tell her, Alex.* She sat down next to Ava and offered her a cigarette, which Ava accepted, and Miriam took one for herself as well. She extended the lighter to light Ava's cigarette, then lit her own.

Ava broke the silence. "I know you said you always tell a different story every time you tell a person how you lost your leg, and I get why that's funny, but I have to know. Was the story you told us tonight the actual truth about how you lost your leg? It felt different, more serious. It had weight behind it."

"Yes, it's the truth, but only part of it. And I'm going to explain everything right now and why I didn't last night on our date." Ava nodded and smoked her cigarette as Miriam continued.

"When I was 18, I did leave home on my birthday. I traveled around before I eventually settled in Pittsburgh. I really am a struggling artist, and I really was a pizza delivery driver there for about eight years. I also suffered from crippling gender dysphoria my entire life, and my desperation to transition led me to make the wrong choices and start gambling, which in turn led to me being attacked.

"On the night of the attack, my best friend Alex Bianchi was at my apartment. We were playing on my PS5, and I confessed to him about having gender dysphoria and my desire to transition; hence my spiraling gambling problem. He was confused but supportive. And then the guys sent for me to take me out killed him right in front of me. Alex never saw it coming. Quicker than a snap of your finger, he was gone.

"The men worked for Mario De Luca, the head of the De Luca crime family. They were bankrolling Leo Rossi's illegal gambling operation, and Leo was best friends with Marco De Luca, Mario's son. They wanted their hundred grand and no witnesses. They didn't know Alex was there. They didn't know he was Leo's younger cousin. Alex didn't know Leo worked for a crime family. I didn't know until a few weeks before I was attacked that Leo worked for the De Luca family. It was a clusterfuck.

"I spent the first eleven days in the hospital unconscious before I finally woke up, and spent weeks in therapy and rehab, both physical and mental therapy. And after about a month, the doctors realized they couldn't save my leg, so we amputated it."

Ava's eyes were wide with horror as she listened to Miriam continue her story.

"A few days later, Assistant U.S. Attorney Amanda Miller visited me in the hospital. She was the lead prosecutor in a RICO case against the De Luca crime family. Because I was a direct victim of De Luca violence and witnessed a murder during the attack, I was a key witness against Mario and Marco De Luca.

"AUSA Miller said I would be placed under federal witness protection headed up by the Department of Justice and the United States Marshal Service, and my case handler would be US Marshal Arthur M. Thompson. I agreed under two conditions: get me as far as reasonably possible away from the De Luca family and fund my transition because if I was going to need a new identity, then I wanted a say in who I was. They agreed, and I became Miriam Ryder, and once I was healed enough to drive and travel I moved here.

"The DOJ and the US Marshal Service cover my gender-affirming care, my laser hair removal, my hormone replacement therapy, my voice training, my car, my house, my wardrobe, my breast augmentation, my stipend, my doctor visits, my therapy sessions, everything. If I make one violation of the program requirements, I lose it all, as well as my protection. If I lose my protection, the De Luca family will find me, and they will kill me.

"This is a lot to believe, I know, but I can prove it. And I'm taking a huge risk, but I want you to understand how serious I am about how much I like you. I didn't want to lie to you for any reason, even if it meant my safety, because I didn't want to hurt you. I want to build this on truths, not lies."

Ava stared at Miriam for what felt like an eternity. She stared into Miriam's eyes as tears streamed down her cheeks. She reached her hand across to take Miriam's hand as she spoke, "You willingly put your very existence at risk, all of that, for me?"

"Yes. Because you're worth it, I feel so alive when I'm with you. I feel I can be my most natural self when I'm with you, and I think you feel that, too."

Ava nodded. "Yes, I feel so free when I'm with you. I can sense your compassion and empathy, and I can see how much you care about me. It's crazy—it's only been two days—but I understand why you couldn't be honest yesterday. Knowing why and the risk you're taking to tell me everything, I trust you. I believe you. And I want us to build on this together, wherever it takes us."

Miriam's phone dinged; it was a text from Rachel. *I'm outside, when is Ava leaving?* Miriam responded, *Come in.* "That's Rachel Lee; she's my local handler. And she's going to be so pissed at me right now." A knock at the door prompted Miriam to say, "Come in!"

Rachel came inside and closed the door behind her. "Miri, can I have a private conversation with you on the porch?"

"Anything you have to say to me can now be said in front of Ava, Rachel." Miriam braced herself, and she felt Ava's hand take hers and gently squeeze it.

"You told her? You promised me this morning you wouldn't tell her! Why did you tell her? Do you realize I'm legally obligated to report this to US Marshal Thompson? You'll lose EVERYTHING! Damn it, Miri! What were you thinking?" Rachel sank into the couch, placing her head in her hands.

"I was thinking that I want to build a life with Ava, and I couldn't do that on lies! She's more important to me than waiting for Thompson's approval whenever that would come! She's a person of tremendous value, not a fucking protocol!"

Rachel looked up, first at Miriam and then at Ava. She knew she was seeing something genuine, and she knew that deep down, Ava would keep Miriam's secret. "Okay, okay. I'll push harder to get Thompson's approval. Just keep your head down, please."

Miriam didn't realize she had been holding her breath, so she breathed a huge sigh of relief. She walked over and hugged Rachel, thanked her, and promised she would keep out of trouble.

Rachel asked, "So, are you two officially a couple now?"

Ava nodded, "I know it's fast, and we swore we'd take things slowly, but yes, we're a couple. Officially."

Miriam added, "Officially."

Rachel offered her congratulations to the pair and said goodbye, and she left. Miriam got up to clean up the empty pizza boxes and put the leftovers in the refrigerator while Ava put up the remaining sodas. The two had the living room straightened up in minutes, and then Miriam started coffee. When it was ready, they moved to the porch swing. They sat there under the stars, listening to the wind lightly blowing through the trees, sipping their coffee, smoking their cigarettes, and enjoying each other's company. *I want every night to end like this.* Miriam smiled at Ava. *I can't tell her yet, but I'm absolutely falling for her hard.*

"Miriam, can I stay over tonight?"

"Yes, you can stay every night. You're free to come and go as you please. I enjoy your presence and want you to always feel welcome here. The lock code to the front door is 1128. You never have to ask permission to come over." *This house is your house,* she added silently.

Ava snuggled deeply into Miriam's side. They sat in the swing until 11:00 p.m., when Ava said, "Let's go to bed." She grabbed Miriam by the hand and led her inside and up the stairs.

Miriam awoke the following day to find Ava not beside her. She looked at her phone, and it was 6:08 a.m. *Did I dream last night, or did that really happen?* She sat up and realized she was completely naked. She imagined Alex saying, *All signs point to yes.* She put her bra and panties on, followed by her prosthetic, and made her way downstairs.

Miriam entered the kitchen to find Ava making breakfast and dancing in her underwear. Ava noticed Miriam in the doorway, rushed over to her, and gave her a passionate kiss. "Good morning, beautiful. There's fresh coffee ready to go, and breakfast will be ready in a few minutes." Miriam smiled, grabbed a cup of coffee, grabbed a cigarette, and went to the front porch.

We did it, we had sex... and it was amazing! Miriam grinned and lit her cigarette. *And she's still here. And she's happy, dancing, making us breakfast!* She sipped her coffee and took a drag of her cigarette. *If I had a family, I would want them to meet her. Alex would love her.*

Miriam wondered how her parents would react to her transition. She remembered when she was four years old, and she told her mother she was a girl. Her mother responded by spanking her and telling her Miriam was sick in the head. Her mother was abusive physically, mentally, and emotionally from the time Miriam was four until she left on her 18th birthday. *Why give a shit what she would think? Mom never wanted a daughter then, I'm sure she wouldn't accept one now.*

Ava emerged carrying two plates and two glasses of orange juice on a serving tray. Miriam smiled as Ava had made bacon, toast, and eggs. They enjoyed their breakfast in silence, sitting on the porch swing in their underwear. They finished breakfast and then had their post-meal cigarettes. Ava finished hers and said, "I have to go get ready for work."

Miriam had forgotten it was Monday morning. She was going to call and plead her case to US Marshal Thompson but had zero idea what she was going to do with her time remaining in the day. Ava could sense she was struggling with what to do and offered a suggestion, "Paint more minis."

Ava went inside to get ready. Miriam took their breakfast dishes inside and loaded them into the dishwasher. She broke out the paint and grabbed a dragon to paint. Ava came back downstairs after forty minutes, kissed Miriam goodbye, and left for work. Miriam checked her phone, and it was 7:45 a.m. US Marshal Thompson would be arriving at his office at 8:00 a.m., and she intended to call at that time. She continued to basecoat her dragon, and her phone alerted her that it was the top of the hour.

Miriam lit a cigarette, went into her contacts, and selected the entry labeled Bakery. After three rings, a commanding voice answered on the other end, "US Marshal Arthur M. Thompson speaking."

Miriam prepared herself for the conversation: "Hi, Marshal Thompson. It's Miriam Ryder. I have a matter of great importance to discuss with you. Is now a good time to talk?"

"Miriam, it's 8:00 a.m. on a Monday. Of course it's not a good time to talk. But you have me on the phone; what do you want to talk about?"

"My girlfriend. I need approval to let her know I'm in witness protection. Please. Sir. Please, sir, Marshal Thompson, sir." Miriam had zero clue how to address him when asking the question. She felt so embarrassed.

There was a pause before Thompson's voice cut through, sharper than before. "Absolutely not. That's not how this works, Ryder. You know the rules."

"But, sir—"

"Miriam, you've been there a week. Do you mean to tell me you've already gotten a girlfriend? You're supposed to be keeping a low profile!"

"Marshal, you told me to keep my head down and to acclimate to my environment. This is me telling you that I'm acclimated. I'm acclimated very well. In a week, I've made friends, been on a date, started a social club with some college kids, started a new hobby, and, yes, I got a girlfriend. And I'm pretty sure I'm in love with her already, and I see a life with her, a real future. She's amazing. I need her to have clearance; please give me the approval to tell her I'm in witness protection. I won't tell her details of the case or about what happened, but I really can't lie to her. She deserves to know."

"Miriam, it's been one week. One."

"Marshal, how long did you know your wife before you knew she was the one you wanted to spend the rest of your life with?" Miriam was met with a long silence. "How long?" She repeated.

"Give me her name so I can vet her and get her in your case file. Any information you can give me will be helpful and make the process quicker."

"Ava Marie McCormick, age 28, birthdate August 7th, 1995. Born in Richmond, Virginia, parents are Ryan and Sophia McCormick, a former attorney turned social justice activist and pediatrician, respectively. Graduate of Mountain View College with a bachelor's degree in fine arts in June of 2018, started teaching art classes at Jasper Hill High School in August of 2018. Would that be sufficient enough?"

"That's extremely helpful, thank you, Miriam. I'll get her vetted and give you the official final word by end of day, okay?"

"Yes, thank you, Marshal Thompson. This means more to me than you can possibly imagine. Goodbye, sir." She ended the call. She squealed with delight, spun around on the spot, and fell onto the couch after losing her balance. She'd done it. She smiled contently and returned to painting her dragon.

Chapter 15: The Art Of Trust

Miriam was laser-focused on painting her dragon. The dragon itself was a classic European red dragon, and Miriam was making lots of progress. She had managed to basecoat all her chosen colors, shade the recesses, and had begun the layering process to brighten the colors back to their original tones while leaving the shadow colors intact. She heard and felt an obnoxiously loud rumble from her stomach, and she glanced at the time on her phone. It was 2:47 p.m.

She walked over to the kitchen and grabbed a slice of cheese pizza and a slice of pepperoni, poured some Mountain Dew, and walked back to the living room, where she had set up her painting area. *Damn, cold pizza is absolutely the best snack. I didn't realize I'd been sitting here painting non-stop for seven hours.* She finished her pizza, lit a cigarette, took her soda and phone outside, and sat in her favorite spot on the porch swing. It was 3:05 p.m., the school was releasing. She would likely hear from Ava very soon. Hopefully, she would hear back from Marshal Thompson within the next two hours with official news.

As she smoked and sipped her soda, a glint of light caught the left corner of her field of vision. Looking towards the source, she saw the unwelcoming sight of a county police cruiser, which was being driven by Deputy Beauregard Harris. Miriam stared fiercely as Bubba continued his makeshift stakeout. She stood up, extended her right middle finger, gestured in his direction, and stormed inside. *Ugh, disgusting piece of shit. What I should have done was record him watching me on my phone.* She peered out of the window only to see that Bubba had departed.

Miriam's phone rang. It was Ava, and she answered, "Hey, how was your day?"

Ava replied, "It was great. A couple of my students apparently saw us at dinner Saturday night and asked if you were my girlfriend. I told them not that it was any of their business, but yes, you were. Was that okay?"

"Of course it's okay! I told Marshal Thompson this morning that I needed approval for my girlfriend to know I'm in witness protection. He said he'd start the vetting process today and hopefully have you approved by the end of the day."

"That's a relief, Miri, I'm glad he's working with you. Hey, I'm going to run to my apartment, would it be okay for me to bring things there to keep at your place? You know, clothes, makeup, pajamas, shoes, those kinds of things?"

"Yes, you don't have to ask. And it's OUR place. I want you to think of this as your home as much as it's mine." She continued, "Oh, so I've been painting all day, and I didn't realize what time it was until a few minutes ago, so I grabbed some pizza and then went outside. And Bubba Harris was parked on the side of the road across the creek, watching me. I flipped him off and came back inside. I thought then I should have recorded him, but he left when I looked outside."

"Miri, you've been painting non-stop for seven hours? I've seen how hyper-fixated you get when painting... are you still in your underwear?"

"Shit... I am."

Ava laughed. "Please get dressed, silly. You're so adorable. Would you like me to pick up some dinner on the way home?"

"Sure, your pick; just surprise me. I'll see you in a little while. Be careful."

"I will. How about subs? I'm craving a sub."

"Sure, tuna on wheat, loads of black pepper, please."

"You got it, my dear, I'll see you in a little while. Bye." Ava ended the call.

Miriam had the biggest smile on her face and pumped her fist in the air to celebrate. *She called it home. She said on the way home!* She placed her phone on the side table and resumed work on her dragon.

Ava arrived home around 6:00 p.m. to discover Miriam still painting on her dragon and *still* in her underwear. She giggled as she closed the door and walked over to give her a kiss. She poured them each a soda from the kitchen, brought them to the coffee table, and handed Miriam her sub, and she took hers. They unwrapped their sandwiches and started to eat. Between bites, Miriam would show Ava her work on the red dragon. Ava's jaw dropped. She was stunned by the amount of detail and progress Miriam had made.

"This is amazing, Miri. Truly amazing. It's nearly complete, and honestly, it's display quality. And you've done all of this today?" Miriam beamed with pride.

"I've been watching a lot of content creators on YouTube for little tips and techniques, combining those things with what you taught me and mixing it in with my own style. Oh, and I have a new saying for painting. 'Slay the gray,' this guy Jon always ends his videos with it."

Her phone rang. *Bakery.* It was Marshal Thompson. Miriam picked up, "Hello, Marshal."

"Hello, Miriam, I just wanted to inform you that Ava has been approved for you to disclose that you're under federal witness protection by the United States Marshal Service. You may not give her any details about your case or why you're in witness protection other than you're a key witness in an RICO case, and she's not allowed to tell anyone those details. Violation of these stipulations will result in your termination from the program. Do you agree to these terms?"

"Yes, Marshal, I agree to those terms."

"Congratulations. You can now tell your girlfriend. Have a good evening, Miriam."

"Thank you, Marshal Thompson. Have a good evening." She ended the call and shared the news with Ava. They hugged and resumed eating dinner.

After dinner, Ava brought in her belongings and she and Miriam put them away. They ended the evening with a shower and their evening porch sitting and went to bed.

The next few days went by uneventfully, with Miriam spending the days building and painting miniatures while Ava was at school teaching art classes. Miriam and Ava found they really enjoyed preparing dinner together each evening. They shared more and more information with each other and spent the evening hours laughing and crying and holding each other, being supportive of one another, and making plans for the weekend.

Miriam's birthday was only a few days away, and Ava had been planning a surprise for Miriam. Sunday night, during dinner, she told Miriam what some of the surprises entailed.

"So, Miri, your birthday is Thursday. 30. Last Day. Carousel. Renew. Renew. Renew."

Miriam grinned. She recognized the reference to the classic sci-fi movie Logan's Run and said, "I promise I won't run from you."

Ava smiled and continued, "I have a surprise for you. I'm taking this week off from work, and I've got plenty of vacation days. We're taking a road trip for your birthday."

Miriam sat upright, "Where are we going?" she asked excitedly.

"Richmond. There are two museums I want to take you to; The

Virginia Museum of Fine Art and the Institute for Contemporary Art at Virginia Commonwealth University. We will tour those on both Wednesday and Thursday, your actual birthday. And then, Thursday evening, I have reservations for dinner for two at The Boathouse at Rocketts Landing overlooking the James River."

Miriam's eyes were exceptionally wide, "That sounds like a fantastic time! Did you get us a hotel, or an Airbnb, or a private rental cabin?"

"Actually, none of those things. I had something else in mind." She smiled, "I want to introduce you to my parents. They want us to stay there with them."

Miriam smiled, but her smile quickly faded, and panic set in. "Your parents? Ava, yes, I'd love to meet them, very much so, but that makes me extremely nervous."

"Why does it make you nervous?"

"Because the last time I met a friend's mother, she despised me. And I'll have to lie to them about my past. Yes, I want to meet your parents, but I assumed that would come later, after the trial, when I'm no longer under witness protection and can freely talk about my life. I want to build a life with you, and I want to do that based on truths, as I said. Your family is very important to you. I don't want to start my relationship with them by lying to them." She gave a worried look to Ava, who smiled warmly back.

"Miri, you have nothing to worry about, I promise. I've got that figured out."

"You do? How?"

"My dad is a former attorney; he may not practice, but he's still a member of the Virginia State Bar. You can place him on retainer to represent you, and you can disclose your witness protection status, and he must by law keep that confidential."

"Okay, that takes care of your dad, but your mom's a pediatrician. I don't think she can treat me for a skinned knee and keep my status private."

"No, but she's dual-licensed. In addition to her general medical license, she's also a licensed professional counselor, so she's also obligated by law to protect your status if you were to disclose that in a session."

Miriam's face glowed with joy, "Holy shit! Ava, you're a genius! It's foolproof! I could kiss you!"

"Well, what's stopping you?"

"Nothing." Miriam took Ava in her arms and kissed her passionately. Their half-eaten dinner was forgotten as they went upstairs.

Chapter 16: Forever Found

Tuesday morning arrived, and Ava's car was packed for their trip. Ava drove a red 2022 Mazda CX-9, and she insisted on driving. She didn't want Miriam to have to concentrate on driving on the interstate and in Richmond City traffic with hand controls during her birthday week. She wanted Miriam to focus on relaxing and enjoying herself. Ava double-checked their bags and travel checklist while Miriam made breakfast, which consisted of hash browns, sausage patties, and toast. After they finished their breakfast, they did one final sweep of the house to ensure they remembered everything.

The drive to Richmond from Jasper Hill was 358 miles and an estimated 5 hours and 35 minutes drive. It was 8:00 a.m., and Ava estimated with gas stops, restroom breaks, and food, they should arrive at her parents' house around 3:00 p.m. A vast majority of the trip would be on Interstate 81 North then Interstate 64 East, so they should avoid any rush hour or lunch rush traffic. They got into the car, lit cigarettes, tuned the radio, rolled their windows down, donned their sunglasses, and pulled out of the driveway heading to their destination.

Miriam and Ava were singing along to the radio, holding hands as Ava drove. Miriam smiled and thought to herself, *This is my first proper road trip in over a decade. This is the first time ever meeting a significant other's parents. I'm so nervous; what if I make a terrible impression? What if they don't like me? What if they—*

"Miri, doll, you're quiet. Why'd you stop singing? What's on your mind?"

"I've never been introduced to someone's parents before. I'm nervous."

"Never? I understand being nervous but don't be. I know they're going to love you. My parents are very supportive of me, they're very supportive of the LGBTQ+ community, they know you're trans, and they know the most important thing of all."

"What's that?"

"That you're good to me, you respect me, and you make me incredibly happy."

Miriam smiled warmly at Ava and squeezed her hand. Ava returned the smile and squeezed back. "Now, less worrying, more singing!"

Unbeknownst to the pair, a county police car tailed behind the whole way to the county line. It stopped there, lingering only for a moment, the headlights staring as if they were a pair of eyes, before turning around.

They stopped for lunch around noon, settling on Wendy's. Miriam got a spicy chicken sandwich with fries and a Coke, while Ava ordered a single combo with everything and a sweet tea. They continued down the interstate, eating and talking, while Miriam would feed Ava French fries between bites of her burger and sips of her tea.

One thing Miriam could do as a passenger was take her prosthetic off to avoid unnecessary discomfort while traveling. To amuse herself and Ava, she used the socket as a cup holder, which caused them both to erupt with laughter. Ava turned the radio down and asked, "Miri, when the trial is over and you don't have to stay in witness protection anymore, what are you going to do?"

Miriam smiled, "Anything we want. As long as we're together, I'm happy.”

Ava smiled, “So if I wanted to move to the swamp and be a bog witch, you’d come with me?”

“I’ve already picked out a large hollowed-out tree for us to use as a hut.”

“Where have you been all my life?”

“Running up gambling debts to the mob and getting beaten to near death?”

Ava laughed wryly. “You literally went there, you silly, adorable, beautiful girl. I was right. My parents are definitely going to love you.”

“I hope so.”

They arrived at Ava’s childhood home at 2:51 p.m., and Ava was pleased they had made it by 3:00 p.m. The pair finished their cigarettes just as they pulled into the driveway on the right side of the house. Miriam put her leg back on, and they got out and stretched. Miriam surveyed the house and took in the details.

The house featured a Georgian Revival style with Arts and Crafts influences. In front of the house was a low stone wall, approximately two feet high, that flanked two square stone columns that were six feet tall, which in turn had square wooden columns on top of them, extending to a height of twelve feet total and supporting a large, sloping roof which doubled as a covered porch. Three tall multi-paned windows were present by the green front door on the porch, all totaling approximately eight feet tall. The second floor featured four shorter multi-paned windows arranged equidistant from each other, spanning the width of the house. Green shutters adorned each window, and the walls were painted a light yellowish tan. On the left side of the angled roof, Miriam spotted a brick chimney. *This house is gorgeous!*

The front door opened, and Ava’s parents emerged to greet them. Ava’s mother, Sophia, was a lovely woman with short brown hair, green eyes, and a fair complexion standing approximately 5'6". Her father, Ryan, was not much taller, standing at 5'8". He wore glasses and had a full beard and mustache, but he had the brightest red hair Miriam had ever seen. It was clear who Ava got her hair color from.

They rushed to Ava and gave her a hug, squeezing as tightly as they could. And suddenly, they were hugging Miriam just as tightly. "Hello, Miriam, we're delighted to meet you! We've heard so much about you! I'm Sophia, and this is Ryan, we are thrilled to have you as a guest in our home for the next few days."

"Thank you. It's a pleasure to meet you, too. I admit, I've been terribly nervous for the past three days about meeting you both."

Ryan scoffed. "Please, Miriam, try not to be nervous. We've been nervous about making a good impression as well, but we're all here together now. You made it safely with our daughter, and we can go out and sit on the patio and have a conversation, tell stories, and learn more about each other. How does that sound?"

"That sounds great, Mr. McCormick. I'd like that very much."

"It's Ryan and Sophia. There's no need for formality."

"Thanks, Ryan. And please, call me Miri. Everyone that I'm close to and love calls me Miri."

Ava was beaming and came to Miri's side and took her hand. Sophia then said, "What would you girls like to drink? I'll bring it around to the patio."

Ava and Miriam exchanged a look then they both said simultaneously, "Coffee!"

Ryan added, "I'll unload the car and take your bags to your room, alright?" Miriam and Ava nodded, and Ava led Miriam to the patio at the back of the house.

Miriam was greeted by a sprawling backyard with a gorgeous flag-stone patio. The patio featured square stone columns identical to the ones in front of the house, supporting another slanted roof to create a covered patio. Stone planters lined the patio, where multiple types of flowers were growing. Miriam was unsure of all the types of flowers, but she knew azaleas, lilies, tulips, and roses and could identify those. She couldn't identify at least five other kinds of flowers.

Ava nudged Miriam and gestured to the left side of the patio, and to Miriam's delight, there was a porch swing. They sat down and got their cigarettes out, and each lit one. After a couple of minutes passed, Sophia and Ryan emerged carrying a tray of coffee with cups, creamers, and sweeteners and a tray with a charcuterie board respectively. Miriam and Ava grinned excitedly and exclaimed simultaneously, "GIRL DINNER!" Ryan chuckled and placed the tray next to the coffee tray on a large glass outdoor table

The pair poured themselves coffee, and Ryan prepared coffee for himself and Sophia. They all sat down, and Sophia asked, "Miriam, where are you from? Did you grow up in Jasper Hill?"

Miriam fidgeted slightly, then answered truthfully. "I'm originally from Northeast Tennessee, I was born there in 1994. My parents divorced when I was five, and my mom got custody of me. She moved us to Southeast Kentucky, not far from Jasper Hill, ironically enough. But the day I turned 18 in 2012, I left in the middle of the night. I didn't have a good childhood." She trailed off.

Ryan picked up and asked, "Where have you been living for the past twelve years? And what brought you to Jasper Hill? Was it MVC?"

"Well, for the first two years, I traveled around a lot, working odd jobs, making my way from town to town, seeing America, never staying more than two or three months in one place. Then in 2014, I moved to P—"

"Dad, before this conversation goes any further, I need you and Mom to do something. Please."

"What is it, sweetheart?" Sophia asked.

"Mom, I need you to officially log this as a counseling session. And

Dad, I need you to take Miri on as a client and be on retainer."

"What's this all about? Retainer? Ava, I don't understand... but fine, Miri, can you give me a dollar?" He extended his hand. Miriam produced a dollar from her purse and placed it in Ryan's hand. "Congratulations, I'm now your attorney and on retainer to represent you as needed."

Sophia added, "I'm officially logging this as one hour of counseling, intake session, from 3:30 p.m. to 4:30 p.m."

Ava nodded, "Thanks Mom, thanks, Dad." Miriam added a thank you as well. All eyes turned to her. She continued on.

"Ten years ago, in 2014, I moved to Pittsburgh. I worked odd jobs to support myself as an artist. I eventually started delivering pizza in 2016."

"But why does that require a counseling session and attorney retention?" Sophia was perplexed.

"Because, Sophia, Ryan, I'm in the witness protection program. I'm a key witness in a federal RICO case. And my identity was changed, and I was relocated to Jasper Hill for my protection until trial."

Sophia's face fell, her brows furrowed in worry. "Witness protection? Ava, do you realize what this means? This isn't just about secrecy—it's about danger. The kind of people Miriam is hiding from... what happens if they find her? What happens to you?"

Ryan leaned forward, his voice calm but firm. "I respect the courage it takes to testify in a case like this, Miriam, but Ava... sweetheart, are you sure this is something you're ready to commit to? Being with someone in WITSEC means living with a constant level of uncertainty and risk. It's not a decision to take lightly."

Sophia shook her head slowly, her hands wringing together. "Ava, I don't think you understand the gravity of this. These aren't just abstract dangers—they're real people who wouldn't hesitate to harm Miriam, and by extension, you. What if they track her here? What if they come after you?" Her voice cracked, revealing the fear bubbling beneath the surface. "You're our only child. I can't lose you, Ava."

Ryan's jaw tightened as he glanced at Sophia. "And what about building a life together? Ava, you've always dreamed of stability, of laying down roots. How can you do that with the constant shadow of danger hanging over you? We're not doubting your love, but this... this isn't a normal situation. You need to be sure you can live with the stakes."

Ava's eyes softened, and she took Miriam's hand. "Mom, Dad, I've never been more sure of anything in my life. Miriam is the most incredible person I've ever met. She's brave, kind, and selfless. Yes, her situation comes with risks, but life without her isn't something I'm willing to consider. She's not just someone I love—she's my person. My soulmate. The one I've waited my whole life to find."

Sophia exchanged a glance with Ryan, her expression softening. "The way you speak about each other... it's clear how much love and respect you share. That's all we've ever wanted for Ava."

Ryan nodded, a small smile forming. "It's clear that you two have something special. If you're all in, Ava, then we'll do our best to support you both. But, Miriam..." He looked at her directly. "Promise us you'll do everything you can to keep each other safe. That's all we ask."

Miriam's voice cracked slightly as she nodded. "I promise. I'll do whatever it takes to protect Ava and our future together."

Ryan smiled gently. "That's all we needed to hear."

Sophia gave Miriam a kind look. "You're welcome here, Miriam. You're part of the family now. And I have to say, your courage is remarkable. It's clear why Ava loves you.

"So you're in witness protection, so obviously, you can't tell us why, and I wager that's what brought you to Jasper Hill. I know Jasper Hill likes to present itself as a friendly, welcoming town, but I've heard stories from Ava and read articles from that area that don't portray

Jasper Hill in the friendliest light, especially towards members of the LGBTQ+ community. In your short time there, has this been your experience?"

Miriam nodded, "On my very first afternoon, the county sheriff harassed me about being transgender. Then on our very first date, his bigoted deputy son harassed us, assaulted Ava, and taunted me. Then the following afternoon, the two of them and the mayor all but told me to get out of town or they'd make me want to get out of town."

"But we're fighting back, Mom and Dad. Miri thought about the college, and the number of students on campus outnumbers the townspeople by a third. So we started the Jasper Hill Equality Coalition. We're going to raise awareness against the mayor and his discriminatory policies and promote equality, fairness, acceptance, and inclusivity. And with Pride month coming up in June, I'm sure we can get a lot of new members to our cause."

"With the student body behind us, we'll vote the bigots out of power. You're a social justice activist, Ryan. Could you give us some pointers or strategy points?"

Ryan's expression brightened as he nodded. "I'd be happy to help, and we can do that after dinner. Sound good?"

Miriam and Ava nodded enthusiastically.

"Miri, Ava tells us you're an artist, do you have a degree in art?"

"No, Sophia, I'm purely self-taught. But I've studied a lot of YouTube videos over the years, learning techniques and developing my own style utilizing what I've learned. It was purely by chance that I was looking for something to read, and the comic store owner suggested that I attend the miniature painting class when I mentioned I was an artist."

Sophia smiled warmly. "Self-taught? That's impressive, Miriam. I'd love to see some of your work while you're here."

Ava added, "The rest is history, as they say."

"I know I was smitten," Miriam said, her voice soft but sincere, glancing at Ava with a hint of a smile.

Sophia leaned forward, her expression warm. "It sounds like a real case of love at first sight to me."

Both Miriam and Ava froze, their eyes meeting as if for the first time. The words hung in the air, heavy with truth.

"I mean... I guess..." Miriam began, her voice faltering as a blush crept up her cheeks. "I—"

"Yeah, we—" Ava cut in, her voice equally uncertain, before stopping mid-sentence. Their gazes locked, unspoken emotions swirling between them.

Neither of them could look away. In that moment, everything else faded—the patio, Ava's parents, the weight of their circumstances. All that mattered was the overwhelming realization shining in each other's eyes.

Miriam's voice was barely above a whisper. "I think I've loved you since that first night, Ava. I just didn't know how to say it... or if I even should."

Ava reached out, taking Miriam's hand in hers, her fingers trembling. "Miri, I—me too. I've loved you for so long, but I didn't know if you felt the same. I didn't want to ruin what we had."

Miriam smiled through the tears welling in her eyes. "You couldn't ruin anything. Not when you're my everything."

Ava squeezed Miriam's hand tightly, her voice breaking as she spoke. "You're my everything, too."

Sophia and Ryan exchanged a knowing glance before quietly excusing themselves, leaving the two women alone to fully embrace the depth of their feelings.

"I love you, Ava. I've loved you since that first night. I love you so much that I couldn't bear to lie to you, so I told you the truth. I love you for your compassion, your empathy, your kindne—"

"I love you, too, Miri; shut up." And Ava pulled Miriam in and kissed her fiercely, exuding every ounce of passion she could muster in her lips, bringing all the warmth possible from her fingers as she caressed Miriam's face. She ached to pour her essence into Miriam.

After several passionate minutes and numerous exchanges of I love you to each other, Miriam lit cigarettes for the two of them and passed one to Ava. "Thank you, by the way."

"For what?" Ava had a quizzical look on her face.

"For not Han Soloing me. When I said I love you. You could have said I know." Miriam smiled. "I would have been totally fine with it, by the way. But thank you. For making the first time you said it to me be exactly what it was."

Ava rested her head on Miriam's shoulder. "Of course, Miri. You're my person. I've finally found you. And I don't want a life without you. I will spend forever with you, or as long as the universe gives us, whichever comes first."

Miriam couldn't stop the tears. She'd never felt such pure emotion from another person before. Nine months ago, she was begging to die in a hospital bed. Now, she was in a moment in time she wished could last to the end of her days.

They sat there in silence, holding each other until Ryan opened the back door to tell them dinner was ready.

Chapter 17: Art, Love, And Acceptance

Sophia and Ryan had prepared a delicious dinner of roasted chicken, grilled asparagus, garlic-infused mashed potatoes, and glazed carrots. Miriam and Ava complimented Ava's parents on the meal. After dinner, they prepared coffee, adjourned to the patio to smoke on the porch swing, and discussed organizational strategies with Ryan for their newly formed Jasper Hill Equality Coalition.

"So, Dad, we're obviously new at this, and we honestly don't have any idea where to start with the JHEC. Can you help us?" Ava asked as Miriam brought up her notes app on her phone to take down details.

Ryan began, "The first thing you need to do is build a diverse coalition and attempt to recruit representatives from multiple marginalized groups. You two represent a portion of the LGBTQ+ community but try to get more members to represent the community's diversity. Recruit racial and ethnic minorities as well, and Miriam, don't forget to recruit disabled individuals. Working together to represent a broad range of these groups will ensure a solid foundation for your coalition."

"Next, you need to nail down your mission statement and make sure it identifies your key issues and goals, the most pressing problems adversely affecting the people of Jasper Hill.

"Once you do these things, you can get to the heart of growing a coalition and grassroots expansion by building relationships with local community members and empowering them to get involved.

"Appoint a social media manager; it's extremely important to utilize social media effectively. Use Facebook, Instagram, Threads, and Bluesky. Those should provide the most engagement. Post daily, multiple times per day.

"Partner with other local organizations and businesses to expand both their reach and yours. The more eyes and ears on you are a net positive.

"Stay up to date and be informed with both local and national news, and be prepared to adapt your strategies because circumstances change in an instant, and be flexible in how you approach each issue.

"Learn to celebrate your victories, no matter how small they seem, because you will face setbacks. Learn from them; they will provide opportunities for growth and improvement.

"And lastly, and this is the most important thing. Prioritize self-care and sustainability, please. Social justice work is both emotionally and physically demanding, and it takes its toll. Set realistic goals for yourselves and the JHEC.

"This is the best advice I can give you. It's hard work, but when you achieve your goals, the results are worth it, and everyone benefits."

"Thank you, Dad. This is a great guide for us to formulate a real plan. It means an incredible amount to Miri and me."

"It absolutely does, Ryan, I don't know where we would have started without your guidance and advice. I'm grateful."

Sophia emerged from the house with fresh coffee for everyone. Once everyone has fresh coffee, Miriam and Ava lit fresh cigarettes. Sophia then asked, "So what's your itinerary for tomorrow, girls?"

"Well, Mom, I have the next two days planned out because, as you're aware, Miri's birthday is Thursday, and I want to make this the most memorable birthday ever for her. So we're going to head out early and get to the Virginia Museum of Fine Arts at 10:00 a.m. and tour it until 1:00 p.m. Then I figured we would get some lunch at the Amuse restaurant upstairs, then go back to touring from 3:00 p.m. to 5:00 p.m. After that, I'll take Miri shopping, and then we'll be home for dinner around 7:00 p.m. if that's okay.

"Thursday is similarly scheduled, but this time we're going to the Institute for Contemporary Art at Virginia Commonwealth University. Lunch from 1:00 p.m. to 3:00 p.m., then more touring the exhibits until 5:00 p.m. And then I've got reservations for two overlooking the James River at The Boathouse at Rocketts Landing at 6:30 p.m."

"That sounds like an absolutely lovely evening. Sunset on the river is divine."

Ryan asked, "Do you girls have any special requests for breakfast in the morning?"

"Pancakes and sausage links would be great if it's possible, Dad." Miriam smiled at Ava, it was the first breakfast she cooked for the two of them.

"You got it. I'm going to go turn in, I'll see you two in the morning." He kissed Ava on top of her head and gave Miriam a hug, then went inside.

Sophia added, "I've got extra pillows and blankets laid out in your room, if you need anything at all tonight, don't hesitate to let us know." She also kissed the top of Ava's head and hugged Miriam goodnight, then retired to the house.

Ava was startled by Miriam's sniffing. "Miri, honey, why are you crying?"

"Your family is incredible. You have such a supportive family. They've made me feel like I belong, like I matter. They've welcomed me effortlessly with open arms. I adore them." She turned to Ava. "Thank you for showing me that family can be a truly wonderful thing."

Ava cradled Miriam in her arms and held her. Never in Miriam's life had she felt so safe and secure. She didn't want to lose this. She couldn't bear the thought of it. After all, she was Ava's person. Now and forever.

Miriam and Ava arrived at the Virginia Museum of Fine Arts promptly at 10:00 a.m. and parked on the covered parking deck for an accessible parking space. The pair walked hand in hand into the museum. Miriam smiled and squealed with excitement. "I've never been to a legitimate art museum before, you know?"

Ava smiled back and replied, "This is part two of my gift to you for your birthday. Part one is being accepted by my parents. I'm going to do everything in my power to give you the most special days ever."

As they walked in, Miriam overheard a museum employee telling another patron that the Virginia Museum of Fine Arts was home to a collection of nearly 50,000 works of art from almost every world culture. "There's no way we could see them all in one day."

What they did see was memorable. Ava made sure to show Miriam some of the more well-known exhibits from the museum's permanent collection. They started by viewing the Art Nouveau section, followed by Art Deco, then Modern and Contemporary American art. Miriam was especially delighted by the areas housing French Impressionist and Post-Impressionist art, but her eyes sparkled when Ava guided her to the East Asian art section of the museum, and as they viewed the exhibits, Ava took pictures of her and Miriam together in the museum. "I want to capture these moments for us to look back on."

Miriam was fascinated by everything the museum had to offer and was surprised when Ava told her it was time for lunch. They made their way to the third floor and entered the Amuse restaurant. Amuse was a seasonal farm-to-table restaurant, and it allowed for sweeping views of the sculpture garden and the atrium.

After lunch, they resumed their tour of the exhibits and collections, marveling at the sheer volume of displays from around the world.

Miriam said, "I can't believe this place exists in Virginia. When I think of museums, my mind always goes to The Louvre or the Smithsonian. And you grew up coming here?"

"Yeah, Mom and Dad would bring me here several times a year. They wanted to instill an appreciation of cultures from around the world at a young age. I think this place strongly influenced my career path."

They departed the museum at 5:00 p.m. and went to the shopping district nearby. Miriam found a shop that designed and sold clay pottery and Ava purchased a set of bowls that featured holes to hold chopsticks in place while eating. They stopped by Stony Point Fashion Park and went dress shopping, with Ava buying Miri a cute purple mid-length dress with half sleeves and a scoop neck.

At this point, Miriam was exhausted. The last time she had pushed herself this hard, she was bedridden the following day. She hoped this time would be different.

Miriam's birthday had arrived and Ava woke her with a gentle good morning kiss. "Happy birthday! How are you feeling this morning, Miri?"

Miriam stretched and moved about on the bed. There was an elevated level of soreness, but nothing she couldn't push through. She had noticed recently that Ava kept her more productive and she was getting her endurance levels back. "I'm sore, but I think I'll be ok today. How did you sleep?"

"Beautifully, absolutely beautifully, thanks to you. Let's go have some breakfast."

They made their way downstairs to find Sophia and Ryan in the kitchen making breakfast. Upon seeing Miriam, they both shouted, "Happy birthday!" and gave her hugs and kisses on each cheek. Ava sat back in a chair and admired how her parents had accepted Miriam; it had been flawless up to that point. Seeing Miriam so happy warmed her heart.

After a rather large breakfast consisting of homemade buttermilk biscuits, sausage gravy, sausage patties, and hash browns, Miriam and Ava retreated to the patio's porch swing for coffee and cigarettes. "Happy birthday, beautiful lady." Ava kissed Miriam's hand and held it to her cheek.

After their porch swing time, they went to get dressed and put their makeup on for the day. Miriam decided she was going to wear her new dress that Ava had bought for her paired with her brown leather knee-high boots. Ava reentered the room wearing a lovely white floral print sundress featuring a halter top with a ruched bodice and pink carnations, her fiery red hair flowing lusciously in contrast. Miriam's jaw dropped slightly and she managed to get out, "You're ravishing!" Ava blushed and took her by the hand and said it was time for them to leave.

They arrived at the Institute for Contemporary Art just before 10:00 a.m. Miriam marveled at the building's architectural design. It featured a double front, with one side opening from the city and the other from the sculpture garden, linking the Virginia Commonwealth University campus to Richmond. Miriam swooned as they entered the sculpture garden, delighted by the bluestone gravel pavement lined with planted ginkgo trees flanking a large reflecting pond.

"I could sit here for hours, and it's so peaceful and lovely." Ava agreed but urged her to follow. They roamed through the gallery, observing the exhibits, noting that there were far fewer than at the Virginia Museum of Fine Arts. Miriam didn't mind. This allowed for more intimacy in observing each exhibit, allowing her and Ava to discuss their interpretations and take pictures together to commemorate the occasion.

They had lunch in the museum's cafe, then returned to the sculpture garden. It was 3:23 p.m. Miriam's body felt it was nearing its limit. "Is it alright if we rest for a while? I'm totally feeling all the walking and standing during the past two days."

Ava responded, "Of course, Miri, please don't hesitate to let me know when you need a break. We can leave early if we need to."

Miriam nodded, "Let's just sit here for a while before we leave. It's so zen. It's speaking to me." They sat hand in hand for the next hour, snuggled together, staring into the reflecting pond. *A year ago, I had to work on my birthday. Alex bought me MLB The Show 23, and I was miserable in hindsight.* Miriam pondered further. *Ava's done a fantastic job. She's poured herself into this birthday celebration. I don't know how she can top it.*

Chapter 18: A Gift Of Love, A Call To Arms

Ava parked the car in the closest accessible parking space she could find. They finished their cigarettes, grabbed their purses, and went into the Boathouse at Rocketts Landing. Ava and Miriam were greeted by the hostess, "Welcome ladies, table for two?"

Ava responded, "We have a reservation for two at 6:30 p.m. under the name McCormick."

The hostess confirmed and said, "Ah yes, very good, please, follow me."

Miriam was relieved to find there was an elevator that took them to the top floor of the three-story restaurant. The hostess led them to a smaller room composed entirely of glass. "Welcome to the Harbourmaster Suite."

Miriam's eyes widened at the table set with candles already burning in the center. "Shall we?" Ava took Miriam by the hand and led her to the table. In addition to the candles, the centerpiece was made of pink carnations to match Ava's dress. Miriam beamed at Ava as they sat down.

After a moment, a waiter approached. He was tall, approximately 6'1", with an athletic build and a short, cropped haircut with shaved sides. "Good evening, ladies. Welcome to The Boathouse. My name is Travis, and I will be taking care of you tonight. Here are a pair of menus. What would you like to drink? "

Ava smiled and said, "Thank you, Travis, I would love a sweet tea, and Miri would like a Pepsi."

Travis nodded, "I'll get those drinks in a moment and be back to take your order."

Miriam looked over the menu and said, "This place is incredible. Do you have any idea what you want?"

Ava nodded, "I do. Would you like to start with a focaccia bread basket?"

"Yes, that sounds wonderful. Are there any specific things that I shouldn't order?"

"Get the lobster, Miri, I am," Ava encouraged.

Travis returned with their drinks and a black and silver box wrapped in silver. He placed the box on the tabletop next to Ava, and they placed their order with him. He departed, and Ava began. Miriam could tell by the way her voice trembled that she was nervous.

"Miri, I have a gift for you, and I hope you like it. I've been working on it secretly at the school for the past two weeks and finished it the first night we were here while you slept. Happy birthday, my love." She presented the box to Miriam.

Miriam smiled and gently unwrapped the exquisitely wrapped gift, then proceeded to open the box. Her breath seemed to leave her as she cupped her left hand over her mouth. She looked up at Ava and then back down.

The box contained a drawing of Miriam done in charcoal pencils. In the drawing, Miriam is sitting on their porch swing with her prosthetic removed and resting against the side table. She is portrayed sipping coffee and smoking a cigarette in her underwear. She exclaimed, "I love it so much, it's stunning! I'm framing this and hanging it in our bedroom!"

Ava was overjoyed. "This is you at your purest, your most laid-bare.

This is how I see you, the fearless woman who's overcome so much and takes time to enjoy a simple cup of coffee and a cigarette while gently swinging. I love you."

"There's one more part of my gift to you." She raised her hand as if to signal someone. Travis returned carrying a violin and bow. He handed it to Ava and departed. Ava said, "I had Mom drop it off here earlier today." She handed Travis her phone and asked him to film the next few minutes. She stood, and stared at Miriam as she began to play an instrumental version of Elvis Presley's 'Can't Help Falling In Love' as Miriam looked on in awe.

Ava attempted to transfer her very soul into the sounds the bow produced as it made contact with the strings. She swayed to the rhythm as Miriam began to sing the lyrics looking into Ava's green eyes.

"...Wise men say only fools rush in, but I can't help falling in love with you. Shall I stay? Would it be a sin if I can't help falling in love with you?"

When they finished the song, Miriam and Ava were both in tears. Miriam rose from her seat and approached Ava to embrace her. She kept humming the tune, and the pair slowly danced as the setting sun cast golden rays onto the surface of the James River in the background while Travis captured the moment with Ava's phone.

Friday morning arrived much faster than they anticipated, and Ava and Miriam were packing their belongings to return to Jasper Hill. They finished packing and went downstairs to the patio to have coffee and cigarettes before leaving.

Sophia and Ryan joined them on the patio and were carrying a beautifully wrapped box adorned with a satin ribbon and a gift tag bearing a heartfelt message: "Happy Birthday, Miri. Welcome to the family. With all our love, Sophia and Ryan."

Miriam opened the box to find a beautifully crafted, handmade jewelry box made from mahogany. The box was adorned with intricate patterns and a delicate latch. Inside, Miriam discovered a letter written on high-quality, textured paper and sealed with a wax stamp bearing their family crest.

Sophia and Ryan also included a custom-made sterling silver necklace with a small, delicate pendant shaped like an interlocking heart and infinity symbol. Ryan said, "This necklace represents our love for you, Miri, and our acceptance of your relationship with Ava."

Miriam opened the letter carefully and read it, and one hand clutched over her mouth as tears freely flowed down her cheeks. The letter read,

"Dear Miri,

We want to express how grateful we are to have you in our lives. From the moment you and Ava met, we knew that you two were something special. And as we've gotten to know you better, we've fallen more and more in love with the kind, compassionate, and strong person you are.

As you celebrate another year of life, we want you to know that we're honored to be a part of your journey. We're so proud of the love and commitment you and Ava share, and we're grateful to be able to support and celebrate you both.

As you look to the future, we hope you know that you'll always have a home with us. We'll always be here to support you, to listen to you, and to love you for who you are.

Happy birthday, Miri. We love you more than words can say.

With all our love,

Sophia and Ryan"

Miriam was uncharacteristically speechless. She gently placed the jewelry box on the side table and got up to hug Ava's parents. They held her as she sobbed, all she could manage to say was, "Thank you."

Ava squeezed in to make it a family hug after giving Miriam a few moments for just her. "That was beautiful, Mom and Dad, but did you have to wait until right before we were leaving?" They all laughed.

Sophia began to wipe tears away from Miriam's face as Ryan asked Ava if their bags were ready to load in the car.

After a joyous and tearful goodbye, Ava and Miriam departed Sophia and Ryan's driveway and began the journey back to their home in Jasper Hill, hand in hand.

On the way home to Jasper Hill, Miriam texted each of the Jasper Hill Equality Coalition members and asked if they could all meet at Miriam and Ava's at 8:00 p.m. Each responded yes in kind, and Miriam was elated. She and Ava reviewed their talking points for the meeting, ensuring that they included the key elements Ryan had discussed with them.

They arrived home around 4:00 p.m. and were happy to be back. As much fun as they had over the past few days, they were exhausted and agreed to nap. The two napped until 6:30 p.m. and woke up feeling refreshed. Ava brought the bags in from the car and Miriam prepared coffee; then they ventured out to their porch swing until the JHEC members began to arrive. Jules was first, followed by Di, Eli, and finally Noah. They each wished Miriam a happy birthday and asked about their trip, then Miriam and Ava covered the strategies they were hoping to enact, when Jules exclaimed loudly, "OH FUCK!"

She showed the others a news article titled "Mayor Winston Proposes Bathroom Bounty."

"A small town in Virginia, Jasper Hill, has proposed a 'bathroom bounty' law, which will allow individuals to sue transgender people for using a restroom that aligns with their gender identity. The proposed law promises a minimum payout of $5,000 for successful claims. This proposed law would be part of a larger wave of anti-trans legislation in the United States, which has been a hotbed for such laws in recent years."

Miriam broke the silence. "Well, now we know our first fight. Let's get to work."

Chapter 19: Building The Resistance

Miriam was shaken. Her body was trembling as anger coursed through her. She knew that the mayor had vowed to make life more difficult for her, but this was dangerous. Virginia was a concealed carry state, and Miriam lived in a town that was considered conservative by all intents and purposes. But she was no stranger to struggling or danger. She sprang into retaliation mode.

"Jules, we need to hold a recruitment meeting, preferably on campus. We need to spread the word and get it in front of as many eyes as possible. Would you be comfortable with this task?"

"I'm on it, Miri. I can think of a couple of locations on campus that can accommodate us. How quickly would we need a space? A week? Two weeks? I don't think we can afford to wait much longer."

"Let's shoot for two weeks. In the meantime, we all need to be feet on the ground, informing people and rallying them to our cause. We want to focus on marginalized groups of people. Primarily focus on members of the LGBTQ+ community because this will affect them first.

"Eli, you have a lot of customers from marginalized groups, could you hang a flyer at Trailblazer and inform your customers about the JHEC and our cause?" Without hesitation, Eli confirmed he would.

She turned to Noah, "Noah, you're the frontman for your band, so you have knowledge of promotion, and I am hoping you promote heavily on social media."

He nodded, "In addition to writing our original songs, I also write our promos for upcoming shows to generate buzz for those gigs. I promote on Facebook, Instagram and Threads."

"Add Bluesky to that. We're going to need an account for the JHEC created for each, with both your personal accounts and your band's accounts to promote the JHEC. Congratulations, you're our social media manager, can you handle the job?"

"Absolutely, Miri. I'd be honored. I'll get started tonight. We need a logo for the JHEC and need to clarify our mission statement."

Jules chimed in. "I've got the logo covered, I'm in graphic design, after all." Miriam smiled; they were becoming a team and accepting roles; she couldn't have asked for more.

Di interjected, "What would you like for me to be doing, Miri?"

"Hang flyers about our recruitment meeting in the cafe and use your extensive knowledge and impeccable intuition to inform potential allies among your customers, please."

"You got it, hun."

Ava asked, "What about me?"

"Well, your job will prevent you from attempting to recruit at the school, so that's out. However, you and I could canvas neighborhoods and the campus together in the evenings to raise awareness. What do you think?"

Ava had a determined look on her face. "As long as I'm by your side, I can do anything. You can count on me, my love."

"So, everyone, what's our mission statement?" Jules asked the room. "It should be a clear and concise summary of our goals, right?"

"Of course, Jules. Ava and I refined the list of our goals. First, we promote LGBTQ+ visibility and acceptance. Secondly, we challenge the conservative attitudes of Jasper Hill's residents. Thirdly, we support LGBTQ+ locals and empower them. And fourth, we advocate for inclusive policies."

"Miri and I felt that our mission statement should be: promoting equality, acceptance, and inclusivity for LGBTQ+ individuals in Jasper Hill."

"Miri, May I offer a suggestion?"

"Of course, Jules, what do you have in mind?"

"I think we should modify the statement. We want all these things, yes, but we also want them for all marginalized groups. With a more inclusive mission statement, the more diverse our coalition can become."

Miri nodded and smiled, "That's an excellent point, Jules. Thank you. Ava, are you okay with that?"

"Yes, Jules is right, and I agree it's a wonderful idea. What do you propose we modify the statement to be?"

Jules replied, "I've been thinking about this throughout our conversation tonight, and I feel this is a great mission statement based on our collective goals, just worded to be more inclusive.

"Empowering and advocating for the rights and dignity of all marginalized individuals in Jasper Hill, regardless of their race, ethnicity, gender identity, sexual orientation, ability, or socioeconomic status."

Everyone nodded in unanimous approval. Miri was thrilled. "It's perfect, Jules. Thank you."

"I'll get to work on a flyer and coordinate with Noah to implement the social media contacts. We can have it for you by Monday morning."

"That's great, Jules. Does anyone have anything to add to tonight's meeting?"

Everyone shook their heads no. Miri concluded, "Then I call this a very successful first meeting and hereby adjourn it."

The group clapped and cheered, and then Di spoke. "Ok, Miri hun, I need all the tea, tell us about your trip and what did Ava do to make it special?"

Ava smiled and rocked back and forth with anticipation as she and Miriam recounted the week's events to the group. Miriam showed off Ava's drawing, jewelry box, and necklace from her parents, and Ava played a video of their violin and song collaboration and silent dance at sunset. There wasn't a dry eye in the room.

At 11:00 p.m., the other members of the JHEC left, and Miriam made coffee. She and Ava went to the porch swing to enjoy some downtime before bed. Both were exhausted but energized from the meeting. After a very long day, they finished their coffee and cigarettes and went to bed, excited for what the next day would bring.

Miriam awoke the following day to find Ava looking through all the photos from their trip. She found her favorite one of her and Miriam and set it as her profile picture on Facebook and Instagram, captioning it, '30th Birthday Celebration With My Love Miri'

Miriam smiled and added, "That's a fantastic picture of us. I love it." They spent the next hour in bed looking through all the pictures as well as the several videos from the trip. Miriam just wanted to lay in bed all day. She was physically drained to the point of exhaustion after the week's events and was feeling the consequences of it all.

Ava noticed Miriam was in pain and gently massaged her stump while lying her head on her shoulder. They would have stayed in bed all day had it not been for a sudden, loud knock on the front door. They got dressed, and Miriam put on her prosthetic and made their way downstairs. Miriam opened the door and was surprised to see Rachel Lee.

"Hi Rachel, is everything okay?"

"Has your phone been off? I've been trying to text you for several hours this morning. Are you alright?"

"Yeah, we're fine; we were just upstairs in bed still. You want some coffee or breakfast?"

"No, I'm fine, thank you. But I did want to talk to you two about something. Yesterday, Mayor Winston proposed a bathroom bounty targeting transgender individuals."

"We saw it last night. We're going to fight back. Actually, we founded an organization, the Jasper Hill Equality Coalition. We're going to rally marginalized groups together, take on the mayor and the sheriff, and vote them out of power. We've got goals."

"Voting those two out is about the only way anything will get better here. As a police officer, I have to remain neutral. But, as a friend and ally, you have my full support. I wanted to give you two a heads-up. But there's more. Mayor Winston is talking about banning Pride events and parades."

Ava was furious, "That asshole... when are they going to try to get this done?"

"He's called for a special town council meeting this Wednesday, followed by a public hearing the following Wednesday. So you have to prepare and know what you're up against."

"Thank you, Rachel, I truly appreciate it. What the mayor fails to realize is that Miriam Dawn Ryder is no stranger to adversity. He wants a fight, and I'll give the old man a fight."

Chapter 20: Diagnoses And Desperation

Gabe sat in a wheelchair in the hospital therapist's office. They had been meeting every day for two weeks now. He was growing increasingly frustrated with each session.

In previous sessions, his survivor's guilt and Alex's death had been deeply discussed. They had also delved into his deep-seated longing for family since his father abandoned him when he was five, and his mother and stepfather abused him until he moved out on his eighteenth birthday. They talked about his addictive personality and gambling issues. But the real underlying issue at hand was his severe gender dysphoria and how he yearned to transition to finally be a woman.

His therapist, Gretchen, was very kind and helped him realize his recklessness was a result of multiple underlying issues that had been untreated for twenty-nine years.

Gretchen was an older lady with graying hair. She wore brightly colored glasses and patterns, accessorized by equally brightly colored earrings and necklaces. Finally, she said, "Gabe, I'm ready to give you multiple diagnoses. Please remember that these are all treatable things.

"Firstly, your history of abandonment by your father and abuse by your mother and stepfather may have led to attachment issues and complex post-traumatic stress disorder, or C-PTSD. These experiences can shape your relationships and behavior patterns.

"Your addictive personality and gambling issues may be coping mechanisms for your underlying emotional pain. This could be a sign of substance use disorder or behavioral addiction.

"Your severe gender dysphoria and desire to transition to female suggest that you may be experiencing significant distress related to your gender identity.

"That being said, Gabe, while treatable, you have a long road ahead of you. Here's what I am proposing as a thorough treatment plan.

"For your C-PTSD, I recommend three things. First, we'll use trauma-focused cognitive-behavioral therapy or TF-CBT. A therapist will work with you to process traumatic memories, reframe any negative thoughts, and develop healthy coping skills.

"Next, we'll utilize eye movement desensitization and reprocessing or EMDR therapy. This therapy can help you reprocess traumatic memories and reduce symptoms.

"Lastly, we'll implement mindfulness-based stress reduction or MBSR. You will learn mindfulness techniques to manage stress and anxiety.

"For your Behavioral Addiction, we're going to try cognitive-behavioral therapy. A therapist will work with you to identify triggers, develop coping skills, and prevent relapse. We'll follow this up with motivational interviewing. You will work with a therapist to explore motivations for change and develop a plan for recovery.

"We will make use of support groups, and you may benefit from attending groups such as Gamblers Anonymous or SMART Recovery.

"Here's the big one, your gender dysphoria. You're absolutely certain you want to medically transition from male to female?"

Gabe nodded rapidly, "Yes, more than anything. I need this. Without it, I think... no, I'm sure I'd kill myself. I can't keep living as someone I'm not."

"That's an extreme feeling of despair. Alright, we can start with gender-affirming care, in which a therapist will continue to work with you to explore your gender identity, develop coping skills, and create a plan for transition. You may be eligible for HRT to help alleviate symptoms of gender dysphoria."

"How much will transitioning cost? Because I can't work right now, obviously, and I don't have great medical insurance."

Gretchen was silent for a few moments. Finally, she answered. "Breast Augmentation is usually $5,000 to $10,000, and gender re-assignment surgery, or GRS, also known as bottom surgery, ranges from $10,000 to $30,000. Facial Feminization Surgery costs anywhere from $20,000 to $50,000. Voice Feminization Surgery costs anywhere from $5,500 to $9,000. So you're looking at $40,500 on the low end to $100,000 on the high end. Those are staggering out-of-pocket costs. In addition to those, HRT can range from $50 to $500 per month, depending on the type and dosage of hormones you'll be on."

Gabe buried his face in his hands. "Why can't I just die?"

Gabe absolutely despised physical therapy. He knew he needed it, and it was beneficial, but it hurt so much that it rendered him nearly unable to move afterward. And after the news about the costs associated with transitioning, he didn't see the point anymore.

The physical therapist was urging him to push past the pain and raise his left arm laterally when he said, "Fuck this bullshit. I don't care. What's the point? I just want to die. Take me back to my room."

Once in his room, Dr. Kapoor approached him and said, "Gabe, I'm told you aren't cooperating with my nurses and have been lashing out."

"I just want to die. Why are you all trying so hard to keep me alive?"

"I'll answer that in a few moments, but I have news for you that will cause distress."

"More than I'm already in? I fucking doubt it."

Dr. Kapoor took a deep breath, her expression somber as she sat down beside Gabe's hospital bed. "Gabe, I want to talk to you about your injury. I know you've been through a lot, and I appreciate your strength and resilience, although your temperament needs work."

Gabe looked up at her, his eyes filled with a mix of fear and anticipation.

Dr. Kapoor continued, "Unfortunately, the damage to your right leg is more extensive than we initially thought. The six compound fractures below your knee have caused significant tissue damage, and despite our best efforts, the wound is not healing properly."

Gabe's face fell, and he looked away, trying to process the news. He knew what she was going to say.

Dr. Kapoor gently placed a hand on his arm. "Gabe, I want to be honest with you. We've explored all possible options, and unfortunately, amputation is the only viable choice at this point. I know this isn't what you want to hear, but I want to assure you that we'll do everything in our power to make this transition as smooth as possible."

Gabe's eyes welled up with tears as he looked at Dr. Kapoor, his voice barely above a whisper. "What about... what about my leg? I thought it was healing. Why is it not healing? Will I ever be able to walk again? See? Why should I bother to go on living?"

Dr. Kapoor's expression was compassionate. "We'll do everything we can to help you regain mobility and independence. We'll discuss prosthetic options and rehabilitation plans to ensure you can adapt to this new situation. You'll have a team of professionals working with you every step of the way."

Gabe nodded slowly, trying to accept the news. Dr. Kapoor handed him a box of tissues and sat with him in silence for a moment, allowing him to process his emotions.

"Why are you all trying so hard to keep me alive, anyway?"

Dr. Kapoor said, "That's better answered by your next guest. I'll show her in." She exited and left Gabe to his thoughts. Five minutes later, there was a knock at the door.

Dr. Kapoor walked into Gabe's hospital room, accompanied by a woman with short, curly brown hair and a warm smile. "Gabe, I'd like you to meet someone," Dr. Kapoor said. "This is Assistant US Attorney Amanda Miller."

AUSA Miller extended her hand, and Gabe shook it weakly. "Nice to meet you, Gabe," she said. "I've heard a lot about you."

Dr. Kapoor nodded. "AUSA Miller is working on a case that involves the De Luca family. I thought it would be beneficial for you to meet her, given your... experiences with them."

AUSA Miller pulled up a chair beside Gabe's bed. "I'm building a RICO case against the De Luca family," she explained. "RICO stands for Racketeer Influenced and Corrupt Organizations. It's a federal law that allows us to prosecute organized crime syndicates." Gabe's eyes widened slightly as he listened.

AUSA Miller continued, "We have evidence that the De Luca family has been involved in extortion, money laundering, illegal gambling, murder, and other illicit activities. We believe they're a significant threat to public safety, and we're working to take them down." Gabe's gaze drifted off, his mind processing the information.

AUSA Miller leaned forward. "Gabe, I want you to know that you're not alone. We're committed to holding the De Luca family accountable for their actions. And we believe you can help us."

Dr. Kapoor nodded in agreement. "AUSA Miller and her team can provide you with protection and support. If you're willing to cooperate, you can work together to bring the De Luca family to justice."

"How can I possibly help, especially from here? I'm just a cripple in a hospital bed."

AUSA Miller replied, "By testifying against them in court for their brutal assault on you and the murder of Alessandro 'Alex' Bianchi."

"And how am I supposed to do that? I can't afford to stay here much longer. My insurance coverage—"

"Has long since expired. Did you think your insurance policy from your pizza delivery job was still covering you? No, Gabe, the United States Department of Justice has been footing the bill. We need you alive to testify."

"So I'm just supposed to let them chop my leg off, sit in this bed until I'm healed enough for a prosthetic while worrying about the De Luca family sending someone else to finish the job?"

AUSA Miller continued, "The DOJ works with numerous agencies, and one of them is the United States Marshal Service. The marshals provide witness protection. They will create a new identity for you, relocate you somewhere safe, provide you with a stipend, and more! And the DOJ will help fund everything. This is how badly we want the De Luca family to pay for their crimes." She continued, "Will you help us, Gabe? Will you testify?"

"How did you even know to contact me? I'm nobody."

AUSA Miller replied with a sympathetic tone. "Gabe, you are someone, and you matter. And yes, we need your testimony." She continued, "As for how we knew to contact you, an anonymous tip was called in the morning after you were attacked. As a precaution, knowing you were a potential witness, we placed you under protective care. Gabe, please, will you help us?"

Gabe thought about the offer. Gabe only wanted one thing in life at this point. He mulled the offer over in his head and thought of his final conversation with Alex. *Alex was supportive. I've got no one else. Disappearing will be easy enough. But I will get a say in who I'm going to be.* Finally, he spoke.

"If I'm going into witness protection, I want as far away from here as possible. But my biggest need is I get a say in who I'm becoming. I've known all my life that I'm a woman. I want to medically transition from male to female, but I can't afford it. But the Department of Justice can, as can the Marshal Service. So, pay for my transition. Those are my terms. Agree to this, and I'm your star witness."

AUSA Miller nodded and replied, "That can be arranged. In fact, your desire to transition would only help with integration into a new identity."

AUSA Miller took out her phone and stepped outside. After a few minutes, she returned. "You have a deal."

Chapter 21: Viral Justice

On Monday morning, Miriam and Ava received a text from Jules reading. *Noah finished setting up all the social media accounts for JHEC, and I designed a recruitment flyer. I sent it to your emails. We need to make as many copies to hand out as possible. Talk soon. J.*

Miriam checked her email, and Noah and Jules had come through with the flyer creation and it looked great.

Join the Jasper Hill Equality Coalition (JHEC)!!!

Empowering Marginalized Voices and Advocating for Change

Mission Statement:

Empowering and advocating for the rights and dignity of all marginalized individuals

in Jasper Hill, regardless of their race, ethnicity, gender identity, sexual orientation,

ability, or socioeconomic status.

Our Goals:

- Promote equality and acceptance for all marginalized groups

- Challenge systemic injustices and discriminatory policies

- Support and empower local marginalized individuals and communities

- Advocate for inclusive and equitable policies and practices

Join us in our mission to create a more just and equitable Jasper Hill!
Whether you're a

student, professional, or community member, we invite you to get
involved and make

a difference.

Membership Benefits Include:

- Opportunities for leadership and skill-building

- Networking with like-minded individuals and organizations

- Access to training and educational resources

- A supportive community committed to social justice

Contact Information:

Email: jhec@gmail.com

Phone: (276) 555-1723

Social Media: @JHEC_JasperHill

Together, we can create a brighter, more inclusive future for all!

"It's great, it's informative, it states our goals clearly, and it lets people
know how to contact us. I can print off a bunch of these during my free
period at work today, and we can distribute them to each member and
get to work hanging them and handing them out."

"How many copies could you get away with printing?"

"If I provide my own paper, 500."

Miriam smiled. It was indeed a start. There were 1,800 students to
reach on campus at Mountain View College and several businesses to
hang these in. They'd need many more copies. "500 to start with is
great, Ava. We'll figure out a way to get more soon."

Ava got up to get ready for work while Miriam went downstairs to
make breakfast. She made them oatmeal, toast, and bacon, and then
they had coffee and cigarettes on the porch swing.

"While you're at work today, I'll go drive around town, get a better
feel for the residential areas, and then I'll talk to Di and Eli about which

local businesses would be best to try to partner with."

"Sounds great. We'll meet back here at 3:30 p.m. and go canvassing then?"

"Sounds like a plan. Have a great day at work today. Be careful. I love you."

"I love you, too." Ava bent down to give Miriam a kiss, then left for work.

Miriam texted Jules and Noah, *Making 500 copies today and will split them up amongst us this evening. Meet at 4:00 p.m. at Trailblazer Comics?*

Miriam spent the next few hours driving around and familiarizing herself with the town limits and all the houses within. She then went to visit Di at the Jasper Hill Cafe. Miriam wasn't surprised to see Mayor Winston in the cafe eating lunch. She decided to get under his skin and strolled straight into the ladies restroom. Miriam didn't need to go but wanted to create the illusion of going. After three minutes, she walked back into the dining room of the restaurant and up to her favorite barstool by the front window.

"What in God's name are you trying to pull?" Mayor Harold Winston exclaimed over Miriam's shoulder. She spun her barstool around to face him. "Hello, Mayor Winston. It's a beautiful day, isn't it?"

He angrily stared and repeated himself. Miriam shrugged. "I'm hungry, and I had to pee, so I went to pee. Now I'm going to order lunch. How exactly is any of that your business?"

"You went into the ladies restroom. That's not designated for you. You belong in the men's restroom. I'm trying to keep our real women safe from people like you!"

Miriam's eyes narrowed, her voice steady. "People like me? Do you mean transgender women, Mayor Winston? Women who deserve the same respect and dignity as any other woman?"

Mayor Winston's face reddened. "You're not a woman, Miriam. You're a man in a dress pretending to be something you're not. And I won't stand for it."

Miriam leaned forward, her voice taking on a sharp edge. "I'm not pretending to be anything, Mayor. I'm living my truth, and I won't let you or anyone else shame me for it. And as for the restroom, I used the one that aligns with my gender identity. It's not about 'real women' or 'safety'; it's about respecting people's humanity and dignity."

The cafe's patrons began to stare, sensing the tension between Miriam and the mayor. Mayor Winston's face turned purple with rage, but Miriam stood her ground, refusing to back down. She reached into her purse and withdrew her driver's license. "You see this? It's a valid Virginia driver's license. Do you see the gender marker? F, for female. My medical records list me as female. So does my birth certificate, the Social Security Administration, my bank, my insurance company, and anyone I deal with. If they can designate me as a woman, surely as a member of the human race, you can treat me as a woman."

Mayor Winston's face twisted in disgust, but Miriam continued her voice firm. "You see, Mayor, I've done my research. I know that Virginia allows residents to change their gender marker on their driver's license or state ID card without requiring medical certification. And I've followed the proper procedures to ensure my identity documents reflect my true self."

The cafe's patrons began to murmur, some nodding in support of Miriam. Mayor Winston's face turned an even deeper shade of purple, but Miriam stood her ground.

"I understand that you may not agree with my identity, Mayor," Miriam said, her voice calm but firm. "But I assure you, I am not pretending to be something I'm not. I am a woman, and I deserve the same respect and dignity as any other woman."

The tension in the room was palpable, but Miriam refused to back down. She had come too far and fought too hard for her rights to let Mayor Winston's bigotry intimidate her.

Miriam fixed him with a cold, unwavering stare, her voice dropping low enough to cut through the murmurs in the cafe. "Mayor Winston, let me make this crystal clear for you. You can puff up your chest, spew your hatred, and thump your self-righteousness all you want, but let me ask you something: When did you become the arbiter of who gets to exist in this town? Who gave you the authority to decide who is 'real' enough to use a public restroom?"

She paused, letting her words sink in, then leaned in slightly, her tone sharper. "You see, Mayor, the last time I checked, this is still America, where people are guaranteed certain unalienable rights—life, liberty, and the pursuit of happiness. Not contingent on your approval. Not subject to your ignorance. And certainly not dictated by your narrow-minded views on gender."

The tension in the room was thick as Miriam continued, her voice steady but laced with a quiet fury. "You keep talking about protecting women, but let's call it what it really is: You're afraid. Afraid of people like me because we challenge your fragile understanding of the world. You want to talk about safety? Let's talk about how often transgender people like me are harassed, assaulted, or even murdered just for existing. And here you are, stoking that fire in a public cafe. You're not protecting anyone—you're putting targets on our backs."

She took a step closer, the air around her electric. "And you want to talk about 'real women'? Real women stand up for what's right. Real women fight for equality, justice, and kindness. So by that measure, Mayor, you wouldn't know a real woman if she stared you down in a public cafe—which, lucky for you, is exactly what's happening right now."

The cafe was silent, every patron's attention riveted on the scene unfolding before them. Mayor Winston spluttered, clearly unprepared for the verbal onslaught. Miriam straightened her posture, her voice rising just enough to carry across the room. "You can cling to your bigotry all you want, but know this, Mayor Winston: You're on the wrong side of history, and deep down, I think you know it. So go ahead and glare, insult, and huff and puff all you like. It won't change the fact that I'm here. I'm not going anywhere. And I will not be silenced."

With that, Miriam turned back to the barstool, the weight of her words lingering in the air, leaving Mayor Winston standing there, his self-righteous indignation crumbling under the scrutiny of the crowd.

"We'll see about that." Mayor Winston turned and stormed out of the cafe. Several patrons loudly sided with the mayor, but a majority of the cafe's patrons verbally encouraged Miriam to show their support for her. Di was beaming in her direction. Miriam felt empowered. She vowed she would see Mayor Harold Winston removed from office.

By the time Ava met Miriam back home at 3:30 p.m., she had already gotten wind of the showdown between Miriam and Mayor Winston. She greeted her with a hug and a kiss, then added, "I am so damned proud of you! I saw it!"

"What? How?"

"One of the diners went on Facebook Live, and the video has been shared several hundred times and watched over 2,500 times in the past three hours. You're going viral, dear."

Miriam laughed as she watched the video as the camera zoomed in on the Mayor's contorted purple face. She then had a thought and texted Noah. *There's a Facebook Live of me confronting the mayor going viral. Share it to all of the JHEC social media accounts, please!*

"That may have just helped our cause."

Miriam's confrontation with Mayor Winston proved beneficial to recruiting members to the JHEC. By Friday, they had over 750 members. Miriam was floored.

Di had posted a flyer on the bulletin board in the Jasper Hill Cafe, and

Eli did the same at Trailblazer Comics. Several other local businesses had also taken flyers and displayed them in their front windows, including the coffee shop, the book store, and the convention center. They had managed to distribute all 500 flyers on Monday and Tuesday and planned to make more.

Jules and Noah were hard at work on campus. Noah would film Jules as she would interview students on campus about their opinions on the upcoming proposed bathroom bounty and Pride celebration bans. Noah would then edit and upload the condensed videos to the JHEC social media accounts. They were gaining traction on campus.

They were not faring as well in the community. Jasper Hill was strongly conservative in attitude, and convincing the townspeople was a monumental task. But with their canvassing every evening, Miriam and Ava had managed to recruit fifty new members from town residents.

The JHEC began holding protests daily outside of Jasper Hill Town Hall, bringing to light the proposed ordinances and spreading awareness. When the Wednesday for the public hearing came around, the town hall was standing room only. The line of people spilled out of the building and onto the sidewalk.

During the hearing, Mayor Winston opened the floor for public opinion. Everyone in attendance urged Miriam to go first. She approached the podium and began speaking from her heart while Ava stood by her side.

"Mayor Winston, esteemed council members, and fellow citizens of Jasper Hill," she began, her voice steady but growing more impassioned with each word. "I stand before you today as a proud transgender woman, as a member of this community, and as a human being who deserves dignity and respect.

"The proposed bathroom bounty and Pride celebration bans are not just attacks on the LGBTQ+ community; they are attacks on our very humanity. They seek to erase our identities, to deny our existence, and to render us invisible. But let me be clear: we will not be erased. We will not be silenced. We will not be denied.

"We are your neighbors, your friends, your family members. We are your coworkers, your classmates, your fellow worshipers. We are people who deserve the same rights, the same freedoms, and the same dignity as anyone else.

"These proposals are not about safety or tradition; they are about control. They are about perpetuating harmful stereotypes, fostering division, and sowing seeds of hatred. Rhetoric like this doesn't exist in a vacuum—it emboldens violence, discrimination, and bigotry. It fans the flames of fear until they engulf entire communities. And let me tell you, those flames burn hotter for the most vulnerable among us.

"The bathroom bounty is not about safety; it's about targeting people like me. Transgender individuals are far more likely to be victims of violence than perpetrators of it. Policies like this don't make anyone safer; they put lives at risk by turning everyday activities into battlegrounds.

"And the Pride celebration ban? It's not about protecting values; it's about erasing ours. It's about suppressing diversity, silencing love, and denying us the right to celebrate our identities and existence. But we see through it, and we will not be deterred. We will rise up, we will speak out, and we will fight for our rights.

"Make no mistake, words and actions like yours ripple outward. They tell young LGBTQ+ people in this town that they are not welcome, not valued, not safe. They create environments where harassment, bullying, and violence are not just tolerated but justified. They tear at the fabric of our community, dividing us when we should be working together.

"But we will fight. We will fight for the right to use the restroom that aligns with our gender identity without fear of harassment, violence, or arrest. We will fight for the right to celebrate our culture and community without fear of persecution or erasure. And we will fight for the right to live, to thrive, and to be treated with the same dignity and respect as anyone else.

"So I ask you, Mayor Winston, and all council members, to consider the true consequences of these proposals. Not just the harm to us, the LGBTQ+ community, but the harm to Jasper Hill as a whole. What kind of legacy do you want to leave? One of division, exclusion, and fear? Or one of compassion, unity, and progress?

"We have a chance here to create a different Jasper Hill—one that is inclusive, welcoming, and affirming of all people, regardless of sexual orientation, gender identity, or expression. Let us choose love over hate, inclusivity over exclusivity, and dignity over discrimination. Let us reject these proposals and instead build a community that values, respects, and celebrates every one of its members.

"Thank you."

A young man in his early thirties, dressed in a crisp button-down shirt emblazoned with the logo of his small construction company, stood up after Miriam finished her speech. He was clearly agitated, his tone sharp and brimming with hostility. Miriam recognized him as the other person from the cafe when the mayor first confronted her with Sheriff Harris and his son.

"Well, I guess we're just supposed to roll over and let people like you tell us how to live, huh?" He gestured dismissively toward Miriam. "I run a family business here in Jasper Hill, a business I built with my own two hands. I've got a wife and two daughters, and I'm supposed to sit here and let you lecture me about 'dignity' and 'inclusivity'? Give me a break.

"You stand up there talking about your rights like you're some kind of hero. But what about my rights? What about the rights of parents in this town who don't want their little girls sharing a restroom with a man in a dress? You can call yourself whatever you want, but biology doesn't lie. A man is a man, and no amount of legal documents or emotional speeches is going to change that.

"This town has values. It has traditions. And we're not going to let a handful of activists come in here and tell us what to believe. You say we're spreading fear? No, we're protecting our community! We're protecting our kids from confusion and God knows what else. You talk about violence like it's something we're responsible for, but you're the one stirring up trouble, forcing your way of life on the rest of us.

"And let's talk about this Pride stuff for a minute. You think the people of Jasper Hill want their streets filled with rainbow flags and parades? You think we want our kids exposed to that? This isn't some big city with your progressive ideas. This is Jasper Hill. We believe in God, family, and hard work. Not whatever agenda you're pushing.

"You say we're dividing the community, but maybe you should look in the mirror. It's you and people like you who are coming in here trying to change everything, telling us we're bigots if we don't agree with you. Well, guess what? We're not changing. We're not bowing down to your demands. This is our town, and we're going to fight to keep it the way it's always been."

He glared at Miriam before sitting back down, his face red with indignation, as murmurs of agreement rippled through a portion of the audience.

Di, the owner of the Jasper Hill Cafe and a lifelong resident of the town, rose from her seat. Her calm, steady demeanor stood in stark contrast to the young business owner's heated outburst. She spoke with quiet authority that commanded the room's attention.

"With all due respect, sir," Di began, "you don't speak for all of Jasper Hill. You certainly don't speak for me. I've lived in this town my entire life, and if there's one thing I know, it's that Jasper Hill is stronger when we come together, not when we let fear and ignorance divide us."

She glanced around the room, meeting the eyes of the council members and several townsfolk. "I've known good, hardworking people in this town who've faced hardship, who've faced judgment, and who've faced loss because of who they are. What Miriam said up there took courage—more courage than most of us have shown in this room today. And yet here you stand, trying to tear her down for it."

Di turned her focus to the young man. "You say you're worried about your daughters sharing a restroom with Miriam. But let me ask you: what are you really teaching them? To be afraid of someone who's different? To judge someone without understanding their story? Or to believe that some people deserve less dignity just because they don't fit your narrow definition of normal?"

Her voice gained strength. "I've run the cafe for years. I've seen all kinds of folks come through those doors. You know what I've learned? People aren't threats because of who they are. They're threats because of hate, because of ignorance, and because of a refusal to listen. I've seen more harm done by that kind of attitude than I ever have by someone like Miriam."

Di gestured toward Miriam, who was sitting quietly but with her head held high. "She's not here to attack your values. She's here to live her life, just like you and me. She's not asking for special treatment—she's asking for basic respect, the same respect we all expect to receive when we walk into a room."

She turned back to the council. "And as for this so-called Pride ban? Since when is celebrating love, identity, and community a threat to Jasper Hill? This town isn't just about tradition. It's about resilience, about coming together in tough times, and about standing up for what's right. We don't have to agree on everything, but we do have to agree on one thing: that every person in this town deserves to feel safe, valued, and seen."

Her voice softened, but her tone remained resolute. "We're not going to grow as a community by building walls around what we don't understand. We grow by opening our hearts, by listening, and by learning. So, to the council members here today: I urge you to stand on the side of love, not fear. Let's show the world what Jasper Hill is really made of."

Di sat down, her words leaving an undeniable weight in the air. A hush fell over the room, and the tension from the earlier outburst seemed to dissipate, replaced by thoughtful contemplation.

Noah, one of the founding members of the Jasper Hill Equality Coalition, stepped forward. Their vibrant outfit and confident stance contrasted with the somber atmosphere that had taken over the room. With a quick glance at Miriam and Di, they adjusted the microphone and began to speak.

"Good evening, everyone. My name is Noah Sawyer, and I'm non-binary. That means I don't fit neatly into the categories of male or female—and believe me, I've heard every argument in the book about how that makes me a threat, how it makes me 'confusing,' or worse, how it makes me 'not real.' Sound familiar?"

They paused, scanning the room, their gaze lingering on the young business owner. "I wasn't going to speak tonight, but after hearing that speech, I realized I had to. Because what we're seeing isn't just an attack on Miriam or the Pride celebration—it's an attack on anyone who dares to live authentically in a world that often demands conformity."

Noah's voice grew firmer. "When I first came to Jasper Hill to attend Mountain View College, I was scared. Scared of being myself in a small town, scared of being visible in a place where I wasn't sure if I'd be accepted. But then I met people like Miriam, Di, and the amazing folks at the Jasper Hill Equality Coalition. They showed me that there's strength in community, even in places where it feels like acceptance is hard to find."

They turned toward the council members. "Let's talk about what these proposals really mean. A bathroom bounty? That's not about safety. That's about control—about policing who gets to exist in public spaces without fear. And a Pride ban? That's not about preserving 'traditional values.' It's about silencing people like me, Miriam, and countless others who just want to celebrate who we are."

Noah took a deep breath, their voice trembling slightly but filled with conviction. "Do you know what's dangerous? It's not me walking into a restroom. It's not Miriam standing at this podium. It's the rhetoric that tells people we're a threat, that we're less than, that we don't belong. That rhetoric is what fuels harassment, violence, and exclusion. And let me tell you, those things are a far bigger threat to this community than a Pride flag or a transgender woman using the bathroom."

They gestured toward Miriam and Di. "People like Miriam and Di are the heart of Jasper Hill. They're the ones fighting to make this town a better place, not just for LGBTQ+ folks but for everyone. They're standing up for the values of inclusion, respect, and love—values this town should be proud to uphold."

Noah leaned closer to the microphone, their voice soft but steady. "To the council, I ask you: what kind of community do you want Jasper Hill to be? One that uplifts its people, or one that tears them down? One that chooses love, or one that gives in to fear? You have the power to make a decision tonight that shows the world what Jasper Hill stands for."

Stepping back, Noah gave a small nod to Miriam and Di before returning to their seat. Their words left a lingering sense of hope in the room, a reminder that the fight for equality was not just Miriam's or Di's but a collective effort that included the younger generation ready to carry the torch forward.

Many of the audience in attendance applauded and cheered. The Mayor attempted to restore order. Once everyone calmed down, more people spoke echoing Miriam's sentiments, although some staunchly opposed, but far fewer in number. The council held a vote on the two proposals.

The room fell into a tense silence as the council prepared to vote, the air heavy with anticipation. Supporters of Miriam's cause sat on the edges of their seats, gripping the arms of their chairs or each other's hands, their breaths held in unison. Opponents exchanged hushed whispers and steely glances, their unease observable. The faint creak of a chair or shuffle of papers sounded deafening in the stillness. Every eye in the room was fixed on the council members, their expressions unreadable as they deliberated. The ticking of the clock on the wall seemed to echo louder with every second, amplifying the weight of the moment.

In a narrow decision, the council had voted 3-2 in opposition to the bathroom bounty and Pride celebration bans. Many of the townspeople erupted in triumphant cheers, and the Mayor and his supporters angrily watched dejectedly as the meeting adjourned.

Miriam stood in the center of the town hall, smiling defiantly at Mayor Winston. She knew Alex would have been proud.

Chapter 22: Reborn In Shadows

Gabe woke up from his anesthesia to excruciating pain. Earlier that morning, Dr. Kapoor and her surgical team amputated fifteen inches of his lower right leg below his knee. He promptly cried out in pain.

"OH GOD, IT HURTS, IT HURTS SO BAD, IT HURTS SO FUCKING BAD! I JUST WANNA DIE IT HURTS SO BAD!" He sobbed and continued shouting. A nurse ran in and administered more morphine, which had an immediate effect. Gabe succumbed to unconsciousness.

When he awoke hours later, he managed to sit up. He looked at the blankets covering him in his hospital bed and saw his left foot sticking up, but no right foot. *That's weird, I still feel it. It feels like it's still there.*

He slowly peeled back the blankets and looked at his leg. He immediately began to cry. His leg was gone. There was a very large bandage wrapped around his knee and some type of pump attached. *Why do I still fucking feel it?*

A few moments later, the door opened. It was Dr. Kapoor. She pulled a chair up to his bedside and spoke.

"Gabriel, I'm glad to see you're awake," Dr. Kapoor said gently. "I know this is a lot to take in, but I want to reassure you that the surgery was a success. We were able to remove the damaged portion of your leg, and you're on the road to recovery."

Gabe looked up at her, tears streaming down his face. "Why do I still feel it?" he asked, his voice shaking. "It feels like my foot is still there."

Dr. Kapoor nodded sympathetically. "That's a common phenomenon after amputation, Gabriel. It's called phantom limb sensation. Your brain is still receiving signals from the nerves that were connected to your foot, even though it's no longer there. It can take some time for your brain to adjust, but it will get better."

Gabe looked down at his leg again, feeling a mix of emotions. "Will I be able to walk again?" he asked.

Dr. Kapoor smiled. "Absolutely, Gabriel. You'll need to go through physical therapy and learn to use a prosthetic, but you'll be able to walk and even run again. It'll take time and hard work, but you'll get there."

Gabe took a deep breath, feeling a glimmer of hope. "Thank you, Doctor," he said, his voice barely above a whisper.

Dr. Kapoor put a hand on his shoulder. "You're welcome, Gabriel. We'll get through this together."

"How long will it take to get a prosthetic? What kind of timeframe am I looking at?"

Dr. Kapoor smiled reassuringly. "We'll start the process of getting you fitted for a prosthetic as soon as possible. Typically, it takes around 2-3 weeks for the swelling to go down and the wound to heal enough for us to start taking measurements for the prosthetic."

She paused, considering Gabe's question. "Once we have the measurements, it usually takes around 4-6 weeks for the prosthetic to be fabricated and fitted. However, this can vary depending on the complexity of the prosthetic and the individual's healing process."

Dr. Kapoor's expression turned encouraging. "But don't worry, Gabriel. We'll work closely with you throughout the entire process to ensure that you get the best possible prosthetic and rehabilitation. You'll be back on your feet in no time."

"I have other good news. I have a meeting scheduled for you

tomorrow morning with an endocrinologist. She will explain the process of HRT. We can discuss everything pertaining to it together when she's here. How does that sound?"

Gabe's face brightened, and his demeanor improved. "That sounds amazing, thank you! I do have a question, though, if you can answer it. When can I get a boob job? Do I have to be on estrogen for a while, or can we just schedule it now?"

Dr. Kapoor chuckled and smiled warmly at Gabe. "Well, Gabriel, I'm glad you're excited about the next steps. However, breast augmentation surgery typically requires a minimum of 12-18 months of hormone replacement therapy before it can be considered."

She leaned forward, explaining further. "This is because estrogen needs time to stimulate breast tissue growth and development. Rushing into surgery before this process is complete can lead to less-than-optimal results and potentially compromise the success of the surgery."

Dr. Kapoor's expression turned reassuring. "But don't worry, Gabriel. We'll work closely with the endocrinologist to monitor your progress on HRT, and when the time is right, we'll discuss the next steps for breast augmentation surgery. Okay?"

"Maybe I can get lucky and have rapid growth?"

Dr. Kapoor smiled and chuckled. "I wouldn't count on rapid growth, Gabriel. While it's possible, it's not the norm. Breast development on HRT is a gradual process, and it's more important to focus on your overall health and well-being rather than rushing the process."

She leaned forward, a hint of amusement in her voice. "Besides, rapid growth can sometimes lead to uneven development or other complications. We want to make sure you get the best possible results, and that means being patient and following the recommended treatment plan.

"Get some rest. You've got a big day ahead of you tomorrow."

The next day, after breakfast, Dr. Kapoor brought a colleague to visit Gabe. "Gabriel, this is Dr. Natalia Alvarez-Santos. She's an endocrinologist here and will be working with you to create a thorough treatment plan for your transition.

Dr. Alvarez-Santos was of Cuban-American descent. She had short, stylish black hair and expressive brown eyes, and she displayed a warm, gentle smile.

"Hello, Gabe, I'm Dr. Alvarez-Santos; let me tell you a little about myself. I completed my medical degree at the University of Florida, and my residency in endocrinology at the .Johns Hopkins University. I have been practicing endocrinology for over fifteen years, and I have a special interest in transgender health and hormone replacement therapy."

"Hi, Dr. Alvarez-Santos. I'm Gabe, legless, hopefully soon-to-be woman."

Dr. Alvarez-Santos smiled warmly and nodded. "It's lovely to meet you, Gabe. I must say, you're quite the optimist, aren't you? 'Legless, hopefully, soon-to-be woman' — I like your style."

Gabe chuckled, feeling a bit more at ease. "Hey, when life gives you shit, don't make shit salad. Make anything better, right? And I figure, why not aim high?"

Dr. Alvarez-Santos laughed. "I couldn't agree more. Now, shall we get down to business? I'd love to discuss your transition goals and create a personalized treatment plan for you."

Gabe nodded enthusiastically. "Absolutely, let's do it. I'm ready to get started."

Dr. Alvarez-Santos pulled out a notebook and began to ask Gabe questions about his medical history, his goals for transition, and any concerns or questions he might have. As they talked, Gabe felt a sense of relief wash over him. He was finally on the path to becoming the woman he was meant to be, and with Dr. Alvarez-Santos's expertise and support, he knew he was in good hands.

Over the following weeks, Gabe underwent grueling physical therapy for both his arm and his leg. Although he couldn't have a prosthetic yet, he needed to keep his strength up with daily exercise in his leg.

He saw multiple therapists and talked about his mindset, new attitude, goals, and transition. During one of these sessions with Gretchen and Dr. Alvarez-Santos, he asked a question.

"When can I start going by my chosen female name and start calling myself a female?"

Gretchen smiled and nodded. "That's a great question, Gabe. For many people, adopting a new name and pronouns is a significant step in their transition. While there's no one-size-fits-all answer, I'd say you can start going by your chosen name and pronouns whenever you feel comfortable and ready."

Dr. Alvarez-Santos added, "From a medical perspective, we can start making those changes on your medical records and prescriptions as soon as you'd like. However, it's essential to remember that everyone's journey is unique, and it's crucial to prioritize your emotional well-being throughout this process."

Gretchen continued, "It might be helpful to consider a few things before making the change. Have you thought about how your friends and family might react? Are there any specific situations or relation-ships where you might feel more or less comfortable using your new name and pronouns?"

Gabe thought for a moment before responding. "I've thought about it a lot. I'm not really worried about my friends. I had one, and he's dead now. My family hasn't been in my life since 2012. So if it's alright with the two of you, I'd like to go ahead and make it official."

Gretchen's expression turned sympathetic. "I'm so sorry, Gabe. Forgive my oversight."

Dr. Alvarez-Santos nodded in agreement. "Of course, we're here to support you, and we'll do everything we can to ensure your transition is as smooth as possible."

Gretchen smiled warmly. "In that case, let's make it official. From now on, we'll use your chosen name and pronouns. What name would you like to go by, Gabe?"

"My name is Miriam. Miriam Dawn Ryder. My pronouns are she/her. And there's no turning back."

Miriam struggled. It was the end of September, and she had been in the hospital for three whole months now, enduring physical therapy. Her left arm was healed but still weak. Her leg was healed, and next week, she would receive her prosthetic.

Miriam's eyes welled up with tears as she gazed at her reflection in the hospital room mirror. She couldn't believe the changes she was seeing. Her skin, once rough and weathered, now felt soft and supple. Her hair, once coarse and brittle, now fell in delicate, silky strands down her neck.

She gently touched her face, marveling at the subtle softening of her features. Her jawline, once sharp and angular, now seemed smoother, more rounded. Her eyes, once sunken and tired, now sparkled with a newfound sense of hope and vitality.

But it was her body that had undergone the most dramatic trans-formation. Her breasts, once nonexistent, now swelled with a gentle, feminine curve. She felt a sense of wonder and awe as she touched them, still marveling at their presence.

Miriam took a deep breath, feeling a sense of gratitude and joy wash over her. She had been on this journey for only a few months, but already she could see the incredible progress she had made. She knew that she still had a long way to go, but for the first time in her life, she felt genuinely hopeful, truly herself. *Estrogen is truly amazing,* she thought.

And next week, she reminded herself, *next week I walk again.*

"Okay, Miriam. Using these parallel bars, walk from one end to the other. It's twelve feet; you've got this." Miriam's prosthetist, Craig, encouraged.

This was it, Miriam's first steps since July 2, 2023. It was the morning of October 2, 2023. She had been allowed to try the prosthetic on the day before and stand to get her balance, but not walk. She started to, but Craig stopped her. "Not yet. Slowly. You have to adjust. All your weight is being supported in an entirely new area than you're used to. You're not going to be able to walk right out of the gate. Be patient."

Now a day removed, she removed her hands from the parallel bars defiantly, extended her palms upwards, and walked to the end of the parallel bars. But she didn't stop; she pivoted on her left foot and walked back, palms extended as she proclaimed, "I'm a goddamn marvel of modern science."

Craig chuckled and uttered, "Holy shit. I've never seen anyone do this before."

Miriam looked at the wooden stairs that were three steps tall, with handrails on each side. "Tomorrow, I take those on."

Craig nodded in agreement, "I believe you. This is remarkable."

In three days' time, Miriam had found her balance, walked without the assistance of parallel bars, climbed steps, came back down the steps, walked to the hospital courtyard, and navigated various terrain: grass, concrete, wood, asphalt, and a variety of sloped surfaces.

"No one does what you've done, Miriam... It's just not done... Where is this coming from?"

Miriam thought for a moment before answering. She thought of how Alex was supportive of her and how he would be angry if she gave up.

Live for yourself, Miri. She heard Alex say in her head.

"I finally have something to live for. Myself."

156

"I finally have something to live for. Myself."

Chapter 23: Witness Protection 101

Miriam hadn't had a cigarette in four months, and she was craving one so badly. The doctors had denied her the use of nicotine patches due to the interference with healing. She couldn't wait to get out of the hospital. The first thing she planned to do was smoke.

She longed to be outside of the hospital walls. She hadn't seen anyone aside from the hospital staff or AUSA Miller in months. She never received visitors. There was no one in her life.

Today, she was meeting with AUSA Miller and her US Marshal handler, Arthur M. Thompson. Marshal Thompson had spoken with her on the phone, and today, they were meeting in person for the first time to discuss how witness protection would work.

Miriam was startled by a knock at her hospital room door. AUSA Amanda Miller and US Marshal Arthur M. Thompson walked in. Marshal Thompson appeared to be a man in his mid-50s, with graying hair and a sizeable, bulky frame.

AUSA Miller spoke first: "Hello, Miriam. I'd like to introduce you to US Marshal Thompson. He'll be your primary handler for the duration of your witness protection."

US Marshal Thompson shook Miriam's hand. He had a very firm grip.

"Miriam, now that you're officially part of the witness protection program, we need to review the rules to ensure your safety and the program's success.

"As a participant in WITSEC, you'll be required to follow specific guidelines to protect your new identity and maintain the integrity of the program.

"First and foremost, you cannot contact anyone from your past life. This includes family members, friends, acquaintances – anyone who knew you as your former identity.

"You'll also need to be careful about sharing information about your past with anyone in your new life. This includes your new friends, coworkers, and even romantic partners.

"In addition, you'll be required to regularly check in with me and follow any instructions I provide. This may include relocating to a new area.

"It's also important to remember that you cannot use your old name or any variation of it. You must use your new name, Miriam Dawn Ryder, exclusively.

"Finally, you need to be aware that if you violate any of these rules, you risk being removed from the program and potentially putting yourself and others in danger."

AUSA Miller added, "We know this is a lot to take in, Miriam, but we're here to support you every step of the way. Do you have any questions about the rules or the program in general?"

Miriam responded, "Yeah, I have a few questions. What about my car? People know that car. Will you provide me with a new car?"

Thompson nodded. "Yes, Miriam, we'll provide you with a new vehicle. We'll also dispose of your old car, so it can't be linked back to you. You'll have a new car with new plates and a new VIN number. We'll make sure it's clean and untraceable."

AUSA Miller added, "And we'll also provide you with a new driver's license, social security card, and other identification documents to match your new identity. We'll ensure you have everything you need to start your new life."

Thompson continued, "Gabe Wilson is officially and legally dead. I presume this won't cause any issues, considering you have no family to speak of?"

Miriam nodded, "No family, so that's not an issue. What about a place to live? The De Luca family knows my old apartment. Where am I supposed to go?"

Marshal Thompson nodded. "We've already arranged for a new place for you to live. It's a secure location, and we've taken steps to ensure that it can't be linked back to your old identity. You'll have a new address, and we'll provide you with all the necessary documents and utilities in your new name."

AUSA Miller added, "We've also set up a new bank account for you, with a new account number and debit card. We'll provide you with a stipend to help you get settled into your new life. And, of course, we'll continue to provide you with medical care and counseling as needed."

Thompson continued, "We'll also be providing you with a new phone and a new phone number. You'll need to be careful about who you contact and how you communicate with them. We'll go over all the details with you, but for now, let's just say that we'll be taking steps to ensure that your new identity remains secure."

Miriam breathed a sigh of relief. "So when does everything go into effect? How soon can all of this be taken care of?"

Miller smiled. "We've already started making arrangements, Miriam. Your new identification documents, phone, and other essentials will be ready for you within the next 24 to 48 hours. We'll also be relocating you to your new residence within the same timeframe."

Thompson added, "We'll have a team of marshals escort you to your new location, and we'll ensure that you're safely settled in before we leave. We'll also be providing you with a secure way to communicate with us in case you need anything or have any concerns."

Miller continued, "Once you're settled into your new life, we'll schedule regular check-ins with you to ensure that everything is going smoothly and that you're adjusting well to your new identity."

"And where is this new location I'll be moving to?"

Marshal Thompson leaned forward, his expression serious. "Miriam, your new location is a small town in Oregon called Bend. It's a beautiful area surrounded by mountains and lakes. We've chosen this location because it's relatively isolated, making it easier for you to start fresh without being recognized. Plus, it's a great place to start over, with plenty of opportunities for outdoor activities and a growing community."

"What if I don't like it there? Can I request a new location if Bend isn't working out?"

US Marshal Thompson's expression turned sympathetic. "I understand that starting over in a new place can be daunting. While we've chosen Bend as the best location for your safety and well-being, we also understand that it may not be the perfect fit for everyone."

Miller added, "If, after a reasonable amount of time, you find that Bend isn't working out for you, we can discuss the possibility of relocating you to a different location. However, please keep in mind that any relocation would need to be approved by the Marshals Service and would require a thorough assessment of the new location's safety and suitability."

Marshal Thompson continued, "It's also important to note that relocating to a new location would require you to start over again with a new job, new friends, and a new community. It's not a decision that should be taken lightly, and we would need to carefully consider the potential risks and benefits before making any decisions."

"So, two days, and I'm out of here?"

Thompson nodded. "That's correct. We're aiming to have everything in place and ready for you to relocate to Bend within the next 48 hours. We'll be working closely with you to ensure a smooth transition and to answer any questions you may have."

AUSA Miller added, "In the meantime, we're moving you today from the hospital to a safe house, and you'll need to keep a low profile. We'll provide you with everything you need, and our team will be there to support you until it's time for you to leave."

Miriam's face beamed with delight. "Can I get a pack of cigarettes before we get to the safe house?"

Miriam inhaled deeply. *Oh, how I've missed this. Four months of no cigarettes was agonizing. I was borderline ready to choke people.*

Miriam was taken to a really nice log cabin in rural Pennsylvania. One wall had large bay windows overlooking a river. The cabin's floor plan was entirely open on the top floor, save for the bathroom, which, to Miriam's surprise, had a hot tub. She was currently enjoying herself in the hot tub.

After a long soak, she gingerly climbed out and dried off, put her prosthetic back on, and admired her body in the bathroom mirror. Her breasts had grown large enough for her to need a bra, and her hips and butt were rounding nicely. *Estrogen is amazing! I am lucky enough to be experiencing rapid growth! I'm already a C cup!*

She got dressed and went into the living room of the cabin. There was a large TV that was connected to every streaming service, so she had entertainment at her fingertips. She stretched out on the couch and searched for something to watch. It was wonderful to relax on a surface that wasn't a hospital bed.

She found her all-time favorite movie, 'The Crow,' and started watching. *I can get used to this. Alex would be happy here, too. I miss him.*

As her stay at the cabin ended, her escorts arrived to begin the cross-country trip to Bend, Oregon. Miriam looked around but didn't see her car. "Umm, where's my car?"

One of her escorts answered her, "It's going to be waiting for us in Oregon, ma'am. They're outfitting it with hand controls. You'll be riding with us for a couple of days."

"When do we leave?"

"Fifteen minutes. I suggest you use the restroom before we go."

The drive to Bend, Oregon, was just over 2,400 miles and would take an estimated 36 hours nonstop. The marshal escorts were instructed to drive straight through, only stopping for restroom breaks and food and to change drivers. While one marshal drove and another rode shotgun, the third marshal slept. Every 8 hours, the driver rotated to the back, the shotgun rider became the driver, and the fresh marshal rode shotgun, watching for anything suspicious.

Miriam quickly discovered that riding with her prosthetic leg attached was extremely painful. She couldn't maneuver it like her left leg to contort to fit into spaces, so she took it off. She did discover that the socket made a perfect cupholder.

Despite orders, Miriam convinced the marshals that she needed to get out and stretch her legs every two hours, and they agreed. It allowed her to walk around and avoid stiffness, get some fresh air, and enjoy a cigarette.

Eventually, after 38 hours, two hours over schedule, they reached Bend, Oregon. Miriam told Marshal Thompson on the phone that she made the marshals stop because of her discomfort with her prosthetic.

They settled her into an A-frame house located on the Deschutes River. *The US Marshal Service certainly has a type, doesn't it? I can definitely get behind that.*

She was delighted to see her new car, a silver 2016 model Honda CR-V, complete with hand controls, in the driveway. Hopefully, she could make a life for herself here. It was early November, and she wondered how long it was considered a 'reasonable amount of time' before her handlers considered relocation.

It was about five months.

Chapter 24: Threats And Consequences

Miriam and Ava celebrated the defeat of the proposed ordinances with the rest of the JHEC founders at the Jasper Hill Cafe. Di had kept the cafe open later than usual for either a victory party or a regrouping session. Ava FaceTimed her parents to share the good news.

"I'm so proud of you girls," Ryan exclaimed as Sophia whooped in the background. "Don't allow yourselves to become complacent. I'm sure your opponents will retaliate, and it will probably be nasty. Keep your wits about you.

"Also, Miri, you showed incredible resolve when the mayor confronted you last week. Sophia and I have watched that video at least ten times now."

"Thank you, Ryan. I didn't realize I was capable of standing up to discrimination like this, but here we are. Your guidance has really paid off."

"We're going to go now, Dad, but we'll talk to you and Mom soon! We love you!"

"We love you two, also! Go have fun, and have a good night!"

Ava ended the call and nestled into Miriam's side. "I'm so happy that we helped rally the town and were part of the catalyst for this, but if I'm honest, I would rather celebrate with you, just the two of us."

"Let's stay ten minutes, then we'll make a discreet exit. Deal?"

"Deal."

Di suddenly unleashed a high-pitched shrieking whistle. Everyone in the cafe turned their attention to her. "If it hadn't been for Miri and Ava founding the Jasper Hill Equality Coalition, it's very likely these ordinances would have passed tonight. So, to show our appreciation, we toast you to Miri and Ava!" She raised her glass in the pair's direction.

Di's whistle startled Miriam. It was just like her friend Alex's.

Numerous people approached them to thank them and congratulate them for their victory. Ava noticed that Miriam was growing over-whelmed, so she motioned for them to leave, and Miriam agreed. Upon reaching Miriam's car, Ava asked if she could drive. Miriam nodded and handed Ava the keys.

"Miri, doll, are you okay?" Ava's voice was fraught with worry.

Miriam replied, "I'm okay... just... for a few minutes there, it felt like I was going to have a panic attack. Thanks for getting me out of there."

As they drove home, the glow of their victory at the cafe began to dim. Miriam stared out the window, her thoughts swirling. For every cheer tonight, she could feel the silent disapproval of those who hadn't come. "We did the right thing," Ava said softly as if reading Miriam's mind. But Miriam couldn't shake the feeling that their fight wasn't over—and that it might cost them more than they realized.

They made their way home, and Ava helped Miriam onto the porch. She guided Miriam to the couch and then started coffee. When she returned, she took Miriam's hand and rested her head on her shoulder.

"Have you ever had a panic attack before?" Ava looked at Miriam quizzically.

Miriam shook her head no. "My therapist, after the attack, diagnosed me with complex post-traumatic stress disorder. She said that panic attacks were a potential side effect of being overwhelmed in stressful or tense situations. The room started feeling so small I was frozen.

My chest became tight, like it was too difficult to breathe or like I had forgotten how to. And Di's whistle kind of reminded me of Alex's; it was jarring."

Ava went to get them each a cup of coffee, lit two cigarettes, passed Miriam one, and kissed her on the forehead. They snuggled in silence on the couch, sipping coffee and smoking. After they finished, Miriam curled up into Ava's lap, and Ava stroked Miriam's hair. She began to hum, 'I Can't Help Falling In Love,' and before she finished the song, Miriam had fallen asleep.

Miriam stirred in her sleep, a vivid memory pulling her into the past. She was back in the cramped apartment she had once shared with Alex on countless late nights. The living room was a chaotic blend of pizza boxes, game controllers, and mismatched furniture. The air was warm, filled with the faint hum of their favorite playlist and Alex's relentless energy.

"Alright, Gabe, final round. Loser buys dinner," Alex declared with a mischievous grin, his thumbs flying over the controller.

"You're on, but don't start crying when I crush you," Miriam—then still Gabe—retorted, her competitive streak flaring.

But before the game could end, Alex leaned back, dropped the controller, and unleashed his signature whistle—a sharp, melodic trill that somehow carried both enthusiasm and playfulness. It was his way of claiming victory before it was even earned.

"Show-off," Miriam muttered, rolling her eyes as Alex laughed, a sound that felt like sunlight bursting into the room.

"Come on, Gabe, admit it—you wish you could whistle like this," Alex teased, nudging her with his elbow. "It's like a secret code. You hear it, and you just know it's me."

She couldn't argue with that. Alex's whistle had always been distinct, impossible to ignore. It was how he'd signal her to come outside when he was in the parking lot or how he'd grab her attention in a crowded bar. It was a sound she'd grown to associate with him.

The memory shifted, the laughter fading into something darker. The whistle came again, echoing in Miriam's mind, but this time it wasn't playful—it was a desperate, haunting call that reverberated in the aftermath of the attack. She couldn't remember if it had been real or if her mind had conjured it in a haze of pain and panic. Either way, it was the last time she'd ever heard it.

Miriam woke with a start, her chest tight, blinking away the remnants of the dream. She glanced at Ava, who was stroking her hair and humming softly.

"You were dreaming, doll," Ava whispered. "Bad one?"

Miriam nodded, her voice barely audible. "It was Alex. His whistle... I could hear it again."

Ava held her tighter, her presence grounding Miriam in the here and now. "He's still with you, love. In the good memories and even in the hard ones. He'll always be with you."

Miriam took a shaky breath, letting Ava's words soothe her. She closed her eyes, imagining Alex sitting there with them, his whistle cutting through the quiet night like a beacon. For a fleeting moment, it felt like he was still close, watching over her, reminding her to keep moving forward.

The following day, Miriam felt much better. She was surprised to see that she and Ava had fallen asleep on the couch. She gently nudged Ava awake. "Good morning, mi amor. Why didn't you wake me? We could have slept in the bed."

"Good morning, my love. I didn't want to wake you because of what you experienced last night; I felt it best to hold you and ensure you felt safe."

"Whatever did I do to deserve you? You're far too good for me. I love you."

"And I love you. As for deserving me, all you had to do was be yourself."

Miriam put her prosthetic on. "I'll start coffee; what do you want for breakfast?"

Ava thought for a minute, then replied, "How about a cheesy omelet with diced peppers and crumbled sausage and some toast?"

"You got it. I'll get started while you get ready for work."

Miriam started a pot of coffee and then diced a red bell pepper and browned sausage. After the sausage was browned, she drained it and shredded cheddar cheese. She then beat three eggs for several minutes, ensuring she incorporated enough air into them to make them light and fluffy.

Ava came back downstairs ready for work and poured them each some coffee while Miriam finished making breakfast. Once it was ready, they went to the porch swing to eat.

They chatted about their plans for the day. Ava had a test to give, and Miriam just wanted to take the day to paint. They had their post-meal cigarettes, and Ava then had to leave for work. She didn't make it to her car when she called out, "Hey, Miri? There's a note on your car!"

Panic set in for Miriam. She looked up to find Ava kneeling by her side, helping her up from the floor of the porch. She hadn't realized she had fallen. Ava handed Miriam a piece of paper. "This was on the windshield of your car."

Miriam looked at the paper and stared in horror at the words staring back at her: *I Know Who You Are*

"Miriam, honey, any idea who this is from?"

She finally managed to get an answer out. "They've found me."

Rachel finished watching the security camera footage. She came into the living room where Miriam was with Ava and let them know what she found. "Whoever it was that left the note on your windshield either knew there were cameras or at least suspected there were cameras. They were dressed head to toe in all black. Mask, gloves, even sunglasses. This could literally be anyone with a medium build."

She continued, "The intruder placed the note at 3:17 a.m. They're only in frame for thirteen seconds, coming in from behind Ava's car to yours, Miri, then back out the way they came. There are eight cameras outside, and none of them caught anyone on them except this one. There are no signs of any vehicles on the few sections of the road the cameras can see. There are no signs of anyone on foot in them. It's as if they were a ghost."

Ava looked extremely worried. Miriam was shaking. "What happens now, Rachel?"

"Well, for now, you have someone here watching you. 24/7 surveillance, multiple eyes. US Marshals. This is just a precaution. Thompson doesn't think you're burned, and neither do I. It's likely some kid playing a prank on a dare or some bullshit to cause paranoia."

Miriam looked up at Rachel, and the fear on her face and in her eyes conveyed all Rachel needed to know. "You think you're burned, " she said. "How?

"Think about it, Miri. Your old identity is gone, declared dead. A funeral was held. An empty coffin was buried in Potter's Field. Your new name, social security number, bank records, driver's license, vehicle registration, work history, medical history, birth certificate-everything has been fabricated with a paper trail tying you to Bend, Oregon, since 1994. Your old car was junked and crushed in a junkyard. Your old apartment was rented out a month after you were attacked. You can't be burned. It's not possible."

Ava nodded, "Rachel's right, Miri. It's impossible for them to have found you."

Rachel added, "Thompson has ordered a psychiatrist to make a house call today. Neither of you are to leave until Thompson gives the all-clear. So, if you need anything, let me know, and I'll get it to you.

"As far as friends and family, you are quarantined with COVID. They don't need to panic."

Miriam nodded and reached for another cigarette. Ava held her in her arms as she continued to shake in fear. "Thank you, Rachel. I'll text you a list soon."

"Hang in there; the psychiatrist will be here in about two hours. Her name is Doctor Molly Ingrid. She'll give you a session, adjust any meds if needed, that sort of thing, and she will be escorted onto the property, so don't worry. I'll leave you ladies be." Rachel left, and Ava noticed an armed officer stationed on the porch.

Miriam finally spoke after first seeing the note. "I thought they had found me. I thought Thompson was going to take me away from you. I thought, at long last, I can be free, I have a life, I have a partner, I have friends, I have a new family... and I thought I was being pulled away from it forever." She looked into Ava's green eyes, "I won't live life if you're not in it. I can't bear the thought of a life without you. The universe has to give us more time than this; it just has to."

Ava held her. "Miriam, love, they're taking me with you if you do go. I won't let them separate us. The universe isn't getting in the way of us." She added, "Besides, I know too much to be left behind."

The pair giggled. Miriam felt the stress leave her body and melted into Ava's arms. *She's right; I'm worried about probably nothing.*

After a week of heavy surveillance and a thorough investigation, US Marshal Thompson gave Rachel the all-clear to lift security on Miriam and Ava. Thompson called Miriam personally. "Miriam, I'm happy to inform you that all of our intelligence reports that investigated the De Luca family and their known accomplices are under the impression that Gabe Wilson is dead. Furthermore, they aren't aware of Miriam Ryder. You're safe."

"Thank you, Marshal Thompson. It's a huge relief."

Thompson added, "I'm not finished. This Jasper Hill Equality Coalition you've founded, you and Ava are to cease involvement. Tell them the stress is too much for you or something, whatever excuse you want. You were told to keep a low profile. The JHEC is not you keeping a low profile. If I get word of you participating in further JHEC activities, you will be removed from WITSEC. You understand what that means?"

"Yes, sir. I'd lose everything. My medical care, my finances, my car, my house, and I'd be left to fend for myself."

"You're goddamn right about that. And Miri, stop smoking! We're trying to keep you alive until the trial." Marshal Thompson ended the call.

"We're all-clear. But we both have to quit the Jasper Hill Equality Coalition. Apparently, I'm not keeping a low profile and attracting unnecessary attention to myself, which is potentially endangering me. I'm sorry, I really liked working in the JHEC."

"Well, I do, too, but we got the ordinances defeated. They have over 750 members now, and they've made the Mountain View College campus more aware of the shitbag mayor and sheriff; this has all happened in weeks. It's grassroots expansion at its finest. It doesn't need the two of us now. Our baby has flown the nest."

"You're right. I'll text the others and let them know the stress was taking its toll, and we have to step away, but with the knowledge, we're leaving it in good hands."

"Perfect. Now, we never did get to celebrate last week. Wanna go have lots of sex?"

"Gods, yes!"

Chapter 25: Fear And Intimidation

Miriam and Ava informed the other Jasper Hill Equality Coalition founders that they, unfortunately, needed to step away from being active. They were all empathetic and understanding but clearly disappointed.

The days following the town hall victory were bittersweet for Miriam. While the Jasper Hill Equality Coalition celebrated their hard-fought triumph, a darker undercurrent began to ripple through the town. Anonymous notes appeared on Miriam and Ava's car windshields, their words dripping with venom: *"You're not welcome here." "Leave before you ruin this town." "We don't want people like you here."*

Miriam clenched her fists as Ava read the messages aloud, her voice trembling. "This isn't the first time someone's told me to leave, Ava. But now they're dragging you into it too. I hate that my fight is hurting you." Ava placed a reassuring hand on Miriam's shoulder, her green eyes burning with defiance. "They can't scare me off, Miri. This is our home. They don't get to take that away from us."

But the backlash didn't stop there. At the cafe, a table of older patrons abruptly left when Miriam and Ava sat down for breakfast, their muttered remarks cutting through the hum of conversation. "We don't need their kind making a scene," one woman hissed under her breath. On another occasion, someone from the shadows whispered *"Freak"* as Miriam walked to her car after grocery shopping.

The worst came one evening as they returned from dinner. A crude, spray-painted slur defaced a large tree at the end of their driveway. Miriam stared at the hateful word, her breath catching in her throat. "Ava..." she whispered, her voice breaking. "How much more of this can we take?"

Ava wrapped her arms around Miriam, holding her close. "We'll take as much as we need to," she said firmly. "We didn't fight this hard to give up now." But as she comforted Miriam, Ava's eyes darted toward the tree, the sharp edges of worry etched into her face.

The anonymous hostility created a sense of isolation Miriam hadn't felt in years. Even in her moments of courage and triumph, the reminders of hate lingered like ghosts haunting the town she'd fought to make better. The small victories sometimes felt swallowed whole by the overwhelming weight of standing firm in a place that seemed determined to reject her existence.

Despite the mounting hostility, Miriam and Ava tried to maintain a semblance of normalcy. Ava returned to work, channeling her energy into her teaching as the school year wound down. At home, Miriam found small distractions in Ava's enthusiasm for her students, even as the weight of the town's rejection pressed heavily on her. One evening, Ava finished designing a creative final project for her classes and brought the printed document to Miriam. "Take a look at this," Ava said, her voice filled with excitement, a welcome reprieve from the tension that had become their new norm

Project Title: "Identity Mosaic"

Objective: To create a mixed-media artwork that represents the complexities of
   personal identity, exploring themes of self-expression, community, and social justice.

Instructions:

1. You will create a large-scale mixed-media artwork (approx. 24" x 36") using a combination of materials such as paint, collage, photography, and found objects.
2. The artwork should represent your own personal identity, incorporating symbols, colors, and imagery that reflect your values, passions, and experiences.
3. You are encouraged to explore themes of social justice, community, and activism in your artwork and consider how your individual identities intersect with broader social issues.
4. The artwork should include a minimum of three distinct visual elements, such as:

- A self-portrait or representation of your physical appearance
  - A symbolic or abstract representation of your personality, values, or passions
  - A visual element that reflects your connection to your community or social justice
  issues
  5. You will write a brief artist statement (approx. 250-500 words) explaining the
  inspiration and meaning behind your artwork.
  Grading Criteria:
  - Creativity and originality of the artwork (30%)
  - Technical skill and execution (25%)
  - Depth and thoughtfulness of the artist statement (20%)
  - Adherence to the project's themes and objectives (25%)
  Display and Celebration:

The finished artworks will be displayed in the school's main hallway, along with your

artist statements. The exhibition will be open to the public during the final week of

May, and a reception will be held to celebrate your creativity and hard work on Friday,

May 31, 2024.

This project is designed to encourage you to think critically about your own identities

and how they intersect with broader social issues. It also provides an opportunity for

you to express yourself creatively and showcase your artistic talents. Project is due on or before Friday, May 24, 2024.

Miriam read the project description and smiled admirably at Ava. "This is really good. Do you think two weeks is enough time for them to finish it?"

"I think so. They're really talented and creative kids." Ava continued, "You're a big inspiration for this project, you know?"

"Me, how so?"

"Your lifelong struggle with your own gender identity and the realization and acceptance of who you truly are, blossoming into the amazing woman who captured my heart, combined with your fight for dignity and respect in a society that wants you to go away. All while fighting for your life, adapting to physical challenges that changed everything for you," She lit cigarettes for each of them and passed Miriam one. "You're my muse."

Miriam's eyes welled up with tears as she looked at Ava. "You're making me blush," she said, her voice barely above a whisper.

Ava smiled and took Miriam's hand. "I'm just speaking the truth," she said. "You're an incredible person, Miriam. Your strength and resilience inspire me every day."

Miriam's face grew hotter as she felt Ava's gaze on her. She looked down, trying to compose herself, but Ava's words had touched her deeply.

"Thank you, Ava," Miriam said finally, her voice still shaking. "That means a lot coming from you."

Ava squeezed Miriam's hand. "I mean every word," Ava said. "You're the love of my life, Miriam. I'm so grateful to have you by my side."

Miriam's heart swelled with emotion as she looked at Ava. She felt seen and loved, and she knew that she felt the same way about Ava.

"I love you too, Ava," Miriam said, her voice filled with emotion.

Ava smiled and leaned in, her lips brushing against Miriam's. "I love you more," she whispered.

As they kissed, Miriam felt a sense of peace and happiness wash over her. She knew that she was exactly where she was meant to be, with her person.

The next morning, Friday, May 10, Ava had gone to work, and Miriam decided to get ready and go out for the first time since the public hearing at the town hall. She showered, got dressed, fixed her makeup and hair, and decided to visit Eli at Trailblazer Comics to pick up some new miniatures to paint and some new books. She also chose to see Di at the Jasper Hill Cafe and have lunch.

She gathered her things, went to her car, and departed, lighting a cigarette for the drive. She made the one-mile drive out of the holler to the main road and pulled out. She glanced into her rearview mirror and noticed a county police cruiser following her. *Great,* she thought, *hopefully, it's not Bubba Harris or his asshole daddy.*

Miriam couldn't shake the feeling that the town was closing in around her. The notes, the whispers, and the graffiti had made it clear that she and Ava were being watched. When she spotted the sheriff's cruiser in her rearview mirror, a chill ran down her spine. This wasn't a coincidence—it was another reminder that they didn't belong.

The county police cruiser followed her all the way to town and continued to follow her through town to the shopping center, which housed Trailblazer Comics. She parked her car and looked up to see Sheriff Tom Harris drive past her, staring intently as she exited her vehicle.

He's just trying to intimidate me. Miriam grinned and waved enthusiastically to Sheriff Harris, who then scowled as he proceeded through the parking lot. Miriam chuckled to herself and then entered the comic shop.

Eli was happy to see Miriam. "Hey, Miri, how are you feeling? COVID is no joke. We were all worried."

"I'm feeling much better, Eli, thanks." Miriam hated lying, but she didn't have a choice. So much depended on her maintaining her cover. "I just wanted to get some new books and maybe a dragon today."

"Oh, I have just the kit for you, then. It's a restock that just came in this week. Let me grab it." He walked over to the wargaming section, pulled a box off the shelf, and showed her. "The Everchosen"

Miriam was impressed with the kit. "I'll take it, it's gorgeous." Eli nodded and took it to the counter. Miriam looked through the trade paperbacks and found the Scott Pilgrim box set and a Hellboy omnibus. She selected those and went to pay.

"Excellent choices. I'm constantly restocking these. Anything else for you today, Miri?"

"No, I think one nosebleed is sufficient." She joked as Eli rang her up. "That comes to $299.25." Miriam handed Eli her debit card.

"I was really sad to hear you and Ava are stepping away from the JHEC. Is everything okay?"

"Yeah, it was just too much for us to handle at the moment. It was a lot of stress, and it was taking a toll on me mentally and physically, and she convinced me of the importance of self-care."

"Trust me, I get that. For years, I worked here six days a week from 10:00 a.m. to 7:00 p.m. Then I finally decided to hire a guy to help out. He's here three days a week, and we started opening on Sundays. Sales are up, and I get time off—a total win."

"I'm glad that it's been a positive development for you, Eli. This place is great, and it provides so much for so many people, but you can't forget to take care of yourself and your loved ones." She thought of Ava, looked at the table where they met, and smiled warmly. "I'm going to go get some food. I'll see you soon. Thanks, Eli. Have a great day!"

"You too, Miri! See ya!"

How do I always end up spending so much every time I go in there? Alex always said I have zero restraints. Miriam got into her car, lit a cigarette, and looked at the car next to hers. There was a young mother struggling to corral her toddler into a car seat. "Beautiful day, isn't it?" the woman said with a quick smile. Miriam returned the smile, grateful for the fleeting normalcy, before spotting Sheriff Harris in her rearview mirror.

What is this guy's problem?

Sheriff Harris followed Miriam all the way to the Jasper Hill Cafe. She parked in the accessible parking spot in front of the restaurant and went inside.

Miriam was pleased to see that her favorite barstool by the front window was available. She sat down and looked around. It was 11:35 a.m., and the cafe was starting to fill up for lunch. Miriam grabbed the menu and was looking at it when the cafe door opened, and Sheriff Harris walked in. To Miriam's disappointment, he sat on the stool beside hers and grabbed a menu.

"Hello, Sheriff Harris. Feeling peckish today?" Miriam reminded herself to choose her words very carefully, but the sheriff didn't make it easy.

"Well, it's about that time. This is the place where people come when they feel like having a cheeseburger, after all." Miriam picked up on his reference to her comments to him on her first day in town.

Miriam forced a smile, trying to appear calm despite the sheriff's unnerving demeanor. "Yes, their cheeseburgers are quite popular. I recommend them."

Sheriff Harris leaned in, his voice taking on a menacing tone. "You know, *Miriam*, I've been thinking a lot about our little chat a few weeks ago. You seem like a smart... *person*... but sometimes smart people can be a little... reckless."

Miriam's instincts told her to choose her next words carefully. The sheriff's eyes bore into her as if daring her to make a wrong move. "I'm not sure what you're insinuating, Sheriff," she said, trying to keep her voice steady.

Sheriff Harris chuckled, a cold, mirthless sound. "Oh, I'm not insinuating anything, *Miriam*." The contempt he used to emphasize her name was obvious. "I'm just stating facts. You see, this is a small town, and we look out for each other. We don't take kindly to strangers coming in and stirring up trouble. Especially mentally ill strangers."

Miriam felt a shiver run down her spine as the sheriff's words hung in the air, heavy with implied threat. She knew she had to be careful, to avoid antagonizing the sheriff further. But she also knew she couldn't back down, not now.

Miriam's eyes narrowed, her mind racing with the implications of the sheriff's words. "Mentally ill strangers?" she repeated, trying to keep her tone neutral.

Sheriff Harris leaned in closer, his voice dropping to a whisper. "Well, you know what I mean, *Miriam*. People with... fragile pasts. People who might be prone to, shall we say, 'flights of fancy'?"

Miriam felt a chill run down her spine when she realized the sheriff implied he knew about her witness protection status. She tried to remain calm, but her heart was racing.

"I'm not sure what you're talking about, Sheriff," Miriam said, trying to sound convincing.

Sheriff Harris chuckled again, the sound sending shivers down Miriam's spine. "Oh, come now, *Miriam*. Let's not play games. I think we both know what's really going on here."

Miriam's instincts told her to get out of there, to escape the sheriff's suffocating presence. But she knew she couldn't back down, not now. She had to keep up the charade, no matter how difficult it became. Miriam's eyes locked onto the sheriff's, her heart pounding in her chest. She knew she had to be careful to avoid giving away her witness protection status.

"I'm afraid I don't know what you're talking about, Sheriff," Miriam repeated, trying to sound calm.

Sheriff Harris leaned back in his chair, a sly smile spreading across his face. "Oh, I think you do, *Miriam*," he said, his voice dripping with contempt and malice. "I think you know exactly what I'm talking about."

Miriam felt a bead of sweat trickle down her forehead as the sheriff's eyes seemed to bore and rip into her soul. She knew she had to think fast to come up with a convincing explanation for the sheriff's accusations.

But before she could respond, the sheriff's phone rang, shrill and insistent. He glanced at the screen, his expression darkening.

"Excuse me, *Miriam*," he said, his voice dripping with menace. "I have to take this."

As the sheriff stood up and walked away, Miriam let out a shaky breath. She knew she had to get out of there to escape the sheriff's overwhelming presence.

But as she turned to leave, she caught a glimpse of something that made her heart skip a beat. A piece of paper on the sheriff's table with a single sentence scrawled on it:

We know who you are.

Miriam texted Ava first. *It was Sheriff Harris. He knows!* She then called Rachel to tell her what had happened. It went to voicemail. "Rachel, it's Miri. Something weird is going on, and I think Sheriff Harris is responsible for the note on my car last Thursday morning. Call me back or come see me at home as soon as you can, please." She added, "I'm really fucking scared, Rachel." She ended the call.

She lit a cigarette, checked her mirrors, and pulled out. There was no sign of Sheriff Harris. Her phone dinged back, and she saw a text from Rachel that read, *In a meeting, out in 5. Be at your place in 15.*

Ava texted back. *I'm leaving work early. Meet you at home.*

When Miriam arrived home, Ava was waiting for her in the driveway. She rushed to give Miriam a hug and was about to ask what had happened when Rachel turned into the driveway. She parked her car and said, "Let's get inside. Hurry."

Once inside, Miriam began pacing back and forth in the living room erratically. "What happened, baby?" Ava's voice was almost pleading.

Rachel added, "Walk us through everything that's happened this morning, please. Take a breath, sit down, have a cigarette. We'll figure this out."

Miriam nodded and sat down, lighting a cigarette. Then, she gathered her composure and began recounting the morning's events.

"After Ava left for work, I took a shower and got ready. I decided to go to Trailblazer Comics and then get some lunch at the cafe. As soon as I pulled out of the holler, I checked my rearview mirror, and Sheriff Harris was behind me. I never saw where he came from.

"He followed me all the way to the comic shop, and I figured I'd get a rise out of him and wave as he passed by. Sheriff Harris scowled. I laughed, and then I went in. I picked up some books and a dragon, chatted with Eli, then left. I exited the parking lot to head to the cafe, but Sheriff Harris was behind me again.

"I parked and went inside. Harris followed me in and sat next to me. He said some things implying he knew I was in WITSEC, and then his phone rang. He was on the call with his back turned, and I saw this." She handed Rachel the piece of paper from the cafe: *"We know who you are."*

As Rachel inspected the note, her lips pressed into a thin line. "I'll admit, this is concerning," she said, her tone sharper than Miriam was used to. "But I've got a few questions for Sheriff Harris. Give me a couple of hours."

Miriam watched Rachel leave, a knot of unease settling in her chest. Ava reached for her hand, squeezing it gently. "She'll figure it out," Ava said softly. Miriam nodded, but the tension in her shoulders didn't ease.

"Why is this happening? I'm terrified, Ava."

Ava held Miriam and replied, "I don't know, dear, but we're in this together. Rachel will get to the bottom of this. Let's defer to her judgment. You know Thompson would rush us to a safe house, and I don't think that's necessary just yet."

Miriam nodded, and they sat there waiting for news from Rachel.

Rachel returned several hours later. Her body language was relaxed, and she asked Miriam and Ava to sit down.

"First of all, there's no need to worry. Yes, Sheriff Harris knows you're in WITSEC, but that's the extent of what he knows."

"How does he know?" Miriam asked.

"As a professional courtesy, US Marshal Thompson contacted the Chief of Police in the town department as well as Sheriff Harris in the county department. He did not tell them it was Miriam who was in witness protection; it was just that there was a new resident in the area in witness protection.

"Honestly, I see that as a lack of critical thinking on Thompson's part. Miri's been the only new resident in town for weeks."

Ava added, "I bet he thought Miriam's arrival would go unnoticed with the college here."

"That's probably it, Ava. But Harris put two and two together, and here we are."

Miriam asked, "But what about the note in the cafe? It was just like the one on the windshield of my car!"

Rachel shook her head. "That's a total coincidence, actually. Sheriff Harris didn't know anything about the original note. He knew you were messing with him to piss him off, so using what he knew about you being in WITSEC, he wanted to make sure you had a stressful day. He wrote the note to fuck with you."

"Wow, that's a dick move," Ava added.

Miriam said, "But the notes were identical!"

"No, they weren't. The original note said '*I Know Who You Are*' with no punctuation and every word capitalized. Sheriff Harris's note said, '*We know who you are.*' with only the first word capitalized and a period at the end. The handwriting is also vastly different.

"GPS records also show that his police cruiser was parked in his driveway all night on the night in question. He may be a dick, but his alibi is solid."

She finished, "And earlier this evening, Jasper Hill PD arrested two high school students caught in the act of placing notes on cars matching the handwriting on the note left on your car, Miri. They've been doing it as a prank, choosing cars at random. I guess they wanted to induce paranoia."

Rachel continued, "Regardless, Miriam, I think it would be prudent for you not to go anywhere alone. Always have Ava or another friend with you. If Sheriff Harris' harassment continues, we'll go through higher channels to shut him down."

Rachel bid the couple goodbye. Ava made some coffee as Miriam sat deeply on the couch, breathing sighs of relief. Miriam heard Ava exit the side door and then return a minute later with Miriam's bag from Trailblazer Comics.

She poured them coffee and lit cigarettes. Then, Ava began reading Scott Pilgrim to Miriam.

Chapter 26: And From Joy Comes Sorrow

Miriam did as Rachel requested and only ventured out in public with Ava. On Sunday, they wanted to go to dinner, so they settled on El Monterrey's and arrived at 6:00 p.m. To their delight, they bumped into Jules, who was already there waiting for a table.

"OMG, you two, it's good to see you! Are you okay? I haven't seen either of you since the town hall." Jules gave Miriam and Ava each a hug. "It's just me eating. Would you like to join me and make a table of three?"

"You know what? Yes, we'd enjoy that very much, Jules."

Miriam said, and Ava nodded in agreement.

They didn't have to wait long, and the hostess led them to their table. Miriam and Ava chose to sit facing the door so they could see if Sheriff Harris or Bubba entered.

"So, Jules, what have you been up to? The semester's almost over. I imagine you've been busy preparing for finals. This is your senior year, right?" Ava inquired.

"Yeah, it's been stressful. We have two weeks left. My first final is Wednesday, but I'm not too worried. Nervous, yes, but I usually do pretty well." She continued, "It's really just everything else that's been going on that has me stressed."

"What, with the JHEC?" Miriam asked.

"Well, that's going well. We're up to 1,000 members now, and it's been incredible. Between that, studying for finals, presentations, and prepping for Pride month at the campus LGBTQ+ resource center, this is the first minute I've had to myself in a while. So it's great to bump into you two."

Ava was curious, "What exactly are you planning for Pride month at the resource center?"

"Get this. Do you know the corner where Di's cafe sits? Well, the cafe's outer wall is just red brick. Well, she owns the building. She's letting us design and paint a mural there, highlighting LGBTQ+ people integrated into the community to help raise awareness and normalize our existence.

"And Sara, who runs the convention center, is letting us set up an art gallery for the last week of the month there that will be open to the public. "And I'm heading up a series of workshops that are designed to teach students and faculty about LGBTQ+ issues, like identity, intersectionality, and allyship." She looked at them, "You're both artists. You could help with the mural and enter pieces into the art gallery."

Ava nodded with excitement, and Miriam was elated. "We'd be thrilled to participate, Jules."

"That's outstanding! I do have one more ask if that's cool." She looked at Miriam. "You're an eloquent speaker. You're also trans. I don't have a transgender woman to provide her perspectives for a workshop. I was hoping that I could talk you into it, Miri."

Ava smiled warmly, and Miriam contemplated her answer. After a moment of silence, she agreed. "I'm in."

Jules let out a slight squeal, "Thank you so much! You're an angel!"

After dinner, Jules said her goodbyes to the couple and returned to her hectic schedule. Miriam and Ava agreed to meet with Jules on Wednesday evening at the resource center for a planning session.

"I know what I'm going to create for the art gallery," Miriam said. The excitement was evident in her voice.

"What's that, love?"

"A delicate sculpture of a butterfly emerging from a cocoon. I feel it will represent my journey in becoming me very well."

"That sounds beautiful, and I can't wait to see you create it. I have an idea, too. But it's not up to me." Ava continued, "I want to enter the charcoal drawing I did for your birthday. Would you be okay with that?"

"Of course, it would be. It's an amazing and thoughtful representation of your love for me. I'd be honored for people to see that. Yes, absolutely. Use it."

They got into Ava's car, lit cigarettes, and drove home. Miriam said, "What about this workshop I've agreed to do? How am I going to approach that? I don't even know where to begin. Do you have any advice for me?"

Ava thought for a moment before responding, "Well, first of all, I think it's amazing that you're doing this, baby. You have such a powerful story to share, and I know you'll make a real impact on those students and faculty."

Miriam nodded, feeling a mix of nerves and determination. "I want to make sure I do it justice, you know? I don't want just to stand up there and talk about myself. I want to make it meaningful and relevant to the audience."

Ava smiled. "That's exactly the right approach, love. Why don't you start by thinking about what you wish you'd known when you were first navigating your transition? What were some of the biggest challenges you faced, and how did you overcome them?"

Miriam's eyes lit up as she began to brainstorm. "Oh, wow, there are so many things... I wish I'd known more about the medical aspects of transition and how to navigate the healthcare system. I wish I'd had more role models and mentors to look up to."

Ava nodded encouragingly. "Those are all great points. And don't forget to talk about the importance of allyship and support. You could share some of your own experiences with how my support and love have made a difference for you."

Miriam's face softened as she looked at Ava. "I don't know what I would have done without you, Ava. You've been my rock throughout this whole journey."

Ava smiled and reached out to take Miriam's hand. "I'll always be here for you, Miri. And I know you're going to knock this workshop out of the park."

June arrived, and Ava's summer vacation had officially begun. Miriam was delighted to have her home during the days, and Ava was fascinated to watch Miriam create her sculpture. She had seen Miriam paint but never sculpt.

Miriam had crafted a delicate, hand-sculpted butterfly emerging from a cocoon, constructed from a combination of translucent resin and jewelry wire. The cocoon was fashioned from clay and textured to resemble the rough, confining walls that once held the butterfly captive.

Miriam hand-drew the wings on acetate and mixed blue ink into a type of water-effect resin used to create dioramas. She carefully poured a very thin layer of the light blue resin over the acetate and let it partially cure. Then, she used a silicone sculpting tool to create striations and separations in the wings and allowed them to fully cure.

Once the resin had cured and the butterfly and cocoon had been painted, she affixed the delicate resin to the butterfly with transparent epoxy. She then perched the piece on a cylindrical black plinth. She smiled with prideful admiration at this piece.

"It's finished." She dared not breathe too heavily in fear of breaking the wings. Ava was taken aback, stunned by the intricacy and delicacy Miriam had utilized.

"This is stunning, Miri, it's absolutely amazing!" Ava' eyes were wide with wonder.

Miriam smiled. "I call it 'Breaking Free,' do you think it's too on the nose?"

"Not at all. It's perfect."

The day of the LGBTQ+ workshop at the campus resource center had arrived. It housed a small auditorium that seated 500. When Miriam and Ava arrived at the center, they were surprised to see the hall was packed, with people standing along the back wall.

They found Jules, who had a delighted expression on her face. "Miriam, these people are all here for you! They've seen the video of your confrontation with Mayor Winston and the video of the impassioned speech you gave at the town hall! You're a rather big deal here!"

A facilitator addressed the audience. "And now I'd like to introduce our next speaker, Miriam Ryder." The auditorium was filled with applause. Ava stepped to the side of the stage with Jules as Miriam made her way up to the podium, surveyed the room, took a deep breath, and began speaking.

"Good morning, everyone. My name is Miriam, and I'm honored to be here today to share my perspective as a transgender woman.

"I want to start by acknowledging the importance of this workshop and the topics we'll be discussing today: identity, intersectionality, and allyship. These are all crucial aspects of creating a more inclusive and supportive environment for LGBTQ+ individuals.

"As Ava, my partner, reminded me, I wish I'd known more about the medical aspects of transition when I was first navigating my journey. I wish I'd had more role models and mentors to look up to. And I wish

I'd known more about how to navigate the healthcare system.

"But most of all, I wish I'd known that I wasn't alone. That there were people like you who care about creating a more inclusive and supportive environment for LGBTQ+ individuals.

"That's why allyship is so important. Having allies like Ava, who support and love me for who I am, has made all the difference in my journey. It's not always easy, but it's worth it.

"So, what can you do to be a better ally? First, educate yourself. Learn about the LGBTQ+ community, our struggles, and our triumphs. Listen to our stories and amplify our voices.

"Second, speak up. When you witness discrimination or harassment, use your privilege to speak out against it. Be an active interceder.

"Third, support LGBTQ+-owned businesses and organizations. Put your money where your mouth is, and invest in our community.

"Finally, be patient and humble. Please recognize that you'll make mistakes, and be willing to learn from them. Apologize when necessary, and move forward with a commitment to doing better.

"In closing, I want to leave you with a quote from Audre Lorde: 'Revolution is not a one-time event, but rather a continuous process.' Creating a more inclusive and supportive environment for LGBTQ+ individuals is an ongoing process, and it requires all of us to be actively engaged."

Miriam scanned the audience. Everyone was focused on her words. She was pleased she had their attention.

"Now, I want to share some details of my journey. As a trans woman, my transition has been a complex and multifaceted process. It's been a journey of self-discovery, growth, and transformation.

"For me, the journey began with a deep sense of discomfort and disconnection from my assigned male identity. I felt like I was living in a body that wasn't mine and that I was pretending to be someone I wasn't.

"It took me a long time to realize that I was trans. I had to navigate a lot of internalized transphobia and shame before I could even consider the possibility that I might be trans.

"Once I began to explore my identity, I started to feel a sense of freedom and liberation that I had never experienced before. I started to see a therapist who specialized in trans issues, and I began to learn more about the trans community and the transition process.

"I decided to start hormone replacement therapy, or HRT, about a year ago. It's been a game-changer for me. The hormones have helped me to feel more connected to my body, and they've allowed me to express myself in a way that feels more authentic.

"In addition to HRT, I've also undergone some surgical procedures to help align my body with my identity. These procedures have been incredibly empowering for me, and they've helped me to feel more confident and comfortable in my own skin.

"Throughout my journey, I've been fortunate to have a fantastic support system. My partner, Ava, has been with me every step of the way, and she's been an incredible source of love, support, and encouragement. I've also been lucky to have an excellent therapist and a supportive medical team.

"Of course, my journey hasn't been without its challenges. I've faced discrimination, harassment, and marginalization. I've had to navigate complex and often hostile systems to access the care and support I need.

"But despite these challenges, I'm proud to say that I'm thriving. I'm living my truth, and I'm feeling more confident, comfortable, and authentic than I ever have before.

"I hope that my story can inspire and empower others. I hope that it can help to humanize and normalize the trans experience. And I hope that it can help to remind everyone that trans people are deserving of love, respect, and dignity.

"Thank you for listening to my story and for being part of this process. Together, we can create a more just and equitable world for all."

The facilitator stepped forward, microphone in hand. "Thank you, Miriam, for sharing your powerful story with us. Now, let's open the floor for questions. Remember, this is a safe space for respectful dialogue."

A student raised their hand, and the facilitator handed them the microphone.

"Miriam, thank you for being so brave. Can you talk more about your experience with healthcare as a trans woman? What were some of the challenges you faced?"

Miriam nodded thoughtfully. "Yes, of course. One of the biggest challenges I faced was finding healthcare providers who were knowledgeable about trans health issues. I had to do a lot of research and advocacy for myself to get the care I needed."

"Thank you, Miriam. Next question?"

A faculty member raised their hand. "Miriam, your story highlights the importance of allyship. Can you speak to how allies can best support trans individuals, particularly in academic settings?"

Miriam smiled. "That's a great question. Allies can play a crucial role in creating inclusive environments. One way to do this is by using correct pronouns and respecting people's identities. Additionally, allies can advocate for policies and practices that support trans individuals, such as inclusive bathrooms and healthcare benefits."

Another student asked, "How can we, as a community, better support trans individuals who are also people of color, or who have disabilities like yourself, or who are low-income?"

Miriam's expression turned thoughtful. "That's a critical question. We need to recognize that trans individuals face intersecting forms of oppression and that we must address these intersections in our advocacy work. This means listening to and amplifying the voices of trans individuals from diverse backgrounds and working to address the systemic barriers that they face."

The facilitator added, "Thank you, Miriam, for sharing your insights with us. Time's running out, so let's squeeze in one more question."

A student raised their hand, looking nervous. "Miriam, I'm so sorry to ask this, but... how do you deal with hate and discrimination? You're so strong and resilient."

Miriam's eyes softened. "Thank you for asking that question. It's not always easy, but I've learned to surround myself with loving and supportive people like my partner, Ava. I've also learned to prioritize self-care and seek help when I need it. I try to focus on the love and positivity in the world rather than letting the hate and negativity consume me."

The room erupted in applause as the facilitator stepped forward to thank Miriam again for sharing her story and insights. Ava rushed forward, embraced Miriam, and kissed her in front of the crowd. Jules smiled onward at the overwhelming reaction from the students and faculty.

The final week of Pride Month featured the art gallery housed in the Jasper Hill Convention Center. The center was a converted movie theater from decades before that also featured a stage for plays, presentations, musical performances, and more. It was operated by a kind woman named Sara, who was honored to host cultural events.

Sara and some volunteers were assisting artists in setting up the gallery for public viewing when Miriam and Ava arrived with their displays. Sara admired Miriam's butterfly sculpture 'Breaking Free' and was particularly moved by Ava's charcoal drawing of Miriam, which she had titled 'My Love, My Heart' which she had placed in an elegant matte black frame and glass cover to accentuate the charcoal drawing.

"These are gorgeous!" Sara said. "I'm going to make sure they're featured prominently." She chose two spots to feature them and thanked Ava and Miriam for submitting them.

The gallery was open to the public throughout the week. Sara received many comments from patrons complimenting the works of art, but none more so than Miriam's butterfly sculpture, second only to Ava's submission, which was the most complimented piece in the gallery.

Miriam and Ava were present for the final night, talking to patrons about their works. They were both having a wonderful evening.

As the evening wore on, the convention center began to close. Attendees had departed, leaving the once-bustling gallery quiet. Volunteers carefully dismantled the exhibits, stacking frames and packing sculptures for safe transport. Miriam and Ava lingered, basking in the evening's success.

"Your sculpture got so many compliments," Ava said, squeezing Miriam's hand. "And your speech at the workshop—it's been the talk of the campus all month."

Miriam smiled, exhaustion settling in. "You should be proud too. People were moved by your drawing."

Sara approached them with a warm smile. "Thank you both for being here tonight. You've made such a difference."

They exchanged pleasantries, and as Sara went to lock up, a sudden, piercing crash echoed through the center. The three women froze, the sound reverberating off the gallery walls.

"What was that?" Ava whispered, her voice tight.

Sara bolted toward the source of the noise, Miriam and Ava following closely behind. As they turned the corner into the gallery, Miriam's breath caught in her throat.

The serene beauty of the gallery had been replaced with chaos. Shattered glass littered the floor, and several paintings hung crooked on the walls, their canvases slashed. A few sculptures lay toppled and broken, jagged edges glinting in the dim light. The once-celebratory space now felt suffocating, heavy with the weight of deliberate destruction.

But it was the corner where Miriam and Ava's pieces had been displayed that stopped them in their tracks.

Ava's charcoal drawing lay face down in a pile of broken glass; the frame shattered into fragments. The once-pristine artwork was smeared and torn, and the paper crumpled as if someone had stomped on it. The image of Miriam—the one Ava had poured her love and artistry into—was unrecognizable.

Miriam's sculpture, Breaking Free, was no better. The delicate butterfly wings, so painstakingly crafted, were bent and snapped, resin shards scattered across the floor. The cocoon lay crushed, its fragments mixing with the broken plinth.

Ava let out a strangled cry, rushing to her drawing. "No... no, no, no!" She knelt beside it, her hands trembling as she gingerly picked up the ruined frame. Tears streaked her face as she clutched the crumpled remains of her work to her chest.

Miriam stood frozen, her heart pounding as she surveyed the damage. Her hands balled into fists at her sides. The destruction wasn't random—it was targeted, deliberate.

"This wasn't just vandalism," Miriam said, her voice low and shaking. "They knew these were ours."

Ava turned to her, her face streaked with tears and anger burning in her green eyes. "How could someone do this? Do they know how much this meant to us? To me?"

Miriam crouched beside her, placing a gentle hand on Ava's shoulder. "They wanted to hurt us, to scare us. But they don't get to win, Ava. We'll rebuild."

Ava shook her head, her voice breaking. "This isn't just about the art. This was my love for you, Miri. I poured everything into this drawing.

And they destroyed it like it was nothing."

Miriam pulled Ava into her arms, holding her tightly as sobs wracked her body. "I know," Miriam whispered, her own tears threatening to spill. "But love doesn't break that easily. What you created is still here, in your heart, in mine. They can't destroy that."

Sara reappeared, her face pale. "The police are on their way," she said, her voice trembling. "I'm so sorry this happened. You didn't deserve this."

The three women stood in the wreckage, a mix of sorrow and fury hanging in the air. When the police arrived, Rachel was among them. She surveyed the damage, her face hardening as she approached Miriam and Ava.

"This was targeted," Rachel said flatly. "We'll find out who did this."

Miriam nodded, though her faith in justice felt tenuous. "I just want to know why," she said softly. "Why do they hate us so much?"

Ava turned to Rachel, her voice resolute despite her tears. "Find them. Whoever did this... they need to know that we won't be scared away."

Rachel placed a reassuring hand on Ava's shoulder. "We will. And you won't face this alone."

As the police gathered evidence and the gallery emptied, Miriam and Ava sat together on the floor, holding each other amidst the remnants of their art. Despite the destruction, a spark of determination flickered between them.

They knew this fight wasn't over.

Chapter 27: One Year

Ava was utterly devastated. Seeing her drawing of Miriam, something she had poured her heart and soul into, destroyed by a vandal in the gallery felt like a personal attack. It was more than just a piece of art—it was a piece of herself, now torn apart and ruined. Her chest ached with the sting of betrayal and sorrow, and tears flowed freely as she stared at the wreckage of her work. For days, Ava was inconsolable, her usual spark snuffed out by the cruel act. Miriam, steadfast and gentle, stayed by her side, offering unwavering support and affection, holding her close as Ava tried to process the pain and find the strength to move forward.

It was now July 2, 2024. Miriam hadn't realized it because she was so focused on Ava, but it was the first anniversary of the brutal attack that changed Miriam's life forever. She was carrying coffee to the porch swing for her and Ava when she realized this.

Miriam began shaking, then crying. She trembled as she handed Ava her coffee, spilling some over the top of the mug. Ava noticed Miriam was distressed and grew concerned.

"Miriam, baby, what is it?"

Miriam looked up at Ava and found the strength to speak. "One year. Today makes a year. A year ago, those assholes killed my friend and left me for dead." Ava lit two cigarettes and passed Miriam one.

"I've never asked because I never want you to have to relive it, but,

Miri, love, I'm here if you want to talk about it. You can talk about your friend, your life before, anything you feel comfortable with. There's no pressure. I am a judgment-free partner." She inhaled from her cigarette, "And if you don't want to talk about it, that's also fine. I'm still going to sit here with you and be here for you. We'll get through this."

Miriam nodded and smiled gently before responding, "Thank you, dear. I have never really gone into all of the details with you about it because of witness protection, and I was ordered not to. I've told you a bit, but you've become such a huge and important part of my life, part of me, that out of respect and my love for you, I never talked about all of it." She exhaled after a drag from her cigarette, "But now is the time to talk about it." She held Ava's hand as she spoke.

"Alex, full name Alessandro Bianchi, he was a great friend. He was 24 and my only real friend. He wasn't mean-spirited but kind, thoughtful, and generous. And fiercely loyal. Very protective. We worked together at a pizza delivery restaurant as delivery drivers. I trained him when he started, and we hit it off.

"He knew I was trying to save money, but he never knew what I was saving it for. I was too scared to tell him I wanted to transition, and I let him assume I wanted a nicer car or a house, that sort of thing. So he told me about his cousin Leo Rossi and introduced me to him.

"Leo seemed like a nice enough guy. He helped Alex support Alex's mom, Francesca, and she never wanted for anything. She adored Alex and Leo, but she hated me.

"Leo was always carrying around this green notebook with faded gold lettering on the cover. I always wondered what it was for. I found out.

"Leo ran an illegal gambling operation. Alex didn't have a clue Leo wasn't legit, and I didn't either for the longest time. It started out with sports betting, baseball, football, basketball, you name it. At first, I made simple bets. But I quickly realized simple bets didn't pay great. So, I got riskier as time went on. Leo kept track of all my transactions in that notebook.

"And for a little bit, I was winning, and winning pretty decent amounts. Eventually, I had saved $20,000.

"So the Kentucky Derby rolled around last year, and the odds on favorite to win was this horse, Angel of the Empire, tremendous favorite, 4-1 odds.

"I bet everything I had on that horse. It was a sure thing. I would have won $100,000.

"But he lost. And I lost everything. Then Leo came to collect. I thought Leo liked me, but he didn't care. He just wanted his money and assured me he would collect it, one way or another.

"About two months went by, and he showed up at my apartment one morning around 7:00 am with his best friend, Marco De Luca, a well-known member of the De Luca crime family. They said I had 24 hours to pay up, or they'd be back, and they would take it from me.

"That was July 1, 2023. The next day, I worked, and then I went home. Alex was there waiting for me. We were playing with my PS5, and I confessed to him that I wanted to transition. He was cool with it and supportive, and then knock-knock.

"Alex answered the door, and six guys showed up. They immediately shot Alex in the back of the head. He never knew what had happened. Then they beat me to near-death."

Ava's eyes widened in horror as Miriam recounted the events of that fateful day. She squeezed Miriam's hand, offering what little comfort she could.

"Miri, honey, I'm so sorry," Ava whispered, her voice trembling. "I can only imagine how terrifying that must have been for you, how traumatizing it was."

Miriam took a deep drag on her cigarette, her eyes welling up with tears. "It's not just what they did to me, Ava," Miriam said, her voice cracking. "It's what they took from me. Alex was my friend, my confidant... he was the only one who truly understood me. They took his future, the remainder of his life."

Ava nodded, her expression somber.

"I'm here for you, Miri," Ava said. "I'll always be here for you. We'll get through this together. I'm not going anywhere."

As they sat there in silence, the only sound being the quiet hum of the porch swing, Miriam felt a sense of gratitude toward Ava. She knew that she could always count on Ava to be there for her, no matter what.

Suddenly, Miriam's phone rang, startling the two of them. It was Assistant US Attorney Amanda Miller. Miriam answered promptly. "Hello?"

"Hello, Miriam, it's AUSA Amanda Miller. Am I catching you at a bad time?"

"Not at all. Ava and I were just enjoying some fresh air on our porch. How can I help you?"

"I need you here in Pittsburgh on Friday, July 5. We don't have a trial date, but I need you here for pre-trial interviews."

"So soon? That's fine, I can be there. But I need Ava to come with me, not for the pre-trial interviews, of course, but to be there for support through everything else. Is that ok? Please?"

AUSA Miller's voice was warm and reassuring. "Of course, Miriam. I completely understand. Ava is more than welcome to accompany you to Pittsburgh. I'll arrange for her to have access to the courthouse and our offices. We'll send a team of marshals to pick you up and escort you to a local safe house."

Miriam let out a sigh of relief, feeling grateful for AUSA Miller's understanding. "Thank you so much, Amanda. I really appreciate it."

AUSA Miller's voice turned serious. "Miriam, I also want to remind you that we'll be going over the details of your testimony during the pre-trial interviews. It's going to be a tough few days, but I'm confident that you'll do great. Just remember to take care of yourself, okay?"

Miriam nodded, even though AUSA Miller couldn't see her. "I will, Amanda. Thank you again for everything." She then added, "How long will the pre-trial interviews take?"

AUSA Miller hesitated for a moment before responding. "The pre-trial interviews will likely take a few days, Miriam. I'd say we're looking at around 2-3 days, depending on how things go. We'll need to review your testimony multiple times, and I'll need to prepare you for any potential cross-examination by the defense."

Miriam nodded, taking a deep breath. She was ready to do whatever it took to see justice served.

AUSA Miller continued, "We'll start on Friday, July 5, and work through the weekend if needed. I'll make sure to give you regular breaks and time to rest. You're doing great, Miriam. Just a little longer, and we'll get through this."

"What are the next steps after the pre-trial interviews?"

AUSA Miller explained, "After the pre-trial interviews, we'll be preparing for the actual trial. We'll use the information from the interviews to finalize our strategy and make any necessary adjustments.

"Once the trial begins, you'll be called to testify as a witness for the prosecution. You'll be sworn in, and I'll ask you questions about your experiences and what you witnessed. The defense will also have the opportunity to cross-examine you.

"After you've testified, the trial will continue with other witnesses and evidence. The prosecution and defense will present their cases, and then the jury will deliberate and reach a verdict.

"And my testimony is a closed testimony, correct?"

AUSA Miller confirmed, "Yes, Miriam, your testimony is indeed a closed testimony. Only authorized personnel will be allowed to be present during your testimony. Ava won't be allowed to participate in the proceedings, but she can wait in our offices during your testimony."

Miriam spoke, "Alright, Amanda, we'll pack and await our escorts. What time do we need to be in Pittsburgh on Friday?"

AUSA Miller replied, "Let's plan for you and Ava to arrive in Pittsburgh by Thursday evening, July 4. That way, you can get settled and rested before the pre-trial interviews start on Friday morning. I'll send a car to pick you up from your safe house. We'll schedule the pre-trial interviews to start around 9:00 a.m. on Friday."

"Thank you, Amanda."

"Thank you, Miriam. I'll see you both soon."

Miriam ended the call and turned to Ava, "Well, we need to pack. We're going to Pittsburgh."

On Thursday, July 4, Miriam and Ava got up at 6:00 a.m. and prepared for the trip to Pittsburgh. Their escort was due to arrive at 9:00 a.m., giving them three hours to make breakfast, have coffee, get dressed, and double-check to make sure they remembered everything.

They had spent the previous day packing and had already placed their bags downstairs. Miriam made breakfast omelets and toast, and they enjoyed their food on the porch swing. They then had coffee and cigarettes. Since they'd be stuck in a vehicle all day, they decided to shower that evening at the safe house.

At 8:50 a.m., two vehicles approached: a blue Chevy Tahoe and a green Ford Explorer. They parked, and a team of four marshals, two per vehicle, exited the cars. The marshals secured the perimeter, loaded Miriam and Ava's bags into the Tahoe, and then loaded Miriam and Ava safely into the Tahoe. They then departed with the Tahoe in the lead.

It was a long five-hour drive to Pittsburgh; the marshals wouldn't stop, and they wouldn't let Miriam and Ava smoke. Miriam's leg was cramping, and she was able to get some relief by removing her prosthetic, but she was highly agitated that she couldn't just have one cigarette. Apparently, the last team that escorted Miriam and let her smoke faced disciplinary action.

After five hours, the marshals alerted Miriam and Ava that they had arrived at their destination. The couple had fallen asleep somewhere in West Virginia, and the marshals let them rest. Miriam put her prosthetic back on, and then she and Ava waited for the marshals to give them permission to get out once the perimeter was secured. Miriam noticed it was the same cabin she had stayed in during her first days in WITSEC.

"Jesus, this is the best cigarette I've ever tasted!" Miriam inhaled deeply, and her eyes were like daggers glaring at the team of marshals as they chuckled.

Ava agreed, "At least during school, I could go to my car during my free period. That was some bullshit."

"That bullshit was for your protection," a voice said from behind them. They turned to see US Marshal Thompson exiting the safe house.

This particular safe house was a log cabin on the Ohio River's edge. Miriam commented, "Marshal Thompson, is it a requirement that all safe houses be cabins on a waterfront? Or is that just a personal preference?"

Thompson chuckled. "It's good to see you, Miriam. It's been some time. May I say that you're a far cry different from when I first met you?"

"And what's that supposed to mean? Is that some weird comment about my appearance?"

"No, Miriam. This is me saying you look happy. I remember a girl ready to die, and now I see a woman fighting for life and conquering it."

Miriam paused, caught off guard by the unexpected kindness. Her expression softened as she looked away, the weight of his words settling over her. Finally, she glanced back at him and said, "Transitioning didn't solve all my problems, Marshal. It's made all my problems worth solving."

Sensing Miriam's discomfort, Ava stepped in and smiled warmly at Marshal Thompson. "Thank you, Marshal. That means a lot coming from you."

Marshal Thompson's expression turned serious, and he nodded. "I'm glad to see you're both doing well. Now, let's get you settled in. We'll go over the security protocols and familiarize you with the safe house."

Ava asked, "And what exactly are the security protocols?"

Marshal Thompson began to explain, "The safe house is equipped with state-of-the-art security systems, including motion detectors, cameras, and alarms. The perimeter of the property is also secured with fencing and surveillance cameras. We have a team of marshals who will be providing 24/7 security, rotating shifts every 8 hours. You'll also have a secure communication system to contact us in case of an emergency." He paused, then added, "And, as an extra precaution, we've implemented a 'no visitors' policy. No one will be allowed to enter the property without prior clearance from me or my team."

"Is there any food here, or can we order something and have you guys bring it to us?" Ava and Miriam were both hungry, having not eaten since 7:00 a.m. It was now 2:15 p.m.

Marshal Thompson nodded sympathetically. "We've stocked the kitchen with some essentials, but I can also arrange for food to be delivered. We have a few trusted contacts in the area who can bring food to the safe house without compromising your location." He pulled out his phone and dialed a number. "Let me call in an order. What would you like? Pizza, sandwiches, or something else?"

Miriam said, "Pizza. It's been a year since I've had decent pizza. Is that alright with you, Ava, dear?" Ava nodded in agreement. "Yes, one pepperoni and sausage and one ham and pineapple!"

Marshal Thompson chuckled and relayed the order over the phone. "Alright, two pizzas: one pepperoni and sausage and one ham and pineapple, both large. And can you make sure they're delivered within the next hour?" He paused, listening to the response, then nodded. "Great, thanks. We'll have someone meet you at the gate to pick up the order." He turned back to Miriam and Ava. "It'll be about an hour. In the meantime, why don't you two get settled in? You can take a look around the safe house, and I'll show you where everything is."

"If it's alright with you, Marshal Thompson, can we stay outside for a few more minutes? Five hours was a long time to be cramped up in the Tahoe." Miriam pleaded her case, attempting to garner sympathy.

Marshal Thompson smiled sympathetically. "Of course, Miriam. You're welcome to stay outside for a bit. Just stay within the designated perimeter, please. We've got cameras and motion detectors set up to alert us to any potential threats, but it's always better to be cautious." He nodded towards the river. "Why don't you two take a walk down by the water? The view's nice and a good way to stretch your legs."

Ava took Miriam's hand, and the two walked to the river's edge. They walked along the bank for a few feet but were afraid to stray out of sight. They sat down by the water's edge and lit fresh cigarettes. Ava broke the silence, "You know, if it weren't for all the security cameras, motion detectors, armed marksmen, and electrified fencing with razor wire, this place would be pretty romantic."

Miriam burst into laughter, and Ava joined her. Miriam toppled over, and Ava leaned in and kissed her deeply. They lay there on the bank of the Ohio River until the pizza arrived.

Chapter 28: Revisiting The Darkness

The next morning, Miriam and Ava exited the secure vehicle and onto the bustling courthouse steps. The morning sun cast a golden glow over the scene, but Miriam's nerves were on edge. She clutched Ava's hand, seeking reassurance as their marshal escorts flanked them.

As they ascended the steps, Miriam's gaze swept the crowded entrance. That's when she saw her – Francesca Bianchi, Alex's mother, standing off to the side, her eyes scanning the crowd with a mix of determination and desperation. Miriam's heart skipped a beat as their eyes met, but only for a fleeting moment. Francesca's gaze didn't linger, but Miriam couldn't help but wonder if she had been recognized.

The marshals guided Miriam and Ava through the security checkpoint, and then Ava was led away to a secure waiting area. Miriam watched her go, feeling a pang of separation anxiety.

One of the marshals, a tall, imposing figure with a kind face, turned to Miriam. "We'll get started with the interviews shortly, Miriam. Just follow me, please."

Miriam nodded, taking a deep breath as she followed the marshal through the courthouse's winding corridors. Her mind, however, was still reeling from the unexpected encounter with Francesca Bianchi.

Did she recognize me? She's been under the impression that Gabe Wilson is dead, and my face has changed since then, but has it changed enough?

As Miriam trailed behind the marshal, her thoughts swirled with anxiety. She couldn't shake the feeling that Francesca's gaze had lingered on her for a fraction of a second longer than necessary. Did she suspect? Miriam's heart rate quickened at the prospect of being discovered.

She replayed the encounter in her mind, analyzing every detail. Francesca's expression had been a mask of determination, but had Miriam detected a flicker of recognition? She couldn't be sure. *What am I going to do? I need to get out of here*!

The marshal stopped in front of a nondescript door and produced a keycard to unlock it. "We're here, Miriam. This is the conference room where we'll be conducting the pre-trial interviews."

Miriam nodded, still distracted by her thoughts. She took a deep breath, attempting to compose herself as she stepped into the conference room. But her mind remained fixated on the encounter with Francesca, her senses on high alert, waiting for any sign that her true identity had been compromised.

Miriam crossed the threshold of the conference room and was greeted by AUSA Amanda Miller and a middle-aged man with a kind face and a notepad in front of him. He stood up, extending his hand to Miriam. "Hello, Miriam. I'm Dr. Elliot Thompson, a psychologist with the Department of Justice. I'll be assisting AUSA Miller with your testimony preparation."

AUSA Miller smiled warmly, her eyes crinkling at the corners. "Good morning, Miriam. I trust you're doing well. Please, have a seat. We have a lot to cover today."

Miriam nodded, taking a seat in the chair dandicated by AUSA Miller. She glanced around the room, taking in the familiar setup of a conference room. But her mind was still reeling from the encounter with Francesca Bianchi, and she couldn't shake the feeling that she was being watched.

"Before we begin, I saw someone outside. Alex Bianchi's mother, Francesca. She saw me. I don't know if she recognized me, but she absolutely saw me."

AUSA Miller's expression turned serious, her eyes narrowing slightly. "Francesca Bianchi, here? That's unusual. Did she approach you or try to make contact?"

Dr. Thompson's eyes flicked to AUSA Miller, then back to Miriam. "This could be a problem. If Francesca Bianchi recognizes you, it could compromise your safety and the entire witness protection program."

AUSA Miller leaned forward, her voice taking on a reassuring tone. "Miriam, we'll look into this immediately. I'll alert the marshals and make sure they're aware of the situation. In the meantime, let's focus on preparing you for your testimony. We'll get through this together."

AUSA Miller stepped out to inform the marshal who escorted Miriam to the conference room about what Miriam just told her. She then returned to the room. "Alright, shall we begin?"

Dr. Thompson nodded, flipping open his notepad. "Yes, let's get started. Miriam, I want to assure you that everything discussed in this room is confidential and for the purpose of preparing you for your testimony. Can you start by telling me about your relationship with Alex Bianchi and the events leading up to his death?" He leaned forward, his eyes locked intently on Miriam's.

AUSA Miller took a seat beside Dr. Thompson, her eyes fixed on Miriam as well. "And please, Miriam, be as detailed as possible. We need to make sure we cover all the necessary points for your testimony."

Miriam took a deep breath and recounted her friendship with Alex with as much accuracy and detail as she could muster. She cited her first meeting with Alex at the restaurant they worked for and how their friendship grew over the three years they knew each other, including all the details Miriam explained to Ava just three days prior.

As Miriam spoke, her voice was steady, but her eyes disclosed a deep sadness. Dr. Thompson and AUSA Miller listened intently, their expressions sympathetic. Dr. Thompson scribbled notes on his pad while AUSA Miller's eyes never left Miriam's face.

When Miriam finished speaking, the room fell silent for a moment. Dr. Thompson looked up from his notes, his eyes locking onto Miriam's. "Thank you, Miriam. That takes a lot of courage to relive. Can you tell me more about the events leading up to the attack? Specifically, about your dealings with Leo Rossi and the debt you owed him?"

Miriam explained how Alex introduced her to his cousin Leo Rossi, who placed bets for people in the neighborhood. She went into detail about the range of sports she gambled on until she had accumulated $20,000 in winnings. Then, she bet all of it on a 4-1 odds horse in the Kentucky Derby, losing $100,000.

She recalled Leo's demeanor changing once she owed such a large sum. She told them about how, on July 1, Leo and his best friend, Marco De Luca, visited her at her apartment and gave her 24 hours to pay, or else.

Dr. Thompson's expression turned grave as Miriam recounted the events leading up to the attack. AUSA Miller's eyes narrowed, her jaw clenched in anger. "And then, on July 2, 2023, Alex was murdered, and you were left for dead," AUSA Miller stated, her voice firm but controlled.

Dr. Thompson nodded, his eyes still locked on Miriam's. "Miriam, can you tell me more about what happened on July 2? What do you remember about the attack?"

"We were at my apartment playing PlayStation. I had just told Alex that I wanted to transition, and there was a knock at the door. He answered it; 6 guys dressed in all black carrying crowbars barged in. He shouted my name and one guy pulled a gun, said no witnesses, and put a bullet in the back of Alex's head.

"Then the lead guy started swinging his crowbar and smashing it into my shin, across my throat, my face, my shin again and again and again and again. I tried to stand, but my leg crumpled like tissue paper. They stomped and kicked me, broke my left arm when I tried to block a crowbar, and repeatedly struck my ribs... I... I... I looked at Alex's body, I heard a frantic woman's voice, and I blacked out."

The room fell silent, the only sound the quiet hum of the fluorescent lights overhead. Dr. Thompson's eyes never left Miriam's face, his expression a mask of compassion and concern. AUSA Miller's eyes had dropped, her gaze fixed on the table as she struggled to maintain her composure.

After a moment, Dr. Thompson spoke, his voice soft and gentle. "Miriam, I'm so sorry you had to endure that. It's unimaginable. Can you tell me what happened after you blacked out? Do you remember anything about the hospital or the aftermath of the attack?"

"I didn't wake up for eight days, was briefly conscious to have my injuries explained to me, and then I passed out for three more days. It was only then that I learned I had been unconscious for eleven days."

Dr. Thompson nodded, his eyes still locked on Miriam's face. "I can only imagine how terrifying that must have been for you. Waking up to learn that you'd been unconscious for eleven days... it's a miracle you survived."

AUSA Miller looked up, her eyes meeting Miriam's. "Miriam, I want to assure you that we're doing everything in our power to ensure that justice is served. The men who did this to you and Alex will be held accountable."

Dr. Thompson leaned forward, his voice taking on a gentle tone. "Miriam, we're going to take a short break. This can't be easy for you. Would you like some water or maybe a few minutes to collect yourself?"

"I really need to see Ava. And I'd like a cigarette. If I can have a few minutes for those two things, I would greatly appreciate it."

AUSA Miller nodded sympathetically. "I'll arrange for you to see Ava. As for the cigarette, I'll see what we can do. We'll need to find a secure outdoor area for you to smoke."

Dr. Thompson stood up, his expression understanding. "I'll escort you to the secure area for your cigarette, and then we'll arrange for you to see Ava. Take a few minutes to collect yourself, and we'll reconvene when you're ready."

AUSA Miller added, "We'll also make sure that the marshal is aware of the situation with Francesca Bianchi, and we'll take necessary precautions to ensure your safety."

Miriam nodded and thanked them. She was exhausted, and reliving those experiences had taken a heavy toll on her. She followed Dr. Thompson to the secure outdoor smoking area. On the way, she asked, "Are you related to US Marshal Thompson at all?"

Dr. Thompson chuckled and shook his head. "No, I'm not related to Marshal Thompson. Thompson is a fairly common surname, and we just happen to share it. I've met Marshal Thompson a few times, though. He's a good man, and he's been a big help in keeping you safe."

When they arrived at the smoking area, Miriam promptly lit a cigarette, taking an intense drag and a long, slow inhale. As she exhaled the smoke, her eyes closed, and her shoulders seemed to relax ever so slightly. The tension in her face eased, replaced by a fleeting look of calm. Dr. Thompson stood beside her, respectfully silent, allowing her a moment of respite from the emotional turmoil of the morning.

As they walked back inside, Miriam's eyes scanned the area, searching for Ava. Dr. Thompson led her to a nearby room, and when they entered, Miriam's face lit up with a warm smile. Ava was sitting on a couch, looking up at Miriam with curious eyes. Miriam rushed over to Ava, sweeping her up in a tight hug. "Hey, baby girl," she whispered, holding Ava close. Miriam couldn't hold back the tears any longer. Once she was in Ava's safe embrace, she let all of her emotions out.

Ava wrapped her arms around Miriam, holding her tightly as Miriam sobbed. Dr. Thompson discreetly stepped out of the room, closing the door behind him to give Miriam and Ava a private moment. As Miriam cried, Ava whispered softly into her ear, "I'm here, my love. I've got you. You're safe." Miriam's tears fell harder at Ava's words, but she felt a sense of comfort and peace wash over her. She held Ava closer, cherishing the warmth and love of her partner, her person eternal.

Ava's expression softened, relief washing over her face. She held Miriam's face in her hands, her eyes locked on Miriam's. "I'm so proud of you," she whispered. "I know how hard this must be for you. But you're doing it, Miriam. You're facing it head-on, and I'm here with you every step of the way." Ava's voice cracked with emotion, and she pulled Miriam into another tight hug.

Miriam felt a lump form in her throat as she wrapped her arms around Ava, holding her close. Breathing in the familiar scent of Ava's hair, she felt a sense of comfort and security wash over her. For a moment, the trauma and pain of the past few months receded, and all that was left was the warmth and love of the woman she loved.

Dr. Thompson knocked on the door. He opened it and said, "Miriam, it's time to return to the interview." Miriam nodded, taking a deep breath as she pulled back from Ava. She wiped away the remaining tears from her face and tried to compose herself.

Ava gave her a reassuring smile and a gentle squeeze on the hand before letting go. "I'll be here," Ava said softly. Miriam nodded, taking one last look at Ava before following Dr. Thompson out of the room.

Chapter 29: The Debt Of Justice

As they walked back to the interview room, Dr. Thompson glanced at Miriam with a concerned expression. "Are you okay to continue?" he asked quietly.

Miriam took a deep breath, steeling herself for what was to come. She nodded, her voice barely above a whisper. "Yes, I'm ready."

Miriam took her seat. AUSA Miller had returned as well. Miriam regained her composure and said confidently, "What's next?"

AUSA Miller smiled, a hint of admiration in her eyes. "Thank you for your resilience, Miriam. Next, we'd like to discuss the events leading up to the shooting. Can you tell us more about your interactions with Francesca Bianchi in the days and weeks before the incident?"

"I only met Francesca Bianchi on three occasions. Once after work, when I was training Alex for our pizza delivery jobs, it was late at night, and he invited me over to his place to hang out. We were playing video games and woke her up. She was pissed and asked me who I was, then told me to get the hell out of her house.

"The second time was about a year later, on Thanksgiving Day of 2021. Alex insisted I show because I didn't have any family, and I brought a shitty store-bought pumpkin pie. She was offended by the gesture, threw the pie away, and told me to get the hell out of her house.

"The third time was when I was looking for Leo. May 6, 2023. The day I made the bet on the Kentucky Derby and lost it all. She hadn't seen me since Thanksgiving Day of 2021, and I thought she would tell me to get the hell out of her house again. But this time was different. She invited me in and offered me lemonade."

AUSA Miller's eyes were fixed intently on Miriam as she recounted her interactions with Francesca Bianchi. When Miriam finished, Miller nodded thoughtfully and made a few notes on her pad. "I see," she said. "And can you tell me more about what happened during that third visit? What did you and Francesca talk about, and did you notice anything unusual about her behavior?"

"She asked me a lot, actually. Where I was from, originally, did I have any family, did I have any goals or plan to go to college, that kind of small talk. It seemed like a normal conversation at the time. Do you think we need to worry about anything?" Miriam looked anxiously between AUSA Miller and Dr. Thompson.

AUSA Miller's expression was reassuring. "No, Miriam, we're just trying to piece together as much information as possible. Your conversation with Francesca might seem insignificant now, but it could be important to our investigation."

Dr. Thompson nodded in agreement. "We're just covering all our bases, Miriam. You're doing great."

AUSA Miller leaned forward slightly. "Can you tell me more about Francesca's demeanor during your conversation? Did she seem nervous, anxious, or calm?"

"She seemed fine, more curious than anything. I tried to be respectful and polite, thanked her for the lemonade, and left. It struck me as out of character based on my minimal interaction with her."

AUSA Miller nodded thoughtfully, making another note on her pad. "I see. So, in your previous interactions with Francesca, she had been hostile and dismissive, but on this occasion, she was unexpectedly friendly and curious. Did you get the sense that she was trying to manipulate you or get something from you, or did it genuinely seem like she was just being friendly?"

"I just thought that as a woman probably around 60, she was just trying to be friendly. I never even thought about it again until today."

AUSA Miller nodded, her expression neutral. "I understand. It's natural to assume someone's kindness is genuine, especially when it's unexpected. Did anything else strike you as unusual about that day, or was it just the change in Francesca's demeanor that stood out?"

"Aside from losing $20,000 and being indebted for $100,000? No, nothing out of the ordinary."

AUSA Miller's eyes widened slightly at the mention of the large sum of money. "I... see," she said, her tone measured. "We'll definitely be looking into that further. Can you tell me more about the circumstances surrounding the bet and the debt?"

"It's like I said before, I placed the bet on the 4-1 favorite to win the Derby, Angel of the Empire, and he lost. Then Leo told me I owed him $100,000, and since he worked for Mario De Luca, I owed Mister De Luca the money."

AUSA Miller's expression turned serious, her eyes narrowing slightly. "I understand. So, you're saying that Leo, who worked for Mario De Luca, told you that you owed De Luca $100,000 after you lost the bet. Did you ever receive any written confirmation of this debt, or was it all verbal?"

"All verbal, to my knowledge. Leo kept a book on him that had the bets and if people won or lost and how much, but I never signed anything."

AUSA Miller's eyes lit up with interest at the mention of the book. "A book, you say? That sounds like a ledger or a record-keeping system. Did you ever see Leo write down your debt in this book, or did he just tell you that it was recorded?"

"No, I saw it. It was a green book with faded gold lettering on the front. Leo always recorded my name inside it. He showed me each time how much I bet, what the odds were, and the payout if I won or what I would owe if I lost."

AUSA Miller nodded, making another note on her pad. "I see. Did you see records of other people's transactions or just your own?"

"Only my own."

AUSA Miller nodded, making another note on her pad. "I see. So, you only saw your own transactions in the book. Did Leo ever mention what would happen if you couldn't pay back the $100,000 you owed?"

"He said I needed to pay it, and I didn't have a lot of time to do it. He refused to let me place any more bets, so he had to know I had no way to pay it back. That was May of 2023. He and Marco visited me a few weeks later, on July 1. That's when they gave me 24 hours to pay."

AUSA Miller's expression turned grave, her eyes locked onto Miriam's. "I see. So, Leo and Marco gave you an ultimatum on July 1, 2023, demanding that you pay the $100,000 within 24 hours. What happened after that?"

"The next day, those guys shot Alex and left me for dead."

AUSA Miller's expression turned somber, her voice filled with empathy. "I'm so sorry, Miriam. That must have been incredibly traumatic for you. Can you tell me more about what happened after you were left for dead? How did you manage to get help?"

"No, I was unconscious. I have no recollection of after the attack until I woke up in the hospital eight days later."

AUSA Miller nodded sympathetically. "I understand. It's not uncommon for trauma victims to experience memory loss or gaps in their recollection. The fact that you woke up in the hospital several days later suggests that you received medical attention in time. Did the hospital staff or police ever question you about the attack, or was it only later, during this investigation?"

"Only later, the day I first met you."

AUSA Miller nodded, her expression thoughtful. "I remember. You were still recovering from your injuries, but you were brave enough to share your story with me. I want to assure you, Miriam, that we're doing everything in our power to bring those responsible for the attack to justice."

"So, what now? Do we have more to cover? Or is that it? I've told you everything I possibly know." Miriam anxiously awaited the answer.

AUSA Miller smiled reassuringly. "You've been incredibly helpful, Miriam. I think we've covered everything for now. Your testimony will be invaluable in building our case against Mario De Luca and his associates. We'll need to get your formal statement down in writing, but that can be done at a later time. For now, you've done enough. Just focus on taking care of yourself and getting back on your feet."

"So Ava and I can go back home? Until you need me for the next phase, that is?"

AUSA Miller nodded. "Yes, you and Ava are free to return home. We'll be in touch soon to discuss the next steps and let you know when we need you to testify. In the meantime, please don't hesitate to reach out if you have any questions or concerns. And, Miriam, please be careful. We'll have protection in place, but it's always better to be cautious."

"Did the marshals find out why Francesca Bianchi was outside this morning?

AUSA Miller's expression turned thoughtful. "Actually, Miriam, we didn't find any sign of Francesca Bianchi outside the courthouse. We had surveillance cameras and agents monitoring the area, but she seems to have vanished into thin air."

Miriam's eyes narrowed slightly, her mind racing with the possibility that Francesca might have been watching her. "Are you sure?" she pressed. "I could have sworn I saw her outside the courthouse."

AUSA Miller's expression turned reassuring. "I understand your concern, Miriam, but I assure you, we've checked all the footage and interviewed witnesses. There's no sign of Francesca Bianchi. It's possible you might have mistaken someone else for her."

Miriam nodded, though she couldn't shake off the feeling that Francesca was still out there, watching her.

Chapter 30: Miriam's Masterpiece

After an emotionally draining and physically demanding few days in Pittsburgh, the team of US Marshals returned Miriam and Ava home on Saturday, July 6. As they settled into their porch swing, Miriam and Ava lit their first cigarettes in five hours.

Ava asked, "So, how long do you think it will be before we have to go back, love?"

"Miller said anytime within the next year," Miriam replied. "It depends on what their investigation uncovers. I think I may have given them something to look for – Leo's notebook."

Ava's curiosity was piqued. "What's so special about the notebook?"

"It's a green notebook with gold lettering, full of my betting trans-actions, and probably other people's too," Miriam explained. "Miller seemed surprised when I mentioned it as if they weren't aware it existed."

Ava's brow furrowed. "That's weird. And what about all the other loose ends? Like, who called 911?"

Miriam's eyes narrowed. "And what about Francesca Bianchi? I could have sworn I saw her outside the courthouse, but Miller said they didn't find any evidence of her being there."

Ava's expression turned thoughtful. "Do you think Francesca could be involved in all of this somehow?"

Miriam shrugged. "I don't know, but I'm going to keep pushing for answers. I want to know what really happened that day, and I want to know who's behind it all."

Ava nodded, her eyes locked on Miriam's. "We'll get to the bottom of it, love. Together."

Miriam and Ava spent the next few days and weeks wondering about the trial developments and who called help for Miriam. As much as these questions plagued them, Miriam had something more pressing on her mind: Ava's birthday.

Miriam realized it was fast approaching—at this point, it was two weeks away. Miriam didn't have fancy restaurants where she could take Ava to dine, but she could cook and create. During these weeks, she wondered what to sculpt. She eventually thought of a design. The final part of her gift would be a poem.

Miriam split her time between Ava and working on the secret sculpture. She would write the poem in her head as she sculpted, glued, and painted. When she wasn't composing a poem in her mind, she was planning a menu.

While Miriam was sculpting, Ava filled her time working on a commission she had received from Sara, the operator of the Jasper Hill Convention Center. Ava created a charcoal drawing of the center, both a view of the outside featuring the marquee and the inside as it exists today with the seating and stage. Sara let Ava take reference photos, and Ava used these to recreate the center with pencils.

Miriam had secretly asked Sara to request the commission be delivered on August 7 so that after she and Ava had dropped it off, Miriam could present Ava with her gifts.

The morning of Ava's birthday arrived, and Miriam gently kissed Ava's forehead to wake her. "Good morning, dear Ava. Happy birthday!"

Ava wrapped her arms around Miriam, rolled her over to climb atop her, and bent down to give her a passionate kiss. They lay there for a few minutes before Miriam asked, "What would you like me to make you for breakfast?"

Ava thought it over. "Crepes with fresh fruit and whipped cream!"

"As you wish, beautiful lady." She gave Ava another kiss and then went downstairs to make breakfast. Ava noticed Miriam forgot to put clothes on and giggled.

When Ava arrived in the kitchen, Miriam had an elaborate breakfast ready consisting of crepes that were rolled and filled with whipped cream and had sprinkled powdered sugar on them, fresh strawberries, blueberries, raspberries, and pineapple, a pot of coffee and a pitcher of orange juice. Ava was delighted.

They had breakfast, then adjourned to the porch swing for coffee and cigarettes. Miriam said, "This breakfast was part one of your birthday celebration today."

Ava snuggled deeply into Miriam's side and took a deep drag from her cigarette. "Can I have a hint about part two?"

Miriam simply said, "It's beautiful out today. Dress in something light and flowy."

They spent the remainder of the morning getting ready for a mysterious day out. Ava was giddy with anticipation and was dancing around the house in every room she entered.

At noon, the couple departed in Miriam's car, and Miriam drove Ava to the convention center. "While you present Sara with the charcoal drawing of her center, do you mind if I dash over and get part two of your gift?"

"Don't be long, love." She kissed Miriam before she exited, then grabbed the matte framed artwork she had created for Sara. Once Ava was inside, she pulled out and drove to the local coffee shop, The Cistern on Main. Their motto was 'A Reservoir of Rich Flavors'.

She walked in and told the barista she had ordered a catered picnic basket. The barista went to the back and momentarily returned with a cute wicker picnic basket with red gingham cloth protruding from the sides. Miriam paid and left to pick up Ava.

Ava was just emerging from the convention center when Miriam pulled in. "Going my way?"

Miriam winked, and Ava giggled as she climbed in. "Yes, I am, love, yes I am."

Miriam drove out of town, and Ava's curiosity was piqued. "Where are we going?" Miriam didn't want to keep her in the dark, so she told her.

"The lake. There's something I want to show you there."

The road to the lake was winding and heavily wooded, and the dense green forest was intensely colored. After twenty minutes, they arrived at a recreation area on one of the many banks of the lake. Miriam parked, and they exited the car. Miriam led Ava to the back of the vehicle. She then pointed to a willow tree near the water's edge.

"See that willow tree? Would you please go on down there and wait for me while I grab a couple of things?" Miriam asked.

Ava responded, "Yes, I am very curious about what you have up your sleeve." She kissed her on the cheek and walked down to the tree.

Miriam opened the rear hatch and retrieved the picnic basket, blanket, wrapped gift, and envelope. Then, she carefully descended the slope to the willow tree, where Ava was waiting.

Ava squealed, "We're having a picnic by the lake!"

Miriam flashed a smile and confirmed, "We're having a picnic by the lake." She set the basket and gift down, then spread the blanket. She then invited Ava to sit down, and Ava obliged.

Miriam handed Ava her gift and an envelope. "Please open the envelope first, " she said. Ava carefully opened the envelope and withdrew a poem Miriam had written.

The poem was written on a sheet of creamy, textured paper with a subtle deckle edge reminiscent of handmade paper. The stationery featured a delicate, laser-cut design along the borders, with intricate floral patterns and intertwined vines.

The calligraphy was done in a beautiful cursive script with varying line widths and flourishes, adding an extra layer of elegance and sophistication. The ink was a deep, rich blue that perfectly complemented the creamy paper.

At the top of the page, a delicate, hand-drawn illustration of a porch swing surrounded by vines and flowers added a touch of whimsy and romance. The illustration was done in matching blue ink, with subtle shading and texture giving it a sense of depth and dimensionality.

Ava studied the sheet, taking in all of the details, and then Miriam recited the poem she had crafted aloud.

"My love, my heart, my shining star,
  You light the way, near and far.
  In your eyes, my soul finds rest,
  With you, my love, I am forever blessed.

"Your brushstrokes dance upon the page,
  A symphony of color, a wondrous stage.
  Your art, a reflection of your beautiful soul,
  A glimpse into the depths that make me whole.

"With every swing of our porch swing's gentle sway,
  I'm reminded of the love we share each day.
  The vines that bind it, like our love, so strong,
  A symbol of our hearts, where love belongs.

"Ava, my love, you are my everything,
  My partner, friend, and guiding light that sings.

I promise to cherish, support, and adore, for certain,
Forever and always, my love, my heart, my person.”

Miriam finished reciting the poem, her eyes moist with tears. Ava's cheeks were wet from tears as well. “Oh, Miri, my heart… oh, it's beautiful. I love it.”

Miriam smiled warmly as she handed her the box. “And here's the last part of what I've planned. I hope you like it.” Ava gently unwrapped the box, carefully opened it, and audibly gasped.

She withdrew a small sculpture of their porch swing, crafted from white resin shaded with light gray. Instead of chains, delicate, hand-painted vines and leaves suspended the swing. Tiny, intricately crafted pink resin flowers dotted the vines, adding a beautiful pop of color to the sculpture.

“Oh, Miri, love, this is exquisite! This is absolutely stunning. Thank you, I love it.”

“We spend so much time there, some of our most intimate moments, some of our most important ones. It's my favorite place to spend in the entire world with you. Happy birthday.”

Ava gently placed the sculpture back into the box and crawled over to Miriam. She took her hands in hers and said, “Miriam Dawn Ryder, you are the poet of my heart, the artist of my soul. Your words, your gift, they mean everything to me. You've captured the essence of our love, of our moments together, in a way that's both deeply personal and universally relatable.

“I'm overwhelmed with emotion, Miri, because I feel seen, I feel heard, I feel loved. You've given me a piece of yourself, a piece of our love, that I will treasure forever.

“This sculpture, this poem, they're not just gifts – they're a reminder of the beauty, the joy, and the love that we share. You're the sunshine that brightens every day, the calm in every storm, and the safe haven where I can always be myself.

"I love you, Miriam, with all my heart, with every fiber of my being. Happy us, happy love, happy life – together, forever, and always."

Miriam looked deeply into Ava's eyes and responded, "Always."

Chapter 31: Missing Pieces

Miriam was home alone, Ava was at work, and summer vacation was over. She was sitting on her porch swing, enjoying a cigarette and the fresh air. She'd grown so accustomed to Ava's constant presence over the summer that these half days with her had led to mild depression.

She thought about her friends. It was Wednesday, August 21. Eli would be at Trailblazer Comics, but Wednesday is new comic book day, so she thought better of going to see him that day. The fall semester had yet to start, so Noah was at home in Richmond. Jules had graduated and had gotten a job in North Carolina. She made the decision to go see Di.

She grabbed her things and drove to the Jasper Hill Cafe. She felt like a bad friend because she hadn't seen Di in a few weeks, but she and Ava went to spend some time with Ava's family before school started again. She knew Di would understand, but it didn't change the fact that she felt terrible.

Di was delighted to see her. "Miriam, it's so good to see you, hun! How was Richmond?

Miriam took her favorite barstool by the front window and replied, "It was wonderful! Ava's parents are so generous and thoughtful. They took us to dinner and to some museums, and we went to a play and took a trip to Monticello. We also went to Williamsburg and other historical sites like Jamestown and Yorktown. They gave us a dose of culture, history, and fun. I'm glad to be back home, though."

"Well, we're glad you're home, too. So, how are things between you and Ava? It seems pretty serious. Just how serious are we talking?"

Miriam blushed, "Di, she's my world. I can't see a life without her. Nor do I want a life without her."

"So, ask her to marry you."

"What?" Miriam stammered, "I... I... I... "

"Miriam, hun, anyone with eyes can see it. You two are it for each other. Ask anybody. Hell, ask Rachel there."

Miriam spun around to see Rachel Lee enter the cafe. She waved her over to the stool next to hers. Rachel sat down and said, "Ask me what?"

Di chuckled, "Should Miri ask Ava to get married?"

Rachel turned to Miriam. "You haven't yet? What's wrong with you?"

Miriam replied, "I've never thought about it before. We're just... we're just... "

"Perfect together? Ask her, you silly girl. She's probably dying for you to ask."

"You think so?" Miriam's mind was racing, her heart pounding. Miriam heard Alex's voice in her head: *Do it, Miri. Propose.* It terrified her, but it made perfect sense. She should do it.

"You two are right. I should ask her. After all, she's my person. I don't want anything more in this world than to spend my life with her."

Di smiled, "I gotta go take some orders. I'll be back."

Rachel asked, "Are you doing ok? No more harassment from the Harris duo?"

"Not a peep. I guess a guardian angel told them to leave me alone."

Rachel responded, "More like a guardian marshal. Word is that

Thompson came down hard on Sheriff Harris. You're off limits to him."

"That's a relief. I'll have to thank him."

She took two menus and handed Rachel one. After a minute, she decided on a patty melt. She asked Rachel, "Have you heard anything about the case? It's been seven weeks since I had to go to Pittsburgh, and I've heard nothing from anyone."

Rachel shook her head, "Not one bit. I may be your handler, but I'm usually not privy to investigation details unless there's a direct threat to you."

"Can you come over to the house after your shift? I was wanting to tell you about something that's been bothering me since Pittsburgh."

"Sure, I'll —" Her phone chimed an alarm. "Shit, I gotta go... Buy her a ring!"

Rachel left the cafe to handle whatever her alarm was about.

After Miriam enjoyed her lunch, she started getting curious about engagement rings. She had no idea what style Ava would even want. She made a mental note to ask Sophia and Ryan the next time she talked to them.

Miriam climbed into her car, lit a cigarette, and drove home. It was only 1:23 p.m. Sophia and Ryan were working. She wanted to talk to them, and that's all she could think about now: Mrs. and Mrs. Ryder. Or would it be Mrs. and Mrs. McCormick? *I don't care which. I just want to marry her and build a life with her.*

She pulled into her driveway and got on the porch when she saw a note affixed to the door. She looked at it and saw it was a religious publication called The Watchtower. Her body relaxed, and she went inside and tossed the copy of The Watchtower into the garbage. She then started some coffee.

What Miriam didn't see was that someone had scrawled a message on The Watchtower that read, *"I KNOW WHO YOU ARE!"*

After dinner, Miriam and Ava were sitting on the porch swing, enjoying coffee and cigarettes. Ava was telling Miriam all about her day. "Ugh, I have the most obnoxious kid in my first class. I don't know what to do." She continued, "He's disruptive, plays dumb, talks over others, and refuses to listen. It's like he wants to be the center of attention at all times."

"I was that way as a kid," Miriam said. "I had a shitty childhood; I've said as much, but I never could pinpoint why. Sure, my parents were awful people that shouldn't have been allowed to breed, but it goes beyond that. Like, I should have been happy to be away from them at school. But I wasn't."

Ava inhaled after a long drag from her cigarette. "Why do you think that?" she said, taking Miriam's hand.

"I honestly believe it boils down to my gender dysphoria. I wasn't happy in my own body. I didn't know how to be a boy, and I knew I was a girl. So, I copied the behavior of other boys and upped the intensity. I overcompensated in presenting as to what I thought a male was supposed to be so much that I overshot and landed in jackass territory."

"I wonder if your parents ever think about you? Like, how can you go twelve years without talking to your kid?"

"I stopped caring years ago. I know what a real family is now, thanks to you. And I don't want that from my own 'family.'"

Headlights were approaching the driveway, and Miriam reminded Ava that she had told Rachel to come by. Rachel came up on the porch and said hello.

"So, Miri, what did you want to tell me about Pittsburgh?"

With help from Ava, Miriam recounted the events of their trip to Pittsburgh, including the sighting of Francesca Bianchi, Leo's notebook, who called 911, and why she was never questioned after regaining consciousness. Rachel was very deliberate with her answer.

"Francesca Bianchi is missing. No one knows her current location, and no one has seen her in weeks."

Ava asked, "Did her family not report her missing?"

Miriam replied, "She didn't have any family, just Alex and Leo. Now Alex is dead, and Leo's in jail awaiting trial along with Mario and Marco De Luca."

Ava inquired further, "If no one reported her missing, then how is she 'missing'? That doesn't add up."

Rachel responded, "Because earlier today, the US Marshal Service executed a search warrant on Francesca Bianchi's home, they found no trace of her. But they found Leo Rossi's green notebook. And Miri, your name is all over it."

"That's great news! This proves that they were running an illegal gambling operation and ties my debt of $100,000 to the notebook, Leo, the De Lucas... this could go to actual trial very soon. Couldn't it? I could finally get out of witness protection! Ava and I could—" Miriam stopped herself short. She almost said 'get married'.

Ava's eyes sparkled with excitement, and she grasped Miriam's hand. "This is amazing news, Miri! We could finally have a normal life."

Rachel's expression was more cautious. "Let's not get ahead of ourselves. While the discovery of the notebook is a significant development, there's still a lot of work to be done before this case goes to trial."

Miriam's enthusiasm was undiminished. "But this is huge, Rachel! The notebook ties everything together. I could finally get out of witness protection and start fresh."

Rachel nodded thoughtfully. "I understand why you're excited, Miri. But we need to be careful. Call AUSA Miller in the morning and see what she says."

Miriam nodded, still grinning from ear to ear. "I'll call her first thing tomorrow. Thanks, Rachel, for letting us know about the notebook.

This could be the break we need to finally put this all behind us.”

Ava squeezed Miriam's hand, her eyes shining with happiness. “We could finally have a life together, Miri. A real life, without all the secrets and hiding.”

Miriam's smile softened, and she leaned in to kiss Ava's forehead. “We'll get there, Ava. I promise.”

The following day, Miriam called AUSA Amanda Miller to get an update on the case. “This is AUSA Amanda Miller.”

“Hi Amanda, it's Miriam Ryder. Could you give me an update on the case proceedings?”

“Yes, Miriam, I was just about to call you. They recovered Leo Rossi's green notebook yesterday. Everything you told us lined up. It's the nail we needed against Leo Rossi and the De Luca family.”

“What does this mean for the trial? Will it move things along much quicker?”

AUSA Amanda Miller's tone was optimistic. “The recovery of Leo Rossi's green notebook is a significant development in the case. Since everything you told us lined up, it's clear that we have a strong case against Leo Rossi and the De Luca family.”

Regarding the trial, AUSA Miller explained that the notebook's discovery would likely accelerate the proceedings. “With this new evidence, we can move forward with confidence. I'd say we're looking at a much quicker trial timeline now.”

Miriam's excitement was palpable. “That's amazing news, Amanda. I'm so relieved that the notebook was found. Does this mean I'll be able to testify soon?”

AUSA Miller reassured her. “We'll be in touch soon to discuss the next steps, Miriam. Your testimony will be crucial in bringing Leo Rossi and the De Luca family to justice.”

“What about the disappearance of Francesca Bianchi? The notebook was in her house, correct?"

AUSA Miller's tone turned more serious. "Yes, that's correct. The notebook was found in Francesca Bianchi's residence. As for her disappearance, we're still investigating. The US Marshal Service is working closely with local law enforcement to try to locate her."

Miriam's curiosity was piqued. "Do you think her disappearance is connected to the case against Leo Rossi and the De Luca family?"

AUSA Miller hesitated for a moment before responding. "We're exploring all possible connections, Miriam. But at this point, it's too early to say for certain. We need to find Francesca Bianchi and get to the bottom of her disappearance before we can draw any conclusions."

Miriam pressed on, her mind racing with possibilities. "But what about the fact that Francesca Bianchi was seen in Pittsburgh, and then she just disappeared? Doesn't that seem suspicious?"

AUSA Miller's tone remained cautious. "We're aware of the sighting in Pittsburgh, Miriam. And yes, her disappearance does raise some red flags. But we need to be careful not to jump to conclusions. We'll continue to investigate and follow up on any leads."

"Are Ava and I in danger?"

AUSA Miller's tone became grave. "Miriam, I want to assure you that we're taking all necessary precautions to ensure your and Ava's safety. However, given the circumstances, it's possible that you both could be at risk. We'll be increasing security measures for you both, and I recommend that you be extra vigilant and report anything suspicious to us at once."

"All right, Amanda. We will. Thank you. I appreciate everything you and your office have done for us."

"You're welcome, Miriam. I'll be in touch soon." AUSA Miller ended the call.

"Well, Ava dear, we're going to be getting increased security measures, whatever that means. Ugh. I just want this to be over so we can—" Miriam stopped herself.

Ava's eyes sparkled with curiosity, and she leaned in, her voice barely above a whisper. "So we can what, Miri? You were going to say something."

Miriam matched Ava's voice level. "So we can have a normal life together, " she said. She took Ava into her arms and kissed her passionately.

Miriam and Ava were so caught up in the moment that neither noticed the glint of sunlight in the woods across the bridge from their house.

Chapter 32: A Mother's Guilt

After an intense moment of passion between the two, Miriam said, "I need to call Marshal Thompson and ask about these increased security measures."

Ava nodded and said, "Put it on speaker. I want to hear this." Miriam dialed Marshal Thompson's number. He answered promptly.

"US Marshal Arthur M. Thompson speaking."

"Good morning, Marshal Thompson. It's Miriam Ryder. I just wanted to touch base with you. I just spoke with AUSA Miller, and she said Francesca Bianchi was missing. As a precaution, Ava and I will be receiving increased security measures. What would that entail, precisely?"

Marshal Thompson's voice was firm and reassuring. "Good morning, Miriam. Yes, we're taking extra precautions to ensure your safety and Ava's. The increased security measures will include a rotating team of marshals keeping an eye on your residence, as well as regular check-ins with you both. We'll also be increasing surveillance in the area and monitoring any potential threats."

Ava spoke up, her voice clear and concerned. "Marshal Thompson, what kind of threats are we talking about? What's going on with Francesca Bianchi's disappearance?"

Marshal Thompson's tone turned grave. "To be honest, we're not entirely sure what's going on with Francesca Bianchi's disappearance.

But we do know that her connection to Leo Rossi and the De Luca family makes her a potentially crucial witness. And that makes her a target. We're doing everything we can to find her and bring her to safety."

"When you say she's a target, a target for whom, exactly?"

Marshal Thompson's voice was measured and deliberate. "We believe that Francesca Bianchi may be a target for the De Luca family, possibly even Leo Rossi himself. Given her connection to them and her potential to testify against them, it's likely that they'll stop at nothing to silence her. And if that happens, and if they find out that she's cooperating with us... well, let's just say that her life would be in grave danger."

"I see. Marshal, how soon can we expect the marshals to be here to keep an eye on our house?"

"They're already on their way, Miriam," Marshal Thompson replied. "You can expect to see a team of marshals arriving within the hour. They'll be keeping a discreet eye on your residence and the surrounding area. Just remember, if you notice anything suspicious or out of the ordinary, don't hesitate to reach out to me or the marshals on duty."

"Okay, Marshal, we'll keep our eyes open. Thank you, sir."

"You're welcome, Miriam. Remember, your safety is our top priority. And Miriam?" Marshal Thompson added, his tone serious. "Be careful, okay?" Thompson ended the call.

Ava looked hopeful, "So we've got an hour. Wanna go fool around?"

"You bet your sweet bottom, I do."

Ava and Miriam were exhausted. They were both sweating and breathing heavily, their bodies weak from the act they had just performed. Ava said, "I'm gonna go start fresh coffee. See you on the porch?"

"I'll be right behind you. Let me put my leg back on."

Ava kissed her as she got out of bed, got dressed, and exited the room to go downstairs. Miriam also dressed and then pulled her prosthetic on. Because she was sweaty, the gripping sleeve didn't create a tight vacuum seal against her thigh. *I'll have to be extra careful going down the stairs.*

As she descended the stairs, a sense of unease prickled at the back of her neck, but not from her prosthetic not being secured. The moment her eyes reached the living room, she froze, her breath hitching in her throat. There, in the center of the room, stood Francesca Bianchi—the woman who had been missing.

Francesca's face was pale but resolute, her trembling hand clutching a gun aimed directly at Ava, who stood motionless, wide-eyed with terror. The air seemed to crackle with tension, and time slowed as the weight of the situation pressed down like a suffocating fog. Ava trembled with terror, and tears streamed silently down her face. She looked at Miriam and said, "I love you."

Miriam's heart skipped a beat, then seemed to stop. Alex's mother was holding the love of her life at gunpoint in their living room. She struggled to find her voice, then finally said, "Mrs. Bianchi, what... what are you doing here?"

Francesca Bianchi spoke, her voice even and tempered at first but with apparent anger behind it. "I'm here to get revenge on the man responsible for my son's death. I'm here for you, Gabe, and I am going to take everything away from you."

"Mrs. Bianchi, I wasn't responsible for Alex's death. He was an innocent victim. He was my best friend, and I am very sorry that he died." *Holy hell, how is she here?*

Francesca Bianchi's expression twisted in rage, her voice rising to a near-shriek. "Don't lie to me! I know all about you. I've been following you for weeks. You two talk very openly out here. It's easy to learn things... your voices carry. I know about your little testimony and how you're going to send Leo and the De Lucas to prison. You think you're so smart, don't you? But you're not smart, Gabe. You're dead." She took a step closer to Ava, the gun still trained on her. "And you're going to die too, just like Alex did."

Miriam's eyes locked onto the weapon, her mind racing with thoughts of how to get Ava to safety. She took a slow step forward, trying not to make any sudden movements. "Mrs. Bianchi, please. Don't hurt Ava. She has nothing to do with this." *Think, Miriam, think.*

Francesca Bianchi's gaze flickered to Miriam, her eyes blazing with a fierce intensity. "You think you can protect her? You think you can save her from me?" She took another step closer to Ava, the gun still trained on her. "I've lost everything because of you. My son, my family, my reputation. You've taken everything from me, and now it's time for you to pay."

Miriam's heart was racing, her mind desperate to find a way to defuse the situation. She took another slow step forward, her hands held out in a calming gesture. "Mrs. Bianchi, please. Listen to me. I'm not Gabe. Not anymore. I'm Miriam. I've been in witness protection this whole time. I didn't kill Alex. Leo Rossi did." *I've got to get the gun. She can't hurt Ava.*

Francesca Bianchi's expression faltered for a moment, a flicker of confusion crossing her face. She looked at Miriam, really looked at her, for the first time. And in that moment, Miriam saw a glimmer of doubt in her eyes. "No," Francesca Bianchi whispered, her voice trembling. "That's not possible. You look like Gabe. I know it's you." But the conviction was gone from her voice, replaced by a hesitant uncertainty.

Ava, sensing the shift in Francesca's demeanor, spoke up in a soft, gentle voice. "Mrs. Bianchi, please. Listen to Miriam. She's telling the truth. She didn't kill Alex. Leo Rossi did."

Please, Ava, don't draw attention to yourself; let me keep her focused on me.

Francesca Bianchi's eyes darted back and forth between Miriam and

Ava, her face a picture of turmoil. She seemed to be struggling to reconcile the truth with her own twisted perceptions. The gun in her hand wavered, and for a moment, Miriam thought she saw a glimmer of hope. But then Francesca's face hardened, and she took a step closer to Miriam. "No," she spat, her voice venomous. "I won't be fooled. You're just trying to trick me. You're Gabe, and you're going to pay for what you did to my son."

Miriam's heart sank as she watched Francesca's face contort with rage. She knew she had to think fast to find a way to calm Francesca down and defuse the situation. She took a slow step forward, her hands held out in a calming gesture. "Mrs. Bianchi, please," she said, her voice soft and gentle. "You're not thinking clearly. You're grieving and angry, and I don't blame you. But I'm not Gabe any longer. I'm Miriam. I transitioned. And I'm telling you the truth. Leo Rossi killed Alex, not me."

Ava spoke up again, her voice firm but gentle. "Mrs. Bianchi, we can prove it. We can show you the evidence. Please, just listen to us." Miriam's mind was racing. *What do I do, Alex?*

Miriam began to speak again, but she heard Alex's voice in her mind. *It was her, Miri. She called 911 that night. You know it was her. Remember!* Then something in her mind clicked as if a light switch turned on. She remembered. She remembered the frantic 911 call. And she remembered who made it.

Alex continued. *Why was she so insistent that I stay away from you? You don't think? No, not Ma, it couldn't have been her...could it?* It was time to try a different approach. *Alex, I'm going to try something. Okay Miri, please be right. Please let this work.*

Miriam's eyes locked onto Francesca's, a sense of determination burning within her. "Mrs. Bianchi, I've been wondering for a long time who could have sent those men to attack me that night. And I think I finally have my answer."

Francesca's expression faltered, a flicker of fear dancing in her eyes. "What are you talking about?" she spat, but her voice was laced with a hint of desperation.

Miriam took another step forward, her voice firm. "I'm talking about the fact that maybe you're the one who sent those men to attack me. You're the one who wanted me left alive but broken. Because you thought I was a bad influence on Alex."

Ava's eyes widened in shock as she stared at Francesca, her face pale. "Oh my god," she whispered. Francesca's face contorted in rage, but Miriam could see the guilt lurking beneath the surface.

"You'll never be able to prove it," Francesca snarled. But Miriam just smiled a cold, hard smile.

"Actually, I think I can. You see, I finally remember the 911 call that night. The voice coming from above my broken body was a woman's. And I think that woman was you."

Francesca's eyes went wide, her face draining of color. "How did you...?" she whispered, "no... no, my boy...."

Miriam's voice was relentless. "You wanted me left alive but broken. Because you thought I was a bad influence on Alex. But you didn't know that Alex was with me that night. And he died because of your actions."

Francesca's face crumpled in sorrow, and she took a step back, the gun wavering in her hand. "No," she whispered, her voice barely audible. "Alex... I didn't know Alex was there. I didn't mean for him to get hurt."

Miriam's eyes narrowed, her voice cold. "You didn't mean for him to get hurt? You sent men to attack me, to break me. And you didn't care who got caught in the crossfire. You're just as guilty as Leo Rossi."

Francesca's eyes filled with tears, and she looked at Miriam with a mixture of grief and shame. "I was only trying to protect Alex," she whispered. "Leo told me to orchestrate the attack, and I was happy to do it. I thought you were a bad influence on Alex. I didn't know..."

Her voice trailed off, and she looked at Ava, who was staring at her in horror. "I'm so sorry," Francesca whispered, her voice barely audible.

"Mrs. Bianchi, Alex was my best friend. My only friend. I cared for him very much. He was the first person to learn about my wanting to transition. I told him minutes before the attack. He was confused but supportive. Alex didn't have a hint of malice or ill intent in his body. He was a fiercely loyal friend, and he tried to save me that night."

Francesca's face contorted in anguish as she listened to Miriam's words. She looked like she had been punched in the gut, her eyes wide with shock and grief. She took a step back, the gun still clutched in her hand, but her grip had loosened. "Oh, Alex," she whispered, her voice cracking with emotion. "My baby. I'm so sorry. I had no idea." She looked up at Miriam, tears streaming down her face. "You're telling me that Alex... that he knew about you? And he was supportive?"

Miriam nodded, her eyes filled with tears. "Yes, Mrs. Bianchi. Alex was an amazing person. He didn't care about my transition. He only cared about me."

Francesca's face crumpled, and she let out a wail of grief. The gun fell from her hand, and she collapsed to the floor, sobbing uncontrollably.

As Francesca Bianchi sobbed on the floor, she began to confess as if to plead with Miriam. "When I saw Alex, I called 911. I knew he was gone, but I had hoped they could have done something, anything. I knew they would try to save you, too. I then realized that Leo would likely pin the attack on me, so I called in an anonymous tip from Alex's phone and told the police that Leo Rossi had ordered the attack. I'm sorry... I'm so sorry... my boy." She added, "You should have died instead of my Alex."

Ava hurriedly moved forward to kick the gun away from Mrs. Bianchi, then rushed to Miriam's side, wrapping her arms around her in a tight hug. "Oh, baby, I'm so sorry," she whispered, tears streaming down her own face. Miriam held her close, her eyes fixed on Francesca's broken form on the floor. She felt a mix of emotions: sadness, anger, and a deep sense of loss. She knew that Francesca's actions had been motivated by a twisted desire to protect her son, but that didn't excuse the harm she had caused. As they stood there, frozen in a moment of raw emotion, Miriam heard the sound of sirens outside. The police had arrived, responding to a call that Miriam hadn't even realized had been made.

She looked at Ava, who nodded, "I dialed 911 and just let dispatch listen to the conversation. The phone's in my back pocket." Together, they waited for the officers to enter the house, their eyes fixed on Francesca's broken form on the floor.

The sirens grew closer and louder, and soon, the house was filled with the sound of footsteps and voices. Miriam and Ava stood frozen, their eyes fixed on Francesca as the police officers entered the room.

One of the officers, a tall, imposing figure with a kind face, approached Miriam and Ava. "Ma'am, are you two okay?" he asked, his voice gentle. Miriam nodded, still holding onto Ava.

"Yes, we're fine. But she..." Miriam gestured to Francesca, who was still sobbing on the floor. The officer's expression turned grim, and he nodded to one of his colleagues.

"We'll take care of her," he said. "Can you tell me what happened here?" Miriam took a deep breath, trying to process the events of the past few minutes. She looked at Ava, who nodded encouragingly. And then, in a calm, clear voice, Miriam began to tell the officer everything.

Miriam's words spilled out in a rush, telling the officer about Francesca's arrival, the gun, and the shocking revelation that Francesca, on Leo's orders, had been behind the attack that killed Alex. The officer listened intently, his expression growing graver with each passing moment. When Miriam finished speaking, the officer nodded thoughtfully.

"I see," he said. "We'll need to take Mrs. Bianchi into custody. And we'll need to get statements from both of you." He glanced at Ava, who nodded in agreement. The officer turned to one of his colleagues, a younger officer with a notebook. "Take Mrs. Bianchi outside and read her her rights. We'll book her for attempted murder and conspiracy to commit murder."

The younger officer nodded and gently helped Francesca to her feet, leading her out of the house in handcuffs. As they left, Miriam felt a sense of closure wash over her. It was finally over. The truth was out, and justice would be served. She turned to Ava, who wrapped her arms around her in a tight hug. "It's over," Ava whispered. "We're safe now."

"Not yet." Miriam said, "There's still the trial of Leo Rossi and the De Lucas."

Ava's expression turned serious, and she nodded in understanding. "You're right," she said. "We're not done yet. But we'll get through it together, okay?" Miriam nodded, feeling a sense of determination wash over her. She knew that the trial would be difficult, but she was ready to face it head-on.

She took a deep breath, steeling herself for what was to come. "Let's do this," she said, her voice firm.

Ava smiled, her eyes shining with pride. "That's my girl," she said, squeezing Miriam's hand.

Thank you, Alex. We're safe. Thank you.

Chapter 33: Aftermath

"How did she find you, Miri, love?" Ava sat on the porch swing, taking a long drag from her cigarette.

Miriam did the same. "Maybe Rachel will know, here she comes."

As they waited for Rachel and their heart rates returned to normal, they surveyed the scene. There were four US Marshals there, along with two state troopers and six county police officers, including Sheriff Harris and Deputy Bubba Harris.

Rachel had been speaking with Sheriff Harris, the state troopers, and the lead US Marshal on the scene. "Rachel, do they know how she found us?"

"She's not talking. We can only speculate right now, and it's best not to do so."

"What happens now? Will Ava and I be moved?"

Rachel's expression turned serious, her eyes locked on Miriam's. "We'll need to discuss that with Marshal Thompson, but it's likely that you both will be relocated to a new safe house. We can't take any chances, not after what happened today."

Ava nodded, taking another drag from her cigarette. "I'm ready to go wherever as long as Miri is safe."

Miriam smiled, feeling a surge of love for Ava. "I feel the same way about you, Ava."

Rachel's expression softened, and she smiled. "I'll make sure to let Marshal Thompson know that. In the meantime, let's get you both packed up and ready to move, just in case. We need to regroup and figure out our next steps."

As Rachel turned to leave, Miriam called out to her. "Rachel, what about Francesca Bianchi? What will happen to her?"

Rachel's expression turned grim. "She'll be charged with attempted murder, conspiracy to commit murder, and a host of other charges. She'll likely spend the rest of her life in prison."

Miriam nodded, feeling a sense of closure wash over her. This part was finally over. Justice would be served. "Can I call Marshal Thompson right now?"

"Yes, go ahead." Rachel nodded.

Miriam dialed Marshal Thompson, and he answered immediately. "US Marshal Arthur M. Thompson speaking."

Miriam took a deep breath before she started, "Marshal, it's Miriam Ryder again. Francesca Bianchi showed up at our house and held us at gunpoint. During the encounter, I remembered her voice was the one who called 911 the night of the attack. She confessed she ordered the men to attack me that night. She's the one that had her own son killed."

Marshal Thompson's voice was calm and collected, but Miriam could sense a hint of surprise and outrage beneath the surface. "Miriam, I'm going to need you to stay calm and stay safe. Can you confirm that Francesca Bianchi is currently in custody?"

Miriam nodded, even though Marshal Thompson couldn't see her. "Yes, Marshal. The police and US Marshals are here. They've taken her into custody."

Marshal Thompson's voice turned firm. "Good. I'm on my way; in the meantime, I'm going to have my team take statements from you and Ava. We'll need to get to the bottom of this and build a case against

Francesca Bianchi. Can you and Ava stay available for the next few hours?"

Miriam glanced over at Ava, who nodded in agreement. "Yes, Marshal. We'll stay available. Are we going to be relocated because of this?"

Marshal Thompson's voice was thoughtful. "That's a good question, Miriam. Given the circumstances, I think it's likely that we'll need to relocate you and Ava to a new safe house. Francesca Bianchi's actions have compromised the security of your current location, and we can't take any chances. I'll discuss it with my team, and we'll make a decision soon. But for now, let's focus on getting your statements and building a case against Francesca Bianchi."

"Alright, Marshal, we'll see you later this evening. Would you like us to make dinner?"

Marshal Thompson's voice was warm and appreciative. "That's very kind of you, Miriam. But don't worry about cooking dinner for me. I'll grab something on the way. Just focus on taking care of yourselves and getting some rest. It's been a long day."

Each department of law enforcement on-site spent the next couple of hours taking statements from Miriam and Ava. Once they had taken statements, all but the team of marshals left. Mrs. Bianchi was taken to the county jail, and Miriam and Ava finally were able to relax and feel safe. After the day's events, they were okay with armed expert sharpshooters keeping surveillance.

Marshal Thompson arrived in person at 4:00 p.m. He was greeted by Miriam and Ava, who were sitting on their porch swing, holding hands.

Marshal Thompson smiled warmly as he approached the porch, his eyes crinkling at the corners. "Ladies, it's good to see you're both doing okay after today's ordeal." He nodded in approval as he took in the scene of Miriam and Ava holding hands on the porch swing. "I'm glad to see you're taking care of each other." He paused, his expression turning serious. "I have some updates to share with you both. Why don't we go inside and sit down?"

Miriam and Ava exchanged a glance, then nodded in unison. They stood up, still holding hands, and led Marshal Thompson into the house. They settled into the living room, Miriam and Ava sitting together on the couch, with Marshal Thompson taking the armchair across from them. Marshal Thompson leaned forward, his elbows on his knees.

"First, I want to assure you both that Francesca Bianchi is being held without bail. She'll be facing a slew of federal charges, including attempted murder and conspiracy to commit murder." He paused, studying their reactions. "I also want to let you know that we're increasing security measures around you both. We'll have a team of marshals keeping a close eye on the house and the surrounding area."

"We're not going to be moved?" Miriam asked hopefully.

Ava added, "What precisely will these increased security measures entail, Marshal Thompson?"

Marshal Thompson nodded understandingly at Miriam's question. "Actually, Miriam, I'm pleased to tell you that you both can stay here. This location has already been compromised, so moving you now would only cause unnecessary disruption. Instead, we'll focus on beefing up security around the house and the perimeter." He turned to Ava, his expression serious. "As for the increased security measures, Ava, we'll have a team of at least four marshals stationed around the clock, keeping watch on the house and the surrounding area. We'll also install additional surveillance cameras and motion sensors to provide an extra layer of protection. Furthermore, we'll have a secure communication system set up so you both can quickly reach us if you need anything."

"What about our movements? Can we go to town, get groceries and food, go to the comic shop, can Ava go to work, and can we have visitors?" Miriam was hoping not to have too many disruptions in their lives.

Marshal Thompson nodded thoughtfully, considering Miriam's questions. "For the time being, I'm afraid there will be some limitations on your movements. We'll need to coordinate any trips to town or other outings with our security team. They'll provide escorts and ensure your safety while you're out. As for groceries and food, we can arrange for deliveries or have our team pick up essentials for you."

He turned to Ava. "Regarding your work, Ava, we'll need to discuss arrangements with your employer. It's possible we can set up a secure remote work arrangement or provide escorts to and from work." He paused, considering the final question. "As for visitors, I'm afraid that will be strictly limited for the time being. We'll need to vet anyone who wants to visit and ensure they're not a security risk."

"Would visitors know about my WITSEC status? How's that going to work, Marshal? This is a tiny town. Wouldn't everyone learn about me being under protection?"

Marshal Thompson's expression turned serious, and he leaned forward slightly. "That's a valid concern, Miriam. To answer your question, no visitors will be informed about your WITSEC status. We'll need to come up with a cover story to explain the increased security presence around your home and the need for vetted visitors." He paused, collecting his thoughts.

"As for the townspeople, we'll work to keep your WITSEC status confidential. However, it's possible that some people might become suspicious or curious about the increased security. We'll need to be prepared to address any rumors or speculation that might arise." He looked at Miriam and Ava reassuringly. "But please be assured, we'll do everything in our power to protect your identities and keep your WITSEC status confidential."

The couple nodded. Ava said, "We can still go outside, right? Can we enjoy our porch time together? Considering we have a team watching out for our safety."

Marshal Thompson smiled, seeming to understand the importance of small comforts. "Absolutely, Ava. You both can still enjoy your porch time together. In fact, our team will be stationed discreetly around the property so you can still have some sense of normalcy and freedom. Just remember to stay within the designated safe zones and follow any instructions from our team. We want to ensure your safety while still allowing you to enjoy your home and each other's company."

A wave of gratitude and relief washed over them. Miriam asked again, "Marshal, are you sure you don't want to stay for dinner?" Ava chimed in, "We're making fried chicken."

Marshal Thompson's face lit up with a warm smile. "No shit? Fried chicken, you say? Well, I'm afraid I'm going to have to accept your hospitality this time. It's been a long day, and a home-cooked meal sounds like just what I need. Thank you, ladies. I'd be delighted to join you for dinner."

The next day, a tech team of marshals arrived to install additional security cameras, motion sensors, and a secure direct communications system. Miriam was impressed with their speed and efficiency during the installation. It took her the better part of a day to install her eight cameras, and she nearly fell off a ladder four times. This team was done in under two hours.

The communications system was identical to the one at the safe house in Pittsburgh, so Miriam and Ava were familiar with it. The tech team integrated Miriam's existing cameras into the surveillance system, so she now had sixteen cameras she could check. In addition, a series of motion sensors was arranged at strategic points on the property.

Ava felt a massive rush of relief. Being held hostage with her life threatened had left her rattled, so the increased safety precautions went a long way to ease her nerves. She turned to Miriam and said, "You know, with all these extra cameras and these men stationed around the property, you're going to have to keep your clothes on. No more smoking outside in your underwear." She wrapped her arms around Miriam and playfully added, "I don't want them distracted from keeping us safe."

"I promise I'll get dressed every morning before coming downstairs." Miriam knew Ava was scared from the standoff with Mrs. Bianchi, and she was too. She didn't want to be the reason a marshal was distracted and risked their safety. *If Francesca found me, who else knows I'm here? And how did she fucking find me? What did I do wrong?*

They had given a list of names of visitors to Marshal Thompson they hoped to have cleared. Eli Marley and Dianna Simmons. Miriam made a mental note to ask about the status of their potential clearance. She also wondered what the official cover story would be. As Ava went outside to the porch, Miriam decided to call Marshal Thompson while it was on her mind.

He answered the phone promptly, "This is US Marshal Thompson speaking."

"Hi, Marshal, it's Miriam Ryder. I was wondering about the status of our visitor requests for Eli Marley and Dianna Simmons. And do we have an official cover story established for my increased security around here?"

Marshal Thompson's voice was professional and friendly over the phone. "Ah, Miriam, good timing. I was just about to reach out to you with an update. We've completed the background checks on Eli Marley and Dianna Simmons, and both have been cleared for visits. We'll work with you to schedule a time that works for everyone."

He paused briefly before addressing Miriam's second question. "Regarding the cover story, we've decided to go with a narrative that you're a witness in a high-profile environmental case, and the increased security is a precautionary measure to ensure your safety due to potential retaliation from parties involved in the case."

"A high-profile environmental case? What, did I witness someone dig up a body that had an endangered plant species growing over it?"

Marshal Thompson chuckled on the other end of the line. "Well, Miriam, I'm glad you're taking this in stride. But, no, nothing quite that dramatic. We're keeping the details vague; we're just saying that you're a material witness in a case involving environmental crimes. That's all anyone needs to know. And, of course, it's not true, but it's a plausible enough cover story to explain the security presence around your home."

"So if anyone asks, I'm a material witness in a case against environmental crimes, and that's all Ava or I can say. Got it." She added, "What about Ava's job? She's an art teacher. Will she be allowed to return to work?"

"That's correct, Miriam. You and Ava can acknowledge that you're a material witness in an environmental crimes case, but you shouldn't provide any further details," Marshal Thompson confirmed.

"Regarding Ava's job," he said, "we've been in touch with the school administration, and we're working on a plan to ensure Ava's safety while she's at work. It's likely that we'll have a security presence at the school, at least for the time being. We'll also be providing Ava with some additional security protocols to follow while she's commuting to and from work."

"And just to make sure, the same cover story goes for Ava's parents, correct? We know we can't visit them, but could we get them on our visitor's list so they can see us?"

Marshal Thompson's response was measured. "Yes, the same cover story applies to Ava's parents, Miriam. It's essential to maintain consistency. As for them visiting you, I can definitely look into it.

However, I need to advise you that it's not a simple process. We'll need to conduct background checks on them, and they'll need to be briefed on the security protocols in place. If everything checks out, we can arrange for them to visit, but it will require some planning and coordination. Let me see what I can do, and I'll get back to you soon."

"That's wonderful news! Any feeling of normalcy really will be helpful. We're both really shaken up about this whole... well, shitshow with Francesca. I mean, what did I do wrong? How did she find me?"

Marshal Thompson's tone turned sympathetic. "Miriam, I want to assure you that you didn't do anything wrong. Francesca's actions are not a reflection of your mistakes but rather a testament to her desperation and determination. As for how she found you, we're still investigating, but it's possible that she had help from someone with access to sensitive information. We'll get to the bottom of it, I promise."

He paused, collecting his thoughts. "But for now, let's focus on keeping you and Ava safe. We'll work on re-establishing a sense of normalcy, and I'll make sure to keep you updated on any developments in the case."

"I actually do have one more crucial question." She looked around to make sure Ava wasn't within earshot. "I want to ask Ava to marry me. Obviously, we can't hold a wedding while I'm in WITSEC, but could I go ahead and propose to her?"

Marshal Thompson's tone softened, and he spoke in a gentle, conspiratorial manner. "Miriam, I think that's a wonderful idea. Proposing to Ava is a personal, intimate moment, and I don't see any reason why you shouldn't be able to do that. And I'm sure she'll accept, and who knows, maybe one day you'll be able to have that wedding you're dreaming of." He added, "I can't believe you haven't asked her yet."

That's as good as I could hope for, and Miriam was ecstatic. "Okay, sir.

Thank you so much for everything. Have a good day."

Marshal Thompson's warm tone lingered as he replied, "You're welcome, Miriam. It was my pleasure to help. I wish you all the best with your proposal, and I'm sure Ava will be thrilled. Take care, and don't hesitate to reach out if you need anything. Have a great day, and good luck!" The call ended with a sense of hope and excitement for Miriam's future with Ava.

Miriam let out a squeal as Ava entered from the front porch. "Who was that on the phone, love?"

Miriam smiled and said, "Marshal Thompson. Both Eli and Di are cleared for coordinated visits, and he's vetting your parents so they can visit us here. As for our cover story, the official word is that I'm a material witness in a high-profile environmental crimes case, and the security is for my safety." She kissed Ava gently. "And you can return to work Monday with a security escort and someone stationed at the school."

Ava's eyes widened with excitement as she processed the information. "That's amazing news, Miriam! I'm so relieved that Eli and Di are cleared to visit and that my parents might be able to come see us, too." She smiled, feeling a sense of hope and normalcy returning. "And I'm glad I can go back to work on Monday. I've missed my students and my routine." Ava's eyes sparkled with curiosity. "But what's going on? You seem... extra happy. Did Marshal Thompson say something else?"

"Oh, just that they're still investigating how Mrs. Bianchi found us, but she's being held without bail, so we should have nothing else to fear from her." *And that I can propose to you!* She thought, already planning the moment in her mind.

Ava's expression turned serious, and she nodded, seeming to process the information about Francesca Bianchi. "That's good to know. I'm just glad she's not a threat to us anymore." She looked at Miriam, her eyes softening. "I'm just glad we're safe, and we have each other." Ava leaned in, and Miriam met her halfway, sharing a gentle, loving kiss.

Chapter 34: Love's Sweet Surprise

ow am I going to do this? Miriam was trying to think of a romantic way to propose to Ava. She was staring at the shiny new engagement ring she had ordered online that had just been delivered. It was Thursday, August 29.

Miriam's eyes sparkled with excitement as she gazed at the engagement ring. She had been thinking about proposing to Ava for a while now, and finally, the perfect moment seemed within reach. But she wanted it to be unique, romantic, and memorable.

She began brainstorming ideas, her mind racing with possibilities. Should she plan a surprise dinner at a fancy restaurant, a sunset picnic in a beautiful spot, or a romantic getaway to a bed and breakfast?

As she thought, Miriam's eyes wandered around the room, taking in the cozy atmosphere of their home. She smiled, an idea beginning to form in her mind. Why not propose to Ava in their own special place, surrounded by the memories and love they had built together? The porch swing. No other place made sense.

With newfound determination, Miriam set to work planning the perfect proposal. She would make it a night to remember; one that would sweep Ava off her feet and leave her feeling loved and cherished. The engagement ring sparkled in her hand, a symbol of the commitment and love she was about to promise to Ava.

She decided to cook a delicious and romantic dinner for the two of them. She wanted a gorgeous lace tablecloth, candles, and champagne. She was determined to make it memorable. Now, what to make for dinner and dessert?

The details were falling into place! Miriam's mind was filled with visions of a candlelit dinner, the soft glow of the candles casting a warm ambiance over the table. The lace tablecloth would add a touch of elegance, and the champagne would be the perfect accompaniment to the meal.

Now, to decide on the menu. Miriam thought about Ava's favorite dishes, and her eyes lit up as she remembered Ava's weakness for Miriam's homemade lasagna. She would make a pan of it, filled with a decadent mix of cheeses and herbs, with a simple yet flavorful sauce made with fresh tomatoes and basil.

For dessert, Miriam knew exactly what to make. Ava had a sweet tooth, and Miriam's tiramisu was always a hit. The creamy mascarpone cheese, the espresso-soaked ladyfingers, and the rich chocolate would all combine to create a dessert that would leave Ava weak in the knees.

With the menu decided, Miriam felt a sense of excitement and anticipation. She couldn't wait to see the look on Ava's face when she walked into the dining room and saw the beautiful table setting, the delicious food, and the champagne chilling in the ice bucket. It was going to be a night to remember!

She made a shopping list and gave it to one of the marshals stationed outside. Miriam had discovered they were surprisingly efficient when it came to grocery shopping, and even though she missed going to the store herself, she didn't mind having everything brought to her. Now, she needed to pick an outfit for the night.

Miriam walked into her closet, scanning the rows of clothes, trying to decide on the perfect outfit for the evening. She wanted to look elegant and sophisticated yet still herself. She ran her fingers over the fabrics, considering her options.

Her eyes landed on a beautiful silk blouse in a deep, rich blue that complemented her eyes perfectly. She paired it with a pair of black trousers that fit her like a glove. The outfit was simple yet chic, and Miriam felt confident that she would look stunning.

She moved on to accessories, selecting a pair of elegant silver earrings and a simple yet stunning silver necklace. She would pair these with her favorite brown leather knee-high boots.

She went to shower while she waited for her groceries to arrive, her thoughts racing as she did. She was proposing to Ava tonight. She was determined to make it a memorable evening. She wanted everything to be perfect.

She finished her shower, toweled off, reassembled herself, and went to get dressed. As she finished getting dressed, Miriam took a step back to admire herself in the mirror. She felt like a million bucks, and she couldn't wait to see Ava's reaction when she walked into the dining room.

She would do her hair and makeup while the lasagna baked, she decided. She was delighted to discover when she went downstairs to see that her groceries had been delivered. She put the champagne in to chill and started preparing her tiramisu.

Once she finished the tiramisu, she began her prep for the lasagna, creating her homemade sauce first. While it simmered, she could focus on her other elements. After an hour, she placed the lasagna in the oven to bake.

She glanced at her phone, which showed that it was 2:30 p.m. Ava would be home in an hour, so she had just enough time to do her hair and makeup.

With the lasagna baking in the oven and the tiramisu chilling in the fridge, Miriam headed back upstairs to start getting ready. She sat down at her vanity, gazing at her reflection in the mirror. She took a deep breath, feeling a mix of excitement and nervousness. This was it, the moment she had been planning for.

She began by styling her hair, curling the ends, and sweeping it to one side. Then, she applied a light layer of makeup, enhancing her natural features without looking too done up. Finally, she finished off her look with a swipe of mascara and a dusting of powder.

Miriam's mind wandered to Ava as she worked on her hair and makeup. She couldn't wait to see her reaction when she entered the dining room. Would she be surprised? Happy? Overwhelmed? Miriam's heart skipped a beat at the thought of it.

She glanced at her phone again, seeing that it was now 3:25 p.m. Ava would be home any minute now. Miriam took a deep breath, feeling a sense of calm wash over her. She was ready.

When she returned to the kitchen, she removed the lasagna from the oven. To her delight, it looked terrific and smelled even better. She allowed it to cool on the counter. Then, she filled a bucket with ice and placed it on the lace tablecloth on the kitchen table. She nestled the champagne bottle in the ice to keep it chilled. She lit two candles and turned off the kitchen lights just as Ava walked through the front door.

Ava walked into the house, dropped her bag on the floor, and called out, "Hey, love! I'm home!" She walked into the kitchen, and her eyes widened in surprise as she took in the romantic setup. The candles flickered softly, casting a warm glow over the table. The champagne bottle chilled in the ice bucket, and the delicious aroma of the lasagna wafted through the air.

Ava's eyes met Miriam's, and she smiled, feeling a sense of wonder and excitement. "Wow, Miriam, what's all this?" she asked, her voice filled with curiosity and delight.

Miriam smiled, feeling her heart skip a beat as she gazed at Ava. She took a deep breath, savoring the moment, and replied, "I just wanted to do something special for us this evening. A nice dinner, some champagne... just a quiet evening together."

"God, you're beautiful, my love," Ava commented, and she took a step closer. Miriam's cheeks flushed with pleasure as she smiled, feeling a sense of happiness and contentment.

"You're pretty stunning yourself," she replied, her eyes locking onto Ava's. The air was filled with a sense of intimacy and affection, and Miriam felt her heart swell with love for Ava. She took a step closer, her eyes never leaving Ava's face. "Welcome home, my love," she said, her voice barely above a whisper.

Ava's eyes sparkled with affection as she gazed at Miriam, her voice filled with emotion. "I'm home now," she whispered, her lips brushing against Miriam's. The gentle touch sent shivers down Miriam's spine, and her heart skipped a beat. She wrapped her arms around Ava, deepening the kiss as they stood there, lost in the moment. The candles flickered softly around them, casting a warm, golden light over the intimate scene.

As they kissed, the world around them melted away, leaving only the two of them lost in the depths of their love. Miriam's heart swelled with emotion, and she felt like she was drowning in the depths of Ava's eyes. She pulled back slightly, her lips still brushing against Ava's, and whispered, "I love you."

Ava's response was a soft smile and a whisper, "I love you too." The moment hung suspended, filled with the promise of forever.

As they stood there, wrapped in each other's arms, Miriam's hand slipped into the pocket of her pants, her fingers closing around the small box that held the engagement ring. She took a deep breath, her heart pounding with excitement and nervousness. This was it, the moment she had been planning for. She pulled back slightly, her eyes locking onto Ava's, and smiled.

"Ava," she whispered, her voice trembling with emotion. "From the moment I met you, I knew that you were someone special. You light up my world in ways that I never thought possible. Will you—"

"Miriam, will you marry me?"

Miriam's eyes widened in shock, and she felt like she had been punched in the gut. She stood there, frozen, the tiny box still clutched in her hand. Ava's eyes sparkled with hope and excitement, and Miriam's heart swelled with love and emotion. She couldn't believe that Ava had beaten her to the punch. She smiled, feeling a sense of relief and joy, and nodded enthusiastically. "Yes, yes, a million times yes!" she exclaimed, tears of happiness streaming down her face.

Ava's face lit up with a radiant smile as she let out a squeal of delight. She threw her arms around Miriam, pulling her into a tight hug. "I was so nervous!" Ava exclaimed, her voice muffled against Miriam's shoulder. "I've been wanting to ask you for so long!" Miriam held her close, feeling a sense of joy and happiness wash over her. She couldn't believe that Ava had proposed to her, and she couldn't wait to spend the rest of her life with the woman she loved. As they hugged, Miriam's hand was still clutching the small box, forgotten in the excitement of the moment.

"I was sure you had suspected I was going to ask you. I almost slipped up several times in the past few days. You picked up on it, didn't you?" Miriam inquired.

Ava laughed, pulling back to gaze at Miriam with sparkling eyes. "I had no idea, none at all," she said, shaking her head. "I mean, I knew you were being sweet and romantic, but I had no idea you were planning something like this." She looked at Miriam's hand, still clutching the small box, and her eyes widened in surprise. "Wait, were you...?" she started to ask, her voice trailing off in curiosity. "You were in the middle of proposing to me just now, weren't you?"

Miriam's face turned bright red as she nodded sheepishly, still clutching the small box. "I was," she admitted, a laugh escaping her lips. "I had it all planned out, and you were one step ahead of me." She smiled, feeling a sense of joy and relief. "I guess we were both thinking the same thing."

Ava's eyes sparkled with amusement as she reached out and gently pried the small box out of Miriam's hand. "I think we make a pretty great team," she said, smiling.

Ava reached into her pocket. "I have something for you, too." She pulled out an engagement ring. "It was my grandmother's. Mom gave it to me when we were in Richmond a few weeks ago. I told Mom and Dad I was going to propose to you, and they had been saving this for me. And now I can give it to you."

Miriam's eyes widened in amazement as she gazed at the beautiful antique ring. She felt a lump form in her throat as she listened to the story behind the ring. "It's exquisite," she whispered, her voice trembling with emotion. She looked up at Ava, her eyes shining with tears. "I'm so touched that your parents gave this to you and that you want me to have it." She held out her hand, and Ava slid the ring onto her finger. It fit perfectly, and Miriam felt like it was meant to be. "I love you," she whispered, her heart overflowing with emotion.

Miriam removed the engagement ring she had purchased for Ava from the tiny box and slid it onto Ava's finger. Ava's eyes sparkled with delight as she gazed at the ring on her finger. She held up her hand, admiring the way the diamond caught the light. "It's beautiful," she whispered, her voice filled with emotion. She looked up at Miriam, her eyes shining with love. "I love you," she said, her voice barely above a whisper.

Miriam smiled, feeling a sense of joy and happiness wash over her. She leaned in, her lips brushing against Ava's in a soft, gentle kiss. "I love you too," she whispered, her heart overflowing with emotion.

Miriam was so caught up in the moment she had forgotten about the food. "Are you hungry, love? I made my homemade lasagna and a tiramisu for dessert."

Ava's eyes lit up with excitement as she smiled. "I'm starving!" she exclaimed, her stomach growling in agreement. "And your lasagna and tiramisu sound amazing. But first," she said, holding up her hand to admire the ring again, "can we just take a moment to appreciate the fact that we're engaged?" She smiled at Miriam, her eyes glistening with happiness. "I feel like I'm on cloud nine."

"Of course! I can't wait to tell your parents! And our friends! Ava, I promise you that I will do everything in my power to make you the happiest woman on the planet every day until my final breath."

Ava's eyes sparkled, and she smiled warmly. "You already do, love."

Miriam's heart swelled with emotion as she gazed at Ava, feeling a deep sense of love and commitment. She smiled, her eyes shining with tears, and pulled Ava into a tender hug. "I promise always to cherish, support, and adore you," she whispered, her voice teeming with conviction. As they held each other, the moment felt like a perfect blend of love, happiness, and promise, a moment that would stay with them forever.

After a delicious dinner and dessert, they adjourned to the porch swing with a glass of champagne. As they settled into the porch swing, the gentle creaking of the chains and the soft sway of the swing created a soothing melody that accompanied the sound of crickets and the rustling of leaves in the evening breeze.

Miriam and Ava sat together, hands intertwined, and sipped their champagne, savoring the sweetness of the moment and the promise of their future together. They lit fresh cigarettes and gazed up at the sky. It was dusk, and the stars were beginning to twinkle in the night sky, and the moon cast a silver glow over the landscape. It created a magical atmosphere that wrapped itself around the two women, holding them close in a warm, loving embrace.

As they sat there, surrounded by the serene beauty of nature, Miriam turned to Ava with a soft smile. "This is perfect," she whispered, her voice barely audible over the gentle rustling of the leaves. Ava nodded in agreement, her eyes glowing with happiness as she squeezed Miriam's hand. They sat in comfortable silence for a moment, watching as the stars continued to twinkle to life in the evening sky.

Then, Ava spoke up, her voice filled with emotion. "I'm so grateful for this life we're building together, Miriam. I promise to always cherish and support you through all of life's joys and challenges." Miriam's heart swelled with love and adoration for Ava, and she knew at that moment that their love would last a lifetime.

"Let's call and tell your parents, dear." Miriam couldn't wait to share the news.

Ava's face lit up with excitement as she nodded enthusiastically. "Yes, let's do it! They're going to be so thrilled." She quickly pulled out her phone and dialed her parents' number, hardly able to contain her excitement. As the phone rang, Ava turned to Miriam with a beaming smile. "I'll put it on speaker so you can hear their reaction," she whispered, her eyes sparkling with anticipation.

As the phone connected, Ava's mom answered on the first ring. "Hello?" she said, her voice warm and familiar.

Ava took a deep breath, hardly able to contain her excitement. "Mom, Dad, I have some news to share with you," she said, her voice fluttering with emotion.

Miriam squeezed Ava's hand reassuringly as Ava's mom's voice came through the speaker, filled with curiosity. "What is it, sweetie? You sound so excited!"

Ava's voice spilled out in a rush of excitement. "Miriam and I are engaged! We're getting married!" There was a moment of stunned silence on the other end of the line, and then Ava's mom let out a loud squeal of delight.

"Oh, Ava! Congratulations, sweetie! We're so happy for you both!"

Ava's dad chimed in, his voice booming through the speaker. "We can't wait to celebrate with you! When's the wedding?"

Miriam said, "Hi Sophia, hi Ryan. We haven't set a date yet, but we wanted to let the two most important people in our lives know first."

Sophia's warm and emotional voice came through the speaker. "We're so honored that you thought of us first, sweethearts. We love you both so much, and we're beyond thrilled to welcome Miriam officially into our family."

Ryan added, his voice filled with excitement. "We can't wait to start planning the wedding with you both! This is going to be a celebration to remember!"

Ava and Miriam exchanged a happy glance, grinning from ear to ear. Ava spoke up, her voice filled with excitement. "We're so glad you're both excited! We can't wait to start planning and sharing this special day with you."

Miriam added, her voice filled with love, "We're going to make this a day to remember, not just for us, but for our whole family." Sophia and Ryan's voices chimed in again, filled with laughter and congratulations, as the four of them basked in the joy and happiness of the moment. They said their goodbyes and ended the call.

"What now, Ava, my dear?"

Ava smiled mischievously, her eyes sparkling with excitement. "Now, my love," she said, "we celebrate! We open another bottle of champagne, and we dance under the stars." She stood up, pulled Miriam to her feet, and wrapped her arms around her waist. "We'll dance to our favorite song and dream of our future together." Miriam's heart swelled with love and happiness as she smiled, knowing that this was just the beginning of their new life together.

Chapter 35: A Little Us

Over the next few days, Miriam and Ava were blissfully happy. Ava was thrilled when her students and coworkers would ask to see her ring, and she was giddy every time she showed it off. Miriam was delighted when Ava told her how happy her students were for her.

On the morning of Tuesday, September 3, Ava was gone to work, and Miriam received a phone call from AUSA Amanda Miller.

"Hello, Miriam, I have some updates for you. Is now a good time?"

Miriam responded, " Yes, it's a great time, actually. What news do you have for me today?"

"A couple of things, actually. First, because of the recovery of Leo Rossi's green notebook and the arrest of Francesca Bianchi, we've made significant progress in the case, and we have a trial date set. It's going to start on Monday, October 7. You're slated for closed testimony on the following Monday, October 14. Because I need to prepare you for trial and because of the nature of your witness protection, I will be flying to you and doing prep there on Wednesday, October 2."

"Alright, I'm sure I'm free that day, "Miriam joked, "What are the steps of my trial preparation since my testimony is a closed testimony?"

AUSA Miller explained, "Since your testimony is closed, we must take extra precautions to protect your identity. We'll go over the details of your testimony, and I'll make sure you're prepared for any questions the prosecution or defense might ask. We'll also practice your testimony to ensure you're comfortable with the process." She added, "I'm also petitioning the judge for additional protective measures to ensure your safety throughout the trial."

Miriam asked, "Will I be testifying in a closed courtroom or testifying remotely?"

AUSA Miller replied, "You'll be testifying in a closed courtroom, but you'll be doing so behind a screen or with your voice distorted to protect your identity. We'll also have a court reporter present to transcribe your testimony."

Miriam nodded, taking mental notes. "Okay, that makes sense. What about the marshals? Will they be present during my testimony?"

AUSA Miller assured her, "Yes, the marshals will be present throughout the trial, including during your testimony. They'll be ensuring your safety and security at all times."

Miriam felt relieved to know that the marshals would be there to protect her. She asked, "What's the expected outcome of the trial? Are we confident that the De Luca family will be convicted?"

AUSA Miller replied, "We're very confident in our case against the De Luca family. With the evidence we've gathered, including Leo Rossi's green notebook and Francesca Bianchi's testimony, we believe we have a strong chance of securing convictions on all counts."

"Francesca Bianchi is testifying against Leo and the De Lucas?"

"Yes, in exchange for a reduced sentence, she has agreed to testify. It certainly strengthens our case."

"How long will the trial preparation take when you arrive on October 2?"

AUSA Miller responded, "I anticipate that the trial preparation will take a few days, depending on how quickly you feel comfortable with the material. I'll work closely with you to review your testimony, practice your responses to potential questions, and ensure you're prepared for anything that might arise during the trial.

"Assuming everything goes smoothly, I expect to be with you from October 2 to October 5. This will give us ample time to prepare and allow for any unexpected issues that might arise. By the time I leave, you'll be well-prepared to testify and help bring the De Luca family to justice."

"Will we be doing trial preparation here at my house or in the local courthouse?"

AUSA Miller replied, "We'll be doing the trial preparation there at your house. Since you're in witness protection, we want to minimize your exposure to the public and avoid drawing any unnecessary attention to your location.

"Conducting the trial preparation in the comfort and security of your own home will also help you feel more at ease and focused on the task at hand. I'll bring all the necessary materials and equipment with me so we can work efficiently and effectively in a secure environment."

A feeling of relief washed over Miriam. "Alright, that works. What was the second thing you wanted to tell me?"

AUSA Miller took a deep breath before answering. "Francesca Bianchi. She tracked you down through Facebook."

Miriam was stunned, "But... I don't have Facebook. I don't use any forms of social media."

Miller responded, "But there are two viral videos of you, one confronting the mayor and one addressing the town council with Ava at your side. I don't know how we missed them, but Francesca didn't. She had seen those videos and recognized you from them on the courthouse steps in Pittsburgh, but she also recognized you as your former identity. The videos were tagged with Jasper Hill's location. She found the profiles of the creators of the Facebook Live videos and traced one to Jules Craft, a mutual friend of Ava's. Ava's profile picture is the two of you. She is also listed as a teacher at Jasper Hill High School. The videos have since been removed from the internet, but there's the very real possibility that the De Luca family has also seen them.

"Remember when you told me Francesca was asking you questions about where you were from and your family while serving you lemonade? She used that information. She drove to Jasper Hill and walked into several businesses asking anyone about the transgender woman who was dating the art teacher, Ava McCormick, while pretending to be your estranged mother wanting to reconcile. Unfortunately, it was a believable story, and Di Simmons was happy to help her and told her where you lived.

"She also heard that the marshals were on the way the day she encountered you and Ava because you were outside and had the call on speaker. She knew she had a window where you were vulnerable. Circumstances could have been very different and very bad that day."

Miriam's eyes widened in shock and horror as she listened. "How... how did she manage to piece all that together?" Miriam asked, her voice shaking slightly.

AUSA Miller explained, "Francesca Bianchi didn't act alone in tracking you down, Miriam. She enlisted the help of several tech-savvy individuals connected to the remaining free members of the De Luca family and their loyalists. They used social media, public records, and advanced surveillance techniques to piece together your new life in Jasper Hill. However, Francesca deliberately withheld the full truth about your identity from the De Luca family. She kept the fact that you had transitioned and were living as Miriam Ryder to herself, likely wanting to confront you personally or exact her own revenge without interference. This calculated secrecy is the only reason the De Lucas haven't been able to exploit her discovery—yet."

Miriam's mind was reeling as she thought about the implications of what AUSA Miller had just told her. She felt a wave of fear wash over her, followed by a sense of anger and frustration.

Miriam's eyes flashed with anger as she thought about how Francesca Bianchi had manipulated and exploited her way into finding Miriam's location. "She's unbelievable," Miriam spat, her voice trembling with rage. "Using my own life against me like that... it's just sickening."

AUSA Miller's tone remained grim but sympathetic. "I know it's a lot to take in, Miriam. But we're going to do everything in our power to make sure she can't hurt you again. We'll be increasing security measures and keeping a close eye on her and the De Luca family."

Miriam took a deep breath, trying to calm herself down. She knew that AUSA Miller and the marshals were doing everything they could to protect her, but it was hard to shake off the feeling of vulnerability that Francesca Bianchi's actions had left her with.

"We didn't have a clue. We made it so easy for them to find us. It's a miracle that Ava and I are still alive."

Miriam's voice cracked as she spoke, the weight of their close call settling in. AUSA Miller's expression turned somber, her voice filled with a mix of concern and admiration for Miriam's resilience.

"Miriam, you can't blame yourself for this," AUSA Miller said gently. "Francesca Bianchi is a master manipulator, and she would have stopped at nothing to find you. It's not your fault that she was able to piece together the information she needed."

Miriam shook her head, still trying to process the events that had unfolded. "But we were so careless," she whispered. "We let our guard down, and it almost cost us everything."

AUSA Miller leaned forward, her voice taking on a reassuring tone. "Miriam, you and Ava are safe now. That's what matters. We'll learn from this experience and take steps to ensure that something like this never happens again."

"She asked me to marry her, you know. We're going to get married...

that almost didn't happen…" Miriam's voice trailed off, and the shock weighed heavily on her.

AUSA Miller's expression softened, and she smiled warmly. "I'm so happy for you both, Miriam. You and Ava deserve all the happiness in the world. It's a miracle that you're both safe and that you have a future together to look forward to."

Miriam's eyes welled up with tears as she thought about how close she and Ava had come to losing each other. She took a deep breath, trying to compose herself.

"I just can't believe it," Miriam whispered. "If Francesca had… if something had happened to Ava… I don't know what I would have done."

AUSA Miller replied, "But nothing did happen, Miriam. You and Ava are safe, and you have each other. That's all that matters."

"Miriam, are you going to be alright?" AUSA Miller asked with concern.

Miriam took a deep breath, trying to calm herself down. She nodded slowly, still feeling a bit shaken. "Yeah, I'll be okay. It's just… it's a lot to process. The thought of what could have happened… it's just terrifying."

AUSA Miller expressed her understanding. "I know it's a lot to take in, Miriam. But you're safe now, and we're going to do everything we can to keep you that way. You're not alone in this. We're all here to support you."

Miriam nodded again, feeling a sense of gratitude towards AUSA Miller. "Thank you," she said softly. "Just knowing that you're all looking out for me… it means a lot."

"You're welcome, Miriam. I'll see you in a month. Remember, this is almost over." And AUSA Miller ended the call.

Miriam walked to the porch swing, sat down, and shakily lit a cigarette, inhaling the smoke deeply while contemplating everything she nearly lost.

Throughout September, Miriam and Ava did as much as they could to keep themselves occupied while anticipating the trial. They were both spending lots of evenings painting miniatures together. Miriam had completed a stunning dragon, while Ava had completed a small army of bugs.

October had arrived before they knew it. Miriam received a call from AUSA Miller, letting her know she would be arriving at the house at 9:00 a.m. the following morning, and they would begin the trial preparation.

After the call, Ava sidled up to Miriam and said, "Miri, love, there's something vital I want to ask you." Her eyes looked into Miriam's longingly.

"Of course, Ava, honey, what is it? You know you can ask me anything."

Ava gathered her nerve before asking. "Well, you've not had gender reassignment surgery, and we know that part of you definitely works. But because you're on HRT, you don't produce sperm. But, in theory, if you came off HRT for a short time, you would begin producing it again." She paused, then quickly continued. "If you would be willing to do that, temporarily, of course, I would like that very much.

"Because I want to have a baby. I want to have your baby, specifically. How do you feel about that?"

Miriam's eyes widened in surprise, and she felt a rush of emotions as she processed Ava's request. She had never considered having a child before, and the idea of it was both thrilling and terrifying.

Miriam took a deep breath, trying to gather her thoughts. She looked into Ava's eyes, seeing the longing and hope in her expression.

"Ava, I... I don't know what to say," Miriam stammered. "I never thought about having a child before. I mean, I've always assumed that it wouldn't be possible for me."

Ava's face fell slightly, but she quickly recovered. "I know it's a lot to ask, Miri. And I know it's not something you've ever considered before. But I couldn't help but think about it, and I feel like it could be something really special for us."

Miriam's heart swelled with love for Ava, and she felt a surge of desire to make her happy.

"Ava, I want to make you happy," Miriam said, her voice filled with emotion. "And if having a child is something that you really want, then I'm willing to consider it. But we need to talk about this more, and we need to think about all the implications. It's not just about me coming off HRT and trying to conceive. There are so many other things to consider."

Ava's face lit up with hope, and she nodded eagerly. "I know, Miri. And I'm willing to do whatever it takes to make this work. I just want to have a child with you, and I'm willing to do whatever it takes to make that happen."

"I want that, too. We'll talk to the doctors about it the instant I have time. I have trial preparation for the next few days. I never thought about kids before, but now, the idea of a little us running around? Yes, absolutely, yes, let's see what we need to do to make it happen!"

Ava's face lit up with joy, and she threw her arms around Miriam, pulling her into a tight hug. "I'm so happy, Miri! I've always dreamed of having a family with you. The thought of a little us running around is just... perfect."

Miriam hugged Ava back, feeling a sense of excitement and possibility that she had never felt before. "We'll make it happen, Ava. We'll talk to the doctors, and we'll figure out what we need to do. We'll make our little family a reality."

As they hugged, Miriam felt a sense of hope and happiness that she hadn't felt in a long time. She knew that there would be challenges ahead, but with Ava by her side, she felt like she could face anything.

Chapter 36: The Weight Of Truth

AUSA Miller arrived promptly at 9:00 a.m. the following morning. Miriam invited her in: "Hello, Amanda. Please come in. Would you like some coffee before we begin?"

AUSA Miller smiled warmly as she entered the house. "Good morning, Miriam. Thank you for the offer, but I'm all set. I've already had my morning coffee. Shall we get started?" She glanced around the room, taking in the cozy atmosphere, before focusing her attention on Miriam. "I must say, your home is lovely. You and Ava have done a wonderful job making it feel warm and welcoming."

"Thank you. We try to put as much of our personality into the place as we can. Oh, look at my engagement ring!" Miriam held her hand out.

AUSA Miller's eyes lit up as she took in the sight of the ring. "Oh, Miriam, it's beautiful! Congratulations again on your engagement. Ava has excellent taste, I must say." She smiled warmly, taking a moment to admire the ring before refocusing on the task at hand. "Now, shall we get started on the trial preparation? We have a lot to cover, and I want to make sure you're feeling confident and prepared."

"Yes, just let me grab a cup of coffee, please, and we'll get started. Where would you like to work? Here in the living room or at the kitchen table?"

"Actually, the kitchen table would be perfect," AUSA Miller replied, smiling. "The natural light in here is lovely, and it looks like we'll have plenty of space to spread out all the documents and materials we'll need to review." She nodded, following Miriam into the kitchen. "And please, take your time getting your coffee. I'll just get settled in and start organizing the files."

"Will it bother you terribly if I smoke? My nerves are shot as is."

AUSA Miller smiled understandingly. "Not at all, Miriam. I completely understand. Please go ahead and smoke if it helps to calm your nerves. We'll be working together for a while, and I want you to feel as comfortable as possible." She paused, adding, "Just open a window if you don't mind. I'm not a smoker myself, but I'm happy to accommodate you."

Miriam thanked her and opened the French doors to the deck and backyard. She lit a cigarette and took the seat closest to the door with her coffee in hand. She said, "Okay, I'm ready, let's start."

AUSA Miller nodded, smiling, and began to organize the files and documents in front of her. "Excellent, let's get started then. As I mentioned earlier, the trial is scheduled to begin on October 7th, and your testimony is slated for October 14th. We'll be going over your testimony in detail, as well as preparing you for any potential questions the defense may ask." She looked up at Miriam, her eyes serious. "I want to assure you, Miriam, that we'll do everything in our power to ensure your safety and well-being throughout this process."

Miriam nodded as she took a drag from her cigarette and inhaled. As she exhaled the smoke out into the open air of the backyard, Miriam's eyes narrowed slightly, focusing on AUSA Miller. "Okay, so what's the plan for today? What do I need to know, and what do we need to go over?" She asked, her voice calm and collected despite the underlying tension that still lingered from the events of the past few weeks.

AUSA Miller nodded, her expression professional and focused. "Today, we'll be going over your testimony in detail, as well as the potential questions you may be asked by the prosecution and defense. We'll also discuss the courtroom layout, the procedure for your testimony, and any other logistical details you need to be aware of." She paused, consulting her notes. "Additionally, I'll be sharing some information with you about the other witnesses who will be testifying, as well as the overall strategy for the prosecution's case."

Miriam nodded, and she prepared mentally. "Let's go."

AUSA Miller smiled slightly, a hint of approval in her eyes. "Alright, let's start with your testimony. Can you walk me through what happened on the night of January 10th when you were attacked by the De Luca family?" She leaned forward slightly, her pen poised over her notebook, ready to take notes.

"It was July 2nd, 2023, when I was attacked, actually." Miriam corrected her. "Wait, was that a tactic defense attorneys might use to cause my credibility to be questioned?"

AUSA Miller's expression turned impressed. "Exactly, Miriam. That's a great catch. Yes, the defense might try to use a minor mistake like that to impeach your credibility. They might try to suggest that if you can't even get the date right, how can you be trusted to remember other details accurately?" She nodded, making a note on her pad. "But you're absolutely right, and I'm glad we could practice this. You corrected me confidently and politely, which is exactly what you should do if something like that happens during your testimony."

Miriam smiled and proceeded to answer the question. "I got off work early that evening and got home right after 8:00 p.m. My friend Alex Bianchi was waiting for me. We went into my apartment, we were playing video games on my PlayStation, we were having a conversation, there was a knock at the door, he answered it, and that's when the attackers arrived."

AUSA Miller nodded, her eyes locked on Miriam as she took detailed notes. "Okay, so let's break this down. You arrived home around 8:00

p.m., and Alex was already there. You were playing video games and chatting when there was a knock at the door. Alex answered it, and that's when the attack occurred. Can you tell me more about what happened next? What did you see, hear, and experience during the attack?"

"Alex shouted my name as the guys made their way into my apartment. There were six of them wearing all black, complete with masks and gloves, and carrying crowbars. Alex tried to reason with them and said, 'Let me talk to Leo. He can sort this all out. There's no need to—,' and those were his last exact words. One of the guys pulled out a gun and shot him in the back of the head, and he died instantly. The gunman said, 'No witnesses,' and then they attacked me with their crowbars. Repeatedly. My leg was snapped. I tried to get up to try to get away, and my leg crumpled. I tried to block blows, and they broke my left arm, eight ribs, hit me in the throat, in the face, on the head, they stomped me, then they left."

AUSA Miller's expression was somber, her eyes filled with empathy as she listened to Miriam's account of the brutal attack. She took detailed notes, her pen moving swiftly across the page. When Miriam finished speaking, AUSA Miller paused for a moment, collecting her thoughts before speaking. "Miriam, I'm so sorry you had to endure that horrific experience. Your bravery in sharing this with me, and soon with the court, is truly admirable." She paused, taking a deep breath. "Now, I want to make sure we prepare you for the possibility that the defense may try to challenge your account of events. Are you prepared to answer questions about the attack and to potentially relive some of those moments on the stand?"

Miriam's voice faltered as she recounted the final words Alex spoke before his death. She fell silent, her gaze distant, as a memory surged to the surface.

It was a summer evening in 2021. Alex and Gabe were sprawled out in the living room of Gabe's apartment, controllers in hand, locked in a heated round of their favorite fighting game.

"Best out of three!" Alex declared, laughing as he narrowly avoided defeat. "I'm not letting you win just because you trained me at work!"

Gabe rolled her eyes. "You mean because I carry you at work. Let's be honest, you owe me."

Alex grinned, the kind of grin that made even a bad day feel tolerable. "Alright, alright. But if I win, you're buying pizza."

"You're on."

Alex leaned back, unleashing his signature whistle—a melodic trill that always meant trouble was coming. "You ready to lose, champ?" he teased, his fingers dancing across the buttons.

The memory softened as Miriam recalled how carefree they'd been, how Alex had always known how to make her laugh, even when things felt overwhelming.

But then, like a storm cloud rolling in, the laughter faded, replaced by the chilling echo of his whistle the night of the attack. This time, it wasn't playful. It was haunting, reverberating through her mind as the memory of his death threatened to overwhelm her.

Miriam blinked, grounding herself as she realized AUSA Miller was watching her with concern. "I'm sorry," Miriam said, her voice shaking. "Sometimes, it just hits me... how much I miss him."

"You don't have to apologize," AUSA Miller replied softly. "Alex was important to you. Let's make sure his story, and yours, are heard."

Miriam steeled herself and took another drag from her cigarette. "I'm ready. Throw everything you've got at me."

AUSA Miller nodded, a hint of a smile on her face. "Alright, Miriam. Let's get started then. I'm going to ask you some tough questions, and I want you to respond as if you were on the stand. Remember, the goal is to prepare you for anything the defense might throw at you." She paused, collecting her thoughts before launching into the first question. "Miriam, can you explain why you didn't call the police directly after the attack? Why did you wait?"

"Because I was incapacitated. My leg was shattered, and I couldn't make it to my phone. I blacked out, trying to crawl to Alex. Someone else called 911."

AUSA Miller nodded, her expression neutral. "I see. And can you tell me more about the person who called 911? Do you know who it was and how they happened to be in a position to make the call?"

"I heard a woman's voice, but I couldn't see anyone or anything clearly because of the blood running into my eyes. She sounded frantic."

AUSA Miller nodded thoughtfully, making a note on her pad. "Okay, so you didn't actually see the woman who made the 911 call, but you heard her voice, and it sounded frantic. That's helpful to know."

"But Francesca Bianchi has since confessed to making the call and orchestrating the attack. Can we use that information in my testimony?"

AUSA Miller paused, her pen hovering over her notepad as she considered Miriam's question. "Francesca Bianchi's confession is significant," she said carefully, "but how we use it depends on several factors. Since she's confessed to making the 911 call and orchestrating the attack, her testimony could be powerful if it aligns with the other evidence we have."

She leaned forward, her tone measured. "However, there are complications. If Francesca's testimony is inconsistent, or if the defense successfully attacks her credibility—given her role in the attack itself—it could backfire. The defense might argue that she has ulterior motives, like cutting a deal for a lighter sentence, or they could suggest her confession was coerced. We need to ensure her testimony is solid and corroborated by other evidence."

Miriam frowned, her grip tightening around her coffee cup. "So, you're saying her confession might not be enough?"

"On its own, no," AUSA Miller admitted. "But coupled with your testimony, physical evidence, and corroboration from other witnesses, it strengthens our case significantly. It establishes a clear connection between Francesca's involvement, the De Luca family's orders, and the events that led to the attack."

Miller's gaze softened as she added, "It's also worth noting that your testimony about hearing a frantic woman's voice adds credibility to her claim that she made the 911 call. It paints her as a conflicted participant—someone who realized the situation had gone too far and tried to mitigate the damage. That could work in our favor."

Miriam nodded slowly, digesting the information. "So, should I mention the confession during my testimony?"

"Not directly," Miller advised. "Your role is to recount your personal experiences and observations. If the defense or prosecution brings up Francesca's confession, it will be addressed during cross-examination or through other witnesses. Your focus should remain on providing a clear, truthful account of what happened to you and what you know firsthand."

Miller gave her a reassuring smile. "Remember, Miriam, the truth is our greatest weapon. Francesca's confession adds weight to your story, but your courage and honesty will be what resonates with the jury."

She paused, looking up at Miriam. "Now, I want to ask you about something that might seem unrelated but bear with me. Can you tell me about your relationship with Alex Bianchi? How did you know him, and how would you describe your friendship?"

"Alex was my best friend. He was my only friend. We met at work. I was working at a pizza delivery restaurant as a driver. He was hired in the summer of 2020, and I trained him. He became like a younger brother to me. I shared everything with him. We did everything together. Pirates games, PlayStation, movies, everything."

AUSA Miller's expression softened, and she nodded sympathetically. "It's clear that Alex meant a lot to you. Losing him must have been devastating." She paused, collecting her thoughts before continuing. "Now, I want to ask you about something that might be difficult to talk about. Can you tell me about any potential conflicts or enemies that Alex might have had? Anyone who might have wanted to hurt him?"

"Alex was a saint. He didn't have any enemies or anything like that. He was a sweet, innocent kid with his whole life ahead of him."

AUSA Miller nodded, her expression understanding. "I can see why you'd think that about him. It's clear that you cared about him deeply." She paused, making a note on her pad. "However, I do need to ask, Miriam, are you aware of any connections Alex might have had to the De Luca family or their associates?"

"His cousin was Leo Rossi. But he knew nothing about Leo being employed by the De Lucas."

AUSA Miller's eyes narrowed slightly, her expression intense. "So, Alex was unaware of his cousin's involvement with the De Luca family. Did Alex ever mention anything to you about his cousin Leo or any interactions he had with him?"

"Alex told me he placed bets for people who were down on their luck. He knew I needed money badly, so he put me in touch with Leo."

AUSA Miller's expression turned grave, her eyes locked on Miriam's. "Alex introduced you to Leo Rossi, and you began placing bets with him. Did you ever suspect that Leo was involved with the De Luca family or that the betting operation was connected to organized crime?"

"No. I thought he was doing it independently through DraftKings or something like that. I didn't have a clue he was working for the De Luca family."

AUSA Miller nodded, her expression thoughtful. "I see. So, you had no knowledge of the De Luca family's involvement in the betting operation, and you thought you were just placing bets through a legitimate platform. Did you ever meet anyone else involved in the betting operation, or was it just Leo that you dealt with?"

"Only Leo."

AUSA Miller nodded, making a note on her pad. "Alright, Miriam. I think that's enough for now. You're doing great. We'll take a break and then come back to some more questions, okay?"

"We can keep going; I'm good," Miriam said as she lit a fresh cigarette. "Don't go easy on me."

AUSA Miller's eyes narrowed slightly as she watched Miriam light the cigarette. "Alright, Miriam. Let's keep going, then. I want to ask you about the night of the attack. You mentioned that the attackers were wearing masks and gloves. Did you notice anything else distinctive about them? Any accents, mannerisms, or physical characteristics that might help identify them?"

"No, nothing that stood out. The lead guy said, 'Mister De Luca said you owe him one hundred grand. He told us to come get it, and if you didn't have it, to take it out of you. So, which will it be, kid?' That's when Alex tried pleading with them, and they shot him. The other one said 'no witnesses,' and they never said anything else."

AUSA Miller's expression turned grim, her eyes locked on Miriam's. "I'm so sorry you had to go through that, Miriam. It's clear that the attackers were sent by the De Luca family to collect a debt. Did you owe Mister De Luca one hundred thousand dollars?"

"I lost a bet to Leo. He said I owed $100,000. And that he worked for Mario De Luca, and because I owed him, by proxy, I owed the De Lucas."

AUSA Miller's eyes widened slightly, her expression intense. "So, Leo Rossi told you that you owed the De Luca family $100,000 because of a bet you lost to him. He made it clear that he worked for Mario De Luca and that you owed them by proxy. Did you ever try negotiating with Leo or the De Lucas about the debt, or did you just assume you had to pay it?"

"No, after about two months, he showed up at my apartment with Marco De Luca and they gave me 24 hours to pay up or else. That was the morning of July 1, 2023."

AUSA Miller's expression turned grave, her eyes locked on Miriam's. "So, Leo Rossi, Marco De Luca, and possibly others came to your apartment on July 1, 2023, and gave you an ultimatum: pay the $100,000 debt within 24 hours or face the consequences. And then, later that day, Alex was killed, and you were attacked. Is that correct?"

"Not entirely. The attack occurred the night of July 2, 2023, but everything else is correct."

AUSA Miller nodded, making a precise note on her pad. "I apologize for the mistake. So, to confirm, the ultimatum was given on July 1, 2023, and the attack occurred the following night, July 2, 2023. Did you report the ultimatum or the attack to the police?"

"No, I was rendered unconscious after the attack. I woke up in the hospital."

AUSA Miller's expression turned sympathetic. "I see. So, you were hospitalized after the attack and didn't have the opportunity to report it to the police. Did the police or anyone else question you about the attack while you were in the hospital?"

"No, no one contacted me until AUSA Amanda Miller told me weeks later that I was in witness protection."

AUSA Miller's eyes locked onto Miriam's, a hint of determination in her voice. "I see. Well, Miriam, I'm glad we're having this conversation now. Your testimony is crucial in helping us take down the De Luca family. Can you tell me more about your experience in witness protection? How have you been holding up?"

"Aside from Francesca Bianchi finding me and Ava and holding us at gunpoint, it's been a positive experience."

AUSA Miller's expression turned grim, her voice firm. "I apologize for the breach in security. Can you tell me more about the incident with Francesca Bianchi? What happened exactly?"

Miriam recounted how Mrs. Bianchi had found them and confronted them and how they were able to survive the encounter.

AUSA Miller listened intently, her expression growing increasingly concerned. "I'm so sorry you and Ava had to go through that, Miriam. It's unacceptable that Francesca Bianchi was able to find you. Can you tell me if Francesca Bianchi said anything that might indicate why she was looking for you or what her motives were?"

"She blamed me for the death of her son, Alex. She wanted to make me pay. She wanted to kill both Ava and me."

AUSA Miller's expression softened, her voice filled with compassion. "I'm so sorry, Miriam. Losing a loved one is never easy, and it's understandable that Francesca Bianchi would be grieving and angry. But it's not your fault, Miriam. You didn't kill Alex. The people responsible for his death are the ones who pulled the trigger. We're going to do everything in our power to bring them to justice."

"One last thing," Miller said, her tone shifting to something more serious. "You will have to testify under your dead name. There's no way around it."

Miriam's breath caught in her throat, her grip tightening around her coffee cup. "No," she said firmly. "Gabe Wilson was declared dead. I am legally Miriam Ryder now. There's no reason for me to use that name in court."

Miller sighed, setting her pen down while leaning forward and meeting Miriam's gaze. "I understand why this is upsetting, but legally, your past identity is crucial to establishing the chain of events. The defense will argue that you—Gabe Wilson—were the one who placed those bets, owed the De Lucas money, and were attacked as a result. If you don't testify under that name, they'll use it to question the validity of your testimony, claiming Miriam Ryder had no involvement in these events. They'll twist it into a credibility issue, and we can't give them that opportunity."

Miriam clenched her jaw, her pulse pounding in her ears. "So what? I'm supposed to sit on that stand and be someone I'm not? Let them erase everything I fought for just to make their jobs easier?"

Miller's voice softened, but there was no room for negotiation. "Miriam, I know how hard this is. I don't want to put you through it, but if we don't present your testimony in a way that aligns with the legal record, the defense will tear it apart. We need the jury to see the full story—your story. And that means connecting who you were to who you are now, without giving them room to manipulate the facts."

Miriam swallowed hard, her stomach churning. Every part of her wanted to fight, to refuse. But deep down, she knew Miller was right. The truth was her best weapon—and to wield it, she had to face her past, even if it meant stepping into a name that no longer belonged to her.

"So what now? What's next?" Miriam lit another cigarette and inhaled deeply.

"Next, you testify in a closed courtroom on October 14."

"When do I need to be in Pittsburgh?"

AUSA Miller checked her notes. "You'll need to be in Pittsburgh by October 12th, two days before your scheduled testimony. We'll arrange for you to be taken to a secure location, where you'll stay until the trial."

"So, just try to stay calm and collected until then?"

AUSA Miller nodded. "Exactly, Miriam. Try to stay calm and focused. We'll take care of everything else. Just remember, you're doing this to bring justice to Alex and to protect yourself and Ava. You're strong and capable, and you'll get through this."

"Thanks, Amanda. Would you like some coffee before you leave?"

AUSA Miller smiled. "That's very kind of you, Miriam. But I should probably get going. I have a lot to do to prepare for the trial. Thank you again for your bravery and cooperation. I'll be in touch soon."

Miriam showed AUSA Miller to the door, and as she closed it, she shuddered. Something told her that the trial was going to go differently.

Her stomach twisted violently, nausea creeping up her throat. *Gabe Wilson.* That name wasn't hers anymore. It hadn't been in over a year. But soon, it would be spoken aloud in a courtroom, recorded into transcripts, burned into the minds of everyone present—including the De Lucas.

They would know.

They would hear her deadname and realize she had survived. That she hadn't died that night like they thought. That she was still breathing, still standing, still ready to take them down.

Her fingers dug into the doorframe as her pulse pounded in her ears. *They'll come for me.* They had already found her once. Francesca Bianchi had hunted her down and held her at gunpoint, and that was before they even knew she was alive. What would stop them now?

A sharp pang of rage cut through the panic. *This isn't fair.* She had rebuilt herself from the ashes of that night. She had fought tooth and nail to become Miriam Ryder, to carve out a life where she wasn't running, where she wasn't defined by the trauma they had inflicted on her. And now, the justice system—the very thing that was supposed to protect her—was forcing her to erase herself just to be believed.

She swallowed against the bile rising in her throat, her breath coming in shallow bursts. *No. They don't get to take this from me.* Not her name, not her sense of self, not her fight. If she had to stand in that courtroom and face them, she would—but she wouldn't do it as the person they had left for dead.

She would do it as Miriam Ryder.

Miriam clenched her jaw and wiped a trembling hand over her face, forcing herself to steady. She lit another cigarette with unsteady fingers and took a deep drag, the familiar burn grounding her. *I'll get through this.*

She had to.

Chapter 37: Veritas

Miriam was nervous over the next nine days in anticipation of the trial. The weight of what lay ahead pressed down on her, but nothing unnerved her more than the knowledge that she would have to identify herself by her deadname in court. It felt like an erasure of everything she had fought to become, an indignity forced upon her by the legal system's rigid necessity. Would she comply, sacrificing a part of herself for the sake of justice, or would she refuse, risking the consequences? The thought gnawed at her, stealing sleep from her nights and peace from her days.

Ava was by her side as much as possible in the evening after school, and her presence made Miriam feel much more confident and at ease. She smiled as she reflected on just how intertwined she and Ava had become in six months. She couldn't wait to plan their wedding and get married. She was adamant she would conceive a child with Ava. She vowed they would have the family they dreamed of. But she had to get through the trial first.

On the Friday morning of October 11, a team of marshals arrived to transport Miriam and Ava to a safe house in Pittsburgh. This is it, she thought. Hopefully, this is my last trip to Pittsburgh. She and Ava climbed into the familiar blue Tahoe, and they departed.

They spoke very little on the trip. Miriam was reviewing numerous theoretical questions from the prosecution and the defense, rehearsing the answers in her mind. Ava sat beside her, holding her hand and gently squeezing it periodically. She knew the best way to support Miriam was to be a steady presence and the rock she could lean on.

To both of their delights, the safe house was the same log cabin on the Ohio River from July. Miriam welcomed the familiarity. The last thing she wanted was the added stress of learning a new location. As they exited the Tahoe, Ava lit their cigarettes and passed one to Miriam, and Miriam's shoulders immediately straightened as her relief washed over her.

"Do you want to get pizza from the same place as last time, Miri?" Ava asked as her stomach grumbled.

"I'd like that very much, dear. Pepperoni and sausage for me, please. And whatever you want."

Miriam knew she'd go for ham and pineapple. Ava gave the order to the marshals stationed on the property, and they waited for the pizza to arrive.

"Miri, love, you've been uncharacteristically quiet for a few days, and I know it's the stress of the trial. Do you want to talk about it?" Ava placed her arms around Miriam's waist from behind.

Ava's arms tightened around Miriam's waist, offering a comforting squeeze. "Hey, I'm here for you. You can talk to me about anything."

Miriam leaned back into Ava's embrace, feeling a sense of safety and security. "I just can't shake off the feeling that something's going to go wrong," she admitted, her voice barely above a whisper.

Ava turned Miriam around to face her, looking into her eyes with concern. "What's making you feel that way? Is it the trial? The testimony?"

Miriam nodded, taking a deep breath. "It's everything. The thought of facing Leo and the De Lucas again, reliving all the horrible things they did... it's just terrifying."

Ava's expression softened, and she pulled Miriam into a gentle hug.

"I know it's scary, but you're not alone. I'm here with you, and we'll face this together. You're strong, Miri, and you can get through this."

Miriam felt a lump form in her throat as she hugged Ava back. She knew Ava was right – she wasn't alone, and she had Ava's love and support to carry her through.

As they stood there, wrapped in each other's arms, Miriam felt a sense of calm wash over her. She knew that no matter what happened, she and Ava would face it together.

On the morning of Monday, October 14, the team of marshals escorted Miriam and Ava to the courthouse for Miriam's testimony. To protect Miriam's identity and shield her from view, they were taken to a guarded back entrance closed to public access. As they pulled up to the unloading area, Miriam was pleased to see AUSA Amanda Miller and US Marshal Arthur M. Thompson waiting. Miriam and Ava immediately lit fresh cigarettes.

Miriam took a deep breath. "One last time—explain the process to me."

AUSA Miller nodded. "Of course, Miriam. Your testimony will be given in a closed courtroom, with only the judge, the prosecutors, the court reporter, and the defense attorneys present. The courtroom will be sealed, and the public will not have access. The judge has ordered for your testimony to be behind frosted bulletproof glass. Your voice, while changed from vocalization surgery, will be further distorted through a modulation device."

Miriam winced at the thought of using her deadname but kept silent as she took a long, satisfying drag from her cigarette. "And Leo Rossi and the De Lucas?"

AUSA Miller's face darkened. "They will be present. However, you will be testifying from behind the glass, so they won't see you."

Miriam exhaled sharply. "Let's get this over with." She nodded, taking one last drag on her cigarette before crushing it out. She was ready to face whatever lay ahead. She gave Ava one last deep and passionate kiss, squeezed her hand, and turned to follow AUSA Miller into the courthouse.

As Miriam walked away, Ava's eyes followed her, filled with a mix of emotions - worry, love, and pride. She watched as Miriam disappeared into the courthouse, feeling a sense of helplessness wash over her. She wanted to be with Miriam, to support her through this ordeal, but she knew that wasn't possible.

Ava took a deep breath, trying to calm her nerves. She glanced over at US Marshal Thompson, who was watching her with a sympathetic expression.

"She'll be okay, Ava," he said quietly. "We'll take good care of her."

Ava nodded, trying to smile. "I know you will," she said. "Thank you."

As she waited outside the courthouse, Ava couldn't help but think about the journey that had brought them to this moment. From the moment she met Miriam, Ava had been by her side, supporting her through the ups and downs of their new life together.

Now, as Miriam prepared to face her enemies in court, Ava felt a sense of pride and admiration for the strong, brave woman she loved. She knew that Miriam was ready for this, that she had the strength and courage to face whatever lay ahead.

As Ava waited anxiously outside the courthouse, she knew that she would be there to support Miriam every step of the way, no matter the trial's outcome.

AUSA Miller led Miriam into the empty courtroom. The witness stand was already outfitted with frosted bulletproof glass to shield her identity, and the microphone had a voice modulation device attached to disguise her voice. AUSA Miller gave her a reassuring nod and said,

"Remember everything we practiced. Stick to the facts only. That's crucial to our testimony. You can do this. You're safe; they can't see you."

Miriam's knees trembled as she approached the stand, each step feeling heavier than the last. She clenched her fists, the phantom pain in her broken arm flaring up as if her body remembered every blow. Her missing portion of her leg throbbed with each step.

She took a deep breath, forcing herself to focus. She had rehearsed this moment countless times, but nothing could truly prepare her for the reality of facing the De Lucas in court. The disgust churned within her at the thought of being forced to use her deadname. It felt like a betrayal—not just to herself but to everything she had fought to rebuild. Yet she knew the prosecution had no choice. The crimes had been committed against Gabriel Wilson. The defense would seize upon any deviation, twisting it to discredit her testimony. Her stomach churned as she weighed defiance against the risk of undermining justice. In the end, she made her choice—not for them, not for the law, but for Alex. For the truth.

AUSA Miller's words of encouragement echoed in her mind as she stepped into the witness stand. The frosted bulletproof glass shimmered under the fluorescent lighting, a reminder of the precautions taken to protect her identity. She adjusted the microphone, her fingers brushing against the modulation device. The courtroom doors shut behind her, and Miriam turned her gaze toward the hazy silhouettes on the other side of the glass. She knew the De Lucas were out there, waiting for her testimony, but she would not let them intimidate her.

The air was thick with tension as the courtroom fell silent. Miriam's heart rate slowed, her focus narrowing to the task at hand. She took another deep breath.

AUSA Miller stood. "Your Honor, the prosecution is ready to proceed with the testimony of our key witness."

The judge nodded. "Very well. Please state your name for the record."

Miriam swallowed against the lump in her throat. "Gabriel Wilson."

A jolt of disgust coursed through her, but she forced herself to remain steady.

AUSA Miller's voice remained calm and steady. "Mr. Wilson, are you acquainted with Leonardo Rossi?"

"Yes."

"How did you meet him?"

"I was introduced to him by Alex Bianchi. They were cousins."

And so it went, question after question. No narrative, just responses—concise and measured. AUSA Miller led her through the horror of that night in painstaking increments, forcing her to relive each moment through direct questioning.

Miriam spoke of the fear, the intimidation, and the violence she had endured at the hands of the men sent by Francesca Bianchi on orders from Leo Rossi, acting for the De Lucas. Her voice remained steady, but the emotion behind her words was palpable.

She described her friendship with Alex Bianchi and how he had introduced her to his cousin Leo Rossi when she needed money. She explained her gambling addiction, her mounting debts—$100,000 owed to Leo. She detailed how Leo had made it clear that her debt belonged to Mario De Luca. Then came July 1, 2023—when Leo Rossi and Marco De Luca came to her apartment and told her she had twenty-four hours to pay or suffer the consequences.

She then went into the horrific details of the attack on July 2, 2023, the day her life was stolen from her. She recounted the blows, the searing agony, the helplessness as Alex lay dead beside her. She described the moment she lost consciousness, waking up eleven days later in the hospital, unrecognizable, broken, and barely alive.

The courtroom was silent, save for the soft hum of the voice modulation device. Even through the distortion, the weight of her words hung heavy in the air.

AUSA Miller nodded, her eyes locked onto the frosted glass of the witness stand. "Thank you, Mr. Wilson. Your bravery and strength are truly admirable."

The judge turned toward the defense table. "You may proceed with your cross-examination."

The lead defense attorney's voice boomed from beyond the frosted glass. "Mr. Wilson, isn't it true that you have a history of dishonesty and deceit?" His tone dripped with skepticism.

Miriam felt a surge of adrenaline but kept her composure. She had anticipated this—knew the defense would try to discredit her.

AUSA Miller promptly rose to her feet. "Objection, Your Honor. Relevance. The defense is attempting to attack the witness's character without establishing any relevance to the case at hand."

The judge raised a hand. "Sustained. Counselor, unless you can directly tie this line of questioning to the events being litigated, move on."

The defense attorney adjusted his tie, his smile tight. "Of course, Your Honor. Let's turn to the events of July 2, 2023."

He paused theatrically before continuing. "Mr. Wilson, you claim to recall every detail of that night, yet you failed to call 911 yourself. Isn't that rather... convenient?"

Miriam inhaled sharply, feeling her pulse quicken, but she forced herself to remain composed. "I didn't call 911 because I couldn't," she said, her voice steady. "My leg was shattered, my arm was broken, and I was slipping in and out of consciousness. Someone else called for help."

The defense attorney leaned in slightly. "But wouldn't someone with such a strong memory have made an attempt, despite their injuries?"

AUSA Miller's voice rang out again. "Objection, Your Honor. Argumentative. The question assumes facts not in evidence and attempts to badger the witness."

The judge's gavel struck the bench lightly. "Sustained. Counselor, rephrase your question."

The defense attorney's tone grew sharper. "You claim you remember every detail of that night, Mr. Wilson," he sneered, "but your memory was apparently foggy enough not to recall the sound of the gunshot. Convenient, isn't it?"

Miriam swallowed hard, the words catching in her throat. "Convenient?" she said, her voice shaking but steady. "Convenient would be forgetting. Convenient would be pretending it didn't happen so I could sleep at night. Convenient would have been dying next to my friend. Instead, I had to change my identity! My entire life! I had to relearn how to walk, get facial reconstructive surgery, and be shifted across the country for my safety... no, that's not convenient. That's my life now."

She paused, eyes locked on the frosted glass. "But to answer your question, the gun loudly went bang."

As Miriam's words rang out, the courtroom fell deathly silent. Even the defense attorney, his smirk frozen mid-retort, seemed momentarily stunned.

For the first time, she felt it—the power of her truth pressing against the weight of their lies.

The defense attorney adjusted his tie, clearly unnerved by Miriam's unwavering resolve. He tried a different approach, his tone almost mockingly polite. "Mr. Wilson, you've painted a dramatic picture of that night, but can you explain why someone like Alex Bianchi—a young man with no criminal record—would associate with someone like you? A man with a gambling problem, deeply indebted to dangerous people?"

AUSA Miller immediately rose, her voice firm. "Objection, Your

Honor. Speculation. The defense is inviting the witness to speculate on another individual's motives, which is inappropriate."

The judge nodded, his expression stern. "Sustained. Move on, Counselor."

Miriam's chest tightened at the mention of Alex, but she refused to let the attorney's baiting shake her. She took a deep breath, her voice steady and tinged with sadness.

"Alex Bianchi was my best friend. He didn't care about my flaws or my mistakes. Alex cared about me as a person. He believed in second chances, in loyalty, and in helping people who were struggling. If you think his kindness and compassion are reasons to question his character, then perhaps you need to reevaluate yours."

"That's enough, Mr. Wilson." The judge admonished her.

She paused, focusing on the hazy figures beyond the frosted glass. The courtroom was silent, the tension suffocating. Sweat poured down her spine as she steeled herself. Then, with unwavering conviction, she added, "And for the record, I am a woman and will be addressed as such."

For a moment, there was stunned silence. Then the courtroom erupted.

Gasps, murmurs, and hushed conversations surged through the room as the weight of Miriam's declaration settled in. The defense team stiffened, their carefully crafted strategy suddenly shaken. They had known who Gabriel Wilson was, but now they understood—beyond the name change, beyond the reconstructed face—exactly what had happened.

The lead defense attorney's mask of composure slipped, his hesitation betraying the realization that their line of attack had just backfired. AUSA Miller's voice cut through the commotion.

"Objection, Your Honor! I move to have the last statement stricken from the record on the grounds that it is irrelevant to the facts of this case."

The judge's gavel slammed down, demanding order. "Enough! The court reporter will disregard the witness's last statement."

But it was too late. The revelation had been spoken, heard, and—despite the judge's ruling—absorbed by everyone in the courtroom.

Miriam exhaled slowly, gripping the edges of the witness stand. She had told the truth, and now they all knew.

The defense attorney adjusted his tie, his composure rattled, but he recovered quickly. He cleared his throat and straightened his notes, avoiding looking at the frosted glass as if unwilling to acknowledge the impact of Miriam's words.

"No further questions, Your Honor."

AUSA Miller stood, smoothing out the lapels of her blazer. "The prosecution rests, Your Honor."

The judge turned to the defense table. "Does the defense wish to present any further witnesses?"

The lead defense attorney hesitated, then exchanged a glance with his co-counsel. "No, Your Honor. The defense rests."

The judge nodded, his voice even. "Very well. The court will adjourn for today. Closing arguments will be scheduled for tomorrow morning."

He turned toward the frosted glass. "Mr. Wilson, you are excused."

Miriam exhaled slowly, gripping the edge of the witness stand as the tension in the room released slightly. The judge's words echoed in her ears, but she hardly processed them. She had done it. She had told her story. Now, all she could do was wait.

The courtroom emptied in slow waves—defense attorneys gathering their notes, the prosecution whispering amongst themselves, and the judge exiting with a sharp rap of his gavel. Only Miller remained.

Miriam stood on unsteady legs, pain searing in her stump due to having her prosthetic on for so long as AUSA Miller approached. The moment the door closed behind the last exiting official, Miller whirled on her.

"What the hell was that?" Miller's voice was sharp, low, her composure barely masking the fury beneath.

Miriam blinked at her, still processing the weight of everything. "What?"

"You know damn well what!" Miller hissed, stepping closer, her frustration radiating off her in waves. "I told you to stick to the facts. I told you not to make this personal, and you went and declared yourself a woman—on the record, in front of the defense, in front of everyone! Do you have any idea what you've just done?"

Miriam clenched her jaw, the fire returning to her eyes. "I told the truth."

"You jeopardized your safety," Miller shot back, eyes flashing. "You think the De Lucas didn't already have enough reason to want you dead? Now you've given them another one. You gave them the missing piece to track you, to hunt you down."

Miriam straightened, her defiance unshaken. "They were going to know eventually. They always do."

Miller ran a frustrated hand through her hair, exhaling sharply. "And now, instead of controlling the timeline, instead of keeping them guessing, you just handed them confirmation on a silver fucking platter."

A sharp knock at the door cut off Miller's anger. The marshals entered, their presence an immediate reminder of the reality of Miriam's situation.

"It's time to move," one of them said firmly.

Miriam stepped past Miller without another word, her pulse steady, her heart resolute.

The hallway was silent save for the echoes of her footsteps and the marshals flanking her. When the doors opened to the secure waiting area, Ava was there.

The moment their eyes met, Ava was across the room, wrapping Miriam in her arms before the marshals could protest. "You're okay," she whispered, her voice shaky with relief. "You did it."

Miriam held her tighter, burying her face in Ava's shoulder. "It's over."

Miller's voice, calmer now but no less serious, cut through the moment. "Not yet. Not until the jury comes back with a verdict."

Miriam pulled back just enough to meet Miller's gaze. "And if they don't?"

Miller exhaled, her expression grim. "Then we start all over again."

A heavy silence hung between them.

One of the marshals cleared his throat. "Let's go. We're taking you both back to the safe house."

Ava squeezed Miriam's hand, her touch grounding, anchoring her to the moment. "Come on, baby. Let's get out of here."

As they were led toward the exit, Miriam cast one last glance down the empty hallway behind them. The trial might have been nearing its end, but a deeper truth settled in her bones.

She had spoken her truth. Now, she would see who dared to silence it.

And she was ready.

Chapter 38: The Road Ahead

"GUILTY ON ALL COUNTS!" AUSA Miller shouted from the lawn of the safe house the next evening. US Marshal Arthur Thompson accompanied her, a relieved but guarded expression on his face.

Miriam and Ava whooped for joy, their voices breaking with the sheer weight of the moment. Miriam's heart skipped a beat, and she felt the stress of the past fifteen months vanish. *We got those bastards, Alex. We got them.* For the first time since that horrible night, she truly believed she could breathe freely again.

"It's over!" Miriam exclaimed, her chest rising and falling with exhilaration. "I'm free! I can live like a normal person again! No more WITSEC! No more hiding! No more secrets and lies! We can have a huge wedding!"

But her joy was short-lived.

Marshal Thompson's smile faded. His posture stiffened, signaling something was wrong.

"I'm sorry, Miriam and Ava, but it's not that simple. You're not being released from WITSEC."

The world tilted.

Miriam's face fell, the hope and joy curdling into confusion and dread. It felt like the air had been sucked from her lungs, like she had been punched in the gut. This wasn't supposed to happen. They won. They got the guilty verdict.

No... no... it's not fair... how?

"What... What do you mean?" She asked, her voice shaking with confusion and disappointment.

AUSA Miller's expression was sympathetic but heavy. Regret flickered in her eyes, but beneath it was a steely certainty.

"The De Lucas have a lot of connections, Miriam. They have a network of associates and loyalists who would stop at nothing to hurt you. Even with the guilty verdict, it's not safe for you to leave WITSEC just yet." Her next words cut even deeper.

"Your testimony let them know exactly who testified. They know Gabe Wilson survived, but they also realized you transitioned. They'll stop at nothing to find you."

Miriam's stomach twisted violently.

Thompson added, "We're doing everything we can to track them all down with the assistance of multiple law enforcement agencies, but their network is vast. And now... they know exactly what they're looking for. A woman, not a man."

It wasn't just that they knew Gabe Wilson survived. They knew who she had become.

Miriam's breath shuddered as realization sank in. Had she been reckless? Had her defiance cost them more than she could have imagined? But what was the alternative? Would she have been able to live with herself if she had let them erase her? If she had let them force her back into a name and identity she had spent the past year shedding?

Ava wrapped her arms around Miriam, her hold fierce and unrelenting. "We'll get through this, baby," she whispered. "We'll figure it out together."

Miriam nodded, but her body felt leaden. The hope she had clung to just moments before was crumbling.

Ava's voice turned sharp, her frustration bubbling to the surface. "How could you not have redacted her deadname from the reports? How?! That's Witness Protection 101!" She turned on Miller, her anger building. "You're telling me that a program built to keep people concealed left a goddamn trail leading straight to her? How does that happen?!"

AUSA Miller stiffened, clearly expecting the outburst. "Because, Ava, the crimes were committed against Gabriel Wilson. The defense would have seized on any deviation from that identity and called her testimony into question."

Ava's nostrils flared. "You forced her to use that name on the stand! Do you have any idea what that did to her?! Do you even care?!"

Miller's patience wore thin. "I do care, Ava. But this wasn't about Miriam's feelings—this was about making sure the case stuck! If we had let her testify under her current name, the defense would have had a field day discrediting her, spinning some nonsense about her being an unreliable witness. We couldn't risk that."

Ava took a step forward, eyes blazing. "Oh, so this is her fault? You didn't even try to protect her identity, did you? You left it out in the open for the defense, for the De Lucas, for anyone to see!"

Miller's expression darkened, her frustration peaking. "We did what we had to do to put the De Lucas behind bars, Ava! And we won! The system worked—"

Ava scoffed, her voice dripping with venom. "Worked? Worked for who? You get your conviction, your big career boost, and we get a lifetime of running! That's your idea of 'working'?"

Miller's fists clenched at her sides. "Miriam—your fiancée—decided to make a grand declaration in open court that she's a woman. That's what happened, Ava. That's why we're here."

Silence.

Miriam's head snapped up, her breath catching in her throat. *Is this my fault? Did I put us in danger?* The thought was suffocating, but so was the alternative—living in fear, in silence, forever bending under the weight of the past. Miriam wanted to speak—wanted to stop this—but what could she say? *Is Miller right? Have I doomed us both?*

Ava recoiled, her expression morphing into disbelief. "Excuse me? You're blaming her for this?"

Miller folded her arms, her tone unyielding. "Yes. I am. She was already protected by the measures we put in place. We had done everything necessary to keep her hidden—until she announced to a room full of people, including the De Lucas' attorneys, that she was a woman."

Ava's fists trembled at her sides. "You absolute *bitch.*"

Thompson took a sharp step forward. "Ava."

"No, don't 'Ava' me!" Ava snapped. Her voice cracked with fury. "You're standing here, acting like Miriam should've just sat there and let them misgender her, erase her, like she was supposed to just—just take it—so you wouldn't have to do extra work?! She told the *truth!* She shouldn't have to hide who she is just because you people can't do your damn jobs right!"

Miller's jaw tightened. "It wasn't about hiding who she is. It was about keeping her alive." She continued. "If we hadn't done things this way, she might not have made it to that stand at all. You think I don't care? I care enough to make the hard choices."

Ava stepped forward, her voice trembling with barely contained rage. "*Alive?* Oh, please, don't you *dare* act like you were doing her a favor! You failed her. You failed both of us. And now, instead of admitting that you screwed up, you're throwing the blame on her for refusing to be erased?!"

Miller took a step forward too, her voice sharp. For the first time, a flicker of doubt crossed her face, her lips pressing into a thin line. "Do you think they wouldn't have figured it out? She made sure they did.

And now? They'll use that information. They'll dig. They'll find the people who knew her before. They'll come for Miriam."

Miriam flinched at the words, and something inside Ava *snapped.*

"So what the hell was she supposed to do, huh?" Ava shot back, her voice rising. "Sit there while they used *him* over and over? While they took the worst thing they could do to her and shoved it in her face, knowing she couldn't fight back? Would you have sat there and let them strip you of your identity in front of the whole damn court?"

Miller's expression tightened, but Ava didn't let up.

"No, you wouldn't have," Ava seethed. "Because *you* get to be exactly who you are every single day. You don't get forced to justify your existence in a goddamn courtroom. She did. And you know what? She *still* played your game. She still went up there, used the name that nearly broke her, and *handed* you the conviction you wanted. But that wasn't enough for you, was it? You needed her to be silent, to be obedient. To just *take it.*"

Miller's mouth opened, but Ava wasn't finished.

"You know what *really* happened, Miller?" Ava continued, stepping closer, her voice a dangerous whisper. "You underestimated them. *You* thought her transition was enough to keep her hidden. You thought, 'Oh, no one's gonna connect the dots,' so you got *lazy.* You didn't seal the reports properly. You didn't anticipate that the defense would dig deeper. And now? You want to shift the blame on her for *your* failure."

Miller's face paled slightly, but her posture remained rigid. "That's not—"

Ava cut her off, fury radiating off her. "No, Miller. You failed her. And instead of owning it, you'd rather pin it on *her.* You'd rather act like the problem was *her existence* instead of your own negligence.

"You didn't protect her properly because you thought she didn't need it. You thought her identity was a smokescreen, and that was enough. And now we're paying the price for your assumption."

Thompson swiftly placed himself between them, his voice a low warning. "Enough. Both of you."

Neither woman backed down immediately. The tension between them burned white-hot, neither willing to yield.

But then Miriam moved. She reached out, gripping Ava's wrist. "Ava. Please. *Stop dear.*"

Ava's breathing was ragged, her body still vibrating with rage. But at Miriam's touch, she exhaled sharply, stepping back.

Thompson exhaled slowly, his expression unreadable. "This isn't productive. What's done is done. No matter how we got here, the reality is that we have a problem—and the only way forward is to deal with it."

Miller's jaw was still set, but her gaze flicked to Miriam for the briefest of moments, something unreadable in her expression. A second of hesitation. Regret? Or just calculation?

Miriam saw it. She wasn't sure which she preferred. Miller conceded. "We don't have time to argue about this. Right now, our focus needs to be on relocating you both as safely as possible."

Ava was still seething, but Miriam gave her hand a squeeze. "We need to focus on what's next, love," she murmured.

Ava exhaled heavily, glaring at Miller one last time. "Fine. But don't think for a second that I'm going to forget this."

Miriam felt a deep pang of sorrow at the thought of leaving Jasper Hill behind. Despite the painful circumstances that had first brought her here, she had come to love this town—the people, the quiet moments, the life she and Ava had begun to build. The idea of starting over yet again, in a place she didn't choose, filled her with a weary kind of grief. But there was no time to dwell. The anger, the frustration at Miller's accusations, the sting of knowing their safety had been jeopardized— those emotions would have to wait. Right now, all that mattered was making sure these people who had failed her made good on their word.

Ava's voice, still tinged with residual anger, softened slightly as she turned to Thompson. "Can we take the porch swing with us to the new safe house? Please?"

Marshal Thompson, who had been watching them closely, let out a slow breath before nodding. His expression softened, and a small, tired smile tugged at his lips. "I think that can be arranged, Ava. We'll make sure to disassemble it and transport it with you. It's the least we can do."

Miriam's eyes welled up as she turned to Ava, who was finally smiling, a small flicker of joy breaking through the storm of their night. The porch swing had been more than just a place to sit—it was where they had stolen quiet moments together, where they had fallen in love, where they had dreamed of their future. Taking it with them meant that, despite everything being torn away, they could hold onto at least one piece of the life they had built.

Miriam inhaled deeply, steadying herself. There was still so much ahead—new rules, new places to navigate—but with Ava by her side, she could face whatever came next.

Miriam and Ava were back home in Jasper Hill. It had been a tumultuous week. Their new safe house was located in the Upstate area of South Carolina. The movers would be there in one hour.

Miriam poured them fresh coffee, and the couple went to the porch. They sat down on the porch swing and lit cigarettes. Miriam had really grown to love this place. She was going to miss it, as well as the people she'd met and the locations she frequented.

"Marshal Thompson said our new safe house was on a lake. Maybe we can get a boat?" Miriam said to Ava.

Ava took a long drag from her cigarette and replied. "Ten years. I've lived here for ten years. I've made a life here. I'm going to miss it so much, Miri, love." She continued.

"But what matters more to me than anything is that we're together. We're going to get married. We're going to have a baby. There will be a little us. We'll build a new life. And no matter where we end up, this swing, this precious porch swing, where we fell in love and have spent so much time together, will be there for us. As we build the life we want, it will be there to comfort us, support us on the rough days, and celebrate with us on the good days. Our child will sit with us in it and grow up with it as a constant in their life. And I'll remain forever by your side, or as long as the universe gives us, whichever comes first. I love you, Miriam Dawn Ryder."

Miriam's eyes welled up with tears as she listened to Ava's words. She felt a deep sense of love and connection to this woman, and the thought of building a new life together filled her with joy and anticipation.

She took a long drag on her cigarette, savoring the moment, and then turned to Ava with a smile. "I love you too, Ava Marie McCormick," she said, her voice barely above a whisper.

As they sat together on the porch swing, wrapped in each other's arms, Miriam knew that no matter where life took them, their love would remain a constant, a source of strength and comfort that would see them through the ups and downs of life.

The sound of the movers' trucks pulling up to the house broke the spell, and Miriam and Ava reluctantly stood up, taking one last look at the only home they had shared together. Hand in hand, they walked back into the house, ready to face whatever the future held as long as they were together.

Epilogue

Miriam and Ava sat on the familiar porch swing, savoring their last few moments in Jasper Hill. The bittersweet ache of saying goodbye hung heavy in the air, but the promise of their future together gave them hope. Despite the anger, the betrayal, and the forced relocation, they still had each other. They held hands, the swing creaking softly beneath them, as they planned for the road ahead.

The fight with Miller still burned in Ava's chest, and Miriam felt the weight of everything they had lost. But they couldn't dwell on that now. Their new home awaited. A fresh start.

Unbeknownst to them, a man in woodland camouflage sat perched high on the ridge, concealed by the dense foliage. His sharp eyes tracked their every movement through the lens of high-powered binoculars.

The man adjusted his position silently, taking care not to disturb the leaves around him. From his vantage point, he could see everything—the swing where they sat, the porch light flickering in the dusk, the red Mazda CX-9 and silver Honda CR-V parked in the driveway, and the movers' truck winding its way up the gravel road.

Lowering the binoculars, he reached into his pocket and pulled out a notepad. His pen scratched quietly as he recorded the license plate numbers of both vehicles. *South Carolina plates.* His lips curled into a grim smile.

WITSEC had tried to erase Miriam Ryder. The federal government had bent over backward to hide her. But he knew the truth now.

Looks like I'll be heading south, he thought, tucking the notepad away. He glanced at his watch, then reached for his phone. *Time to inform Mr. De Luca.*

Reaching into his vest pocket, the man pulled out a burner phone and dialed a memorized number. After a single ring, a voice answered.

"Speak."

"It's me," the man said in a low, gravelly tone. "I've got confirmation. The location is accurate. But there's something else—something you'll want to know."

The voice on the other end grew sharper. "What is it?"

A wicked grin spread across the man's face as he leaned back against a tree trunk, savoring the moment. "Francesca Bianchi lied to you. She held something back."

A pause. Then the voice growled, "Explain."

"Oh, she gave you the basics," the man said, relishing his power. "She led you to believe that the witness hiding under your nose was nothing more than a runaway with a debt. What she didn't tell you— what she tried to keep hidden—is that your so-called dead debtor didn't just survive. He transitioned. Gabriel Wilson isn't a man anymore. He's a woman now. A woman named Miriam Ryder."

The voice on the other end was silent for a beat, then exploded with fury. "What did you say?"

"You heard me," the man replied, his tone smug. "The De Lucas' key witness didn't just disappear—she rebuilt herself entirely. Francesca thought she could use that information for herself. Maybe to strike a deal. But now... now it's yours."

The voice grew cold, deadly. "And you're certain?"

The man chuckled, his eyes narrowing as he watched Miriam and Ava laugh together on the porch swing. Their happiness, their belief that they were safe—it made him almost pity them. Almost.

"As certain as I am that she's right in front of me, saying her goodbyes."

Another pause, longer this time. Then the voice spoke, calm but seething with malice.

"Good work. Stay on them. I'll handle Francesca later."

The line went dead.

The man slipped the phone back into his pocket, his grim smile returning. He watched as Miriam and Ava stood to greet the movers, blissfully unaware of the predator watching them from the shadows—blissfully unaware that their escape had already failed before it had even begun.

The man whispered to himself, "South Carolina's a lovely place to visit this time of year."

To Be Continued...

Maya Fisher

About the Author

Maya Dawn Fisher is a transgender woman, below-the-knee amputee, writer, and professional procrastinator residing in rural Southwest Virginia. When she's not dodging deadlines or avoiding adult responsibilities, Maya enjoys unapologetically chain-smoking on the porch, sipping coffee, and yelling at her three cats to stop plotting against her—one of whom is deaf.

She's been partnered with the same unlucky woman, Misty, for 20 years, and they're both still baffled by their teenage daughter's ability to survive (and thrive) despite their best efforts to mess her up.

Maya's debut novel, **Reborn in Shadows**, has been **selected for inclusion in the Library of Congress**, a milestone that ensures her voice and storytelling will be preserved among the literary record.

Her writing is a mix of humor, heart, and occasional profanity, which she hopes will make you laugh, cry, and possibly question her life choices.

You can connect with me on:

- https://authormayafisher.com
- https://x.com/AuthorMayaF
- https://www.facebook.com/AuthorMayaFisher
- https://www.instagram.com/author_maya_fisher
- https://www.threads.net/@author_maya_fisher
- https://bsky.app/profile/author-maya-fisher.bsky.social